WAKING BRIGID

WAKING BRIGID

Francis Clark

TOR®

A TOM DOHERTY ASSOCIATES BOOK
New York

WAKING BRIGID

Map by Jennifer Hanover

A Tor Book
Published by Tom Doherty Associates, LLC
175 Fifth Avenue
New York, NY 10010

www.tor.com

Tor® is a registered trademark of Tom Doherty Associates, LLC.

Library of Congress Cataloging-in-Publication Data

Clark, Francis, d. 2007.
    Waking Brigid / Francis Clark.—1st ed.
        p.   cm.
    "A Tom Doherty Associates book."
    ISBN-13: 978-0-7653-1810-7
    ISBN-10: 0-7653-1810-5
    1. Nuns—Fiction.   2. Satanism—Fiction.   3. Murder—Fiction.   4. Savannah
(Ga.)—Fiction.   5. United States—History—1865–1898—Fiction.   I. Title.
    PS3603.L363W35 2008
    813'.6—dc22   2007040737

First Edition: February 2008

Printed in the United States of America

0 9 8 7 6 5 4 3 2 1

For Amy

ACKNOWLEDGMENTS

As with any work of fiction, there are more people to thank than can fit into a brief paragraph, but there are some that must be mentioned.

Thanks to Reg, Jim, Terry, and Miranda for helping me see my own story more clearly. Special thanks to my wife, Amy, for patience; my agent, Nat Sobel, for perseverance; and my editor, Claire Eddy, for doing the magic that editors do.

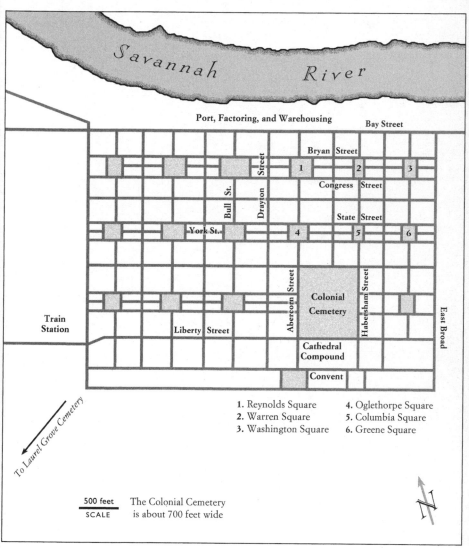

S a v a n n a h   R i v e r

Port, Factoring, and Warehousing

Bay Street

Bryan Street

1   2   3

Congress Street

Bull St.

Drayton Street

State Street

York St.   4   5   6

Abercorn Street

Colonial
Cemetery

Habersham Street

East Broad

Train
Station

Liberty Street

Cathedral
Compound

Convent

To Laurel Grove Cemetery

1. Reynolds Square   4. Oglethorpe Square
2. Warren Square   5. Columbia Square
3. Washington Square   6. Greene Square

500 feet   The Colonial Cemetery
SCALE   is about 700 feet wide

N

Map of downtown Savannah in 1874.
The city extended to the south, east, and west.

CHAPTER ONE

Savannah, Georgia
Friday, October 9, 1874

THE dream always began the same, and, though he recoiled in terror even inside the dream, he could never escape the outcome. He was walking toward the hospital tent. Around it were men broken in battle, arms and legs smashed by rifle balls, sword cuts already infected with the filth of the battlefield. Cannons rumbled in the distance. Couriers rattled back and forth on the muddy trails of the camp. Beside the tent was the inevitable harbinger of his trade—a stack of arms and limbs sawn from men as they screamed. The Confederate doctors rarely had laudanum or whiskey to dull the patient's pain while the saw rasped its way through the flesh and bone. Cutting the bone was always the most agonizing part. Some cried out. Some just cried. The ones who screamed seemed to do the best, though the screams haunted him as they did every doctor. In his dream he would enter a tent, a vague concoction of the tents at Shiloh, Antietam, and a half-dozen lesser battles where the men of the South died for "the Cause." Someone he thought he knew handed him a saw and a scalpel. Somnolent, deadened, he walked to a table where a patient lay, his pants crudely ripped back, revealing a shattered right leg.

"Hold him," he muttered to the two Negro orderlies who stood at the head of the table, like waiters at a crude feast. As they moved to hold him down, the boy raised his head, and Gaston saw that he was young, maybe sixteen.

"You're not gonna take my laig," he cried through the pain.

"No choice, son." He repeated the litany, "It's your leg or your life."

"You're not gonna take my laig." Stubbornly repeated.

"Hold him." The orderlies tightened their grip, yet the boy struggled to raise his head.

"Butcher." He said it calmly, pronouncing judgment on the doctor.

The screaming began when he cut into the flesh with his scalpel. So much like cutting up a cow or a pig, only this flesh lived, this flesh screamed with a human voice.

Until then the dream had been true to reality, so close to what he had seen and done a thousand times, even down to his feeling of cold detachment as he sliced away a part of a man who might never feel like a man again. But then the insanity started; the tent began to drum as things fell against the canvas. The poles swayed; the oil lamps rocked with the impact. Where the objects struck, each left an imprint of blood. The tent began to sag under the strain. The blood leaked through the canvas. A seam over his head split, and shattered arms and legs fell on him. Some were mangled stumps, some putrid with gangrene, some freshly removed. Some limbs were tattered, some cleanly cut. The tattered ones betrayed the work of a soldier. The cleanly cut were the work of doctors. All the limbs fell straight at him. A putrid thigh slapped him in the face, blinding him in one eye with its trail of gore. As the limbs cascaded through the rent canvas and beat him to the floor, he saw a fervid look of victory in the face of the boy.

"Ain't gonna get me. Ain't gonna get mine."

Then Gaston was swamped in the onrush of limbs, buried in a mound of bone and blood and torn meat. He clawed madly for the surface, but it was out of reach; the tide was endless. He tried to breathe, but his mouth and nose were blocked by a putrefying gore that made him retch.

He would wake up gasping for air. The sour mash whiskey he kept by his bedside was the only thing strong enough to wash the taste out of his mouth.

It had been almost ten years since Appomattox, and Savannah once again grew rich on the cotton trade. But Gaston's dream and his memories never let him enjoy the peace and the new prosperity. He always remembered that one-half of the budget of the state of Mississippi was spent to pay for artificial limbs in 1866. That fact reminded him that for three years he had not been a doctor, just a meat cutter and an expert at the final game of triage.

He heard his boy running up the stairs.

"Doc Gaston, Doc Gaston, you needed."

Ezekiel began knocking loudly at the door; he knew the doctor was normally a heavy sleeper.

"Come on in. I'm awake."

Ezekiel's dark eyes took in the bedroom quickly. "Been havin' that dream?"

"Yeah."

"Well, you needed. Mistah Richardson took real bad."

"I'll get dressed."

"I be downstairs." Ezekiel turned to his small room to get dressed.

Ezekiel's relationship with Dr. Gaston went back eight years. He knew well enough that he had to go with the doctor to the hospital, even though Zeke was nowhere near fond of the Saint James' Ward. Saint James' was the "lockup ward" at Saint Joseph's Hospital. In the ward were those too crazy to be left on their own. What made Ezekiel specially afraid was that Saul Richardson had gone from being a respected man to someone screaming about the Devil overnight. And now it was near the black of the moon again.

"White people too smart to believe in the Devil," Ezekiel muttered as he pulled his clothes on. "They willin' to talk about him, but don't believe. He sets his traps just the same, and Mistah Richardson fall into his snare." He finished dressing quickly. Doc Gaston usually got ready too soon for him anyway.

In a few minutes they were on their way. Gaston walked steadily, though not quickly. The war years had aged him prematurely, though at sixty-two he was hardly a young man anymore. He didn't carry a bag. Saint Jo's would have everything he needed, not that they had anything to help Saul Richardson, except enough laudanum to knock him senseless. Gaston and Ezekiel walked the few blocks to the hospital in silence. The fog that often rose in the city at night enveloped them, so that the light of the gas lamps was diffused, leaving much of the street in darkness. The fog swallowed the sounds of conversation and even dulled the sounds made by the few horses and carriages abroad at this hour. The sharp tap of hooves on stone was transmuted into a dull clopping sound. As they walked through the shroud of fog, Ezekiel was concerned with his fears. Gaston was concerned with his patient.

David Gaston was one of Saul Richardson's circle of friends, not merely his doctor. They had known each other for many years. Richardson's family was part of Savannah society, and, as such, was one that Gaston frequently saw at the various gatherings. They had become close friends since the war, which had left too many empty seats for them not to have. Yet Gaston had not really been part of Richardson's daily life, any more than Richardson had been part of his. They saw each other socially, and they might play cards together on occasion. The business world of cotton factors and the medical world of doctors did not overlap to any great extent.

Richardson had begun screaming almost a month ago, on the night before the new moon. He'd been taken to the Saint James' Ward and given enough laudanum to quiet him. It had taken a large dose, three times more than Gaston usually used for an amputation. The next day Gaston had gone to see Mrs. Richardson. Her elegant home looked out over one of Savannah's many squares.

His wife had let it slip to Gaston that it was odd for Richardson to have been at home on the night it started. He had been going out to his gentlemen's club on the first or second night before the new moon since before their marriage. He had failed to attend only when pressing business had called him from Savannah. Since he had not gone two nights before the new moon, she had expected him to have gone the evening before the new moon. Instead, he had locked himself in the study shortly after dinner. His screams had brought her downstairs. When she was unable to persuade him to unbolt the door, she had sent the cook's son for the police. From that point, Gaston knew the story. The police had summoned him almost as soon as they had arrived. Mrs. Richardson could not, or would not, add anything more of substance to the story. She had not known where her husband went or for what purpose on those evenings, merely that he arrived home long after she had retired. Savannah had always been a city of secrets. That a wife did not know where her husband might be or that a husband was not precisely sure of his wife's whereabouts was merely a matter of good manners in a city whose sophistication was greater than its devotion to moral standards. Certainly few had known of the negotiations with General Sherman that assured that the city managed to surrender to his army without a shot being fired or a house being burned.

Gaston's reverie was broken by their arrival at the front entrance of the hospital. It was brightly lit as usual. He turned up the stairs of the hospital. The flicker of the many gaslights made the brick front seem to waver in the darkness. Ezekiel hung back.

"I wait for you heah."

"Come on in and go down to the kitchen, Zeke. They'll have hot coffee down there."

Ezekiel hesitated, fear gleaming in his eyes.

"Suit yourself, Zeke, but I might be a while. Besides, there's a lot more bright light in the kitchen than you're likely to see out here." Faced with such a persuasive argument, Ezekiel followed the doctor into the hospital and immediately turned down the stairs to the kitchen.

Sister Mary Francis was waiting for the doctor at the front desk, her stocky hips balanced, as always, by a rosary, a crucifix, and a heavy ring of keys. Her hands fluttered more than usual, and a strand of gray hair had escaped the confines of her wimple, a certain sign that she had been roused from sleep for the emergency. Yet none of her disarray served to lessen the stern devotion to her patients that gleamed like frozen candle flames in her green eyes.

She gave an almost imperceptible nod of her head to the doctor and led the way to the Saint James' Ward. As they walked down the long corridor to the ward, Gaston noticed an unusual number of nuns about for the hour. Whispering like black doves, they stayed in the shadows at the sides of the corridor, out of the way of the aged nun and the physician in tow. For them, what resided in the confines of the Saint James' was terrifying. It was damnation itself, the Devil come to roost. They had heard the screams in the night, and they knew that no secular potions could safeguard Richardson from that which stalked him.

"Damn you." Richardson's screeching cry echoed down the hallway the moment the heavy door to the Saint James' was opened. "Kill me and be done with it."

Gaston barely recognized Richardson's voice. It was hoarse with screaming. He looked at the nun beside him. She was crossing herself. He took refuge in clinical thought.

"How long?"

"Since just before ten."

"Have you given him any laudanum?"

Her face creased a bit more deeply. "He's too dangerous at times for many of the sisters. But he is rational much of the time. The orderlies won't go near him, even after I put the fear of God in them." She sighed. "But we did give him his dose at nine." As if on cue, the screaming from Richardson's room suddenly ceased. The sudden silence startled both of them.

The nun looked at the doctor. "As I said, he is rational much of the time."

The doctor shook his head. This case troubled him more than he wanted to admit. "So at nine you gave him the full dose I prescribed."

"The full dose."

Gaston frowned. With that much laudanum in him a man could have his leg sawn off and not have his drug dream interrupted. "Are you certain he drank it all?"

A moment's irritation at Gaston's question flickered through her eyes. She let it pass before replying in a neutral tone, "I saw him drink it. I took the bottle back from him. He . . ." She stopped.

"Yes?"

"He said, 'Thank you, Sister. Better have a priest at hand. This could be my last night as your guest.' He smiled at me with a look I've seen before." She turned to the doctor. "They know when they're about to die. I know he's not really sick, but it was that look of death."

Gaston knew the look she referred to too well to question her judgment.

When they reached the door to Richardson's room, Gaston rapped on it. "Saul? It's David."

The hoarse voice came through the iron door. "I am sorry I cannot receive you any better, David. But please come inside. It's safe enough now. Regardless of what those nuns and half-witted darkies tell you, I have not become the Devil."

Gaston opened the small view hole cut in the door and looked through the grille. Richardson's face blocked the view into the room. Gaston was aghast at the changes in the two days since he'd last seen Richardson. He had the drained look of a man who was only hours from death by internal bleeding.

"But David," Richardson said, "you have to promise one thing. You have to leave when I tell you. The Devil will come for me, and I will know when he's coming. But he may get you if you're with me." A slight flash of humor passed through his eyes. "I know quite well that you think me insane. I assure you I am not, but if you fail to swear that you will leave when I tell you, I will knock you sense-less the moment you set foot in this room. Then the boys can drag you out of the way of harm."

"Saul, it's me."

"David, I don't have time for politeness. Do you swear?"

He nodded. "I swear."

Richardson turned away, and Gaston reached for the door handle. "Stay here, Sister. Be ready to let me out."

She bowed her head and clutched her rosary.

A shadow darkened the viewing port. "And David," Richard-son whispered, "wear a cross."

Gaston stepped back from the door, only to find a crucifix pressed into his hand. It was Sister Francis's. It was her only valu-able possession. The heavy silver crucifix had been on her waist from the first day that Gaston had met her in the better days of the 1840s. He resisted taking it from her.

She pressed it into his hand. "If the Lord doesn't recognize me as one of his own without it by now, he never will."

Gaston started to put it back into her hand.

She stopped him. "If praying over a thing can make it holy, then that's as holy as you'll find. It might serve to protect you. Please, wear it."

He drew the chain up over his head until the heavy silver cross dropped down on his chest. Then he did something he had not done for years. He crossed himself.

The door opened into a room that was totally vacant except for a bed, a chamber pot, and a chair. Richardson sat on the bed. A complete view of his patient did little to reassure Gaston. Dark circles of exhaustion marred Saul's patrician face. Saul had always been thin, but now he was emaciated. His skin had the sickly white tone of the seriously ill. He was sweating feverishly. A poorly healed cut on his cheek hinted at something more, as did the cuts on his hands and abrasions on his wrists. "I'm glad you came. Sorry I can't offer you a drink, but the staff here seems somewhat lax."

Gaston grimaced at the forced humor. "Hello, Saul. How are you?"

"Uh, a little dry now. Could I have some water?"

"Sister," Gaston called over his shoulder, "might you bring us some water?"

"Of course, Doctor." Her response was muffled by the thick door.

"It's all right, David," Richardson said. "It really is. I intend you no harm. The sisters are less confused than they act. Every one of them knows what's happening here. They know it as well as I. They know who it is that I am facing."

"And who's that?"

"The Devil, a demon, a minion of the netherworld."

"Saul, I can't believe—"

Saul interrupted. "But the nuns can. They know. Look in their eyes. They know. The nurses avoid me. It is always two that come. One stays in the hall. Half the time, the one who comes in is clutching her crucifix or her rosary. Any amulet that might give them some protection."

The sound of the door opening behind him caused Gaston to turn and see a frightened nun with a carafe of water and two glasses on a tray. She set the tray down just inside the door and scurried out. A second nun held the door for her. She swiftly shut the door, and the latch clicked as the door shut. It couldn't be opened from the inside.

Gaston's nervousness was obvious, and Richardson smiled. "You're not in any danger really. I can tell when I'm about to lose control. They'll have time to get you out of here."

"Lose control?"

Richardson got up from the bed and walked to the barred window that looked out over nothing more interesting than another wall of the hospital. "They don't let the people on the street see in here," he grimaced, "probably some sense of delicacy. My keepers are made uncomfortable by the situation. One minute I am a Richardson, someone to be reckoned with. A few minutes later I'm the most violent patient on the floor, like an animal—biting, clawing, defecating."

He moved back to the bed and sat down, grimacing as a bruise or cut took his weight. "It's all done to shame me, to shame one who would break faith with them."

Gaston waited.

"When I first came here, when you first admitted me, I was too afraid to say much. But in the past few days, I've become certain that they are going to kill me. So I don't have much more to fear. And I want to tell someone."

He stared across the room at the iron door. "You won't believe me, but I'll tell you anyway. I don't have much time for the story." He looked at Gaston. "But it will be a story without names. If you knew the names, you might say something. Then your life would be at risk as well."

Gaston remained silent and let Saul continue. "Before the war, I joined a club, a very exclusive club. It seemed something grand, like a Hellfire Club. We donned robes and chanted, engaged in all manner of perversity, bowed to a statue of Satan, reveled in our superiority.

"Some seven years after I came home from the war, I was invited into the inner circle. Much hurrah, blood poured on burning sulfur. Even greater fun. I advanced to the special meetings, held after the new members departed. There I began to see things that made no sense to me. Some of the women who were brought in for our little rituals were of the lowest class. They always arrived in a drugged haze, but still screamed most convincingly. I thought it was part of an act, that they were prostitutes, hired for the evening of fun. Probably made a month's pay for a night of debauchery." He took a sip of water. The glass was unsteady in his hand. "Until we killed one of them." He looked at Gaston. "One of our more prominent citizens did the actual killing, though the job wasn't very hard. The poor girl had been used and used and was half out of her mind. Two men held her up, and he slit her throat from behind." A look of distaste passed across Richardson's face. "He seemed skilled at the task. The blood shot out of her neck, and one of the women in the group came up with a bowl and caught it. The blood splashed into the bowl and down her arms. Like beasts, others came to rub their hands in it, dunking them into the bowl, painting their faces with the hot blood while the woman died.

"I was horrified. Drunk or not, I backed away into a corner of the room and crouched there. I couldn't believe what I was seeing. Then they passed the bowl, leaving the draining corpse in the middle of the floor. Like a perverted acolyte, the woman brought the bowl to each of them; each of them tasted the blood. The last person that she took the bowl to was our leader, our high priest. I watched him drink from the bowl, then paint his face with the blood. He took the bowl from her and turned to pour it over the small fire they had built near the center of the room.

"That's when one of the others stopped the priest. He said, 'One has not partaken.' He pointed to me. I was vomiting." He looked at Gaston. "You can't imagine the smell, so choking, so overwhelming. . . ."

"I can."

"That's right; you were at Antietam. I forgot. You'd know." He ran his hands over his head, pushing his dirty hair out of his face. "The priest stood over me, all drenched in blood, and held the bowl over my head. He said, 'You've sworn. You are one of us. You cannot deny the sacrament.' Then he poured some of the blood onto my head. The rest he gave to the fire."

Gaston was too shocked to respond immediately. He knew that among the prostitutes of Savannah, some would go missing from time to time. But no one paid it much mind, thinking the girls had perhaps moved on to where they could make more money. Or maybe they had gotten drunk and fallen into the river. In a few hours they would be well into the Atlantic. But those that went missing were never the courtesans who serviced the upper class. The missing ones were the girls who met the cotton ships, who lived in the worst brothels of Indian Street, or who seemed to live nowhere at all.

There was always a ready supply, both colored and white. The white girls came from the ruined farms of South Georgia, daughters of sharecroppers. Many had been orphaned by the war. The black girls were former slaves or the children of slaves who had found themselves free in 1865. They had no knowledge of how to cope with their new world, even if they did have their freedom and a small piece of land. Both groups lived a precarious existence. On a whim or a failed crop, the entire family of a sharecropper might be turned out. If the man of the family was dead or if he had some accident while farming and the women couldn't make up for his work among themselves, they had to find a way for the family to survive. These girls, without education, breeding, or family ties, had but one thing to sell. Once they did, their families would have no more to do with them, even if most of the money they made was sent back to help the family. The girls were condemned by the ruthless Baptist morality that ruled the red clay Piedmont.

Richardson continued his story. "I was trapped. I had sworn myself into the club, done all manner of things that would place me in the grip of the law or earn me social ostracism. So I could not betray them. But I had to get out. I'd seen too much death already."

Gaston interrupted. "Saul, I can't believe . . ."

Richardson ignored the interruption. "They warned me that I would die if I left the group." He paused, then continued, "Now I know it's true. Over the past month, the visions have become worse. I see the face of a demon, some creature, over and over again. It comes in the night. Sometimes I lose consciousness. That's when the sisters say I go insane." He shook his head with exhaustion and shame. "You see, tonight may be my last night."

"Why?"

"It's the night before the new moon. The time they do their rituals."

A silence fell between the two men. Gaston noticed the stale smell of the bedsheets, the faint reek from the chamber pot.

"So why did you call me here?"

"A priest seemed unlikely to hear my confession, but a doctor could hardly refuse to come."

"But you've told me nothing I can use."

"Nor will I. But you have brought something I can use." His hand reached out to grab the crucifix that hung around Gaston's neck. "A nun's crucifix, worn smooth with prayer . . ."

"It's not mine; I can't."

"I need it." His hand clasped the crucifix like a soldier in his first battle grasps his rifle.

Gaston reluctantly slipped the chain over his head.

"Thank you, David. The sister won't mind. No nun would mind having her crucifix in the hands of a sinner when he meets the Devil." A sardonic grin crossed Richardson's face. He raised his voice. "Would you, Sister? I know you're listening."

She responded, her voice muffled by the door, "I hope it serves to burn his hands if he comes for you."

"He will come," Richardson answered with certainty. Suddenly he turned his head to the side and seemed to peer through the wall. He cocked his head, as if listening.

Richardson's face grew more somber. "Get out, David; get out now." He withdrew into the far corner of the room and folded himself around the crucifix. "Get out," he screamed. "Get out."

Gaston stood, but did not move. He wanted to help, but had no idea how. The room became cold, and the light from the oil lamp near the ceiling seemed to dim. Then the door crashed open, and the formidable strength of Sister Francis dragged him out into the corridor. One of the other nuns, Sister Mary Brigid, emerged from the shadows to pull the door shut. Sister Francis threw the latch on the door and tried to look through the small viewing port in the door. The lamps were already extinguished, and a dull red glow suffused the room. The last thing she saw was Richardson, cowering in the far corner. The air turned chill, gelid, as if all of the warmth had been sucked from the night.

Sister Francis turned for help, then stopped. A low, animal growl emerged from the room, mated with Richardson's first scream. She turned back to the door. The slide that covered the view port in the door slid shut, driven by an unseen hand. Then the door shuddered as something, perhaps the bed, slammed against it from the inside.

Richardson's incoherent screaming reverberated down the hall. The orderlies ran toward them. They stopped when something like an animal's roar erupted inside the room. It did not sound like Richardson. Sister Francis desperately tried to open the slide in the door, but could not budge it. Regardless of the chill that suffused the air, the door was hot to the touch. The chamber pot shattered against the wall in the room. Dark laughter came through the door, though it was hard to distinguish beneath Richardson's screams. Then the laughter stopped, to be replaced by an unmistakable bellow of rage. Richardson screamed once more; then there was the sound of a heavy object striking the wall.

They heard the sound of shattering glass, and it was over. The silence was so sudden that they almost fell into it. The chill that had clung to the air vanished, to be replaced by the warm and humid air of a normal October night.

Gaston and Sister Francis crossed themselves. The orderlies became unfrozen. Some made the sign of the cross. Others made signs from different religions, but they were all signs of warding off evil.

Gaston looked at them. "Boys, get this door open." They reluctantly came down the hall.

The larger of the first two orderlies, the one they called Elijah, reached for the latch, slid it open, and pushed the door. Nothing happened. Elijah was a big man, well over six feet. He threw his shoulder into the door. Nothing. Then he motioned to the other orderly, Sam, who came and lent his shoulder to it as well. Both were big men, heavily muscled. Together they weighed well over five hundred pounds, yet they had to hit the door five times with their combined weight to open it far enough for a man to enter. Then they backed away from it.

"Sister, fetch me . . ." Gaston stopped. Sister Brigid had two oil lamps in her hands, both already lit. She handed one to Gaston. As he took it, he glanced into her eyes. He had never seen eyes that deep a shade of blue, nor could he read the expression on her face. Unexpectedly, she seemed calm and self-possessed. He turned to enter the room, and was not surprised that Sister Brigid, not the re- doubtable Sister Francis, was the one to follow him.

The room had been destroyed. The chamber pot had been smashed against the left wall. The twisted frame of the bed had been blocking the door. The glass in the windows on the far wall had shattered outward, leaving few shards within the room. Parts of the one chair were still recognizable. But it was the right wall that drew their attention. Richardson lay on the floor, one arm twisted behind him at a grotesque angle. He appeared to have been thrown against the wall. He had struck with enough force to shatter his skull. On the right side of his skull, blood, brains, shattered bone, and hair were intertwined. Gaston looked at the corpse almost dis- passionately. He had seen too many.

Thinking of the nun, he turned, expecting her to be upset by the condition of the corpse. Instead, he saw her standing near the opposite wall, her head bent down.

"Sister Brigid, are you all right?"

"Yes," she said, almost distractedly. "Come look at this."

He walked over to where she stood, realizing that she was not cringing from the sights in the room and wondering at her self- control. She pointed to something on the floor. It was Sister Fran- cis's crucifix. He bent down and reached toward it.

"No." Brigid stopped him with that cool voice of hers. "It's too hot. See, look around the edges; it's partially molten."

He peered at the object on the floor. She was right. Part of the cross had indeed been melted. He looked up at her. The expression on her face was pensive. Then he stood, looking from the crucifix to the twisted body on the opposite side of the room.

Gaston said, "I would never have thought that he would let go of that cross."

"I think it unlikely he had much choice." With that Brigid left the room, walking in unhurried steps through the twisted furniture.

Gaston was struck by her calm. He thought he knew why the corpse had not bothered her. She had seen far worse in the war, but this situation was nothing like anything she would have seen in the war—the brutalized corpse, the molten crucifix. She saw the impossible, the unbelievable, with an equanimity that he could not achieve. He wondered what was the source of her self-control. Even with all of his experience, he had no explanation for the events in the room, at least not one that he could believe.

CHAPTER TWO

Ireland, the 1840s

BRIGID Rourke was the second daughter of Tom and Nessa Rourke. Born in January of 1840 and preceded by two brothers and a sister, Brigid was their fourth child. There would be only one more, her younger brother, Roy. The Rourkes were tenant farmers on land that their family had been farming for generations, yet their land was no longer owned by them or by any other Irishman. It was now part of a large estate owned by an absentee English lord. He visited once every two or three years. His only concerns were that the rents were paid and that the crops paid him a good profit.

As Tom was a competent farmer, the family had little to fear from year to year, though they lived in a state of poverty that most Englishmen would never see. Their home, a two-room cottage, was better than what many Irish had. Parents, children, and the occasional pig slept together. They lived in County Mayo, near the sea on the western coast of Ireland. Good fortune at fishing, and the luck of the sea god, Lir, afforded the families who lived near the sea a better diet than many of the Irish. But the mainstay of their diet, like so many Irish, was the potato.

On the day of Brigid's birth, her great-aunt Emer, the village midwife and much more, had named her after one of the brightest and fairest of the old goddesses. The name was well chosen, for the infant was beautiful. Her eyes would become dark blue, and there was a porcelain clarity to her skin, even as an infant. By the time she was four, her eyes had turned the promised blue, and her hair was as black and shiny as a raven's wing. When neighbors visited the Rourkes, they often left Brigid small presents—carved toys or a bit of sweet bread. Many of the presents were given because she was favored by Emer.

Emer was regarded with respect by those who lived nearby. She was called "the old mother" by almost everyone, except a few of the strictest Catholics who called her "the witch" behind her back and in the privacy of their homes. None did so in public, as Emer was the only one with the true hand of a midwife for many miles. The babies she brought from their mothers were more often straight and true than those delivered by the doctors. She knew the potions to ease the pain of labor. And she knew the herbs that would keep a woman from conceiving. No one wanted too large a family when the food supply was so limited.

Brigid loved to visit with her great-aunt Emer, who, like her, had deep blue eyes. Emer told the little girl the stories of the old gods and the warrior kings, of Cúchulainn, and of the cattle raids. Sometimes Emer would take Brigid with her to listen to the men play the boisterous music that was interwoven with the daily life of Ireland. The little girl was entranced by the music and the dancing. Regardless of the material poverty of her life, the little girl had another kind of wealth that few others had. She had the music and the stories of centuries of Irish history and legends to fill her heart. One or another of the *seanchaide,* the singers, would visit once or even twice a month. Then the entire village would gather and listen as he wove his stories. His words built castles of gold, painting pictures of times before the English came and stole Ireland away from them. He sang of the ancient heroes and the elder gods, of kings in their castles and battles against the Fir Bolg.

Everything began to change in 1845. That year, some of the potato crop failed. Belts were tightened, the community grew closer, and those that had enough food shared what they had so that none would starve. The men made more trips into the Western Sea, and there were more fish on the table, though they had been bought with a few more lives than were normally given to the storms. Father Ferguson, the priest at the Catholic parish, tried to convince the villagers that it was their remaining pagan ways that had brought them this punishment from God. But the people remembered that the Tuatha Dé Danaan had been their gods for many years before Christianity, the English, and the potato made their way to Ireland. In the old days, before Catholicism came to Ireland, there had never been a time of starvation as there had been in 1831, when almost half the potato crop had failed.

In 1846 the crop began well. It looked better than that of the previous year. Then, in the last week of July, the blight struck again, only this time with greater force, withering crops in a few days. Where before a farmer might count on his field bringing in a ton or more of potatoes, now he had to do with less than fifty pounds. No amount of fishing could make up for the almost total loss of their main food supply. Other food could be bought, but not by people who had no money, who bartered for the few things that they needed. The Great Famine had begun.

Some small help came from the Church. Some, unexpectedly, even came from the English lord who owned the land, but it was not enough. As the winter came and the winds that blew from the Western Sea seemed colder than ever, disease began to take its toll on a population weakened by hunger. Even all of the medicinal skill of Emer could not keep the children and the old of the village alive. What use was medicine to one who was already starving to death? Brigid's younger brother, Roy, was barely two when he caught a cold that became pneumonia. He was buried in the first week of 1847. Across Ireland this story was repeated over and over in the years of the famine. By the time the famine was over in 1851, a million would have died from starvation or the diseases that ran rampant over the starved population. Another million and a half Irish would have immigrated to another country out of desperation.

Father Ferguson surely thought he was doing a good thing when he came to the cottage of Tom and Nessa. He offered to send seven-year-old Brigid to the convent school in Dublin. There she would be educated and fed. True, he could send only one child, and the reasons that Brigid was singled out were obvious to everyone.

Brigid was Emer's chosen one. Though Emer had another village girl to whom she had taught her skills, Brigid was different. Even Brigid's older sister, Siobhan, did not have her gifts. Brigid had the blood. Some said she was even showing signs of "the Sight," a highly respected gift. One with the Sight could see health or illness, would know if a baby was turned, and could occasionally glimpse the Old Ones.

The Sight was a matter of blood. You were born with it or you were not. For centuries the priestesses had tried to teach the skill, but with little success. Emer had the Sight, but Nessa, the daughter of her sister, did not. It was Nessa's daughter Brigid who had been blessed with the gift.

Brigid was the descendant of a line of women with the Sight that went back farther than any could remember. The signs of the Sight had begun to show earlier in Brigid than they had in Emer. Even as a child, Brigid seemed to have a special way with animals. At times, she seemed to see things where others saw only empty air. Father Ferguson knew that she could easily grow into a formidable adversary for him or his successors. So the offer to send her to convent school was less than an act of kindness. It was, at least partially, a maneuver to increase the Church's hold over the local population.

Father Ferguson had come to accept that Ireland was a country that was both Christian and pagan. For hundreds of years, the old ways and Catholicism had lived in a state of uneasy truce. At times the Church and the belief in the Tuatha Dé Danaan coexisted peacefully. Such dual beliefs did not trouble the Irish. Like all Celtic peoples, the Irish have never had much difficulty believing in two incompatible truths at the same time. The priestess, or the "Old Woman," had always had her place in the community. The Church could not totally dislodge the beliefs in the old ways. Part of the endurance of the old beliefs was based on the special skill with herbs that the woman in the priestess role possessed. But a greater part was based on her "special" abilities—her ability to glimpse the future, to know which disease caused a sickness, and to midwife with a skill that defied the doctors. A priest would not dare touch a pregnant woman's belly. The Old Woman would, and then tell if the birth would be easy or hard, if the child was sound, and if it were boy or girl.

After the priest's visit, Nessa went to Emer to discuss Brigid's future with her. Nessa said little when she entered the cottage of her aunt. Her gaunt figure spoke for her. Emer was aware of the family's suffering and the loss of Roy a few weeks before. Nessa sat down within the cottage. Unlike countless visits before, this time she had no gift of food with her, and that made her uneasy, though food was more precious than gold.

Emer breathed heavily in the hazy peat smoke that curled up from the small fire. "Don't worry, Nessa; you know you are always welcome." She managed a small smile. Then her voice became more distant. "I have been the village woman for almost forty years now. It has been hard. The English and the Catholics rule this world."

Nessa had nothing to say. She had come to ask a question, but she knew that Emer would get around to that question in her own way and time.

"This famine will become much worse before things are better. Many of our people will die. Ireland will change, too." Her gaze wandered, as though she were seeing scenes from her dreams. "We have held on to the old ways for many years. We still hold the stories of the old gods in our minds and hearts. But, for a while, it may be necessary that we forget them."

Nessa was shocked by what she was hearing, though she herself had often made the argument that the old ways were dying. To hear Emer say it was a different matter.

"It is cloudy in the future. There are too many decisions before us all. And now the hunger looms stronger than anything in our hearts. Perhaps the Old Ones will return. Perhaps they will sink into the sea. But that is not for an old woman to decide."

She refocused on her niece. "Send Brigid to the convent school. At least it will assure that she will live. I have taught her enough that a spark of the old ways will survive. Perhaps she will find her way; perhaps she will not."

Nessa thought that Emer was through and began to get up.

"Wait." The deep blue eyes of Emer held her. "I will die within the year." She held up her hand to stop Nessa's response. "Do not be sad. It is simply my time. I tell you so we can prepare. Do not let Brigid know until you must." She drew a deep breath. "But you must always be certain that she has a way to find one of us, or someone who is taught by us. She may have need."

Nessa nodded. She had been taught in the old ways. Death held little fear for her. It was only a change to a different realm. In time, you would return and breathe the air once again. Maybe it would be a time when there was joy and not a time when everyone was starving.

"Emer, should I make preparations?"

The old woman smiled. "No, dear, it's not that soon. But when I pass, I want no gifts of food buried with me. Give food to the children. Flowers would be nice, but make them foxglove or hemlock. Nothing you might eat."

The two women, both starving, chuckled a bit. Like all Irish, they could find a touch of humor in any situation, no matter how horrible.

CHAPTER THREE

Savannah
Saturday, October 10, 1874

MONSIGNOR Robert Henry was the highest-ranking official of the Catholic Church in Savannah outside of the bishop himself. Others often referred to the monsignor as the "eyes and ears" of the bishop. As such, he had been told of the strange happenings in the asylum ward of the hospital even before the bishop himself knew. Or perhaps Robert had been the first to learn of the events because the mother superior preferred to disturb his sleep rather than that of the bishop. After his visit to the hospital, the monsignor had carefully questioned the mother superior about the events surrounding Richardson's death and had not been able to sleep during the remainder of the night.

As the pink light of dawn appeared, he had dressed and gone to the refectory, more for coffee than for breakfast. As soon as the hour became acceptable, he made his way to the home of David Gaston. The walk was not a long one, as the monsignor's lodgings in the cathedral compound were not far from the home of his old friend. Robert walked quickly, his long legs gliding over the irregular sidewalks of the awakening city. It was a Saturday morning, so few people were on the street.

Gaston had been the monsignor's doctor since before the start of the war. The years had been far more kind to the priest than they had been to the doctor. Robert had been shocked at the change that had come over Gaston in the years he had been away. When David had left the city to tend to the army in the field in 1861, he had been in his late forties, contented and well married. When he returned, only four years later, he looked as though a decade had passed. The death of his wife while he was away had been a harsh blow, and his duties in the field had affected his physical health. He was stooped from hours of surgery, often fruitlessly trying to save a young man's life. Even more important, his spirit seemed broken by the constant company of death and the brutalities of medical necessity. The loss of his wife had left him without the companionship that might have helped him recover from the horrors of war. In the months after his return, Robert Henry had been his primary visitor, part confessor and part friend.

At first, the monsignor did not really understand what Gaston had experienced during the war. Robert had seen the war from the relative quiet of Savannah. While the city had been deeply affected by the war, with shortages and rationing almost constant, there had been no combat in its graceful streets. The city had seen its share of death, often in the form of wounded soldiers who had come home to die. In the later months of 1864, the wounded fleeing from Sherman's advancing army had found their only chance for medical care in Savannah. For many weeks the streets around the hospitals had become unsheltered wards, where women ministered to the sick and wounded with no more than water, whiskey, and fresh bandages.

Robert's conversations with Gaston had made him aware of the butchery that had occurred on the battlefields to the north. Gaston had sat in his empty house, drinking heavily, and, after much prompting, had told Robert of the things that he had seen as a field doctor for the Confederate Army. Robert came to realize that what he had seen in the streets of Savannah was nothing more than Purgatory and that true Hell had lain farther to the north. As Robert made the last turn onto the street where Gaston lived, he knew that he would find out the truth of what had happened to Saul Richardson, free of any spiritual overtones, for David Gaston no longer had faith in anything.

Robert turned up the short flight of stairs that led to Gaston's home and office. One of the two front rooms was a consulting room. The other was David's sitting room, where he could almost always be found during the day. Robert knocked on the front door and was soon rewarded with the sound of feet coming slowly down the stairs. Ezekiel opened the door and smiled out at the monsignor.

"Mistah Henry. Good to see you. Come on in." Ezekiel meant what he said. As gruff as Gaston usually was, a visit from the monsignor usually meant that the doctor would be in a better mood for the rest of the day.

Robert entered the dimly lit hallway. He noticed that the door to the sitting room was shut. Ezekiel, as usual, missed nothing. He had seen the monsignor's eyes glance toward the sitting room door.

Ezekiel was a freed slave. He had spent the first forty-five years of his life as someone's property, a servant on one of the inland plantations. When he was emancipated, he had not the slightest idea of what he should do with his freedom. Fortunately, the widow of the deceased plantation owner had sent Zeke to Robert Henry. Henry realized that Ezekiel would be the perfect servant for his friend the doctor. Ezekiel was still rather astonished to be paid money for doing an easier job than the one he had done on the plantation, but he was hardly fool enough to turn down free food and lodging, along with a small paycheck each week.

Ezekiel said, "He's been in there since we got back from Saint Jo's. He mighta moved around while I slept. But not much." He thought for a moment. "Fresh bottle of sour mash is missin' from the pantry."

"Guess I better go in," Robert said.

"Better you than me," Ezekiel replied. "Like some coffee, Mistah Henry?"

"For me and the doctor."

With a slight grin Ezekiel nodded and turned toward the kitchen.

Robert grasped the handle to the sitting room door and slid it open. He saw David asleep in a chair, one foot propped on an ottoman.

David stirred at the noise. "Dammit, Ezekiel, I don't want to be bothered," he said without opening his eyes.

"Ezekiel is too smart to bother you when you're like this. I'm not."

David's eyes snapped open, and he struggled upright in his chair. He was fully awake almost instantly.

"I still am amazed when I see you do that," Robert said.

"Try being a doctor for forty years. You'll learn it, too." He gestured to a chair. "Have a seat. Don't wait for me to get up. Might take a while. Damn leg's asleep."

Robert smiled at his friend and took the chair nearest him. In a few moments, Ezekiel came in with a tray with coffee, sugar, and cups. He hadn't bothered with cream, since he knew neither of the men took it. "Want me to fix up some breakfast?"

David looked at his guest. Robert said, "Not me, I've already eaten."

"Nothing for me, Zeke."

"Yassuh," he said, though as he turned back to the kitchen he mumbled, "Probably wouldn't set well on that sour mash."

Gaston watched him leave. "Sometimes I wonder if you got me the best servant or the rudest."

As he poured coffee for them both, Robert replied, "Not certain there is a difference."

Gaston chuckled. "Probably right."

They sipped their coffee together in the quiet for a bit. Robert knew that David couldn't be rushed. Finally he spoke. "Guess you came to ask about what happened last night."

Robert nodded. David sat back in his chair and wove his fingers together. His fingers were short and thick, a workman's hands.

Robert's hands were long fingered and expressive. They seemed made for the finest of work. But it was Gaston who was the surgeon.

"I've been Saul Richardson's doctor for years. When all of this started, I just thought he'd gone crazy. A lot of men did who saw what we saw. One day it just catches up to them, and they blow their brains out or lock themselves in a room. Saul was different. He said the Devil was coming for him."

"And was he?"

"I don't know. All I can tell you is that my visit with Saul ended when he seemed to sense something. He said I had to get out of his room. He pulled Sister Francis's crucifix off of my neck and screamed for me to get out. Sister Francis came in and dragged me out. One of the other nuns slammed the door shut behind me. Then we tried to get back in, but the door was jammed. So was the viewing port."

Gaston fell silent as the memories of the night washed over him. Remembering the strange sensations that he had felt while they waited outside the door, he shuddered briefly. The monsignor did not miss his friend's reaction. Over the years he had seen Gaston angry, depressed, jovial—the full range of emotions—but he had never seen him afraid until now.

The doctor went on. "I tell you, Robert, it sounded like an animal was in there with him. The air was incredibly cold. Not Savannah winter cold, but a bad Virginia winter cold. We heard the sounds of a struggle, we heard Saul scream, then there was a thump, and everything got quiet. Glass shattered and the cold left us. It took us a while to get the door open, but, when we did, Richardson was dead, slumped below a bloody spot on the wall."

"Had he killed himself?"

"Couldn't have. A man can't inflict that kind of injury on himself. His head had been smashed against the wall. Parts of his brain were there. Even if he could injure himself like that, he couldn't do it, smash open the window, and then return to the spot on the wall where his head hit. Not possible."

"Then what killed him?"

"I don't know. But I'll tell you what he told me when he was still alive." David reached for the sour mash to "sweeten" his coffee. He poured a healthy slug into the cup and offered it to Robert, who, unusually, put some whiskey in his coffee. "Saul said he'd belonged to a group that met each month on the new moon. He gave me no names. If I knew names, he said, repeating them would put my life in danger."

"Why?"

"You'll see. His companions in this group prayed to a statue of Satan, and apparently took it pretty seriously. When Saul got invited into the inner circle he found out they were having debauched rituals, bringing in prostitutes for their ceremonies, but it sounded like an orgy to me." David took a healthy slug of his coffee. "He got frightened when they killed one of the girls. They slit her throat, drained her blood, and drank it."

"They actually killed someone?"

"That's what he said," Gaston replied. "Saul refused to drink the blood. He'd seen too much on the battlefield. After that ritual, he told them he had to leave the group. They reminded him that leaving wasn't permitted, but he left anyway. The next new moon, his nightmares about a demon coming for him started."

"So you think he was killed by a demon?"

David sighed and leaned back in his chair. "I don't know what to believe. I just know what he said and what I saw. But whatever happened in that room when the door was shut is something I don't want to know. Likely it's more your department than mine."

BISHOP Francis Marion Shea had been the head of the Catholic Church for both Georgia and Florida for almost twenty years. From his new cathedral in Savannah, he administered the Church throughout both states. Many of the Catholics within his large diocese were Irish, though the first Catholics in Savannah had been

French. They had come to Savannah in the last years of the previous
century, fleeing the revolution in France and the slave revolts in
Haiti, but there were also many Catholics spread throughout the
formerly Spanish territory of Florida. Annually he would tour the
major parishes of Florida. He visited the northern part of his diocese
rarely. There were few Catholics there. His duties usually kept him
within the confines of his compound in Savannah. His Spanish-
speaking staff members tended to the needs of his Florida parishioners. Though his Florida parishioners were polite when he spoke
Spanish, he knew that his American tongue did not do justice to
their beautiful language. He had tried to do better with Spanish,
but his Latin kept intruding. Besides, they had enough difficulty
seeing him as a bishop. His blond hair, now peppered with gray,
seemed a curiosity in Florida. Fortunately the liturgy was in Latin,
which was something of home ground for the bishop.

Bishop Shea had been born in Charleston. His mother had assured him that he had been named for her favorite relative, the
Revolutionary War hero. The bishop was actually descended from a
brother of Francis Marion, which was close enough to prevent his
full name from being an embarrassment; rather, it was an assurance
of a good reception in the old colonial cities.

He would shortly be seeing Mother Superior Mary Margaret of
the Sisters of Mercy. She ran Saint Joseph's Hospital near the cathedral and was one of the bishop's most trusted advisors. That morning he had granted her request for an immediate audience. He felt
certain he knew what it would be about. The monsignor had already told him of the strange events in the hospital the previous
night.

The mother superior met with the bishop before lunch. As they
exchanged their formal greetings, she bent to kiss his ring. Then he
motioned to her to sit on the long sofa that ran along one side of his
office. As she sat, she arranged the skirts of her habit around her.
The bishop moved to join her on the sofa.

As the bishop sat, he said, "Mother Superior, I don't think I have ever received a request from you that contained the words 'earliest possible opportunity,' even during the recent war."

"Your Grace, nothing like this has ever happened to us before." She took a deep breath and released it slowly. "The events of last night have shaken much of the sisterly community. Had the events not been attested to by no fewer than five of the sisters, including Sister Francis, I would not have troubled you. However, I have no doubt that the situation is serious."

"Go on," he said.

"Last night Saul Richardson died. That, in itself, is not a matter that I would have brought to your attention. It is the manner of his death that troubles my community."

"I imagine that it would. Monsignor Henry has already discussed the events with me."

"He has?" The mother superior was surprised.

"Yes, and he gave me a detailed enough account that I am forced to believe that we may be confronting something that I have never faced before."

"So you are convinced?"

"Reluctantly," he said.

"I was reluctant to believe as well, but the physical evidence was unquestionable."

"What specifically?"

"The viewing port in the door has a slide that can be moved from the inside or the outside of the room. It had been slammed shut from the inside with so much force that it had warped. Even our strongest orderly can't slide it open. And the lamp in the ceiling was extinguished. How? Richardson could not reach it." She paused and reached into her habit. He could not see what she was grasping in her pocket. "And there is one more thing." She withdrew the damaged crucifix of Sister Francis and handed it to him. As he took it, she went on. "See how the edges are melted?"

He looked down at the heavy crucifix. When he saw the molten edges, he dropped it. Then he quickly picked it up from the floor, embarrassed by his own reaction. "The monsignor did not tell me about this."

"Dr. Gaston carried that crucifix, Sister Francis's crucifix, into the room with him. It was undamaged. But he left it behind with Richardson. There is no way which I am aware of that this crucifix could have been melted in the short space of time in which these events occurred. No matches or fuel were in the room. It simply could not have happened. But it did."

The bishop handed the crucifix back to Sister Margaret. He did not want to hold it any longer. Perhaps her faith was strong enough to believe that the crucifix could not be desecrated by anything. He was not certain of his. After she took it, he stared at the far wall in the room, looking for a way to deny that any of this had happened. None came easily. None came at all. The nun interrupted his thoughts.

"Your Grace?"

He looked back to her.

"You do believe me?"

"I do not wish to, but I do." The bishop stood and walked slowly to his window that looked over a garden. "About an hour ago, the monsignor told me Dr. Gaston's perspective on the events of last night. Combining his story with yours, I cannot deny that there is an evil influence at work."

"Then, Your Grace, what are we to do?"

"All those involved are to talk to no one about it. There will be enough rumors without our assistance." He paused. "As for dealing with this presence, the Church has its means."

"An exorcism."

"Perhaps that is what is called for, perhaps not. Whatever killed our patient did not seem to possess him. If that is true, then the situation is more serious than one that can be handled by an exorcism. We will need someone with special skills. There is a Benedictine monk, Father Benito, in Saint Augustine. I will send for him, as he is far more expert in these matters than I."

"Do you think that Father Benito can help?"

The bishop looked at her sadly. "That is a question he will have to answer. If it is beyond his abilities, rest assured that he will know whom he must contact.

"I will send for him. In the meantime, I would suggest that everyone who was present write a description of the events while they are still fresh in their minds. Father Benito will need all of the information that he can obtain. As for the room . . ."

"I have already had it sealed," she said.

"Good. We must discuss this further. Tonight, after vespers, bring those you have mentioned to me. Before you arrive, I will have sent for Father Benito."

Mother Superior Mary Margaret nodded, stood, and left the bishop's chamber. The bishop stayed seated on the sofa, absorbed in his thoughts. He had never expected to face the kind of situation that he was facing now. As a bishop he, of course, knew about the special resources that the Church had at its disposal. While he knew of them, he had never expected to call on them.

In the Bible, Jesus had cast out demons. He had exorcised spirits that were in possession of the body. But the Savior had also faced more fearsome opponents, ones that did not need the anchor of human flesh. If such a creature had come to the bishop's city, it must be thrown back to the place where it belonged.

The presence of such evil in his city was a reminder to him of human evil. It was more than probable that this demon had been summoned, which meant that hidden in his city were men who would open the doors that would let such evil in. Had he passed them on the street? Had they smiled at him? Were they in his own congregation?

He wondered how well he would sleep until Benito's arrival. Anyone might be in danger. Because of the bishop's position in the Church, he himself could face special hazard. His faith would have to sustain him. Without thinking, he began saying the words to a hymn written by Martin Luther:

"A mighty fortress is our God, a bulwark never failing,
Our helper he amidst the flood, of mortal ills prevailing,
But still our ancient foe, doth seek to work us woe,
His craft and power are great, and armed with cruel hate,
On earth is not his equal."

The hymn gave him comfort, which, he was certain, was precisely what Luther had intended.

CHAPTER FOUR

SISTER Brigid sat alone in the nuns' chapel until late Saturday morning. She should have had recourse to the simple comforts that were available to the other nuns—prayer and the quiet telling of the rosary beads. But she did not. What she had seen and heard had shaken her much too deeply, and the events had awakened memories from the earliest years of her life.

Brigid had experienced the events of the night in a way that no one else had. She had not merely felt the cold generated by the passage of the creature; she had sensed its presence and known its thirst for human blood. It was a being of merciless evil. She knew all of these things because the potency of its presence had awakened her Sight, which had long lain mostly dormant in her. She did not feel the need to reach for her missal and crucifix to assuage the horror of Richardson's death. Instead, she found herself seeing her great-aunt Emer's face through the smoke of a peat fire.

When she had been six years old, her great-aunt had begun Brigid's training. Emer had planned that Brigid would one day take her place. Brigid's deep blue eyes were a mark in her family, a mark that was always paired with special abilities. She could see and hear things that others could not, and Emer patiently spoke with her niece about the "other world" that she could see.

For Brigid, her aunt's tiny cottage was a place of peace, a peace rooted in the land itself. Many nights Brigid would visit the cottage alone, and she and her aunt would look into the smoke of the fire in the cottage. Within it, there were shapes that hung just on the edge of Brigid's vision, small faces that wished her well. She was beginning the training that would enable her to become her aunt's successor.

Then the famine had come and changed her destiny. Brigid had been sent to the convent school in Dublin when she had been seven. She still remembered her tearful departure from her home, and she had never seen her parents or her aunt Emer again. While the world Brigid had entered was so much more comfortable physically than the one she had grown up in, it was a strange world to one raised as she had been. There was plenty of food and warm clothes to wear in Dublin, but the convent school was cold emotionally. She had learned quickly, sometimes brutally, that the stories, even the names, of the old gods were forbidden. Things that she had seen her aunt do were dismissed as "stories." Brigid quickly learned that the talents of the Sight were not welcome in her new home, and she repressed her reactions to things that she saw that others could not see. After a few years, she stopped seeing them. At least most of the time. In the intervening three decades, the Church had become her home. Her special skills had been put away. They had no place in the Catholic Church. The Church was not a place of magic; it was a place of ritual and prayer.

Brigid could not tell even the Mother Superior what she had perceived on the night that Richardson had been killed. From the dark recesses of her memories, Brigid knew that magic was what was needed to deal with the spirit that had been summoned from a dark quarter of the universe to kill Richardson. The magic that was needed was that of the old ways, part of a religion whose origins were lost to her.

Brigid decided to write to her sister, Siobhan, who lived with her husband in a village not many miles from where they had been born. From her letters, Brigid knew that Siobhan still retained contact with some few who held to the old ways. Brigid's niece, Nessa, was apparently studying the old traditions, since she had been the one to inherit the powers that Emer and Brigid shared.

Once resolved, Sister Brigid left the small chapel, fetched paper and pen, and wrote her letter. By late afternoon, she had mailed it at the post office on the waterfront. The reason for her haste was simple—mail took two weeks to reach Ireland. She did not want to explain, even to herself, why it was important that the letter to her sister be sent in secret.

Brigid knew that the letter would be on its way to Ireland soon, regardless of the fact that it was a Saturday. Almost two thousand ships a year left Savannah. Most were destined for Liverpool or Belfast, delivering the precious cotton to the looms of an industrialized Great Britain. With typical English thoroughness, the postal service between Great Britain and important overseas ports, like Savannah, was excellent. Even the post within Ireland traveled rapidly, since the English lords liked to keep in close touch with their Irish holdings, particularly in the harvest season when the price of both cotton and corn varied by the day.

Brigid knew that Siobhan would take the matter seriously. The question was whether or not she could do anything about the situation. This demon was not a matter for the local village priestess. Though Emer had seemed immensely powerful to Brigid as a child, she knew, with more perspective, that this matter would have been beyond her aunt's capabilities.

Her letter mailed, she walked slowly back to the convent. She had no further duties until that evening when she would work in the hospital. As she walked, she finally examined the thoughts that had led her to mail the letter. The impulse had been an undeniable vestige of her past. She had been raised a pagan; at least that was what the Church would have called her upbringing. Her namesake, the goddess Brigid, had belonged to a much more complex pantheon than the Christian one. The Celtic gods often feuded with one another. They drank, they fought, and they sometimes killed for the love of a mortal. They had so much laughter, so much life. She stopped. She could not believe what she was thinking. She nervously crossed herself.

"Blessed Mother," she thought, "what am I doing?" But all she saw was Emer's eyes, glittering through the smoke.

Several people passed by the nun as she walked. The men doffed their hats, and the ladies smiled. The occasional colored servant passed by, stepping aside to allow the white woman to pass. The seriousness of Brigid's visage told everyone that she was deep in thought, and no one was rude enough to disturb her. The streets she was traversing were quiet ones, away from the business districts of Broughton and the waterfront. A few carriages rolled by, their horses' hooves tapping on cobblestones or thudding on sand. Even the sharp taps on the stones were absorbed by the moss-hung oaks that shaded the streets and squares.

The very air seemed alive. The humidity of Savannah was no burden in October, when the days were pleasant. The heavy trunks of the oak trees, many over a century old, stood like sentinels in the sandy soil of the squares. Each was draped with the gray cloak of Spanish moss that thrived in the city's mild climate. The branches gave shade in the squares, and, to someone raised as she had been, put her in mind of the sacred groves in Ireland. To Brigid, the open squares seemed like natural churches, places where worship or introspective thought would be appropriate.

Brigid turned down another street that she knew would take her farther from the convent, not closer. She didn't pause to wonder why she needed to be away from the convent to think clearly. All that she knew was that she could not imagine that the suffering Christ could come down from his cross to fight the demon that had come last night. But one of the great heroes, perhaps Manannán mac Lir, son of the god of the sea, seemed a more likely champion. In the old legends, his lance, once thrown, never rested until it tasted blood.

She was dazed by the currents in her thoughts. She knew that they sprang from the events of the previous night. In a few moments, her safe, Catholic world had been shattered. Since she had been a small child and introduced to the convent school, she had lived in a world of spiritual order. Neither good nor evil reared its head too strongly. There was no passion, except the passion of prayer. In fact, the spiritual life of a nun was not one of revelations and visions, but one of dogma, liturgy, and meditation. She did not expect to see any denizen of another world. She did not expect to see Christ appear before her or a statue of Mary weep blood.

How different were the Catholic beliefs from the old ways of Brigid's homeland, where every bush might hide a spirit, where one left offerings at the springs out of respect for the Old Ones who dwelt there. To the pagan Irish, the world was alive with the presence of the gods and the thousands of smaller spirits who crowded one another on that great island. Laughter and dancing, mischief and sorrow, all cascaded around their lives in a way that only one raised to it could comprehend. It was chaotic, sometimes a bit frightening, but then, was that not the nature of life? The gods could surely see the sense of it. Meanwhile, it was the business of mortals to get on with life itself.

Brigid's Catholic world had no room for the events of the previous evening. A demon had come from somewhere, perhaps from Hell itself. In the middle of a building filled with nuns, it had taken a soul, taken a life, and the crucifix that had been given to the victim had done nothing to protect him. Forty years of Sister Francis's prayers had not made that cross holy enough to slow the demon that had swept from who-knows-where to crush Richardson. The demon had melted the edges of the crucifix. Had it done that because its power was too limited to destroy the sacred symbol, or because it had wanted the crucifix left intact, but damaged, to show that it meant nothing, that it was only a piece of silver to the demon?

In that moment, though she did not recognize it, she had started remembering. She had started becoming Emer's great-niece again.

She had walked into Richardson's room when others dared not, simply because she knew the creature had gone. The melted crucifix was only a piece of metal to her. In her thoughts, dredged from childhood memories, had been a protective chant in Gaelic that would surely bring forces to protect her. Emer had taught her that there was no Devil, no Lord of Evil. Beings bent on causing harm would flee from the presence of the least of the gods.

Brigid sat heavily on a bench in one of the squares and tilted her head back, raising her eyes upward. A movement in one of the trees drew her attention. She thought she had seen, from the corner of her eye, a small human shape ducking behind one of the massive branches. Brigid looked at the branch more closely and focused her vision on the space just above the branch. Her Sight was reawakening and Brigid was amazed and a bit afraid. She sat and waited. Soon she saw a small, slightly triangular face above and behind the branch. Judging by the size of its head, Brigid knew it would stand perhaps two and a half feet tall. It was human-like, though its skin and hair were uniformly tinged a greenish brown. Brigid was surprised, but not astonished. She had not seen a little one for many years, not since she had been a child.

Shy, and somewhat afraid, the small creature smiled at her. It was beautiful, childlike, and a bit mischievous. Brigid opened her mind to it, as Emer had taught her. A sound like a young girl's laughter floated through her. The little one was like a child in many ways, eager to please, but also in search of fun. It was also far, far older than Brigid. Barring accident, the little ones were immortal, or at least many thought so. Emer had told her that they could be killed, though she had met many that were hundreds of years old.

The little creature in the tree was entranced that a human had taken notice of it. So few did. Then another came up beside it. They giggled together for a moment, then vanished behind the thick branch. Brigid had been well schooled in the lore of the little ones and treated them with respect, as she should any living being. Fools often disregarded them and failed to greet them graciously, which was a grievous error of judgment. Your luck would not go well if you offended them. Angering them was to be avoided. Fortunately, angering them was a difficult thing to do.

Impelled by the sight of the little ones, her mind wandered to other thoughts. She was thirty-four years old, separated by decades from her lessons with her aunt. Although Brigid was no longer as beautiful as she once had been, she knew that beneath her habit was still the slender shape of a dancer, yet she had never known the touch of a man.

"Mother of God." She thought to herself, "Is one night all it takes to awaken the pagan in me? I have not thought of having given up the pleasures of a man for over a decade."

She shook her head, as if trying to dislodge the thoughts that had found a home there. Brigid needed to move, if only to help change her thoughts. She stood and continued her walk in the late afternoon, as the day was one of those exquisite ones that made Savannah such a blessed city.

BY six Brigid's letter was in the postal pouch aboard the *John J. Stevenson,* a steamship bound for Belfast. The ship headed out to sea with the early evening tide, her engines propelling her rapidly down the channel, against the wind. The *John J. Stevenson* was one of the newest ships on the Atlantic routes. She carried less than a full complement of sail, as sail was, for her, rarely the primary propulsion. When the wind was strong and favorable, she might sail to save fuel, though the sails were mainly there to provide emergency propulsion should the steam engines fail. Even in 1874, few shipbuilders were willing to trust steam as the only source of propulsion, but the advances in engine power and reliability since the crossing of the first steamship in 1819 were remarkable. In that year, Fulton's grand gamble, the steamship *City of Savannah,* had been the first steamship to cross the ocean, though it had made most of the crossing under sail rather than steam. It was no accident that the first "transatlantic steamship" sailed from one of the great cotton ports. That crossing to Liverpool had taken twenty-eight days. The *John J. Stevenson* would make the crossing to Belfast in nine or ten days. From there, the letter would reach Siobhan in a few more days at most.

Brigid had found her way to the high bluffs that overlooked the river. She watched a ship depart down the Savannah River. She did not know if her letter was on board that particular ship, though she did know it was likely that the letter had begun its crossing. She was sitting above the river on the bluffs as the slow twilight began to descend. Normally a woman would not be in this place alone. But nuns rarely had to fear what most women might. As a nun, Brigid was unlikely to be in any danger. Nor was it normal that she was outside of the convent or the hospital by herself at this hour. However, the mother superior had granted her permission to take time to reflect upon the recent events. Mary Margaret was well aware of the stress placed upon the nuns who had been present when Richardson had died, especially Sisters Francis and Brigid. They had been closest to the events.

Sister Brigid held her rosary, more to have something to do with her hands than to pray. Her problem was that she did not know to whom she should pray. The more she thought of the Christian God to whom she had been devoted, the more she saw his face turn into that of one of the Tuatha Dé Danaan. She felt alone and surrounded, all at once. As the darkness began its final descent and the gaslights along Bay Street were lit, she realized that she would need many more hours to come to terms with all that had been awakened by Richardson's death. She thought of Emer, of her sister, Siobhan, and of her niece, Nessa, whom she had never met. She wondered what her life would have been like if she had stayed with her family. Would she have been one of the ones who fell to the famine, or would she have been a survivor, now married and raising her own children?

She stood and began a circuitous walk back to the hospital, where she could avoid these thoughts by absorbing herself in her work. It was good work, helping the sick, regardless of what god's name it was done in. She came to Washington Square. Not in the mood for the many people who would be out on Broughton Street, she turned right onto Saint Julian Street. The street was quiet and res- idential, with a few modest homes and many of the grander homes of the wealthy planters and factors. Some of the homes were already shuttered; others were open to the night, with conversation drifting onto the quiet, beautiful street. The foot and carriage traffic had al- most come to a halt at this hour, leaving the street nearly deserted.

She was aware of the eyes that had been following her since she had entered the square. The little ones were watching her, finding her more interesting and more confusing than most of the humans who passed by them. As they watched Brigid, one of them looked to another, a question in its glittering eyes. The other one shook its head. "No."

Deep in thought, she was not paying attention to the blocks that she was passing until a chill swept through her body. She stopped in the middle of Warren Square. She had walked through this square many times before without sensing anything unusual, but then, she had never before walked it at night with her Sight reawakened.

Lying like a pall across the section of Saint Julian in front of her and covering almost the entire block was a dark mist, something that could not be seen by normal sight but was there nonetheless. It was not alive; it did not react to her. Like smoke after a fire, the darkness swirled in upon itself, a manifest residue of evil. Trapped inside of it were the final thoughts of people just before their gruesome deaths— pain, fear, and mindless horror. Their dreadful thoughts swirled out of the cloud and penetrated into her mind, bringing with them their terror of an inhuman thing, a creature with a chill fascination with their suffering and a brutal enjoyment of their pain, reminding her of the presence that had swept into Richardson's room.

She wanted to scream. She pushed the thoughts of others out of her mind. She held herself still and controlled a desperate urge to run. When she had pushed the nightmares from her, she walked toward the noise of Broughton Street, toward the people thronging the thoroughfare. She would take a much more brightly lit route back to the hospital, where the welcoming figure of Saint Joseph would greet her at the door. She would return to the safety of the routine—the bedpans, the coughing, and the illness.

The Sight, as always, was a mixed gift, one capable of bringing laughter and beauty that others did not see. It was also the bringer of horrors that other people would, thankfully, never be aware of. Here in the dim street she had encountered a residue of evil and a sure knowledge of a creature that fed on the pain and fear of others. The fear haunted her as she made her way back to the hospital.

CHAPTER FIVE

Monday, October 12

JAKOB Streng ruled his factoring house from a mahogany desk set in front of the windows, looking out over his employees' desks. In most other cotton factors' offices, the owner had a separate office, but that custom had never set well with Streng. He felt he had to be aware of the events of the day. Only then could he control the events around him and remain a successful cotton broker. For his rare private conversations, he had a small room set aside on the second floor.

Adjacent to his desk was the desk of his nephew, Frederick Kuck. When Jakob was present, Frederick's job was to keep his eyes and ears open to the changes in the market. When Jakob was absent, young Freddy ran the office with the assistance of Samuel Black, the manager, who occupied a second desk near Streng's. Some of the other factors in the city thought it odd that Jacob's manager should be a Jew, but Jakob didn't give a damn about his manager's ancestry. What he cared about was making money, and Samuel was very adept at helping him do just that.

Jakob was often absent, and only a few of those who worked with him were aware of his "avocation." Even his nephew knew nothing of the rituals that Jakob conducted in his basement, and the dark powers that he summoned. All that Freddy knew was that Jakob was often absent for one or two days a month because of some vague illness, which he had gathered was some form of severe headache.

Streng & Co. had been founded by Jakob's father, Herman. Jakob's grandfather, Heinrich, had emigrated from Germany in 1790 and had become a successful grocer. He had two sons. Otto had taken over the grocery business. The other son, Herman, had seen the money that could be made in the cotton trade, so he had created the factoring house in 1823. Based on the foundation laid by Herman, Jakob had built Streng & Co. into the most successful factoring house in the city. Its success was based on two things— Samuel's efficient management and Jakob's uncanny ability to predict fluctuations in the price of cotton.

Jakob had to laugh when he saw the astonishment on the faces of the other factors when he correctly predicted a shift in the price of prime Sea Island cotton. True, he was very good at guessing the trends in the market, but that guessing was aided by the telegraph on the second floor, which could send him the prices on the London market before the main exchange in Savannah even opened. The telegraph service was expensive, but had paid for itself many times over.

Every morning at seven, Jakob joined Frederick, Samuel, and two other of his employees at his business. Many of the critical decisions of the day were made in these early hours. The remaining employees came at eight. Promptly at nine, Jakob would walk the few blocks to his house for breakfast, returning by eleven. Whenever he left the office, an unsettling tension left with him. Though he paid his employees better than the other factors did, he was not an easy man to work for. He was demanding and exacting, prone to sudden anger and quick firings of those who did not meet his standards. His employees would not admit, even to each other, how much they feared the man. They knew his temper and his precision, but those characteristics were not the seat of their fear. It was his nature that frightened them. In business dealings he was bloodless, cold. While he might publicly bemoan the collapse of a competing factoring firm, his eyes always seemed to be laughing when he spoke of it. His employees knew that he had as little concern for their own future as he had for that of other factoring firms, but he did pay well.

When the clock struck nine, Streng rose from his chair and slid the document he was working on into a drawer and locked it. Freddy and Samuel were at their desks, as they always managed to be at nine.

"Freddy, Samuel." He nodded to each in turn, then took his hat from the stand behind his desk. He did not need to explain his actions to the two men. They knew where he was going and what would be expected of them in his absence. The others in the office watched Streng as he strode out of the office. After he shut the door behind himself, the sound of muted conversation sprang up in the office. They did not talk about him, merely began the normal conversation that would take place in any office where the owner was not feared.

As Jakob walked to his home, he was relieved to be away from the office. The ritual that he had conducted Friday had tired him. As he walked home, he automatically responded with a smile and a wave to others who greeted him. Since he was one of the preeminent cotton factors in the city, he was well known. Knowing human nature as he did, he suspected that many of the ones who greeted him were doing so because he was wealthy, not out of any sense of personal regard. Greed was one of the sins that Jakob knew well.

CHAPTER SIX

Saint Augustine, Florida
Monday, October 12

FATHER Luis Benito was a Benedictine monk, living in a small monastery near the old city of Saint Augustine, Florida. Like many in his abbey, his native language was Spanish. Florida had been a part of the dwindling Spanish Empire, except for a brief period of British rule, for hundreds of years. In 1819 it was formally ceded to the United States. In the year of his birth, 1829, Spanish was still the first language of many Floridians, even though the official language of this former part of New Spain had become English. Now the Spanish Floridians were increasingly becoming fluent in the new language, having found themselves at a disadvantage in matters of business and government to the Anglos who were moving to their state. Father Benito had learned the new language as a child, though he still preferred the more graceful cadences of Spanish to the harsher tones of English. Truth be told, however, he preferred Latin to either of them.

In his calling he had learned other languages. Knowing Greek was a tremendous advantage in studying the old texts that dealt with magic. He had a passable reading knowledge of Aramaic, French, and German, though he considered it a blessing that he had never actually had to converse in German. It was, to his ear, a decidedly ugly tongue.

The monastery where he lived was only a few miles from where he had been born. He was happy to have returned to the rural quiet of Florida, for in his years with the Church he had seen much of the world and he was grateful for the serenity of his homeland. When he was twenty-one, the Church had sent him to the Vatican to study. He had remained there for almost a decade before being posted to Spain, where the Benedictines had a monastery that served the bishop of Toledo. The immense Gothic cathedral of Toledo loomed over the city. Under Arab rule Toledo had been one of the intellectual centers of Europe. When the Arabs and Jews had been driven from Spain in the fifteenth and sixteenth centuries, the city had lost its scholarly prominence.

Benito had found Toledo to be a city filled with ancient pain. Much of the Spanish Inquisition had been run from Toledo, and the cathedral, for all its Gothic majesty, was a place that no one with Benito's perceptual abilities could stand to be within for very long. Along with the black residue of centuries of soot from candles and incense was a different residue, one lain down by confessions, torture, and fear. He was also disturbed by the old synagogue, whose entire congregation had been either killed, driven off, or converted during the Inquisition. The building had been made into a small church, which seemed to Benito a second injury lain over an older one.

After a few years in Toledo, he had requested to return to Florida. The Church was gracious enough to grant his request. For over a decade now he had been living quietly in the small monastery. It was his home. He had first begun his life in the Church at this very monastery.

His family had deep roots in Saint Augustine. His great-grandfather had come to Florida almost a century before, bringing with him his trade as a saddle maker. Father Benito's grandfather had expanded the business. The horse-loving Spaniards always needed saddles, especially the superbly crafted ones made by Benito and Sons. Their trade had assured that the family had weathered the turns of fate that haunted the old city.

Since its founding in 1565, Saint Augustine had survived attacks by the English, the Indians, and even the occasional pirate. Benito's great-grandfather had come to Saint Augustine shortly after the city's return to Spanish rule in 1783. His son, Benito's namesake, had married a Seminole Indian woman, a frequent occurrence among the Spanish. Benito was therefore one-quarter Seminole, and his family was large, with relations extending into both the European and the Indian community. The yellow fever epidemic of 1821 had struck down many in the city, though the Benito family had suffered less than most.

Benito's garden was his pride. He had studied medicinal herbs since his childhood. His mother had taught him the knowledge that her mother had brought from Spain. So he knew of foxglove and its use to calm the heart, that comfrey speeded healing. But he had added additional herbs to the list of those known in Europe. Some of his Seminole relatives had avoided the removal of their tribe to west of the Mississippi. Those who remained freely shared their medical knowledge with him. While the Europeans knew of tobacco only as something to smoke, the Seminoles used it to reduce bleeding and infection. Father Benito relied heavily on the native herbs that grew much better in the hot and damp climate of Florida than his European transplants.

He was in his garden, removing some of the native weeds that seemed partial to the carefully tilled soil of his herbarium, when the letter from the bishop arrived. It was carried to the garden by Prior Richard. The prior was somewhat irritated that a letter had been specifically sent from the bishop in Savannah to Father Benito. It had been hand-carried by the bishop's emissary, Monsignor Henry, who was now waiting with the abbot. What made the letter all the more infuriating to the prior was that it had been delivered with the instruction that it could be opened only by Father Benito and that its contents could be discussed with the abbot and Monsignor Henry, but no one else.

Father Benito saw the prior approaching through the mid-afternoon shadows. Benito rose from his garden and wiped his hands on his cassock, partially to see the expression of distaste that would pass over the prior's face. The prior did not care for tilling the soil. Benito folded his hands before him and made a slight bow.

"What brings you to my garden, Prior?"

"A letter, Brother Benito. From the bishop himself."

He extended his hand. "Well, let us see what he has to say."

The prior did not move to hand the letter to him. Instead, he said, "Its contents must be discussed only with the abbot."

"Well, Prior, I will find it a great difficulty to discuss it with anyone until I have had a chance to read it."

Acting as if he were astonished to still find the letter in his hands, the prior gave it to Father Benito.

"Thank you." Benito began to open the wax seal on the letter, only to find the prior still standing over him.

The prior looked at him with great seriousness. "I am to take you to the abbot as soon as you have digested the contents."

"You may have to wait a bit, Brother Prior. Digestion can take time, especially when the words come from such an important personage."

The prior stiffened. "I will wait." He doubted the day could possibly bring a more interesting event than a letter from the bishop.

Father Benito nodded and finished opening the letter. When he saw it was written in Greek, which the prior could not read, he turned away from the prior and was rewarded with a peek over his shoulder and a sudden drawing back when the prior realized he could learn nothing, even if the letter were in his hands.

All of the amusement faded from Father Benito's face when he read the letter. It was a summons. The bishop said that Father Benito was to come to Savannah to meet with himself and the mother superior of the convent of the Sisters of Mercy. The purpose of the trip was to deal with a dark spirit that had the ability to kill. Father Benito's abbot was to make arrangements for him to travel to Savannah with all possible speed, and Monsignor Henry, the bishop's secretary, was waiting to escort him.

Father Benito was troubled by the letter. The bishop was a steady man, yet the tone of the letter implied that the evidence surrounding the events left no room for doubt. That the bishop had written in classical Greek meant even more, as it implied that he did not want the letter to be read if it fell from the messenger's hands. The more conventional Latin would not have protected the letter from being read by any number of people. To write it in Greek meant that the bishop was concerned with keeping the contents very private, and it also meant that the bishop knew something about Father Benito. Few enough knew biblical, Koine, Greek, much less the classical Greek the bishop had used to write to him.

Benito looked at the prior. "If you would, Prior, please take me to the abbot."

The prior was surprised to hear the formal tone in Benito's voice. Usually the monk joked with him, often teasing. Benito's formality made the prior realize that this was a matter of some concern. Now he was even more irritated that he had not been able to read what was in the letter. His face showing nothing of his irritation, he led Benito to the abbot.

The interview with the abbot was brief and to the point. He, too, had received a letter from the bishop. It contained few of the normal formalities, but did impress upon the abbot that Father Benito's presence was needed immediately. The bishop did not need to explain his reasons, but he had given the abbot enough information to understand the urgency of the matter.

Within an hour Father Benito was on his way to the train station in the company of Monsignor Robert Henry. The afternoon northbound train passed through Saint Augustine at 4:17, and the two priests boarded the train for Savannah. Though the trip was only about two hundred miles, they would not be at their destination until dawn. This last run of the day had many stops on its route. The journey gave Father Benito time to make the acquaintance of Monsignor Henry and to understand the gravity of the situation. It also impressed Benito with the bishop's thoroughness. Monsignor Henry spoke Latin as well as he spoke English, and he was also quite knowledgeable in classical Greek. As a result, they could discuss the matter in public with little fear of being understood. The passenger cars had few riders for the trip, which made their conversation even more private.

The first few miles passed without conversation. Benito was allowing the monsignor to approach the topic at his own pace. Benito was well aware of the discomfort this topic caused for some priests. For a good half hour, the monsignor spent his time looking out the window at the beauty of this section of northern Florida. When he was finally ready to talk about the matter, he turned to Benito.

"Father Benito, do you feel a part of the modern Church?"

Benito was pleased by the direct but graceful inquiry. "Monsignor, what I and others like me do must seem to you like something left over from a different time. But I can assure you it is real."

"How much of this have you seen?"

"I was present at four exorcisms before I was allowed to lead one. There were those times, of course, when we were called in to perform an exorcism and nothing was present. But I do not count those instances. I myself have been the primary priest at seven exorcisms."

"You've seen eleven?" Robert could not keep the surprise from his voice.

Benito had learned that his unusual occupation was not accepted by the entire priestly community. "Monsignor, I have become accustomed to the reaction. Today, even some priests often find the presence of the supernatural to be as normal, or perhaps I should say natural, as we once did."

"I don't want to seem that I disbelieve you, but did you actually see the creatures that were exorcised?"

"Not always. But on three occasions, I definitely did."

"Did they have a physical reality?"

"Again, not always. But at two of these three exorcisms, the spirit attacked me as soon as it left the body of its intended victim. The spirit attempted to possess me in turn. In both of these cases, my struggle with the spirit became physical. I wrestled with the demon, 'casting it out' in a most literal sense."

"You touched and felt it?"

"Yes. It was not a strong physical presence. It could cause me no harm physically, but it was tangible."

The monsignor was shaken. "I fear I do not know much about this realm. But even this small amount of knowledge frightens me."

Benito sought to assuage the fears of the monsignor. "Your reaction is a common one. I have seen it before. The Church has realized that such things exist since its beginning. Now, as then, priests are prepared to deal with the problem. Thankfully, such problems are rare."

As the monsignor absorbed the answer, Benito reflected that the Church had distanced itself from its own spiritual heritage. Things that had been accepted for thousands of years as part of the human experience now seemed like fairy tales to some.

Having given the monsignor time to reflect on what he had said, Benito asked, "So, Monsignor, what can you tell me about the events in Savannah?"

The monsignor provided a thorough summary of what had occurred, including the perspectives of those who had been present. His account made it clear that the situation was worse than Benito had imagined. When Henry finished his tale, Benito focused on the details of the death.

"So Richardson was killed by impact with the wall?"

"That is the opinion of those present, including the doctor," the monsignor said.

"And Mr. Richardson said that the presence came and went?"

The monsignor nodded.

"And the glass was shattered outward after the impact?"

"Yes."

"Then, Monsignor, this situation is likely more serious than you have imagined."

"How so?"

"When a person is possessed by a spirit, normally the spirit does not come and go. It stays with the body, as that is its link to this world. Nor will it kill its host, except very rarely. And the creature should not be able to perform so potent a physical act as smashing a window outward without the aid of a host's body. Based upon what you have said, we are dealing with a powerful spirit, more than likely a demon. It was able to affect the physical world without the need of a human medium. This situation does not call for an exorcism, but something far more potent."

"Are you saying you can't help?"

"No. Only that it is not likely that exorcism will be enough."

Like most priests, the monsignor tended to group any banishing of any spirit under the rubric of exorcism. "There are other options?"

"Yes, but, I regret to say, answering your question will have to wait until we are in a more private place than a railcar." Benito did not trust the screen of foreign languages to protect them from a casual listener when discussing this particular matter.

He saw the concern in the monsignor's face. Fortunately, Monsignor Henry had been sufficiently alarmed by the conversation to be inclined not to press the Benedictine for more information. Benito did not care to reveal how ill-equipped he himself was to deal with such a creature alone. He would need a great deal of help.

They spent the rest of the trip discussing other matters, sleeping, or thinking. The monsignor was attempting to rearrange his worldview to accommodate this new information. Benito began making plans. On Tuesday morning, as the train pulled into the station in Savannah, Father Benito was awakened from his few hours of sleep by Monsignor Henry.

"Father, do you need to rest before seeing the bishop?"

"No, Monsignor, I can see the bishop at his convenience. However," he smiled, "if he desires me to wait, I may perhaps doze off."

Monsignor Henry returned the smile. He liked this Benedictine. Laughter on the outside, and a profound devotion to his faith and to his calling on the inside.

The two priests exited the station onto West Broad Street. The staging yard for the station was below them. It was busy at this hour. Heavy wagons jostled for position as they sought to deliver their cargoes to the loading docks. Whips snapped as the teamsters drove the wagons toward the docks. Wheels sometimes slammed against each other as the wagons moved, and the air was punctuated by the calls of the drivers, shouting and cursing at one another while others laughed at the shows of anger, none of which could be taken seriously.

The two priests made their way to the archdiocese through streets that were awakening to the calls of the fishmongers and the bustle of servants who were on their way to work. Small carts darted back and forth, loaded with the early catch. The vendors sang rhymes to the freshness of their grouper or the color of their snapper. Live crabs tried to climb out of the carts. Shrimp were fresh enough that they still snapped in miniature anger at their captivity. Servants bought food as they walked, seafood being a part of the breakfast menu in many homes. Benito smiled at the profligacy of the life displayed. He had missed the rhythms of a city.

As they walked, Benito considered the situation. A thought occurred to him. He realized that he could be more thorough in his briefing of the bishop if he could examine the room where the events had happened.

"Monsignor, will we pass near the hospital on the way to the cathedral?"

"Within a few blocks."

"Then perhaps I should see this place where the patient died before I meet with the bishop."

"I don't know that you can learn much there that I have not already told you."

Benito smiled. "I will be viewing it in a different manner than you might."

"I understand," the monsignor replied, not certain that he did. "If we continue on this street, we will pass the hospital shortly."

Benito began to expand his senses even as they walked, performing the mental exercises that were needed to engage his Sight. As he did so, he unavoidably felt the city around him. He had never been to this city before, so all that he knew of it was its reputation for beauty and its prominence as a port. Its reputation for beauty was more than justified. Benito had seen many of the great cities of Europe, and few rivaled Savannah. The wide streets were complemented by graciously proportioned buildings. The oak trees stood over the city streets like sentinels, cloaked in their gray robes of Spanish moss, which was as common here as in his beloved Saint Augustine. However, what he apprehended with his Sight was almost shocking. The city seemed to be on the verge of consciousness, reaching out, just below awareness, to embrace him in welcome. The currents of life itself buzzed about him. He knew that this place had been occupied for thousands of years and the Indians had left a strong trace of their lives in the ground. He could still sense the suffering that many had felt when the Yamacraw Indians had been decimated by the smallpox virus that the Europeans had brought with them in the years just prior to the founding of the city. The air was misted with arcane memory and the sunlight was slightly dimmed by the thoughts and magic that had slid through the air over the centuries. However, beneath the benign beauty and the sadness of plague was a dark thread of evil that he could not trace. Underneath the warmth of the welcome that the city offered was a current of danger, strong enough to put Benito on his guard. He could almost taste blood on his tongue.

The monsignor stopped, and Benito, absorbed in his perceptions, bumped into him. "Sorry."

"Is something wrong, Father Benito?"

"No, Monsignor. It's just that this city is magical."

The monsignor smiled. "You don't need special powers to know that." He waved at the redbrick building in front of them. "This is the hospital. Are you ready to see the room?"

"Yes."

The monsignor led him up the stairs to the lobby of the hospital, not bothering to stop at the front desk, as no one would think of questioning his reasons for being there. He took the stairs to the second floor, leading the monk down the hall to a very solid iron door. Over the entrance was a sign, "Saint James' Ward." The monsignor rapped on the door.

Sister Francis peered out of the viewing port and opened the door for them.

"Monsignor, welcome," the nun said.

"Sister Francis, let me introduce our visitor from Florida, Father Benito."

She nodded her head in greeting. "Ah, yes, we have been expecting your arrival. A pleasure to meet you." She turned immediately to lead them down the hall.

The monsignor leaned to Benito as they followed her down the hall. "You will find that there are no secrets within a cathedral compound."

Benito nodded in return. "Yes, I remember now."

Sister Francis stopped near the end of the hall. She withdrew her keys and opened the door to what had been Richardson's room. "This is where he was killed."

"Thank you, Sister," the monsignor replied, noting that Sister Francis seemed certain that what had occurred had not been a normal death.

"Please call me when you are ready to leave," she said. "The mother superior has been quite firm that no one should enter the room without her permission or yours."

"A wise course of action," Benito said.

The nun turned and left the two men in front of the open door.

"Should I go in with you?" the monsignor asked.

"No. It is best that I do this alone. Please let no one disturb me."

"Of course."

Benito had felt a cold touch of evil before they had reached the door. His stomach clenched at the touch. Before entering the room, he constrained his Sight. His senses were still heightened, but not as greatly as they might have been. He knew that what lay in the room might be strong enough to overwhelm him if he did not pull back. Every magical act leaves behind impressions in the physical objects around it. For those with the Sight, these remnants were like a book that could be read, telling the story of what had happened. He steeled himself and entered the room.

Boards covered the shattered window. Otherwise, the room was the same as it had been the night that Richardson died. Benito took inventory of the few items in the room in a glance. What immediately caught his eye was the dried blood on the wall. He walked over to it, noting how little broken glass was on the floor. Clearly the window had been shattered from the inside. He reached the bloodstained wall and touched the plaster. Immediately a flood of sensation ran through his heightened senses. First he sensed the impact, then the sudden darkness, then the void as the man's spirit had flown from his body. Benito, now attuned to the events of the night, faced back into the room. Facing him was a shadow of what had been there, a leering bloodred face with pointed teeth, surmounting the immense figure of a demon. He knew he was not seeing something that was there, merely something that had been. Nonetheless, he was frightened.

He inhaled deeply, waiting for his pulse to slow. He crossed his arms across his chest, curled his fingers, than slowly moved his arms downward in one of the oldest warding gestures. As he did so, he exhaled in a rush. When he opened his eyes, he saw the monsignor staring at him.

Benito looked at him. "It's worse than I thought."

PROMPTLY at 9:15, Jakob Streng was about to enjoy his breakfast. His house, 454 Saint Julian Street, was not remarkable. For those without the Sight it was a distinguished-looking Savannah row house much like the others that occupied the block. The dark green velvet of its window hangings and the complex fleur-de-lis detailing of its wrought iron made it clear that the occupant of the house was wealthy, even by the standards of this genteel neighborhood. The first floor of the house was elevated perhaps five feet above the street level and was accessed by a short flight of steps from the sidewalk. The ground floor, sunk a few feet into the soil, served as a basement. These partially buried basements were a common feature in Savannah, where the water table often rose almost to street level. Though most of the small basement windows on the street were curtained, the ones on this house were unique. The heavy black drapes on these windows thoroughly blocked prying eyes from seeing anything in the basement.

Inside the house, Essie, a Negro servant, was serving breakfast to Jakob and his guest, George Long, at a table in the dining room on the first floor. George was young, about twenty-five, and somewhat in awe of his mentor. Streng was over sixty, with close-cropped, iron gray hair. Most men of his girth give the appearance of being "soft." Streng gave no such appearance.

George Long acted as Streng's eyes and ears about the city. Long brought information back to him and their group about what was being said that might affect their activities. Streng would occasionally send him on fact-finding excursions. In the two years that Long had performed this service, he had become adept at ferreting out information.

While George nervously waited for Essie to finish bringing his eggs, bacon, and grits from the sideboard, he looked about the room. The signs of wealth were all about them—the velvet draperies, the inlaid mahogany furniture, even the heavy silver that sat on the table. Yet the furnishings were far less intimidating to Long than what he had seen Streng do. The man possessed a power that Long could not begin to fathom. Long was as frightened by that power as he was drawn to it.

As soon as Essie left the room, Streng began eating his large breakfast platter. Long pecked at his meal, eating a few small mouthfuls of eggs and occupying himself by taking a biscuit from an ornate platter and buttering it.

Gathering up his resolve, he began the conversation. "Jakob, I have important information."

"Well, it must be to interrupt a meal as important as breakfast." Jakob smiled at his young disciple.

"The bishop has summoned an exorcist. He arrived earlier this morning."

"Um," Streng grunted around a strip of bacon. He swallowed. "I expected that."

George was startled by the response. "If you expected that, then why did you have us proceed with killing Richardson?"

"As an example. We have a few other weak members. They need to know that once they have joined in the rituals, there is no leaving. Membership is a lifetime affair."

"But an exorcist?"

"He presents no danger to us. Our brother groups in other cities have dealt with them before."

"I didn't know."

"Of course you didn't. You didn't have any reason to know, until now." He reached for a biscuit and split it open. "But don't be too comfortable; the Church can present a danger to us." He paused as he buttered the biscuit and added black cherry preserves, enjoying the discomfort on Long's face as the young man waited for him to continue. "Nowadays, the danger from the Church is temporal, not magical, which is why I want you to be alert to events about the cathedral. An exorcist does not have the arcane power to deal with a minion as powerful as Belial. Our demon is, after all, a hand of Satan on earth. Even the magicians in the Church can offer little resistance. The Church's secular power is of greater concern. Powerful magicians have been trapped before by the temporal forces that the Church can command. That was why we had to silence Richardson.

His death places a permanent seal on his lips. The information that he had might have been dangerous in the wrong hands."

Long's face showed relief. "So what we must do is simply be silent. That shouldn't be too hard to manage."

"Especially with the shining example of Richardson's grisly death to inspire those of faint heart."

Streng smiled grimly. Long relaxed. "So we have nothing to fear magically?"

"No. Not anymore."

George was confused. "You mean the Church once had the power to threaten us?"

"Long ago there were potent ceremonial magicians in the Church. We defeated them. But magic was not a long-term concern for the Church. Their temporal power had grown to be too great. That is when the Church started its great campaign, the Inquisition. Where the Inquisition thrived, many of our members died. So we learned to be rigidly circumspect. After all, we were their most obvious target, even though most of the people that the Church killed had nothing to do with us. They weren't followers of Satan. They were pagans whose practices the Church wanted to end, or Jews, or rival factions within the Church itself."

A strange smile played at the corners of Streng's mouth. "The Church has never been overly fond of competition for the souls of men." He stepped to the sideboard and poured himself another cup of coffee. "Unintentionally, they did those of us that worship the left hand, the Lord of Evil, a great favor."

"A favor?"

"They killed our greatest enemy. There was once an order of pagan magicians in Europe that battled with us. They were apparently effective. But the Church, in their pursuit of one faith, destroyed them by early in the eighteenth century. At least, that is the last time we heard of them. The Church's campaigns also destroyed over half of our circles, but many of us survived."

"Because of our power?"

"Yes, and also because we have stayed hidden from the eyes of men. What the Church cannot find, it cannot destroy. Besides, the Church has become far more concerned with the terrors that men inflict on each other." He looked in Long's eyes. "How many casualties were there at Gettysburg?"

"Almost thirty thousand."

"And if you include the Yankees?"

"I don't know."

"Fifty thousand," Streng said. "Think about it. Over fifty thousand men killed, wounded, or missing in a few days. What difference does a handful of men falling to magic matter in the grand scale of things?"

"But that's an unusual instance."

"Not really. During the Thirty Years' War in Germany entire cities were destroyed. Some historians say that at the battle of Magdeburg in the 1600s, there were three hundred thousand casualties. The entire city was destroyed. If Satan himself were in charge of things, could he have done a better job?"

Long was silenced by the magnitude of the numbers.

"So you can see why the Church pays less attention to things that once concerned them greatly."

"But there were other magicians who opposed us?"

Streng went to sit in an overstuffed leather chair. "You ask many questions, George."

George feared that he had overstepped his bounds with his host.

Streng saw the fear cross his face. He did not want George to be afraid, at least not now. He was still about the business of tying the boy ever closer to the circle. For Streng, control and seduction were the greatest aphrodisiacs. "It is all right. You need to ask questions."

Streng steepled his hands as he began his tale. "Our real magical enemies, if they even existed, left few traces behind them. They served the old gods." He saw the expression on Long's face.

"No, I'm not talking about local village witches. They still have a few of those in Ireland and other rural places. They are good for casting out the small possessions, for a little medicine, for the local festival fire. These others were different, though they served the same gods."

Streng's eyes focused on his student. George was so young, a firebrand, filled with his own importance and the excitement of the "evil power" he would someday attain. George had no knowledge of the tests ahead. He would find that their pleasures had a price.

"These other magicians were called 'walkers.' The name came from the reputation they had for traveling on foot. They rarely identified themselves, except to the local witch. They were one of the reasons that lone travelers in Celtic lands, at least those on foot and decently dressed, were rarely bothered. Everyone had heard of the walkers, but no one knew precisely who they were. The legend of their power was enough to protect travelers."

"Could they threaten us?"

"The last incident with them is said to have happened in the 1720s. One of our groups was meeting in England, near Manchester. They customarily met in an abandoned farmhouse. During a meeting, the farmhouse burned to the ground. Fourteen men and three women died. No one escaped."

"Couldn't it have been an accident?"

"Of course. But for a fire to sweep through a house so quickly that not even one would escape? Unlikely. Besides, the first of our order to arrive there found a strange mark on the ground, a mark associated with the walkers."

"You believe that these magicians existed?"

"I don't know. But there is always some truth in legends."

Long nodded. The silence drew out in the room.

Streng rose. "Time to be about our business in this world instead of discussing history."

"Well, thank you for your time; I feel much less worried than I did when I came this morning."

"Think nothing further about it, George. Just remain obser-
vant." Streng paused. "But repeat nothing of what we've said, even
to another member. I must decide who knows these things."

"Of course."

Streng nodded and showed Long out. He watched the young
man merge with the traffic on the sidewalk. Then he returned to the
dining room.

"Essie," he called.

The black servant appeared at the door from the kitchen almost
instantly.

"Lock it," he said.

She did as she was told. As she returned to the main part of the
room, a metamorphosis began. Her gait changed from the slow and
subservient gait of a servant. She became light on her feet. She went
to the sideboard and got a fresh cup and filled it with coffee. She
went to one of the leather chairs and sat down. Streng still stood by
the window, gazing out at the street.

"So," he said. "Did you hear it all?"

She nodded.

"What do you think?"

Her voice changed. Her customary accent, which was almost
indistinguishable from the accent of any other Negro in Savannah,
adopted some of the gentler sounds of a Haitian-French accent. "I
don' think the boy will be a problem. Probably nevah would have
been."

"We need to find out about this new priest from Florida."

"I have some folk I can trust. What about you?"

"You know I have someone in the diocese. They had already
told me that he was coming. I'm sure they will tell me more."

"You sure?"

"I am," Streng said.

"What about that story you told the boy?"

He looked at her questioningly.

"The one about these 'walkers.'"

"Oh, that is an old tale we use from time to time. I'm sure there were walkers or some other order of magicians once, but they are long dead, and they were never that powerful."

She nodded unconvincingly.

"Do you doubt that?" he said with an edge to his voice.

"I doubt everythin'," she said. "I had too many surprises in my life not to expect one more. There's too many magics around to think there might not be one more."

"So you fear the walker?" Streng asked.

"No. But if there is one, I'd be careful round him."

"If he comes for us, he will come for you. This is a time we should work together."

"I'm sorry, Mr. Streng. It won't work. Like I said before, Voudon magic is different from yours. Don't mix well."

Streng was irritated by her customary rebuff, but he didn't show it. He had too much respect for voodoo. Besides, she was useful. Colored people could go and listen where a white man would be noticed and raise questions. All he said was, "Let me know if you hear anything."

"You know I will." She went to the table and set down her cup. Reassuming the demeanor of a Negro servant, with bent shoulders and a slow walk, she disappeared through the door and down the back hallway to the kitchen. Her mind was moving faster than her feet. What she had overheard was important. There might be magicians who Streng really feared. If so, then perhaps the city could get rid of Streng and his kind. And high time, too. Regardless of the power she and the others of her faith shared, she could not confront the spirit that Streng and his group summoned. Regardless, her people looked to her for an answer. She was the *mambo,* the high priestess. Though her religion was hidden from the eyes of the white men, many turned to her for leadership and counsel. She was able to protect those who came to her, to make certain they were not out on the nights that Streng and his people hunted, but she wanted to do more. To be able to remove Streng and his kind? She smiled, just slightly, as she moved to the kitchen. Now that would be an accomplishment.

Streng's thoughts remained focused on Esmerelda after she left the room. He knew she was a powerful voodoo priestess. Over the years, she had provided him with much useful information. He did not understand why she did not aid him magically. Perhaps she was right, that their magic did not mix with his. He grunted. That question was one he wouldn't answer today. He had at least managed to deal with one problem by assuring himself that Long could be trusted. Next he would head to the factoring house and check on the activities of his firm. Then he would busy himself in learning more about this Catholic priest.

CHAPTER SEVEN

THE bishop stood where he always stood when confronted with a problem, at the window in his office that overlooked his garden. Behind him, Monsignor Henry and Father Benito sat in silence. The sunlight coming through the windows illuminated the bishop's thin blond hair, now turning to gray. He turned back into the room, facing his visitors. Over the past hour Father Benito had told him things that he found almost impossible to accept as describing events here in his own city.

"Father Benito," he said, "I am certain that you have faced a reluctance to believe in people before when delivering such news."

"I have, Your Grace," Benito replied.

"Your Grace," the monsignor said, "I am staggered. A demon? One summoned by black magicians. And to think that the Church harbors its own magicians to fight them? It all seems so . . . medieval." The monsignor faltered.

The bishop's face softened as he took his seat. "Monsignor, sometimes I fear that you are too much a part of the secular world. There is much wisdom in the Church that we find hard to believe. Many mysteries are part of our faith, and, if the Church finds it necessary to train such men as Father Benito in these arcane skills, then such skills are needed."

"Thank you, Your Grace," Benito said.

"Father, I assume you know how to find the assistance you need within the Church?"

"Yes. The Church has a small group of men and women who, like me, are trained in the arts needed to fight such creatures. We are drawn from many different orders."

The bishop said, "We are in your hands. What must we do?"

"I will talk to those who witnessed the events. Then I must send a telegram to a certain individual and let him know what we are facing."

"To whom?"

"To the head of the Church's mages in North America. Your Grace, with all respect, the man that I will contact is within the Church, but his 'other talents' are not well known. I must ask that you keep his name secret. Many would not understand the need for such men in our modern Church."

"Of course."

Benito looked to the monsignor, who nodded as guarantee for his silence on the matter. The priest continued, "You will meet him in the course of affairs. His name is Father Joseph Rimaldi. He resides in Maryland. He is the one who will contact the others."

The monsignor interrupted. "Is this Rimaldi a Jesuit?"

The monk smiled. "Yes, the Father Provincial of Maryland, to be precise."

Monsignor Henry sat back in his chair. This development was interesting. He had long wanted to meet Rimaldi, but these were hardly the circumstances in which he had imagined the meeting might occur. The presence of such a preeminent scholar in the group of magicians, or, as Benito referred to them, mages, did much to remove the last doubts in his mind.

The bishop asked, "How many others?"

"Unless I discover something that implies a weakness, I would estimate that we will need six or more to deal with this creature."

"That many?"

"Father Rimaldi will make the final decision, but it is better to have more than we need than less."

The bishop rose, and the other two came to their feet as well. "Father Benito, you have my full support in whatever is needed." He looked to the monsignor. "Please, Monsignor, place the resources of the archdiocese at his disposal. And Father, please keep me informed as you deem appropriate. These are matters in which I confess my ignorance. As I said earlier, we are all in your hands."

"Your Grace, I shall do everything in my power to assure you are not disappointed in the trust you have placed in me." He bowed his head. "Pax vobiscum."

"And to you, Father."

The monk and the monsignor left together. The bishop remained in his office. He walked back to the large window that overlooked the garden. He stood where he had spent many hours contemplating what he had thought to be important issues. Compared to the evil that they now faced, those other issues were reduced to trivial administrative details.

He knew that such power as their enemies possessed did not arise instantaneously. The group that was summoning this demon must have been present for some time. They might even be part of the social elite in this rigidly stratified city. Though he knew they must have taken steps to remain secret, the people who lived in this city were very capable of keeping secrets. He walked to the side table where he kept his whiskey and poured a drink into a waiting glass. He wrapped his hand around the glass, gently warming the amber liquid inside it. Bringing the glass up to his nose, he smelled the Irish whiskey, whose name came from the Gaelic word *usquebaugh*. As he returned to his place in front of the window, he took his first sip, enjoying the gentle fire and complex flavor of the drink. This whiskey was imported directly from Ireland. Each year his old friend Aaron Goethe sent a small barrel of the whiskey to him on the first day of Hanukkah. Aaron had a highly developed sense of irony, though he might have chosen the date just to make sure that the bishop knew when the first day of the festival was, since it changed each year with the Jewish calendar. With the arrival of the gift, the bishop was aware that many of the businesses in the city would keep irregular hours, or none at all, for the next week.

The smile from the memory and the taste of the whiskey faded from his face as he thought of the business at hand. He was glad that Benito was here. As he thought in front of his window, a quote swam up to the surface of his mind, a quote from the *Malleus Maleficarum,* the infamous *Hammer Against Witches,* which had played such a critical role in the Inquisition:

> *The belief that there are such beings as Witches is so Essential a part of the Catholic faith that Obstinacy to maintain the Opposite Opinion manifestly savours of Heresy.*

According to that same book, these Witches invariably commanded demons drawn from Satan's ranks.

CHAPTER EIGHT

Wednesday, October 14

FATHER Benito began the day with prayer, as always. Then he went to the refectory for breakfast, which was a rare pleasure for him. At the monastery in Saint Augustine, breakfast was a simple affair of bread and cheese. Perhaps as a vestige of English influence, breakfast in Savannah could be called nothing less than sumptuous. Eggs, ham, bacon, muffins, breads, tarts, fresh fruit, hominy, and often some delightful kind of seafood were arrayed along the serving table. This meal was the most complex of the day.

While he ate, he looked about the large room. One side of the refectory was filled with the customary long tables, each of which sat about fifteen. These were the tables that the nuns used. On the other side were scattered smaller, six-person tables, which were used by the priests and staff. Few were occupied at this time. When Benito glanced toward the nuns' tables, he saw that someone had been staring at him. She quickly turned her eyes away and rejoined the conversation at her table. He received a similar reaction from other tables as well. He was the stranger, the outsider, and a natural object of curiosity. But he recognized something more in their eyes, something he had seen before. They were afraid. He had long ago stopped being upset by such reactions. He had come to understand that his presence always garnered the twin reactions of curiosity and fear. Others did not want to be reminded of his work. His very existence reaffirmed something that others did not wish to be reminded of, that there was active evil in this world.

He finished his breakfast in silence, endeavoring not to look too closely at any of the other tables. In the closed atmosphere of a convent, his glance could lead to gossip, which might lead to hysteria. In the coming days they would all find enough to fear without false rumors and speculation.

His previous day's work had not been entirely satisfactory. The day had been tiring and had offered him little of value, other than what he had perceived during his visit to Richardson's room. He had interviewed the doctor and the orderlies who had been present on the night of Richardson's death. Dr. Gaston had been as uncommunicative as the monsignor had warned he might be. The orderlies had been too frightened by the events to provide any useful information. However, Benito's visit to the scene of the death had, in itself, been enough to justify the sending of his telegram to Rimaldi. He hoped that help would be coming from that quarter soon. He was seriously overmatched, though he must do his best to hide his fear.

As Benito was finishing breakfast, the monsignor entered the refectory. He smiled when he noticed Benito and crossed the room to join him. He pulled out the chair opposite Benito. "Good morning, Father."

"Monsignor." Benito smiled in greeting.

"Have you sent your telegram?"

"Earlier this morning."

"Good," the monsignor said, then paused, unsure of himself.

Benito waited, quietly sipping his coffee. The monsignor would speak when he was ready.

Reaching his decision, the monsignor said, "Father, there is a book that I would like to show you."

"Yes?"

"It's a journal, a record of events kept by some of my predecessors. Strange things have occurred here as far back as anyone can remember. It is the efforts of different priests over the last century to keep some record of the unusual events that have occurred here. These events are . . ." he searched for the right word, "I guess you would have to call them puzzling."

"I would very much like to see this journal."

"I thought you might. Would now be a good time?"

In response, Benito pushed his chair back from the table. The monsignor rose with him and led him from the dining room. He took Benito down a hall, turned, and then led him down another passage, deeper into the cathedral compound. They were well away from any trafficked areas. Only an occasional window provided any light. The monsignor stopped at a small table to light a lamp, then led Benito down a flight of stairs to a door. He drew a key from his cassock. Unlocking the door, he gestured for Benito to follow him into the room. He set down the lamp and went to light a second one.

Benito gazed around the room. It was musty, even though a ventilation shaft allowed some air circulation within the room. Only a dim fragment of light came down the shaft, which told Benito that the shaft did not open directly to the outside, but rather to a larger shaft, which itself opened to the outside. The room was a collection of old records and volumes that were likely overflow from the library. The scholar in Benito was intrigued. If he did not have more pressing interests, he would have liked to spend some time discovering what might be sent to this almost hidden room.

The monsignor went to a small cabinet set into the wall. Unlocking it, he withdrew a slim, leather-bound volume. It was old and well worn. He handed the book to Father Benito.

Benito sat in a chair near a lamp, opened the slender volume, and read the first entry. "'Sixteen October, 1786. Prostitute murdered in alley off State Street. Throat slit, no blood was found at site.'" He read on. "'Fourteen February, 1788. Statue of goat-footed Satan found in abandoned home. Family left area suddenly. Rumored to have moved north into Cherokee lands. Cannot contact.'"

The next entry. "'Twenty-six May, 1792. Discovered cleared circle south of town. Area had standing pillar, some traces of voodoo drawing on ground. Will observe as time permits.'"

Benito looked up, excitement in his eyes.

The monsignor had expected this reaction. "Some of the descriptions are as brief as the ones you've seen. Others are quite detailed. Some are cryptic. For many years there are no entries at all, which I think reflects that no record was kept. I don't know if it is of value, but I thought it could be."

"Robert, you have given me a great gift. This book may give us a real opportunity to discover something about our opponent."

"I thought it might. This record has been kept by a senior member of the bishop's staff for decades. Prior to that, it was kept by a member of the Catholic community who was simply interested in odd occurrences. We now pass it on to each other, and it has grown in detail over time. It has become something of a legacy. This city has both its good and bad sides, as most places do, but there is one series of unexplained, but similar, events that have taken place over the years that indicates something unusual has been happening. We have more than just the normal number of killings that might occur in any seaport town."

Luis looked at him questioningly.

Robert scratched the side of his nose as he thought of how he might best summarize the events. "As you will find in reading through the record, numerous corpses of women have been found in alleyways and propped against walls. Some of these are not relevant to what you are doing, but there is a pattern to certain of these killings, mainly in the eastern part of the city. I don't know what incited the suspicion of the first person to record the killing, but since then each succeeding keeper of the diary has been fairly diligent in recording unusual events and similar killings. In each of these cases, a woman's throat has been slit and very little blood was found near the corpse. So the corpse must have been drained of blood, then carried to where it was found. Saul Richardson said that a woman was killed and her blood drained in the August ritual."

Benito could not hide the shock on his face. "So the first similar killing was nearly a hundred years ago?"

The monsignor nodded.

"Then this is a very old evil."

"Four things made these killings eerily similar," the monsignor said. "First, it is clear that the bodies were carried to their final location after they had been murdered. Little blood is near the corpse. Second is the location of the bodies. They are in the upper part of the town, above the bluffs of the port. If a sailor killed a girl, he would not likely carry her up from the river to deposit her above the bluff. So these murders are not the random killings one finds in a seaport. Third, the women have almost all been murdered in a similar manner. Their throats were cut with near surgical precision. Bodies of others, ones found nearer the port, have the usual assortment of wounds you would expect—a knife wound in the stomach, a blow to the head, ragged cuts inflicted by a variety of knives. The killings we are concerned with speak of someone carrying on his work with precision."

"And the police have shown no interest?" Benito interrupted.

"This is not a town where the police become concerned with the deaths of prostitutes or the occasional sailor. Seaports are violent places. If no one of substance raises questions, the investigation will be perfunctory at best. They are easily discouraged by members of the upper class, which is one of the reasons that they take only a cursory look into things. There's a chance they might reveal too much."

"Sad."

"Yes, but that is how it is."

"And the newspaper?"

"The press here is good at covering society weddings and the price of cotton," the monsignor replied with an edge to his voice. "I think they consider news of unsolved crimes to be 'distasteful.' Anything they might have to say about such events will be buried in the interior pages. However, Savannah is a small city, and murders, even those not reported in the press, will be the subject of gossip. Within the Church we have our own informal sources of information."

Benito digested the statement before continuing. "You said there were four distinguishing features."

"The fourth is the pattern. These killings occur at about even intervals. If one is killed on the fifteenth of a given month, then the next one will be found a few months later on the eleventh, or thereabouts. If the interval stretches out longer, to say six months, then the killing would be near the seventh of the month."

The monk looked carefully at the monsignor. "So the intervals are based on the lunar month, not the calendar month."

"Yes. I surmise they are slain the night of a ritual."

"Perhaps if we had a lunar calendar?"

"I've already looked at one. These events are occurring just before or on the new moon."

"Are you certain?"

"Richardson was killed on the ninth. The moon was dark that night and the night of the tenth. So he was killed on the last night of the waning moon. I assume the astronomical new moon was sometime in the day on the tenth. He had been admitted to the ward almost exactly one month before, at the preceding new moon. Adding to that, an unidentified woman's corpse was found in mid-August. Since the lunar month is about twenty-nine days, that would make her death just before the new moon as well. It would also make that killing the one that Richardson described to Dr. Gaston."

Benito unconsciously crossed himself. He also performed another gesture with his hands that the monsignor was unfamiliar with. The monsignor didn't ask what the gesture was. He assumed it was some kind of protective spell and hoped it included him.

The monsignor went on with his narrative. "But there is another disturbing factor. Even though they are all found around the time of the new moon, the time interval between the killings has become shorter. Forty years ago, we would find a woman killed in this manner every year or so. Over the past ten years, the interval has shortened.

Now we find one every few months. Whoever is doing this has become more bold."

"And more certain of his power," Luis added.

Robert nodded, then stood. "Now you know what I know. Please keep the journal as long as you need to." A slight smile crossed his face. "I have a feeling this is what it was intended for."

The monsignor stood and led Benito from the room, carefully locking the door behind them. Benito followed him back to the more frequented areas of the building.

Father Benito looked at the book in his hands. He already knew that the task before him was beyond his capabilities. He hoped it would not be beyond those of Father Rimaldi.

❦

FATHER Joseph Rimaldi was the leader of the Church's mages in the United States and the Canadian provinces, though that job occupied very little of his time. He also headed the Jesuits who formed the main academic staff at a university near Baltimore as part of his duties as the Father Provincial of the Maryland Province, one of the oldest of the Jesuit provinces, tracing its beginnings back to 1634. Under his purview were some of the finest scholars of the Catholic Church to be found outside of the Vatican. Rimaldi was approaching sixty, though it could hardly be told from his appearance. His black hair was barely peppered with gray, his walk was that of a much younger man, and his penetrating glance still caused the most brilliant of his scholars to doubt their conclusions.

He had come far in life, all thanks to the Church. Born in an Italian slum in New York City, tall and gangly as a youngster, he had matured into a powerfully built man, someone seen as a likely candidate for the boxing ring or the varied groups of toughs that roamed the Italian neighborhoods. But Rimaldi had taken a very different turn, deciding to become a priest. His intelligence drew the attention of others at the seminary, where he proved himself to be a highly capable scholar. The Jesuits found Rimaldi before his ordination and quickly claimed him for their own. Rimaldi was discovering his voracious intellectual appetite at the same time. Through the Jesuits, he had entered college and now possessed two doctoral degrees, one in philology and the other in history. His rise through the Jesuit ranks had been rapid.

At the age of thirty, he had been transferred to Rome. In his decade and a half in Europe, all of the remnants of the boy from the slums had been overlain by an increasing European sophistication. It was in Rome that he had discovered the "secret order" of magicians in the Church. His dogged research skills had led him to uncover what was supposed to be securely hidden. However, the mages of the Church had found him to be no threat. He became a willing recruit. He had been transferred to their school, which was located in an isolated castle in the Italian Alps.

The students there were drawn from many different orders of priests and nuns. Benedictines and Jesuits studied alongside Dominicans. At the school, Rimaldi had undergone instruction in ceremonial magic, emerging a few years later as a particularly adept member of this hidden group. He resumed his duties as a Jesuit, though, of course, maintaining contact with others trained in magic. After his return to the United States and a succession of posts in the varied Jesuit provinces, he was appointed to the position of Father Provincial of the powerful Maryland Province in 1866.

The years had not dimmed Rimaldi's formidable intellect. He was supremely confident in his abilities, too confident, some of his students thought. They often joked about his air of absolute certainty. The joking was always done as a veiled compliment, but some were not comfortable with a priest who had too much of the taint of pride about him. Yet few would question him. His razor-sharp mind and the breadth of his reading had earned him their respect.

Rimaldi was alone in his study when the knock came on his door.

"Enter." He spoke over his book.

Father Phillipe de Montferrat, Rimaldi's secretary, entered silently and came to stand beside his superior. Phillipe was the scion of an old family of French aristocrats. His composure was rarely ruffled, a characteristic that made him the perfect secretary for the sometimes volcanic Rimaldi. Over the years the bond between them had become strong. Rimaldi trusted him absolutely. As a result, Phillipe was privy to many of the private aspects of the province's business.

After finishing the paragraph he was reading, Rimaldi looked up at the hovering priest, who held a telegram.

"Father Provincial," Phillipe said, "I thought I should bring this to you immediately. It is from one of the people whom you said warranted special attention, a Father Benito."

Rimaldi marked his place and reached up for the telegram. He noticed that it had been sent from the office of the bishop in Savannah rather than the abbey in Saint Augustine. He placed his book to the side and sat more upright as he unfolded it with anticipation. Father Benito was one of his favorites within the mages' circle.

Father Phillipe turned to go. He did not expect any word from Rimaldi, as they spent little time on pleasantries. He was surprised when Rimaldi's voice came from the chair.

"Wait, Father Phillipe; I may have need of you."

Phillipe turned and sat in the second chair in the room, facing the other priest. He did not think he had ever seen his superior so focused, and he patiently waited as Rimaldi translated the telegram, not once, but twice.

The telegram would have looked unintelligible to almost anyone else. Though it was composed with standard English characters, it was actually written in classical Greek. It also contained one of the special words that the mages of the Church used between themselves. He put the telegram down and stared off into the distance for a minute. He then turned to the younger priest. "Father Phillipe, do you believe in Satan?"

Phillipe might have been amazed had he not been aware that Rimaldi never asked spurious questions. Rimaldi often began a conversation in a lateral direction, only later leading back to the main point. "Of course, Father."

"And would you like to meet him?"

"Of course not, Father. I have met several Protestants, and that is quite close enough for me."

Rimaldi smiled thinly at the joke, even though it betrayed a weakness in his Church that he would rather forget.

"This time, Phillipe, it is a more serious matter than that." He handed the telegram to the young priest.

Phillipe read it quickly, as he was familiar with the transpositions that scholars used to write Greek with English characters. "What does the word 'gorgon' mean in this context?"

"It means a very powerful demon."

"It can't be true," Phillipe said, handing it back.

"But I take it you would not like to convince a bishop, three nuns, and a Benedictine of that fact?"

Phillipe looked at Rimaldi blankly. He had no idea of what to say.

"You think as many others would think, Phillipe. Our Church has become too certain of its place in the world. Even in the Church, some are too much a part of these modern times to believe in evil. Yet, without our estimable consent, evil continues to exist." Rimaldi held up the telegram. "I know Father Benito well. He would not raise a false alarm. He needs my help and the help of others whom the Church has trained to deal with such creatures."

"What do you need of me, Father?" The young priest did not ask the obvious question, as he knew that the Father Provincial would tell no more than he wished to in any event.

"First, I must speak with Father Ryan. He will be in charge in my absence. He can also take over my classes on the works of Saint Augustine. Father Brogan can take my ethics classes. But there are other matters that must remain confidential. So I have special instructions for you. This work I will undertake is dangerous. In the event that I do not return, Father Ryan will know what to do with regard to the Jesuit order. But there are others who must know.

"A cardinal in Rome, Cardinal Termignoni, must be informed if I do not return. I will give you a letter for him. It will be sent only in the event of my death. You will send Benito's telegram with my letter, if it comes to that. I will also have several letters and a few telegrams for you to send before my departure. I will be leaving for Savannah in a few days.

"Do you have any questions, Phillipe?"

"No, sir."

"Good. But you have become knowledgeable of our secretive cadre of mages, something that few in the Church know about. I know that I can count on your discretion; your obedience is unquestioned. But you are also a Jesuit, and I am not equally certain that I can restrain your eventual curiosity."

The young priest did not respond. He merely waited.

"That was the response that I'd hoped for. You know yourself well for one so young." Rimaldi smiled. "But you must remember—speak to no one about this matter. Discussion of these topics is generally not welcome within the Church." He paused before continuing, "Now, do you have any immediate questions?"

"Honestly, Father, I do not know where the questions that you have raised would begin or end," the younger priest said. "It is all rather much to understand."

"For now, let us leave this as a beginning to a future discussion. I have work to do, and they are waiting for me in Savannah. We can discuss this matter further on my return."

"I look forward to your return. May God bless your endeavors."

"Thank you, Father Phillipe."

The young priest rose to seek Father Ryan.

A SLIVER of the waxing moon dimly illuminated the salt marsh that lay between Savannah and the ocean. A small boat with a single passenger ground against the mix of shells and sediment that bordered a tree-covered island. Esmerelda was late. Streng had insisted on a late supper. But she had no worry that the ceremony would start without her. She was the *mambo,* the priestess.

Esmerelda had been sent to Savannah from Haiti by her own high priestess almost ten years ago. The Voudon community in Savannah had not been leaderless since their last *mambo*'s unexpected death in 1859. Riley had been the *houngan,* the priest, and had led the practitioners until a new *mambo* could be sent. Normally a circle's priestess would have trained her own replacement, but she had died young and there had been no one here able to train a replacement. The theology and magic of Voudon were complex. Little was written down. Almost all of it was held in the mind of the *mambo.* In Voudon, the *houngan* was not expected to know what a priestess did.

Tonight was one of the early nights of the growing moon, a night for prophecy, for hearing what the *loa,* the gods of Voudon, had to say to them. Only the initiated of the followers of Voudon met on the island for this ritual. The other ceremonies, those on the night of the full moon, were open to any interested in Voudon. Tonight was for finding guidance from the gods. Esmerelda hoped they would speak clearly. She needed direction.

The path to their ceremonial site twisted through the vegetation to the center of the small island. The growth was thick. Though the site was as close as fifty feet from the edge of the island, no one could see it from any of the brackish creeks that wove through the marsh. Besides, it was unlikely that anyone would be out on so dark a night.

She came to the edge of the clearing. In it was their ceremonial circle, their *hounfour.* The *houngan* was already in the circle. It would be rude for her to enter the circle without being recognized by him. She stopped, just as he would have stopped if she had arrived first.

He looked up and a smile came to his face. "Welcome, sistah. Welcome, *mambo.*"

She entered the *hounfour* and embraced Riley. She had high respect for this man. He had been a slave and yet had kept to their faith, even without a *mambo* to guide him. Such loyalty gave him great credit in the eyes of the *loa*. For her, it had been different; she had come from Haiti after the Americans had outlawed slaving.

She raised her voice and addressed the others waiting there. "Move to the east of the circle; the *houngan* and I mus' talk."

Riley looked at her questioningly. This was strange, but he followed her. They sat near where the west fire would be lit, perhaps thirty feet from the others, who grouped on the opposite side of the circle. The others talked together so as not to hear what the *mambo* and the *houngan* said to each other.

"What the problem, Esmerelda?"

"Streng's gone crazy with his power. He drunk. Too much fire, no earth."

"He gonna kill some more?"

"He's always gonna kill more. This priest they call from Saint Augustine, he's here to throw out the demon, but I doubt he got the power to deal with Streng. If Streng kills him, he gets even more drunk. Nobody be safe, not even our folk."

The *houngan* nodded. "So you want to ask the *loa* if we should do somethin'?"

She nodded.

"Streng scares me," Riley said.

"Me, too. But he's killin'. Maybe the *loa* want him stopped."

They looked at each other. Fear and determination were shared in their eyes. Then he looked back over to their assembled worshipers. He called out to the others with his deep voice, "Light the fires."

A student of Voudon, a *hounsis,* picked up a flaming brand from the small fire near the east edge of the clearing. He walked around to each of the other points of the compass and lit the piles of kindling and wood that they had built earlier. Each fire was fifteen feet from the *poteau-mitan,* the post in the center of the circle.

Esmerelda stood. "Circle round."

The worshipers spread themselves evenly around the *hounfour,* forming a rough circle.

"Sarah," she called. One of the young women, also a *hounsis*, stepped forward. "Draw the *veve* for Ogun Balanjo."

Sarah picked up a stick from the ground and stood next to the center post. She began drawing on the ground. The *veve* were doorways through which the *loa* might enter into this world. First she drew the *veve* for Legba, the *loa* of the crossroads, who opens the way for the other *loa*. Once she finished the first *veve*, she would draw the *veve* for Ogun Balanjo, the spirit of healing and prophecy.

While she was drawing, the *houngan* nodded to three other of the *hounsis*. One picked up the cooling pitcher and went into the woods. He would fetch water to cool the center post. The other sat before the drums and began a slow and heavy beat. The third picked up a bound raven. He carried the flapping bird to the center post and tied it to a rope that was wrapped around the post. The *houngan* and the *mambo* went to stand near the center post, staying clear of Sarah, who was now drawing the second *veve*.

Daniel, the student with the cooling pitcher, emerged from the woods. He bowed to the priest and priestess, then took the cooling pitcher to the east fire, where he held it up in salute. He did the same at the south, the west, and the north. Then he came to the center post, poured a little water on it, and waited for Sarah to finish.

The drums kept up their incessant beat, but the tempo slowly increased. The fifteen or so other worshipers began to sway with the beat.

Sarah stood, indicating she had finished both *veve*. Esmerelda looked at them. They were perfect. "Good job, girl."

Sarah gave a quick smile and retreated back to the circle of worshipers.

The priest spoke. "Daniel, wash round the *veve*."

Daniel walked carefully around the *veve*, pouring a thin stream of water to the ground. He was careful not to wash away any of the *veve*, just circle it with water to show respect. When he finished, he stood by the *poteau-mitan*.

Esmerelda stamped her feet on the ground three times. Then

she walked to the entrance of the circle, spun around, and walked slowly, carefully, back to the center post, holding the *veve* of Legba in her mind. When she touched the post, the drums increased in rhythm. The worshipers all then followed the lead of the *houngan* and began to chant in time to the beat. The sounds were low and guttural, an old chant in Fon, the language of Dahomey, the western African kingdom that had been a seat of the slave trade.

Now the dancing began in earnest, and all of the worshipers, except Daniel and the drummer, started to slowly circle the center post. Each time the *houngan* passed in front of the drummer, the rhythm would speed up and the chant would grow louder.

Esmerelda's face glistened with sweat. She knew a *loa* would come tonight. As she danced with the others, she could feel the power building. She nodded to Daniel, who poured more water on the *poteau-mitan*. She could feel the heat coming from it. Their chant was working. She felt more than saw the arrival of Legba. He "mounted" Daniel, taking possession of his body. Legba-Daniel began dancing, still holding the cooling pitcher. Now he poured the water on himself as much as on the center post. Esmerelda started to go to Daniel, who was now Legba, but the *loa* waved her away. Legba set down the cooling pitcher and went to stand before the drums. He widened his stance an almost impossible amount. Then he began to lift his feet one after the other, goading the drummer to a faster rhythm. Legba-Daniel joined the dance, whirling inside the circle of worshipers. Then he went to the entrance to the circle. In the air he scribed part of the *veve* for Ogun Balanjo, then reared back as if struck by a wind. Sarah fell from the circle of dancers and began to writhe on the ground, thrusting her hips upward as if making love to a man, trying to draw him deeper inside of her. Legba-Daniel went to her and began speaking in a tongue that Esmerelda could not understand. The drumming went on as Legba whispered to Sarah, soothing her and the *loa* that was mounting her body.

Riley motioned to the third *hounsis,* John, who went to the center post and sliced the head from the raven. Then he cut it free from the post and carried the twitching body to where Ogun Balanjo–Sarah lay on the ground. Legba-Daniel still whispered to her. John let the blood spout out over the two *loa,* then handed the bird to Esmerelda, who had left the dance to come before the *loa.* The *houngan* joined her and they bowed together, then knelt over the twitching body of Sarah, letting the blood from the bird spurt out over the girl. Daniel fell backward into the sand. Legba had left him. Sarah's eyes grew wide and she sat up, then pulled her feet under her and sat on her heels, facing the *mambo* and *houngan.* She placed her hand over her mouth. The *houngan's* voice ripped over the drumming and chanting. "Stop. The *loa* will speak."

In the sudden quiet, Sarah stood, trembling. The blood of the bird ran down her arms. She reached out for the raven and took it from Esmerelda. Sarah pressed her lips to the severed neck, then tossed the corpse away and laughed. "*Mambo,* you have given me a beautiful mount." Sarah's hands rose and pressed over her breasts. "This one made for pleasure." The worshipers murmured to each other. This was a high blessing for Sarah, coming from a *loa.*

Ogun-Sarah looked at Esmerelda. "But tonight not for pleasure. You want to know about the white man with the devil." He made it a statement. "Sistah, you stay away from his magic. You and *houngan,* don't do nothin'. Talk's fine. Watchin's fine. But work no magic, 'less you have to. Let 'em fix it themselves." Sarah swayed; then she fell to her knees and collapsed as the *loa* left her.

None but Esmerelda had ever seen a mount like this. None but her had heard a *loa* speak like this. The *houngan* stood and spoke to the amazed worshipers, startling them into movement. "Fetch water for Sarah and Daniel. Run like the Baron behind ya."

They picked up the cooling pitcher and several other pots that lay about and went to fill them with cool water for the two who had been mounted.

Riley leaned close to Esmerelda. "Sistah, I never heard such, never hear a *loa* speak so plain."

"I hear it once before," she said. "When I was a little girl, I heard the *loa* speak this plain." Though the night was warm, she shivered. "Lotsa men died."

✿

BISHOP Shea could not sleep. The events of the day had disturbed him too much. During the day, he had caught himself repeating Luther's hymn as something of a chant. In the night it became a prayer to ward off the evil the bishop was aware now roamed the streets of his city. He knew that he could not control this creature, nor could Benito, except with a great deal of help. The bishop got up from his bed and went into his office, which was adjacent to his bedroom. Though the moon had already set, the votive candle in the small shrine in his office gave him enough light to move around such a familiar place. He poured a small amount of whiskey in a glass, thinking that perhaps it might help him sleep. He downed it quickly and set down the glass.

The bishop was not a man who tended to pace or to sit when he thought. Rather he went to stand by the window that overlooked the garden. The walls blocked much of the light from the street lamps, leaving the area dimly lit, though he could still make out the geometric pattern of the pale concrete sidewalks. Almost immediately, he saw a shape moving across the walk and thought that someone else might be having trouble sleeping, perhaps the monsignor. Then the shape moved off the sidewalk and through a rose bed, which the monsignor would never do. Francis Shea loved his roses too much. The shape emerged onto the concrete walk on the other side of the rose bed.

The bishop was angry. Someone was callously walking through his flowers in the night. Then he noticed the shape, which had stopped moving. It was far too large to be the monsignor. In fact, it was too large to be human. The bishop's blood chilled as he looked at the unmoving shape, certain that it was regarding him with a feral intelligence. The shape began to glow a faint red, and the bishop could see that it was no creature of this world. It was the thing that had been haunting his thoughts, the thing that had killed Richardson. It was not bothered that it had been seen; rather, it locked eyes with the bishop until the priest glanced away.

When he looked back, the creature had turned and was continuing on its way in the garden. When the shape reached the far wall it disappeared into it. The bishop remained standing, frozen. The aura of menace that he had felt dissipated, but his fear was more durable. With shaking hands, he went to his desk and began lighting candles. When the room was brightly lit, he poured himself a full glass of whiskey and sat. He was ashamed as well as afraid. He had done nothing, remaining frozen in fear. Every protection—every prayer, every psalm, every hymn—had fled from his mind in the face of the beast. He felt violated that the beast had come to destroy his roses and peer into his mind. It must have looked inside of him while he slept. How else could it have discovered that the roses were a source of comfort to him?

This creature was the face of darkness that Benito and his kind had sworn to confront. They had a courage that Francis could not understand. At least in an exorcism, you knew where the enemy was. It was inside its victim. This demon could be anywhere, behind you, in front of you, around the next corner. It could not be exorcised. It must be fought and defeated. In the presence of such evil, Francis realized that he was impotent. He hoped that Benito and his kind were not. He prayed that Benito's help would arrive soon. In prayer Francis found some solace, though he still found it difficult to push the horrid face from his memory.

CHAPTER NINE

STRENG had chosen the hours between sunset Wednesday and dawn on Thursday to begin sowing the seeds of doubt in the minds of his enemies. He had sent Belial to haunt the cathedral compound in the darkness. Streng himself had a very specific goal in mind. In the hours before dawn, the darkest hours of night, he separated his essence from his body and went to visit the priest from Saint Augustine.

⁓⋈⁓

FATHER Benito awoke in his chamber, certain that he was not alone. He could see nothing in the pitch-black room, but he could feel the presence of another. Cold sweat broke out on Benito's back as he prepared to defend himself. Using his Sight he could detect the movements of the presence. He recognized it as the projection of another magician's consciousness. The shade moved about the room, then came to hover over Benito's bed, floating a few feet above him. Benito could have reached out to it, but concentrated on his own shielding in case of attack.

An impression formed in his mind. Subtly but clearly, he was being warned to leave the city, to escape his own death, which was inevitable if he stayed.

Its work done, the other presence faded away, leaving Benito alone with his fear. He now knew that he was being watched. Even his sleep would not be safe from their opponents until more of his order arrived. Whoever these magicians were, they were outside of his experience. They were very skilled. They could project their presences, invading even the sacred space of the cathedral compound.

With shaking hands, he lit the candle at his bedside. He did not try to sleep again. The effort would be pointless. He read until dawn, then dressed and went to the chapel to pray. That duty offered some reassurance. When he at last felt the fear was cleansed from him, he went to the dining hall.

While he ate breakfast, he considered the events of the previous day, if only to forget the events of the night. He had spoken with four of the five nuns present on the night of Richardson's death and learned little from them. Perhaps today would be better. After breakfast, he would talk to the final nun, Sister Brigid. As he finished his breakfast, the monsignor entered the dining hall. He joined Benito.

The monsignor could not help but notice how drained Benito looked. "Are you well, Father?"

"I slept poorly. Bad dreams."

The monsignor did not want to know what bad dreams might trouble the sleep of a mage.

Benito forced himself to appear more cheerful than he felt. "Don't be concerned, Monsignor." He smiled and changed the topic. "However, you may find it of interest that I was able to mine something valuable from your little book."

"What did you discover?"

"The most important thing is what I have been able to deduce," Benito said.

"Which is?"

"If we assume that the ones who are killing these girls do not want to be discovered carrying a dead body, then they would not carry the bodies far. But they also would space the bodies so they would give no clue as to where the killings were done. For a while the bodies appear in one area. For a while in another. If it were not for your historical record, we would not be able to come up with even a rough location for the murders."

"But with our 'historical record'?"

"I cannot be precise, but they appear to be in the eastern area of the city, a few blocks south of Bay Street and four or five blocks east of Bull."

The monsignor frowned. "That would imply that we are dealing with men of means. There are few poor families in that area."

"Would you expect them to be otherwise?"

"No, but it will make them difficult to deal with. The police would never believe that a prominent family would be involved in a thing such as this."

"Would they believe us in any event?"

"I suppose not."

"It is always that way. The police are like other men. They go to church and believe in God. They ask him to protect them against Satan, but don't really expect that they will ever confront him. When he shows up at their door, they invite him in for a glass of wine."

Monsignor Henry nodded in agreement. "Even without the police, would we be able to do something ourselves to catch them? Perhaps if priests were to roam the area on the appropriate nights?"

The monk shook his head. "Most priests would not notice anything out of the ordinary. These men we are working against are cautious. If they saw a priest in their area, they would cancel their ceremony for that evening. Also, I would suspect the room where the killing is done has thick enough walls that little sound would escape. The only ones who could know that they were at work would be those of us who can sense the use of magic. I am presently the only one here who could sense such things. And if I 'saw' them, they would likely 'see' me."

"So there is nothing we can do?"

"We need to assemble enough priests with magical talent to be certain that we can overwhelm them. I have already begun that task. That we have an approximate idea of where they are and the nights on which they do their magic will be of tremendous value. Your little book may be the key to defeating them."

"I am glad it will be of service," the monsignor replied. He began to rise from his chair.

"If you would stay a moment longer, there is something else that I would like to ask."

The monsignor resettled in his chair.

The monk continued, "I have spoken to all but one of the five nuns who were present that night."

The monsignor inclined his head in a slight nod.

Benito continued, "Three of the nuns stayed as far away from the door as they could and tried to block out the sights and sounds. They had little to tell me. Sister Francis mainly confirmed what I already knew. I must say, though, that she is quite courageous. She showed little fear in relating the events of the night."

"I am not surprised," the monsignor said. "I think that if the Devil himself appeared in her room late one night, Sister Francis would attempt to put his eyes out with a candlestick. Her faith is deep. She is one who truly does 'trust in the Lord.' I have seen her dealing with battle casualties so badly wounded that their screaming could be heard throughout the hospital. Her expression and compassion never wavered. If there is anything she fears, I don't know what it would be."

The monk sat back and thought for a moment, remembering his interview with Sister Francis. He doubted neither her faith nor her courage, but Benito was certain that the monsignor was wrong about one thing. Sister Francis was afraid. She was doing a notable job of hiding her fear, but the events of the night had frightened her more than she would admit.

"So," the monsignor continued, "only Sister Brigid remains."

"I left her to the last because she was the first to enter the room, other than the doctor."

"She entered before Sister Francis?"

"Yes."

"That is unusual, so unusual that I didn't even ask about it." The monsignor rubbed his brow. "I mean, I have no reason to doubt her, but Sister Francis has always appeared to be made of sterner stuff than Sister Brigid. Brigid is Irish, and the Irish nuns are the first to give credence to otherworldly forces. It seems unlikely that she would be the first to enter."

"Yet she was."

"That is interesting, Father." He paused. "But does it mean anything?"

"Perhaps I will find out when I meet with her."

"When will that be?"

"She's waiting for me now."

The monsignor rose. "Then I think it's time you interviewed our courageous young nun. Please let me know if anything comes of it."

"Certainly, Monsignor." He rose and bowed slightly to the monsignor before turning to go to his meeting with Sister Brigid. Something in Benito quickened as he walked to the meeting; he was unusually alert.

༺࿉༻

SISTER Brigid was waiting for Father Benito in what the nuns referred to as the "contemplation room." Sister Brigid had always loved this small sandstone-walled chapel that jutted into the convent garden. Three stained-glass windows adorned the north, south, and east walls. However, the room remained dim, even on the brightest of days. A simple stone altar, adorned with a brass cross, was before the largest of the windows, which faced to the east. Four small pews were in front of the altar. Each could hold five people. The austerity and beauty of the room made it a favored place both for prayer and for meditation. Sister Brigid was sitting in the first of the pews, awaiting Father Benito. As she waited, she began to probe what lay beneath her thoughts and feelings of the past few days. She knew that the answer to the riddles in her mind was in her past. She called to mind the image of her aunt in her simple home. As Sister Brigid tried to bring the image into clarity, she accidentally engaged her Sight.

An image of her aunt appeared in the air before her. The face was just as she had remembered. She was seeing her as the old woman had appeared the day that Brigid had said good-bye to her before leaving for the convent school. The image wavered from the tears that had fallen from Brigid's eyes so long ago. She had been so frightened, going away to a strange place and unfamiliar people. She knew that she would not be happy. Yet her aunt's face had held the calm that it always had. She was telling her, "Remember that you will always be who you are, and that there will always be a few of us to help. The old faith will remain. The gods cannot die. They are part of the land."

Those words had been spoken almost thirty years ago, yet they brought more solace to her than anything else she had been told. Perhaps this old memory had lain behind her letter to Siobhan.

Father Benito was approaching the room along the corridor from the convent. He was enjoying the texture of the stone and the beauty of the view from the windows. The morning sun, having crested the eastern wall of the convent, slanted in through the windows. The carefully tended garden lay between the corridor and the east wall. He stopped before one of the windows, halfway down the hall to the door to the small chapel, and looked out at the roses that grew in profusion across the face of the pane. He admired the skill of whatever unknown gardener had trained the roses to arc across the window opening. The red and white roses, each part of separate bushes, intertwined. The morning sun illuminated them brilliantly. The effect was one of having created stained glass from living materials. He drank in their beauty, reflecting that no human craftsman could have created the delicate beauty of these flowers. No stained glass could mimic the exquisite colors that the flowers displayed so flagrantly. If he had needed proof of the existence and love of God, there was no better evidence than what he saw with his eyes. Father Benito always saw the hand of God around him, most often revealed in nature's casual displays of her awesome beauty. Here in Savannah, as in Saint Augustine, he could see the pure profligacy of nature.

Others did not see it, and so their faith wavered or became insubstantial. Benito had seen it in a thousand landscapes and many countries. Here or in the austere hills of Spain, God had left his signature of beauty. It was up to man to decide what to do with it. In some places, the people had chosen to scar the land. They lived without hope or color, trudging to their jobs at some nameless factory or mine. In other places, men had worked to bring the beauty into their lives, as had the unknown gardener who had woven the roses into this exquisite framework around the window. Luis had seen the Sistine Chapel and the beauty that had been created by Michaelangelo. That fresco had been inspired by a vision. The delicate arc of God's hand as he reached out in the very act of creation was breathtaking in its beauty. Luis also remembered an olive grove outside of Toledo, a part of the Church's property that was rarely visited, except for garnering the yearly offering of olives. When the politics and corruption of the cathedral had become too painful, he had often ridden out to the grove, which had been placed to give a view of two valleys. Each had harbored a small stream. Both were a cool respite from the heat of the Spanish sun, as he had often visited them in the heat of the day when many of his colleagues were taking their siesta. His horse wandered about him, sampling the grasses as Luis enjoyed the cheese, bread, and wine the monks of the nearby monastery had provided him. Sometimes he dozed, only to be eventually wakened by his horse, ready to move on to another place. Sometimes Luis woke on his own, feeling a little dazed by waking in a place that was much like he imagined paradise would be.

He found it strange that no one ever came to this place, which to Benito was as sacred as the cathedral itself. The others stayed behind at the offices and apartments in the city. He found it odd that none of the many there ever came to this place, which possessed a more subtle beauty than any of the great art that hung on the walls of the cathedral and its offices, even the haunting visions of El Greco.

The memory washed through him, refreshing him like cool water. However, he had business at hand and turned his attention from the window, continuing down the hallway. Something immediately passed across that part of his consciousness that had been awakened by his magical training. Magic was in use somewhere close at hand. After a moment of anxiety, he understood that this magic was not directed toward him, nor was it directed at all. It was merely someone using his ability to look more deeply into something. It could be the efforts of a trained magician, or it could be the efforts of one of those few who were born with the Sight. Those born to the art always made the best magicians. Even the most rigorous training could not give someone the potency of vision that those born with the Sight possessed naturally.

Luis made use of a simple spell that rendered him difficult to perceive by magical means. Now he could move securely, as his own presence would not intrude into the consciousness of the one using the Sight. Then Luis moved toward the source of the magic. He was not surprised that he was moving closer to the chapel where he was to meet Sister Brigid. Raising his own Sight to its most acute level, he silently opened the door to the room, so as not to disturb the nun who was sitting in the first pew, her head rigid in concentration. Floating in the air between her and the altar he saw the face of an old woman before an indefinite background. Undoubtedly, the nun could see more.

The image vanished. Brigid sat upright in the pew and turned to face the monk. She had sensed his presence, regardless of his spell. She was embarrassed to have been lost in thoughts of her aunt when Church business was at hand.

The Benedictine was amazed that an untutored magician could have detected him, even though he had made an effort to remain invisible to the Sight. She had also been projecting an image, a different skill from the Sight. Her gifts were strong. He wondered if she had ever been trained. If she had not, which was likely, she had been born with remarkable abilities. He would need to be careful around her. There would be no point in deceiving her or telling her half-truths.

She stood up rapidly, covering her expression, and said, "Father Benito, I am Sister Mary Brigid."

Father Benito replied, "I am pleased to meet you, Sister. Could you tell me who the old woman was?"

"You could see her?"

"Yes."

She stuttered, "Then . . . you have the Sight?"

"Yes."

She was speechless. She had never expected to meet a priest with the Sight.

Sensing her emotions, he smiled to her before turning to close the door behind him. Then he gently asked again, "Who was the woman?"

"My great-aunt."

He walked down the left side of the room, finally seating himself on the opposite end of the small pew upon which Brigid had been sitting. "Please," he said, "sit down."

She sat back down in the pew, facing him. She remained silent, unsure of what, if anything, she should say.

"Would you tell me about your aunt?"

A silence drew out between them in the room. He was waiting for an answer, his curiosity raised by what he had seen, wondering if she might be of assistance in dealing with their opponent.

She was afraid. If he could see an image that she had accidentally projected while thinking of her aunt, what else could he discover? Would he find out about her crisis of faith? Could he, a priest, possibly understand her background? Might he react with the same harshness that she had experienced as a small child?

He tried to calm her. "As you should know, Sister, I cannot see into your mind." He smiled. "Perhaps I should tell you about your aunt?"

She nodded dumbly.

"She was a village wisewoman, what some might call a witch. She followed in the old religion of your people. You admired her, looked up to her. But, as a young child, you were sent away to Catholic school. Perhaps in a place distant from your home?"

She nodded again, the fear still hanging on her face like a mask.

"You have nothing to fear from me. I, unlike many others in the Church, recognize that God has many faces. Perhaps your family was one that chose to see many faces of God instead of one. What concerns me isn't what might concern many priests. I am not concerned with what you believe as much as I care about whom you serve. Do you serve good, or evil? Since you are a nun and minister to the sick, what you do is good. Therefore you are good. What you may believe in to sustain yourself is of less concern to me than who you are."

She stared back dumbly, though the tension was draining from her.

He asked, "So, was I right about your aunt?"

"Yes. She was the wisewoman. She worshiped the old gods. As a child, I was to be trained to walk in her footsteps."

"What happened?"

"The famine," she replied. "When the village priest came to my family and asked if they would like to send me to Catholic school in Dublin, my parents had no choice. It wasn't even a question of one less mouth to feed. At that time, we did not know if any would survive. Of my parent's five children, only three survived the famine."

Benito nodded. He knew more than he wanted to know about the famine, about the Church's inaction when so many of the faithful were dying for want of the simplest need of all, food. And he understood, with some distaste, why the village priest had chosen this particular girl.

"So, Sister, you were the one that your aunt had chosen to train?"

"Yes, Father."

"Because?"

"Of all of the children in the family, I was the one with the strongest gifts."

"Did you go far in your training?"

"No, not at all, or perhaps I should say not since I was seven. My aunt had just begun my training when I was sent to Dublin."

"What a waste."

"What do you mean?"

"You have almost no training, certainly no encouragement, yet you have magical abilities that many strive for years to attain. You are an hereditary. Your gift came to you at birth. Just a few lessons from your aunt began its development. Though left without nurturing for years, it is still strong enough that another magician can sense its workings." He mused. "How powerful you could have become."

She interrupted. "Another magician?"

"Yes, Sister, the Church has its own magicians, though we prefer the term 'mage.' I am one of them."

"But I have never heard of them."

"Our existence is kept secret, except from those who must know. In your case, you will find out about us whether I tell you or not. Other mages from within the Church will gather here very soon. We will fight the creature that killed Mr. Richardson. In order to achieve that, the working that we do must be very powerful. With your gift, you could no more ignore our efforts than you could ignore an artillery shell falling on the convent."

"Where does the Church get these magicians?" she asked, her curiosity overwhelming her shyness.

"We look for people who have an aptitude for being trained in the arcane arts. An hereditary is the most prized find, which is what makes our not finding you such a loss. Your local priest was trying to disrupt the pagan community in your village, a foolish tactic. Instead he should have alerted his superiors, and they would have contacted us. Perhaps we could have recruited you, perhaps not.

"Whatever the source of the candidate, after we find one, we begin the process of training. If the training is successful, he or she becomes one of those who are called in special situations. It is rare that we can find one who is an hereditary like you. Hereditaries can quickly master what it takes others years to learn. Does this gift run in your family?"

"My ancestors have been the wise ones of the village, sometimes the district, for longer than the *seanchaide* can remember."

Benito knew the abilities of the Irish storytellers. Some of their stories had been unchanged for hundreds of years. Their memories were legendary. So it was likely that this nun's ancestors had been the pagan priestesses of their village for centuries. It was a pity that his order had not found her before. Now they were facing a deadly enemy, and a potentially powerful hereditary magician was with them. However, she was untrained and probably useless.

In the silence she had found her own question. "Why does the Church have magicians?"

"It has been necessary, from time to time, to deal with things that cannot be handled by an exorcism."

"So the rite does not always work?"

"The official position is that it does. But the power of the rite is controlled by ability as well as faith. Enacting a ceremony, speaking the words, and invoking the powers are all done far better by a mage than by a priest untrained in the arts. If the priest has been trained as I have, there is more power at hand, since the priest is the conduit for the powers he invokes. There are also other rituals that we use. They are much more powerful than an exorcism. Sometimes an exorcism is not enough, no matter who is performing it."

She nodded. Her acceptance of the complex explanation surprised him. She must have gained some understanding of how these things worked, either from her aunt or from the culture of her childhood.

She asked, "What are these things that can't be dealt with by exorcism?"

"Something like what we are facing now. The creature that came for Richardson did not possess him. It simply killed him. A traditional exorcism would have no effect on this creature, since this demon can leave at will. It is not tethered to the body. Exorcism is for the removal of a spirit that inhabits a human body. The demon that killed Richardson was independent of his body. In all likelihood, the creature had been summoned by other magicians. We can assume that they are evil and, quite probably, worshipers of Satan."

Again she listened quietly, not questioning the explanation, seeming to file it away in her mind for later examination.

He thought for a moment. "Now I understand why you were the first nun to enter the room. You had no fear that it would attack you because you knew that it was gone."

"Yes."

"And the fact that it had been there at all did not surprise you?"

"I never thought about it that way."

"Sister, most people would have been terrified just to know that such a thing was close. They would run from it or try to deny what they were perceiving."

"It was there. I felt it. But it had not come for me."

"You were certain?"

"Of course."

"Your perceptions are remarkable."

"Is there something wrong with what I felt?" She bristled a little at his comment.

"Not in the least. You were absolutely right. What makes your reaction so odd is that few others would react that way. The Irish tend to accept the presence of the unseen, the manifold nature of a spirit realm, where some are good and some are evil. In most places in the Christian world, all that is unseen is suspected of being evil."

"That seems so," she paused, "odd."

"To you it is. But much of Ireland is still only thinly Christian-ized. Sometimes I think that it is a veil that hides a pagan heart." He asked, "And who is your namesake, Brigid?"

"A saint, one of the patron saints of Ireland."

"I know that. I mean, who was Brigid?"

"The goddess of mothering, of help, and of the hearth. Some say of love."

"Precisely. And because we could not remove her from the Irish, we made her a saint, so her worship could continue within the sanctions of the Church."

Sister Brigid was becoming more and more unsure of this conver-sation. Father Benito was not reacting to the things she was saying as she expected a priest would. Though he was outside her own experi-ence, she also realized that no matter how open-minded he might seem, he was still a priest. She was unwilling to share all of her thoughts with him. Her aunt had warned her about priests, that they were often well-meaning but still dangerous. They were intent on re-placing the old religion. What was said to one had to be guarded carefully, and Brigid was afraid that she had already said too much. She shifted ground.

"Father, what was the thing that killed Mr. Richardson?"

"That is what I have come to talk to you about. It was a demon, a spirit of evil. I don't know what else to call it. Because you were there, you may be able to contribute some understanding that we do not have. I perceived the remnants of its presence in the hospital room. I know the creature is very powerful, I know what it seems capable of, but I was not there."

"Father, I think you know most of what I know already. I felt it come and go. I felt a strong chill when it was there. It was powerful and did not mind entering a place of nuns and priests to do its will. The sanctity of our hospital seemed to pose no barrier to it."

"Why do you say that?"

"It happened so quickly. There was no sense of struggle. The only delay in killing Richardson seemed to be for the thing's own amusement. It taunted its victim before it killed him. Its terrible laughter ran through the corridor."

This information was what Benito could not have hoped to gain except by speaking with someone with the Sight who had been present on that night. The information was frightening. This creature was very strong if it could end a human life with no more effort than a human would need to kill an insect.

"Are you certain?" he asked.

"Yes."

"Then I and my brothers face a formidable challenge. We do not know where this thing comes from, what its name is. . . ." He drifted into silence.

"I think I know where it comes from."

He sat upright as if cold water had been thrown on him. "You do?"

"I'm not certain, but there is something I saw."

"Please, go on."

"The evening after the murder, I was walking in the city around twilight. As I returned to the hospital for my shift that evening, I happened to walk by a certain street. I almost turned down it. But I sensed something there, something evil and dark. With the Sight, I could see a dark mist hanging over the street, like a cloud of black smoke."

"Where?"

"It was in front of a house on Saint Julian Street. I saw the cloud while I was standing in Warren Square."

The name of the square was within the area he had laboriously defined by going through the monsignor's journal. "Sister," he said, "you have given us a great gift. Such knowledge can help us. Could you lead me there?"

"Yes."

Another thought struck him. "Were you observed?"

"I don't think so."

"Sister, I would like you to consider something, though you are under no obligation to pursue it. You have a potent talent. Perhaps you could put it to further use in our work?"

She looked at the priest levelly. Her eyes seemed to pierce him. For several seconds they held their positions, until her gaze softened.

"Father, that is not something that I can decide now. Could I have some time to think about it, perhaps offer a prayer?"

"Certainly. But please, do not mention anything of our conversation other than that I asked you about the events of the evening. I may have need to discuss your special gift with the mother superior so that she can understand why I need you to take me to the place where you saw the darkness. Other than that small exception, what we said—about magic, your aunt, and what you saw—needs to remain between us and God."

"You can count on my silence, Father." She hoped she could count on his.

"And Sister, before you go, I have one more thing I must tell you. You may be in some danger. If there are potent magicians abroad, they will not take kindly to someone who has the ability to perceive them."

"What should I do?"

"If you perceive anything that might be called magical or spiritual threatening you, come to me immediately, day or night."

"Yes, Father."

"Go with God," he replied.

She rose and left the chapel. As the door shut behind her, Benito's thoughts stayed with the surprising woman he had just met. The most remarkable part of the conversation was the part that had never occurred. He had identified the ones who had summoned the demon as worshipers of Satan. He was relatively sure that was what they were, but only in the sense that they themselves thought they were honoring Lucifer. When Benito had called them satanists, the nun had been concerned with the other points that he had made, not with the implied presence of the Lord of Evil. Why not? Was it because she did not believe in Satan?

Though it was contrary to Church doctrine, Benito knew that many within the Church, himself included, did not believe in one encompassing Lord of Evil. The priest used the term "Satan" in the old sense of the word, meaning "adversary." It was a convenient shorthand that conformed to doctrine. Benito thought it likely that Brigid shared his perspective.

He was convinced that the creature that they were dealing with was frighteningly strong. The working that they must do would be dangerous. He would be glad when Rimaldi and the others arrived. He did not feel safe in this city, no matter how pleasant its outward aspects might be, especially after his disturbing nighttime visitor.

He went back to the monsignor's office, surprised to find that Father Henry was with the bishop. Henry's secretary said that Benito could wait for the monsignor in his office. She was certain that the monsignor would not be long. Benito had just settled himself in a chair when he heard Father Henry's voice in the outer office.

"Katherine, you need to find Father Benito for me." The monsignor's voice was rushed, yet had an edge. He sounded upset.

"Father," the woman replied. "He's here, waiting for you."

Benito was already at the door to the monsignor's office.

"Thank God," he said, looking at Benito. He took a moment to gather himself into a more composed frame of mind. "Oh, and Katherine, I'm sorry I was abrupt."

"It's all right, Father. Is the bishop not feeling well?"

"I just need Father Benito."

"What is it?" Benito asked.

"I don't know if I can explain, but if you could come with me . . ."

"Of course."

The monsignor led him down the corridor quickly. They were in a part of the compound that Benito was unfamiliar with, though he knew they were below the bishop's office. They emerged through a beautifully detailed oak door into a small garden. The only other exit was into a corridor on another side. Two sides of the garden appeared to end in flat walls with no doorways, which Benito assumed were outside walls of the compound. The small garden was graced with a smooth concrete path and enough roses to dazzle the eye with their wealth of colors. The only mar on the garden was in one of the rose beds, which had a streak of destruction running through it.

Benito went immediately to the roses. The monsignor followed. The gardener in Benito was incensed at the destroyed plants. Someone had walked directly through the bed of flowers, ignoring the thorns and callously snapping the branches. Some plants had been uprooted. All of the plants along the path of destruction were desiccated and blackened, seemingly poisoned.

The monsignor did not wait for Benito's comment, but said, "This is the bishop's private garden. No one has access to it during the night, when it is locked. The bishop, the day gardener, and myself have the only keys. At sundown yesterday, the doors were locked and the plants were undamaged."

Benito stood. "But someone came into the garden and did it intentionally. These plants have been destroyed. But no poison could have stripped the life from these plants so quickly."

"Then what happened?"

"I think you already know."

The monsignor nodded and led Luis a few feet to a bench along one of the outside walls. They sat as the monsignor told his story.

"Last night, the bishop had trouble sleeping. He went into his office, to the window that he often stands by to think. It looks down on this garden. Bishop Shea loves roses and has had this garden carefully tended for years. During the day he often leaves it open for others to wander in. But last night, late in the evening, he looked down into the garden and saw something moving in the near darkness. It was a large, manlike figure, but too large to be a man. It walked through this bed, then turned and looked up at the bishop, as if it knew that he would be watching at that very window." He pointed to the window, where Bishop Shea was now standing, look-ing down at them.

Benito nodded to the bishop in acknowledgment.

Monsignor Henry continued, "The figure glowed a dull red. It turned away from the bishop and walked down this path and through that wall."

Benito said, "Our opponents were busy last night. I had a warn-ing visit. It was the bad dream that I told you had troubled my sleep. Apparently, one of the human magicians visited me, and the demon visited this garden."

"Why?"

"To do what it has done. Frighten us."

"How did it kill the plants? I mean, I understand how it broke them, but it did more than that."

"It pulled the life from them. Everything that lives has that elu-sive quality of life to it. This creature sucked the life from the plants."

Comprehending what Benito was saying pushed the monsignor to the verge of hysteria. Here, in the privacy of the bishop's garden, Monsignor Henry let more emotion show than he would have in another location, and his fear was clearly written on his face. In a strained voice, he asked, "Can it do that?"

"Yes, a demon has that ability. It can drain life from a plant, from an animal, from a human, from almost anything."

"My God, what are we facing?"

"A powerful demon. We are joining battle with an opponent of great strength." Benito looked him directly in the eye, attempting to steady him as he spoke. "Nothing will be the same after this is all over. This is not the last of the things you will see, and it is definitely not the most terrible. You must trust in God and in the priests that the Church will send to deal with this. I alone cannot defeat it. But the priests that Father Rimaldi will summon can."

The monsignor visibly calmed. "What do you need of me?"

"Courage and constancy. Even if you may have your doubts of

what we can do, you must not let others, particularly those under you, see that. You must show belief and assurance."

The monsignor nodded. "That I can do."

Benito smiled. "Good."

The two men sat for a moment longer in silence. Then the monsignor raised his head and looked at the Benedictine. "But tell me, Father, is that what you are doing now, showing belief and assurance?"

Benito regarded him carefully. "Robert, to another I might lie, but to you I cannot. The only answer I have is another question. Would it do any good for me to show my doubts?"

"No, it wouldn't."

༄

AFTER lunch, Benito went to see the mother superior. Her office was near the front of the convent, as would be expected. She would have visitors who should not pass through to the places where the nuns lived and slept. He stopped before her iron-bound oak door and rapped lightly.

"Come in," she called from inside.

Father Benito entered the office. It was pleasingly austere.

She stood as he entered. "So you must be the mysterious Father Benito."

"I am, Mother Superior."

"Please, please, come in and sit down. I'm Mary Margaret. Or, for simplicity, 'Margaret' will do."

"And I am Luis."

"A pleasure to meet you." She smiled as she regained her chair. "I've been looking forward to your visit. Perhaps you can give me some words of comfort for my nuns. They are afraid, and I have little to offer them."

"I hope I can." He took the offered chair. "But first, I must apologize. In my hurry to interview the nuns who were there the night of the events, I failed to first pay a call on you. It was impolite of me."

"No matter, Father. Everything has been at sixes and sevens

since that night. I have spent an unusual amount of time dealing with my own charges. It seems that many of the sisters have been rather astonished to find that being a nun might one day cause them to come face-to-face with an occupant of the nether regions. We were fortunate that Sister Francis was there that night. She is as steady as a rock and has helped calm the others."

"And Sister Brigid?"

She looked at him a moment before replying, "Her reaction puzzles me. She seems untroubled by the events, except that she is more inwardly turned than she normally is. I wonder what might be going on inside her mind?"

"I can assure you a great deal."

"Please, go on."

"I just spoke with her. She is Irish, native born in one of the more pagan regions of the island. She has had less to adjust to than many others might. She grew up believing the spirit realm was just around the next hill, so she seems more ready to accept what happened." He carefully avoided much of the content of the conversation. "She is still frightened by the events, even if she has little trouble accepting that they occurred."

The mother superior nodded. "For myself, the problem was to accept that the events occurred so close at hand. Perhaps it is some weakness in my faith, but I had not expected such a manifestation."

"Yet it is here nonetheless."

"The bishop," she said, "was reluctant to accept that these events were occurring in his own domain, but he did. He implied that it might not be a case of possession."

"He was correct. This creature is beyond the reach of an exorcism. Simple faith and ritual are not protection enough against what we are facing."

"Sister Francis thinks it is, even though her crucifix is one of the things that convinced the bishop otherwise." She smiled to herself ruefully. "I do not have her abiding trust. I have tried, but the world is too much with me. Especially after the war years."

"How so?"

"It is difficult to believe in an almighty and caring God when you see so many men who have been wounded or maimed. In the later years of the war we often had so many casualties that every bed in the hospital was filled and we had to leave men on the floor. At the worst times, we had patients lying in the street. There were many soldiers that we could do nothing for." She spoke slowly as she remembered that time. "All we could do was watch them die. Some died slowly. The minié ball is a terrible adversary. It shatters bone and leaves a path for infection. There were times, some as long as a month, when the hospital was never silent. There was always a man screaming or moaning in pain."

The priest bowed his head. She had seen a vision of Hell far worse than he had. "That is much to endure, Sister."

"It is hard to believe with the same naive force that you once did when you have seen such horror. At least, it was for me. Sister Francis could manage it. I could not. War reminds us that, even in man, the drive to evil exists. Something must be the source of that evil."

Benito realized that this nun had opened her heart to him, but he had no ready words of comfort.

"Forgive me," she said, her voice rough. "I think the recent events have all drawn us to remember our own visions of evil." She paused, and her tone became more personal. "I mean, I understand war. It is horrible, but it is a thing that men do to themselves, to one another. This demon is a thing I do not understand. How can God let such things loose? Richardson's head was shattered when he was thrown against the wall."

"God did not let it loose. Men did."

"What men?"

"We don't know yet. This creature was summoned by men who are performing their own evil magic. It did not slip from the netherworld; it was called. Their objective is not to have it possess someone, but to use it to terrify and kill. They worship it. They kill in its name."

"Kill?"

"Yes. Their rituals often involve human sacrifice."

She looked at him with horror on her face.

"The victims are the ones whom no one would miss," he said. "Over the past several years a prostitute has been found dead about once every four months in the same general area of the city. All of them had been murdered in a similar way."

The nun took some time before responding to what Benito had said. "It is hard to believe, but I do."

"It is harder for me to accept that no one noticed."

"Poor girls." She crossed herself. "I will pray for their souls." Her eyes hardened. "When you have been a nun as long as I have, you know that some of the girls who take orders do so because it is a last resort. A broken marriage, an illicit affair, there are many reasons. Some come because it is the only option other than the brothel. The girls who were killed by these men might have just as easily been nuns. I know it is odd to think of the choice to take orders in that way—the nunnery or the brothel. Perhaps that is why we sisters do not condemn the sisters of that other order as vociferously as our society does." She looked at Benito. "How did Richardson come to be a victim?"

"He was one of their members who tried to leave."

"They could have found a way to kill him that would have drawn less attention."

"I'm certain they could have, but they chose to do it this way to make an example of him, probably to assure the loyalty of other members. Or they may have done it just to prove that they could."

"So the Church awakens its own magicians to deal with them." She noticed his reaction. "Father, your secret is safe, but I have been in the Church too long not to know some of its secrets. Though, until you sent your telegram, I was not sure that your informal order of magicians existed."

"I can say nothing about that."

"I know, even though I do confess to the sin of curiosity." She smiled. "But none of this is what brought you to me. You have need of something I can provide? Sister Brigid, I would assume."

He smiled. "One day I will learn not to underestimate the insight of a mother superior."

"Thank you for the compliment, but it was easy to see. She has a gift that we are all aware of. Even the doctors have come to rely on it more than they would care to admit."

"You mean her abilities have been used?"

"Not in a formal way, but we found out early in the war that she seemed to know about a person's health, about his chances for survival." She continued, "Often the most difficult choice that a doctor has to make in treating gangrene is where he should cut. Can he save the knee? Must the knee go to protect the patient's life?

"She always seemed to know if the doctor had cut enough. It was as though she could see the infection in the body. Some of the other nuns were frightened by her peculiar skill, but we were in a war, and there were many men coming to us for help. Her special sense was simply too useful to ignore."

"Her senses might make her valuable in our work."

"If she can help to defeat whatever this thing might be, she is yours. There may be too few nuns now as at any time, but I want to keep my charges very busy in the wake of Richardson's death. Their minds should not be idle. Giving Sister Brigid's duties to others will serve my purposes, as well as yours."

"Thank you, Mother Superior."

"I will send her to you once I have made the arrangements. She will be assigned to you as long as you need her."

"I appreciate your understanding."

The mother superior's voice took on an unexpected edge. "I saw the melted crucifix of Sister Francis. Can faith and prayer really protect a person from this thing that has been unleashed here?"

He paused before responding. "In almost every case, faith and prayer offer enough protection. But here, at this time, they are not enough. Only a mage is safe from this thing, and only a potent one at that."

"I always prefer the truth, even when it is unpleasant."

"I will not make that mistake again," he apologized.

"May God speed the others that will help you."

"They cannot arrive too quickly for me," he said. "Once they arrive, you and your nuns will be safer, because the demon's attention will be diverted by more powerful opponents. Until then, none of us are truly safe. Perhaps you should tell your nuns that the Church has a means of defending them, but you might refrain from telling them that we must wait for others to arrive."

Benito excused himself. As he walked down the corridor, he felt helpless. Everything around him told him the danger they were in. His nighttime visitor and the destruction of the roses meant that the opponents were trying to create fear and hysteria. The enemies were unpredictable. The normal circumspection that restrained them did not seem to apply here.

CHAPTER TEN

Friday, October 16

SISTER Brigid awoke at five to the sounds of the convent's dormitory. Relieved of her duties, she could stay in her cot and listen to the whispers as the nuns prepared to go about their work. These morning sounds had always been a comfort to her. She kept her eyes closed as she listened. She knew the other sisters by their whispering voices as well as by their spoken ones. They did not know why they whispered, but morning had always been a time for quiet.

She rolled onto her back and stretched. This morning she noticed that the sisters were quieter than usual. Even the whispered morning conversations were less frequent. And there was no laughter. On most mornings some humorous observation would bring amusement and a soft laugh. But not this day. She knew fear was the reason for the change. The few muted whispers were about Richardson's death or about the arrival of Father Benito. She also heard indistinct mutterings about the bishop's roses.

Suddenly the quiet was shattered by a scream. Brigid threw the covers off and ran out into the corridor. A small group was gathering outside of Sister Francis's room. Some of the nuns were dressed for their shift in the wards. Some were still clad in their nightdresses. Brigid joined the back of the group and looked over their heads into Sister Francis's cell. The nun was dead, her eyes gouged out, the empty sockets surrounded with dried blood.

Sister Maria, who had found the corpse, had backed against the wall opposite Sister Francis's door. Her fist was crammed into her mouth beneath her shocked and staring eyes.

"Fetch the mother superior," Brigid said.

Sending for her was not necessary. Mother Superior Mary Margaret was already in the dormitory, quickly walking down the hall to see what had broken the quiet of the morning. She pushed through the nuns to the door of Sister Francis's cell and was shocked by the mutilated body.

"Is she dead?"

No one responded.

Margaret whirled to face the nuns. "Most of you are nurses and no one thought to find out?"

They backed away from the angry mother superior, giving Brigid a chance to come to the door of the room. Brigid looked into the room at Sister Francis. "She's dead, Mother Superior."

"Don't you need to touch her to be sure?" Margaret asked angrily.

Brigid entered the cell and leaned over the corpse. She attempted to lift Sister Francis's arm to detect a pulse, but rigor mortis had begun and the corpse resisted movement. The skin temperature alone was enough to confirm what Brigid's Sight had already told her. "It's been some time since she died. The body is cold."

Now facing into the cell, the mother superior had her back to the other nuns. Brigid saw how tightly she held herself in control.

Margaret spoke over her shoulder, her words carefully measured. "Sister Teresa, tell the monsignor. Then find Father Benito and bring him here. The rest of you, get back to your cells. Do not leave the dormitory."

The nuns scurried away, both in obedience and in fear.

"And finish getting dressed," she called. "There will be men in the dormitory in a few minutes."

Brigid made her way out of the room. Margaret stopped her. "I'm sorry, Brigid. I know you didn't need to touch her to be sure. But I was angry. . . ."

"I understand, Mother Superior. I share your feeling."

"I want you here when they arrive. I would feel safer."

"Of course. It will only take me a moment to get dressed."

The mother superior stepped back into the corridor. Brigid went to her room, emerging a minute later, wearing her habit and donning her wimple. The two stood, waiting. Brigid stared into the room, using her Sight to see what she could.

"What do you see?" the mother superior asked.

"I can't be sure, but I think it was the same thing that killed Richardson."

Brigid kept her other thoughts to herself. The mother superior did not need to know that the death of so faithful a nun as Sister Francis had brought questions to Brigid's mind. Faith would not stop this demon. Only magical power could do that, and magic did not seem to be the property of any one religion. Father Benito had implied as much. She resolved to trust him, since he obviously knew that Christianity itself did not possess any special potency. It came down to whether you served good or evil. He had told her and she had not heard. She had withheld what she thought from him, fearing that he, as a priest, might present a danger to her. She now saw her opinion as understandable but foolish.

The monsignor appeared at the end of the hallway, striding at a speed close to running for most men. He was out of breath when he arrived.

Margaret pointed into the cell. The monsignor's eyes followed her hand.

He crossed himself. "Mother of God."

The mother superior's anger had dissipated, overwhelmed by sadness. Sister Francis had been her oldest friend in the convent. She had been there long before the mother superior had come and had welcomed her new superior with open arms and an endless supply of energy and compassion. Without Sister Francis's constancy, Margaret might not have been able to manage the hospital during the horrors of the war years.

Sister Teresa entered the corridor at the far door, bringing Father Benito into the dormitory. They joined the other three. Benito immediately went to the door of the cell. He crossed himself silently, then lowered his head as he engaged his Sight.

Having completed her task, Sister Teresa was unsure what to do. "Mother Superior, is there anything else?" Teresa was one of the older nuns, a rock almost as stable as Sister Francis had once been.

"Please take charge of the others," Margaret said. "They need to get to breakfast and relieve the morning shift on the wards, but they are not to talk to anyone else about what has happened. I know that they will talk to each other. We can't prevent that. But no one else can know about this until the monsignor and the bishop discuss it."

"Do you wish me to tell the bishop?"

"No, I will do that," she said.

Sister Teresa left to pass the mother superior's instructions on to the other nuns.

Father Benito had been absolutely still, staring into the room. Now he turned and faced Brigid. "Was it the same thing that killed Richardson?"

Brigid nodded in affirmation.

Margaret blurted out, "This was done by the creature you told me about?"

"Yes," Benito replied.

"Monsignor," the mother superior said, "I must tell the bishop."

"I agree."

She began walking away down the hall slowly, then picked up her pace as she focused on the task at hand rather than the corpse she was leaving behind.

The monsignor looked at Benito and Brigid. "Did it have to put out her eyes?"

Benito answered, "It did that to horrify whoever found her."

"It succeeded," the monsignor said.

❦

BRIGID joined Benito in their meeting room at eleven. In the intervening time, they had both managed to overcome some of the morning's emotions, but certainly not all. Brigid felt vulnerable. She did not think she could withstand an attack on her own, and she thought she would be the next one to feel the anger of their opponents. It was difficult to avoid recalling the image of Sister Francis's ravaged face. Brigid had often found compassion and strength in Sister Francis's eyes, but those eyes were now destroyed, as was the kindly but stern person that had lain behind them.

Their meeting was the first in the room that the bishop had assigned to Benito and the others of his order. It had been well chosen, isolated from the normal traffic within the compound and easily large enough to hold all who had been summoned. The heavy oak table in the middle of the room had the patina of age. It had been cared for lovingly, and glowed as only well-rubbed wood can. Around it were about a dozen chairs.

Other matters were foremost on Benito's mind. "Brigid, do you think that you can work today?"

"I feel compelled to work today. I want to do something that might help bring those responsible for killing Sister Francis to justice."

Benito looked at her carefully. "You are afraid."

"Shouldn't I be? Only two nuns entered the room that night. One is dead."

"We face powerful opponents here, and your ability to sense others might have made our opponents take note of you. You sensed the demon. You saw the cloud on Saint Julian. Perhaps you have been seen as well."

"I don't need to be reminded."

"I am almost certain that one of our mages will be another nun.

If so, I would like you to stay with her. That would offer you better protection, but the best protection is for me to teach you what you need to defend yourself. The techniques will probably be very potent in your hands. After all, you are born to it."

"You would teach me magic?" she said, surprised.

"I have no choice. You could be in danger. The men we face are part of a cult that has been in this city for over a century. We do not know what power they might have accumulated. Members of my order are traveling here right now from all over the country, but, even when assembled, we may not prove to be up to the task."

"You might fail? I thought God would not allow that."

"The fault lies in us. We must be capable of calling down power that can combat this danger. If we fail, it is because we fail, not because God has failed."

"And what would happen if you were to fail?"

"It is likely that we would die."

"And would your soul be forfeit to the demon? Would it then possess you?"

"For the first to die, no, the demon would be occupied with defeating the others. The last to die would be in danger of his soul being taken."

Brigid was unnerved by the solemn pronouncement. "I was taught that this type of thing could not exist, a creature that could fight a priest, much less many priests, and possibly defeat them, even come to control one."

Benito said, "When you take it upon yourself to fight such a creature, you expose yourself to its magic. Unfortunately, that is precisely what we must do. And there is the matter of those who summoned it. They, too, can strike against us, and they are powerful in their own right."

Brigid realized that she was learning things that seemed to be in opposition to all of what the Church had taught her about the power of Christ, about the power of faith. These new thoughts meshed with the thoughts that had been awakened from her past.

The priest understood the play of emotions across her face. "I know this is not what you expected to hear. We do not know why some of these things are so, only that good men have fallen before in dealing with such magicians."

She changed, not in any obvious way, but some of the obsequiousness of a nun fell from her. Something within her had turned in the current, driven by the death of Sister Francis and all the other things Brigid had seen and felt. She placed both hands on the edge of the table. "Then there is something wrong with your magic."

Benito was not prepared for the transformation that had occurred, for her contradicting him. "No, you do not understand how this is; we—"

She interrupted. "No, Father Benito, I cannot accept your vulnerability. True, I was only seven when I left my home, but I had already seen things that were more than the product of a child's imagination. My aunt could summon sprites that would dance in the smoke. I have seen the spirit creatures by the streams when I went to gather herbs. You are a good man, an honest man. I know that from looking at you. If you fail, the fault lies in your ritual, in your understanding, not in your inability to be a 'good vessel.'"

He rose to the defense. "These rituals have been developed over hundreds of years. They have been used to defend the Church for centuries."

"Then why did I never hear of such things in my childhood? In all the tales of the old gods there is no creature that the hero cannot overcome, no demon too powerful for the gods."

"Those are only legends; this is reality. We are not gods; we are only men."

A silence fell between them. She wondered if she should go on. She felt something rising inside her, a memory, a surety. He could see the change and wondered what he had awakened.

"My aunt told me a tale when I was six, a tale about a demon. I thought then that she was merely trying to frighten me. But I came to find it was true."

Father Benito kept silent. She had struck a place that contained his doubts as well as hers.

"About ten years before I was born, a man sought to do magic against the English. He did his magic at a place close to a village that lay ten miles from my own. He managed to open a doorway into another world and release something that was half man, half beast. He could not control it, so he was the first to die at its hands. Then it roamed free every night near the place where it had been summoned. It was seen by hundreds in the twilight and the dawn, in torchlight and lamplight. For four nights it killed animals, children, even adults. It was said to laugh when it killed, just as this demon laughed when it killed Richardson.

"The terrified people huddled around the Old Woman of the village. They hoped that her wisdom could protect them. True, she could offer some protection, but they could not spend every night with the Old Woman. There were flocks to protect from prowling dogs and wolves, horses to soothe when storms came. My aunt went to that village to help, but she could only help the local woman hold the thing at bay. The local Catholic priests were as fearful as everyone else and hid in their churches.

"On the fifth day, an old man came to the village. He looked frail and old to my aunt. She said that he seemed a creature of gray cloth and gauze. Without his walking staff, it seemed he could hardly hold himself erect. He was tired from the road, but would only rest long enough to take refreshment. Then he went to the place where the magic had been done.

"As twilight began to settle, he climbed up onto the small rock outcropping where the one who had summoned the beast had died. My aunt and one of the men of the village had to help the old man with the climb. But once on the rock, he sent them down, away from what he knew would happen.

"As full darkness descended, they heard the beast shuffling closer. My aunt, who was near the base of the outcropping, was only thirty feet from the old man. She could tell that the beast was approaching. She was more afraid for the old man than for herself, since he seemed like a sacrifice being offered up to the beast.

"As the beast came closer, she heard the horses and sheep in the nearby village pens become restive. The horses began to scream in fear. The air became still. Then the beast ascended the rocks, going for the old man.

"When the creature reached the top, a light suddenly flared, illuminating the old man. My aunt ran back from the rock and looked up. The old man was standing erect. A dim light the color of moonlight surrounded him and revealed the beast standing opposite him. The creature was roaring to frighten him, but the old man held up his hand, and the roaring stopped. The beast tried to attack the old man, but his feet were frozen to the rock. All it could do was swat uselessly at the old magician. Then the old man muttered something and spread his arms. Light sprang up at his feet and ran up his body. Balls of bright, swirling colors grew about his hands. When he was ready he pointed his hands and the swirling light wrapped around the mute beast, who beat helplessly at them. The old man lowered his arms, and the colors condensed onto the beast. For a moment there was complete stillness. Then the creature burst into flame. Its voice was released and the screams could be heard as they echoed off the rocks and rolled down the hills to the sea. When the screaming stopped, the creature was gone. The light dimmed and went out. All that was left was a frail old man at the top of the rock.

"My aunt went up to him and helped him down. She took him to the village, where they gave him poteen and a bed. He did not say a word until my aunt began to cover him for the night. All he said was, 'I fear I'm too old to do that many more times.' He smiled and fell asleep. The next morning, he was gone. No one ever saw him again."

She pinned Benito with her gaze. "Can you bring us a magician like him?"

Benito tried to reconcile the story with what he knew. Every image, every gesture, of what Brigid had said had implication to him.

Her recounting reflected what he had read of legendary magicians, but he did not want to accept her story. "It can't be true."

"It is true."

They sat together in the silence after her story. She was certain all that she had said was true, all the more so because she had not remembered the tale until she had begun to tell it. As for Benito, he was lost in remembering things that he had discovered years ago, during his training. For part of that time, he had had access to the greatest magical library in the world, the one deep beneath the Vatican. No one went there but the members of his order.

His voice was sad when he spoke. "Sister, we cannot bring you a mage like him." He paused and took a deep breath, for the things he was about to reveal would be hard for him to say. He even feared to say them, for by their nature they were almost blasphemous. "Did such men ever exist? Yes, if the legends of many cultures are to be believed. There are records of actions performed by these magicians from the Caucasus to the British Isles, everywhere the Celtic peoples have lived. Though they have different names in different places, they're usually called 'walkers.'"

Brigid smiled. "That's what my aunt called him, 'the walker.'"

Benito went on. "The stories, looked at individually, are unbelievable. Even within my order they are usually dismissed as embellishments, folktales, but when they are looked at together, there are too many similarities to be disregarded. These magicians seemed to appear in times of need and disappear just as soon afterwards. They were solitary men and women of power, who must have had some communication with one another. They were never part of organized rituals or rites.

"The stories about them began to become less and less frequent starting in the ninth century. The position the Church takes, if it takes one at all, is that people became less superstitious as the Christian faith assumed ascendancy. These old tales of powerful magicians and dragons and things that walked the night were relics of a dark time before the coming of the faith."

Benito looked away. He did not want to see the reaction in her eyes as he went on. "But there is a more insidious possibility. As the Church's power grew, believing in these things and telling these tales became heretical. These magicians, whoever they were, would have needed to work more and more away from public view. Exposed, they would be branded as heretics or wizards and persecuted. For all of their power against those things that can haunt us, they would not have been able to withstand the secular power of the Church.

"Perhaps such men were needed less. As the magical knowledge was leached out of the general population, there would have been fewer magicians and fewer fools to summon things they could not control. But, to our shame, it is more likely that many of these solitary magicians were apprehended and converted or killed by one of the innumerable campaigns waged as we sought to abolish competing forms of religion."

"The Inquisition," she said.

"Yes, the Inquisition and other efforts." He fell silent for a moment, and she respected his privacy. Then he continued, "Whatever their knowledge was, it was never written down. For a tradition such as theirs to continue, it must be passed on. That passing on of knowledge would have been difficult in the Christian world. Perhaps they felt that the world had turned away from them when the people converted to a new religion. I had believed that their knowledge was lost, that there would be no more of these men, since the last stories we had of them were from the fifteenth century. That is," he said, "until I heard your story."

There was an edge to her voice when she spoke. "So now the Church will seek out the old man and others like him, now that you know."

He shook his head. "No, the Church will not do that again. And they cannot do it in this case because they will never know. I shall not repeat your story of the walker."

Brigid regarded the priest with increased respect. Her decision to trust him had been right, even though he was part of a Church that had taken her away from all she had been born to.

Benito continued, "If their magic exists at all, it must be allowed to survive. I, we, all of us, have an obligation to keep it alive. If even part of the legends is true, these walkers could do things that we cannot imagine. We must summon many priests and perform complex rituals to raise the power needed to try and fight against demonic creatures. They did not."

"Does that mean your opponents are more powerful than you?"

"No, I do not believe that they are more powerful, at least not once we are fully assembled. But their creature may be stronger than us. You see, it is easier to control a thing that you have summoned than to fight against a thing that has been summoned by another. And they may not even control it. Perhaps all that they do is open the door for it. Their power could be less than ours and yet be strong enough to summon a creature that we cannot destroy."

She nodded and sat quietly for a moment. "I wonder, why were the old magicians called 'walkers'?"

"They seemed to be constantly on the move, generally on foot. They are mentioned in numerous texts, though little is said about them in any one place. The information is so vague that it is difficult to piece anything together."

"What gods did they serve?" She had intentionally said "gods," not "God."

"The gods," he replied.

"No, I mean which of the old gods?"

"I know what you meant. But the answer is the same. Does it matter if a goddess was called Athena in Greece and Minerva in Rome? It was still the same goddess. Does it matter if the god of the underworld was Hades, Bran, or Pluto? They were all the same gods throughout Europe, just with different names."

"If Christ surpassed all of the old gods, why is your power not greater?" She could not keep an edge of sarcasm from her voice. In her question was contained her anger at the silence that had been enforced on her since she had been seven and at the convent school. It was also fueled by her regrets—the life she might have had, the lovers that she would have known, the children who might have carried on her line.

Sadly he said, "I don't know. I have never known. From the first time that I suspected that the walkers were real, that there were powers we could not attain, that their magic dwarfed our own, I have wondered." He looked at the nun. "But what choice do we have? We are here; we are part of the Church. And the remnants of the old religion are just strands, single threads out of a vast pattern that we glimpse but whose heart we cannot know. Can you call one of the immortal Celtic god-heroes, like Nuada of the Silver Hand? Can you ask him to dispatch this demon? And if you could, would he laugh in your face for the millions who no longer know him? Did the old gods leave us, or did we leave them?"

They both let the sadness of that statement hang in the air. She stood and walked to the window that looked down on the garden. She could see the small nuns' chapel where they had previously met on the opposite side of the walled garden. Her bravado, which had been so strong a few minutes ago, had faded.

"Father Benito, all that we have said today . . ." She trailed off. "I am afraid of what we have said. I am confused. I'm no longer sure of what I believe."

"I know that," he replied.

"I have told you about my doubts." Fear played across her face. "You won't tell anyone else?"

"No, I wouldn't do that. We are no longer nun and priest; we are two magicians—friends, I hope." He smiled. "Besides, I am too close to apostasy to reveal anyone else's secrets."

Brigid said, "You know I have no control over what I do and see. It comes and goes as it pleases."

"Control." He nodded. "Yes, that I can teach you, and protection."

She turned away from the window and faced him. "Good. Then teach." She walked back to her chair and sat down facing him.

He fell easily into the rhythms of the lesson. "First you have to know your own body. Your body is a reflection of your spirit. In order to know the spirit, you must know the body. In order to harness the power of the spirit, the body must not intrude upon the flow of energies. But do not be deceived into thinking that the body is unimportant. It is part of the magic as well. It helps create the energy. Do you understand?"

"I think I do."

"The principle will become more clear as time goes on. For now, you must learn how to be as clear as water, to learn the passages through your body."

"How do I do that?"

"Lie on the table and relax. Loosen any clothes that bind you. You must be as comfortable as possible to be able to sense the movements inside your body. Physical sensations will disturb you now; later you will learn what they are and be able to ignore them."

She assumed the position that he had requested, adjusting her position to assure that nothing was rubbing against her skin.

"Comfortable?"

"Yes, though it feels odd to be lying on a table in a room with a man who is not a doctor."

He laughed lightly. "Don't worry; you are safe with me."

She smiled in response, feeling no need to speak.

"Now, try and look inside yourself. You will find that there are bright pathways that connect the different parts of you. These are the paths along which your real power passes. The main one will be behind your solar plexus."

"I see them."

"Already?" he asked, thinking that she was deceiving herself.

"They are like small flows of light that connect into something, I don't know what to call it."

"'Nexus' for one, 'nexuses' for more than one."

"I see different nexuses, where the colors of the light blend together. Some white, some pale blue, some yellow."

"Those are nexuses. For you to see them so quickly is . . . well, it's odd."

He had never had the pleasure of training an hereditary. Her ability to see her own paths so well would make the training go quickly. He decided to try a more advanced technique.

"Look along the pathways and see if there are any areas that seem blocked, unable to allow the free flow of energy. It will look like an area where the flow of light is restricted or invisible."

"I see two of them, both just above my stomach. There is a line going up to the area, but it doesn't connect to anything."

Benito frowned, knowing that these were the areas that were often cut off by emotional distress. "Is there a line going down toward it from above?"

"Yes, but it doesn't connect to anything."

"All right. Imagine that there is strong energy flowing up the bottom line. Now you have it push through the dark area to connect to the line coming down."

He watched as she focused her attention, her face becoming tense as she pushed.

"No," he said, "don't waste energy by letting your face show what you are feeling. Focus on the line and the flow of energy only."

Her face relaxed. He raised the potency of his sight so that he could see her progress. Slowly the line from the bottom began to inch its way upward. Then, with startling speed, it jumped through the dark area in the abdomen and joined the other line.

Brigid involuntarily gasped as a combined sense of pain and pleasure shot through her. The pain quickly faded. Benito pulled back his sight to look at her with normal perceptions.

"Better?" he asked.

She sat up suddenly. "I feel dizzy, a little nauseated, but that is fading away. I feel more complete, like things are the way they should be, if that makes any sense."

"It makes perfect sense. And that is enough for today. Please, don't try and work on this alone. The results can be surprising."

"But I feel fine; I can keep going."

"Trust me, it's enough for today. You are a remarkable pupil. Most students take weeks to get this far; sometimes it takes many sessions even to see the lines of strength."

"Why am I so different?"

"You are an hereditary, and a powerful one at that. Besides, you were trained, even though only a little, as a child."

"I understand. I think." She still seemed dazed as she slipped off the table and went to the door and unlocked it. Before she left, she turned and looked at him one more time. "I feel like I am finding something inside of myself."

"You are. Rest well tonight. You will probably feel very tired soon."

He watched her leave, unsurprised that she was an apt pupil but aware that she might be too adept for him. He was trying to train an hereditary, and the rules and pace of progress that he was accustomed to did not apply. She learned very quickly, maybe too quickly. Had he known the full truth, he would have been worried at what else he was unknowingly awakening in her.

As she returned to the convent dormitory she thought about what had just happened. The exercises had been a revelation. She could still see the bright paths of energy in her body. They were still connecting, and, as they did, they fed on one another and began to grow. She had not told him about the deep red paths, the ones that were almost the color of blood. She did not know why, but felt they were for her and her alone, at least for now. These lines joined together much lower in her body and whispered of passion.

She had been right to trust Benito. He was a good man. For the first time since her childhood, she was seeing a man as a friend. In teaching her, he was revealing much about himself. Brigid could see what lay inside him. Though a man of deep faith, he was also someone committed to the pursuit of knowledge, a trait that she regarded highly. Like all of the Celts, the Irish respected men of knowledge. But Benito was not only a man of knowledge; he was also a man of deep compassion. She had nothing to fear from him, even though there were other feelings still veiled behind his dark eyes.

CHAPTER ELEVEN

Friday Evening, October 16

JAKOB Streng sat lazily in the armchair of his private study. He had spent significant time during the day learning what he could of Father Benito and his plans. Streng's mind was not eased by what he had discovered. The priest from Florida had dispatched a telegram, and he was spending time in the private library of the archdiocese, often accompanied by the bishop's secretary, Monsignor Henry.

Another member of Streng's group, Lilith Claire, had attempted to observe the activities of Benito. Her efforts, regardless of her subtlety as a magician, had not gone well. She had been detected by Benito. However, she would try to observe him a few more times. Even when she was detected, her observations served a purpose. The monk would know that he was being watched.

In response to the old nun's death Streng had detected no workings from within the diocese. Streng, as well as three other of his most competent magicians, had been observing the compound where Benito resided. He had not been able to goad Benito into action. Benito was biding his time, something that made Streng uneasy. Streng did not understand those who could wait so easily. He would have been pushed to action by now. Benito was obviously holding something back. Was it possible that he and his kind might present a danger to them?

Streng and some of his senior members were part of the closed confines of Savannah society. The police knew better than to look too closely at anything that might lead to a member of that group. In his probing of Benito he had discovered little, other than that he was a competent magician. Jakob could estimate the extent of his power, though he had seen no signs that Benito would be a challenging opponent. But Jakob did not like knowledge without certainty, and he had little of that.

Essie's reports from her own people had served only to confirm what he had discovered. For once, her ubiquitous sources of information had come up with no new facts for Jakob. He could not even find where Benito's telegram had been sent, though he had little doubt that it was a request for help. Jakob was worried. The Church's arms were long. Had the Church learned better ways to train their magicians? Would they be a real danger to his group?

He resigned himself to not having an answer now. Besides, he was not interested in sifting through the scraps of information that he possessed. He had come to his private study for relaxation. He picked up the opium pipe from the side table and noticed that the ball had gone dead. He scratched a match against the side of its box and brought the flame to the bowl. Drawing gently, he lit the opium mud and inhaled a steady stream of the sweet smoke into his lungs. As the drug penetrated into his system, his anxiety and pain faded.

Jakob lived with pain many days of his life. It was part of the price he paid for his pleasures and for the power that Belial brought. Jakob's joints ached. Other pains clustered around his heart and deep within his bowels. He knew he was deteriorating physically. He had an increasing sense of sickness within him. The feeling was not unexpected; after all, he had joined the cult in his teens.

Jakob's father, Herman, had joined the satanic cult when he had been in his twenties. Even then the coven had been old. It had been founded in the late 1700s, though no one knew much of the early years, other than the name of the founder, a Mr. Lamont. The coven had proven useful in business and in many other ways. The members were usually very successful financially. But they tended to die young and in poor health. Jakob's father had died in his fifties from a wasting disease no doctor could identify. Herman's death had been a difficult blow to Jakob's grandfather, Heinrich, who was, at the time, an unusually vital man in his late seventies. Herman's brother, Otto, had lived into his eighties. Jakob wondered if his inability to have children was a result of his joining the cult when he had been so young, before he had experienced sex. He had certainly had opportunity to conceive a child with one of the many women that he had taken pleasure in, but there had been no son, no daughter, to carry on his business.

Jakob's pain was always more severe after a summoning ritual, and the day after a ritual was no longer a normal day for him in other ways. He spent much of it asleep, dazed and drained of energy. He rarely summoned Belial on successive days, something he might have to do again as this struggle continued. While the demon's arrival always brought a heady burst of energy to him, the creature's departure left him weakened.

On the days after a summoning, Jakob could not seem to focus his mind on the decisions at work. To be mentally slow was a fatal flaw in his business. The price of cotton fluctuated on the world markets in response to changes in the quality and quantity of the supply available. The price of the prime Sea Island cotton that was Streng's primary business was particularly volatile. In previous years, Streng's uncanny ability to predict the price of cotton had made him a wealthy man. Now he had lost much of that innate skill and depended more and more on the telegraph line to give him a business advantage.

Fortunately, his nephew, Frederick, was there to take care of business. Without children of his own, Jakob had turned to his sister for help. She had been pleased to send her son to work for his wealthy uncle. Frederick knew nothing of his uncle's rituals or personal habits. The young man only knew that on some days his uncle suffered too severely to spend much time at the offices of his factoring house. On those days, Frederick took control of the office. He had learned the cotton market quickly, especially the critical skill of making good guesses on future prices. Over the years, Frederick had learned his job well enough so that Jakob's presence was not often needed. But Jakob was not fool enough to trust that Frederick would always make the right decisions. He was still young. Nor did Jakob trust that the boy might not find a way to divert more than his generous salary into his personal account.

Jakob looked at the three doors that led out from the study. One gave entrance onto the hallway, another to his bedroom. The other opened directly into another bedroom. Customarily, the room was occupied by a young woman, who most were led to believe was his maid. In reality, she was his whore. But Sally was not there now; he had lent her to Jarred Cawthorne for the week. He was Streng's closest friend and an avid participant in their monthly rituals. Jarred was the one who wielded the knife so expertly that he made draining the blood of their victims simple.

Obtaining Sally had been ridiculously easy. Jakob had sent an agent into the countryside to find a young girl. Sally had been fourteen and was showing the first signs of beauty. She had been the best of his agent's finds. She was hired as a "serving girl" and brought to Savannah. The parents had been willing to let her go with few questions, especially after they were given the massive sum of one hundred dollars as their part of her "first year's pay." Jakob chuckled in his opium haze. They had known damn well that she would be no "serving girl," but, in their poverty, had no compunction about selling their little girl into white slavery.

Controlling her was simple. Jakob had treated her kindly. The girl was mystified that she was given such a fine room to sleep in and such fine clothes. Her meals were even brought to her. But Jakob had assured that each meal was laced with laudanum. Soon she was addicted. It was then that Jakob and Cawthorne had taken her to a small house deep within Cawthorne's plantation. The two men held her there and waited for the drug withdrawal to begin making her skin crawl. They explained to her that she was addicted to laudanum and had two choices. She could become their plaything and have all the laudanum she wished for, as well as money, clothes, education, and an eventual chance for freedom. Or they would let her go, and she could fend for herself.

She had resisted for a while, but it took less than twelve hours without the drug to change her opinion. Then they had dosed her with the laudanum she craved and explored the pleasures she could offer. Sally had turned out to be very different from the other girls they had obtained. She was more intelligent and more sensual. Soon, practices that the other girls had always been reluctant to perform became commonplace, even desirable, to her. Her appetites grew. She even had a taste for pain, a taste that Cawthorne was pleased to satisfy. When her two-year mark had come, the time when they would have normally replaced her with another, neither of the two men was tired of her. So she was not sent to a brothel madam to become one of her "girls." Now approaching seventeen, Sally was an accomplished slattern with no desire to change the opulent lifestyle she purchased by giving the two men and their friends free access to her body. She even seemed to enjoy it.

Thinking about Sally, Jakob felt the accustomed hardening in his pants and regretted that Sally was not here to serve him. Instead he relit his pipe and dove a little deeper into the opium-scented waters that encased him. His mind drifted from Sally to other topics. He began imagining what they might do with that irritating monk from Florida. The information he needed would eventually come to him. Until then, Jakob felt there was little sense in worrying about him.

CHAPTER TWELVE

Saturday, October 17

BENITO knew that Father Provincial Rimaldi would be the first of his order to arrive. He should be here soon; of that Benito was certain. But, even together, they would have to be careful of any actions that might draw the notice of those who had summoned the demon. Until Rimaldi's arrival, Benito would have to be very discreet.

He spent part of the day examining the contents of the library at the archdiocese. Other than the diary that had been given him by the monsignor, Benito found nothing that would be of any assistance. As the afternoon drew to a close, he walked to the main police station. He hoped the police might have information that would be of value, and he could think of no better time to unearth it than on a quiet Saturday. The police were more than happy to chat with a priest, but could offer him no help and were apparently surprised that there had been any increase in the deaths of prostitutes. They paid little attention to such crimes.

Disappointed, he left the police station. As he walked back through the twilight, he reflected on the day. It was sad that human life had so little value that a series of similar deaths would not be noticed, but it was to be expected. The poor were always disenfranchised, and the poor who lived in the shadow of society's morals would be even more routinely ignored. Prostitution was nominally illegal in Georgia, but Savannah was a seaport, and sailors expected prostitutes for their relaxation. In a city such as Savannah, prostitutes were a valuable asset. Without them, the sailors would find other ways to "enjoy" their shore leave, and those other ways would probably be more destructive.

When he came to the square in front of the cathedral he sat in the quiet. The soft breeze that blew up from the marshes rustled the leaves in the oaks that overshadowed the square. Spanish moss hung gracefully over many of the branches, swinging almost hypnotically in the soft wind. In the air was a faint, indefinable scent, both sweet and alive. Benito doubted that he had been in any other city that possessed such dreamlike beauty. The city seemed to watch its inhabitants and desire to protect them. No wonder the city was a destination for so many travelers. Few of the residents showed much tendency to leave. The city's beauty was seductive, even soporific, luring residents into a false feeling of confident lassitude. Benito again felt the almost sentient nature of the city, tainted with the dark undercurrent that he could now name. The satanist cult had been in the city for many years, operating in anonymity. The very loveliness of the city allowed great darkness to go unnoticed.

Benito was uneasy. Were the dark currents stronger or was he only imagining it after the death of Sister Francis? As the light faded, his perspective on the majestic oaks with their curtains of moss began to change. He sensed that they, rather than feeling warm and embracing, were looming over him, poised to strike. Knowing that such perceptions do not change without a reason, he focused his attention. For a moment he sensed that someone was watching him, something he had felt before. He reached out to define it, and it vanished.

Whoever had been watching him had slid away when he had felt the focus of Benito's attention. But the observer had not moved fast enough. Benito had detected a presence, though he could not discern anything more about the observer. Or perhaps, Benito thought with a slight shudder, the observer merely wanted him to know that he was being watched. If so, he had timed his actions well. Benito had been quiet, at peace, until he had been reminded that he could not afford to let his guard down for any reason.

He was frustrated by his lack of knowledge, but he did not dare use his magical abilities to probe their opponents. He could not face them alone. All he could do was endeavor to protect himself and stay alive until more of his order arrived.

Brigid was a bright point in his time in the city. She was born with immense talent and was mastering the flow of energies in her body at an astonishing speed. In their next session, he would have to move to the basics of defense. He had never had a student like her, one that learned so rapidly and to such a powerful effect. Quite possibly she would need no spells to defend herself. She might have an intuitive mastery of her talents. Then she would be safe, more safe than he himself could be.

She was a rare creature, an orchid. He felt that he had been wandering in the woods and found an unexpected flower of entrancing beauty and purity. She was also changing rapidly under the effects of the events around them and his training. The shy nun was becoming something else entirely, something that almost seemed from another time. He was not aware of the deeply creased smile that crossed his face.

His mind jumped to another, less pleasant topic as he walked back to the cathedral. His efforts during the day had been unsuccessful. He needed more information and thought again of the monsignor's diary. Had he overlooked something? As he thought through the entries, he realized that he had. The entries in the diary often spoke of locating a Voudon ritual site. Apparently a very active Voudon cult existed in Savannah. Benito had previously had little contact with the religion that the slaves had brought with them from Africa.

Few former slaves lived in Benito's home state of Florida. As a result, the African religion did not usually have a large enough concentration of adherents to remain active. Here in Savannah, where there had been a large population of slaves concentrated in the city and on the plantations, the underground worship of the African gods still flourished. Many of the gods of Voudon had been given Christian names in their ceremonies, but they retained many of the same characteristics that they had possessed in Africa.

Though much of the supposed magic of Voudon was little more than showmanship, Benito knew that there was real magic in their practices. The priests and priestesses might well have enough magical knowledge to detect the activities of other magicians. The local Voudon community might even have knowledge of the satanists. The difficulty for Benito would be in finding a way to contact them. Any white man would have trouble making contact with the leaders of the cult. For a white priest it would be even more difficult. He would have to convince them he was not trying to trouble them in any way, only find out if they had any information that would be of use. The best place to start would be close at hand, with the colored staff who worked in the diocese itself. He also realized that he had a ready ally in the search. Sister Brigid had been working at the hospital for years. It was likely that she had formed some kind of connection with a few of the colored people who worked alongside her.

Sister Brigid was becoming an increasingly important part of his plans. She had agreed to take him to the place where she had seen the darkness lying across Saint Julian Street. Seeing the nature of that darkness would tell him something about the power of the cult. He did not really need Brigid as a guide, but he did want her company, if only for the pleasure of it.

His desire might be selfish. Having her along could expose her to danger. His wanting to have her with him was possibly driven by his own fear. Even in the light of day, he did not want to face the cult alone. Before he and Brigid went, he would have to work on her defensive abilities. That way she would be safer. Besides, having a second person with him might give the others pause, especially if they detected that she was an hereditary. Everyone knew that hereditaries were able to conceal the extent of their power.

Visiting the dark miasma that hung over Saint Julian Street was not a task that he looked forward to. He was taking a risk, but continued ignorance would place them in even more danger.

CHAPTER THIRTEEN

Sunday, October 18

WHEN Brigid entered the dining hall for breakfast, she saw Father Benito and the mother superior in conversation with the monsignor. They were sitting at one of the smaller tables, well apart from the others. Brigid went to the far end of the room and loaded a small tray with a light breakfast. Then she turned back into the room.

She paused. Her long training in the Catholic hierarchy demanded that she not interrupt the monsignor and mother superior at their table. However, Brigid's new status as a magician-in-training urged her to join them. She felt that she belonged with them, not with the sisters who were her ostensible equals. An edge of resentment crept into her thoughts. She felt that she did not really belong with the sisters, who would be gabbing, like hothouse flowers, of the recent events with no understanding of the real implications or the danger. Even the death of Sister Francis had not warned them of their own personal jeopardy. Brigid realized that she was being neither humble nor charitable, but she did not care. Humility and charity no longer seemed like admirable emotions.

The old training as a nun won out, and she turned to join some of the other nuns, planning to sit where she might be able to see when Benito's conversation ended. She had just begun to move in that direction when the mother superior called to her, "Sister Brigid, please join us." She turned to join them, happy for the summons, and only barely conscious of the nuns behind her. They had begun whispering to one another about this new event as soon as her back was turned.

Father Benito and Monsignor Henry stood as she approached the table, and Benito indicated the chair on his right. "Please." She nervously sat down facing the monsignor, who, as the bishop's secretary and principal assistant, would generally have little to do with one of the nuns, except through the intermediary of the mother superior. Brigid's sense of daring seemed to slip before the gaze of the monsignor, but he smiled as she sat, welcoming her to the conclave. Father Benito brought her into the conversation. "Sister, I suspect you know that there is an active Voudon, or voodoo, cult here in Savannah?"

She nodded.

"It doesn't surprise you?" the monsignor asked.

"No, Monsignor. When you work closely with people you can't help but hear things that they didn't intend for you to hear. Over the years I have heard enough to know that their religion still has followers."

"And that doesn't frighten you?" the monsignor said.

"No," Brigid said, as if mystified by the question. "I have never thought of them as evil. They merely follow another faith." Her innocent response sprang from her new confidence. Christianity was not the only source of good.

"And their different faith doesn't concern you?" the monsignor asked.

Benito turned the conversation away from what could be a troublesome topic. "They might have some information to offer us, perhaps might even know who our opponents are. I asked Monsignor Henry what he thought might be the best way to try and contact them. We're not often seen as allies by the Voudon community."

The monsignor added, "A priest is unlikely to be successful in the attempt." He looked at Brigid. "The mother superior thinks you might be the person for the task."

Margaret said, "You have friends among the staff, at least more so than I do."

"As a woman, you will be less threatening to them," Benito said.

"So," the monsignor asked, "will you help us?"

The conversation had gone better than what she had anticipated. Apparently, Benito had not told the monsignor anything about her personal dilemma. Relieved, she answered, "Of course, Monsignor, I will talk to some of the staff."

"Good," the monsignor said, and rose. "I have to see the bishop, so I must leave. But I want to thank you for your willingness to help."

"You're welcome," she said automatically, though she was not accustomed to having a monsignor ask if she would do something.

As Monsignor Henry left the table, his thoughts stayed with what had just occurred. It was odd to him that Sister Brigid was so unaffected by the events of that night, and she seemed to be quite comfortable with the assignment to find out more about voodoo in Savannah. There was obviously more depth to her than he had thought, but depth alone was not the answer to this riddle. Still absorbed in his thoughts, he turned down the corridor that led to the bishop's offices.

In the dining hall, Benito watched the odd play of expressions move across Brigid's face as she finished her breakfast. She was reacting as if she were two people. One was the nun who would always obey the requests of a monsignor. The other was only beginning to show, but she was a woman who made her own path.

Finishing her breakfast, Brigid asked the priest, "Are you sure that the Voudon cult will have more information?"

"I am not certain that they will know anything. Still, they may prove to be helpful."

"Helpful?"

"Yes. They may have perceived something that night."

"They have real power?"

"Voudon has practitioners of magic in it. So there is a chance that they have perceived something, just as you did."

Brigid found herself in territory that made her uncomfortable in the presence of the mother superior. The world that was opening to Brigid through the intermediary of the Benedictine priest was not new to her, but it was not the one she had been taught to believe in for the last twenty-seven years of her life. Benito represented her new life and the mother superior her old one. Within the mother superior's realm was obligation, obedience, and duty. Within Benito's was collegiality, purpose, and a sense of waking from a long sleep. In that sleep, Brigid's feelings had been muted, redirected, inaccessible.

Sensing Brigid's discomfort, the mother superior rose and excused herself, trying to ease Brigid's concern by saying, "Don't be concerned with your other duties for now, Brigid. Your primary task is to help Father Benito."

Brigid was left with Father Benito, who said, "If you're done with your breakfast, we have work to do."

Brigid nodded. He rose, and she followed him out of the dining hall. They turned down a corridor and went to the workroom to continue with Brigid's training.

She entered the room first. He followed, locking the door behind them. They sat, facing each other.

"What are we going to do today?" she asked, obviously excited about her training.

"I've given this a lot of thought," he said. "We may be rushing things a little, but we need to begin working on your ability to protect yourself."

She did not need to ask why, as she shared his concern. She had already realized that she might be in danger, especially after Sister Francis's death.

"And," he said, "you may be ready to move into shielding now." He paused. "Can we begin?"

"Yes," she said, her eyes glittering.

"I want you to close your eyes and lean back in the chair. Try to see the pathways in your body, just as you did in the last lesson."

She closed her eyes and turned her Sight inward. With some effort she could see the differently colored pathways. "I can see them," she said.

"Is your vision of them clear, or are they faint?"

"They are becoming more visible to me as I concentrate."

"Good. Is there any place where the lines are interrupted?"

"No. That surprises me; there was at least one that had seemed cut off before."

"Even when you are not consciously working, your mind will try and connect the paths. It's obviously been busy, so you are ready for the next step. For now, just breathe easily and stay focused on the pathways in your body."

He was quiet as she fixed the images in her mind; then he said, "Now comes the harder part. Think of the lines in your body growing brighter. With each breath you take, you draw new energy into the body. When you exhale, you hold the energy while letting the air out. Start doing this and let me know what happens to the lines."

She strained as she breathed, taking in overly large breaths.

"No," he said. "Stay relaxed as you breathe. Breathe deeply, but not unnaturally."

Her breathing settled down to a more normal pace, though with slightly longer breaths.

"What is happening to the paths?"

"They are growing brighter, stronger, with each breath."

"When you feel they are as bright as you want them to be, stop adding to the lines and hold the strength inside of you."

Again, he waited, his attention focused on his student. He watched her carefully with his Sight. For most students, the problem was getting them to be able to see and bring power to the paths. He felt her problem might be the opposite, adding more power than she could handle.

When he saw the first shimmering of power about her, he said, "Hold that power where you are."

"But I can add more," she protested.

"That is enough for now."

The air around her was charged with her power in his Sight. She had the strength to do what was needed.

"We are going to try and build a protective shell around you. It should be large enough to protect your entire body from head to toe. It should be shaped like an elongated sphere, almost egg shaped. Now slowly feed the energy out through the solar plexus and spin the shield around you, like a moth's cocoon."

He could see the power coming out of her as it fed out into the air. It layered upward, and soon a glittering sphere of pale yellowish light surrounded her. He had not expected it to be so intense. As he had been told, hereditaries often had unsuspected power.

"That's good. Now I am going to test it by pushing against it." He got up and walked around the table, bringing his own shielding up as he went. For him, calling up shielding took but a second or two, speeded by years of practice. He kept walking until his own shield was only a few feet from hers.

He moved slowly until the shields touched, and continued to move forward. For a moment, both shields bent slightly where they met; then his shield began to bow inward, adapting to the stronger shield of Brigid. Benito was shocked. He was very adept at shielding. Even the moderate shielding he was using was strong, stronger than that of most mages. Without thinking about it, he moved closer and sent more power into his shield, expecting that her shield would deform under the additional pressure. For a moment it did; then, when he reached the original limit of her shield, a stream of dark red energy flowed out of her and reinforced her own shield. Almost instantaneously, the color ran up Brigid's shielding like a streak of blood. Her shield snapped to its original shape as the color took hold. With mind-rending suddenness, his own shield collapsed before the wave of red that reached almost to his body.

When his shield broke, its energy was driven back on him. Unprepared for the influx of energy, he fell backward, catching himself as he hit the floor. Then he was overwhelmed by a dark wave of unconsciousness.

Brigid was sitting with her eyes shut, unaware of what had happened. She knew only that she had pressed back at Benito's pressure on her shield. Everything she had done in her defense had been instinctual. She could no longer feel his shield and opened her eyes. She was horrified to see Benito lying on the ground, unconscious and unshielded. She did not even know how to bring down her own shield, he hadn't yet taught her how, but her hands knew. She crossed her forearms and brought her hands down, exhaling as she did. The deep red glow around her faded back into the ethers.

She went to kneel beside Luis. She was no longer a mage in training, but a nurse. She felt for a pulse immediately and found a reassuringly steady beat. She immediately went to the door and unlocked it, running down the hall to a small bathroom, where she wet a towel with cold water. When she arrived back in the room, Benito was beginning to awaken. She shut the door and went to him.

"Don't try to get up," she said, and placed the damp towel on his forehead.

He opened his eyes, dazed, and said drunkenly, "Your eyes are the most remarkable shade of blue."

She didn't know what to make of his remark.

An embarrassed smile came to his face. "Sorry, I was dazed." He used humor to cover his faux pas. "I was warned about hereditaries." He tried to laugh and winced. "My head feels like a railroad spike went through it."

"I am so sorry." She was too concerned about her responsibility for his injury to see humor in the situation.

"Don't be. I should have known not to push against your shield. You're only learning control. Your reaction was automatic, to push back, but doing that drew on a deeper level of power."

"I didn't mean to," she apologized.

He sat up, even as she tried to stop him. "You don't need to apologize. I'm fine, just need to get over this headache. Give me a hand."

She helped him to his feet. Once standing, he began a series of motions that she did not understand, moving his arms in wide arcs, rolling his shoulders back, and dropping his head back. When he was done, he said, "Much better."

He pulled a chair out from the table and sat, indicating that she should also sit.

"Are you sure you're all right, Luis?"

"I'm fine, especially since you stopped calling me Father Benito."

"I didn't intentionally do that."

He smiled again. "That's all right, too. We need to work together, not stand on Church formalities. Being formal would slow your learning, and that would be a waste. We are both mages. I am trained; you are an hereditary. But we are both the same thing. I forgot that hereditaries are born with certain aptitudes that require little to awaken them."

"I just felt pressure and responded without thinking."

"I know that, but I also know that you didn't tell me about the deep red pathway you saw last week."

"How did you know that?"

"That kind of strength could not have gone unnoticed in all that you saw."

"I was afraid of the color. I thought it might be something bad."

"Don't make that kind of association. Colors in this realm often mean many things. Powerful hereditaries have a strong coloring to their shields and in the paths in their bodies."

"Does that mean that I am powerful?" she asked hesitantly.

"Without a doubt, but you are still untrained. As for your defense, you may even be strong enough to withstand the demon on your own. In any event, I could not shield you better than you can shield yourself. Practice your shielding on your own; just be careful not to hit anyone with it."

She grinned, returning to her normal good humor. "Then that's all for today?"

"It's more than enough."

She rose and went to the door to the room and grabbed the handle. She stopped and looked back at him. Sounding almost coquettish, she said, "Do you really think my eyes are a remarkable shade of blue?"

"Most remarkable."

He was rewarded with a glimpse of a smile as she left.

THE deep hours of the night were quiet. The few up at midnight were mainly in their homes. Silence held sway in the streets.

Margaret did not need anyone to wake her. She became fully awake every evening at midnight, then donned her habit and began her evening rounds. She had been visiting the varied locations of her domain at midnight for years. She would walk through the nuns' dormitory, adjacent to her own quarters; then she would go to the contemplation room, often stopping for a moment of reflection. Finally she would leave the cathedral compound and take the short walk to the hospital. There she would pass through every corridor, greeting the nuns on the evening shift and making herself available to talk if any of them were troubled. Since Richardson's death, the routine had taken longer than it once had. The situation had become worse since Sister Francis's death. The nuns, in particular the younger ones, needed reassurance. They were nervous, especially in the dead hours of the night.

As Margaret entered the nuns' quarters she steeled herself for the walk down the quiet, dimly lit passage. This walk had once been pleasant. But all sense of comfort was banished by having to pass by Sister Francis's room. Margaret could not pass the door in the silence of the night without remembering the way her friend had looked when she had first seen her body. The ugly memory gave her a chill. The image of the blinded nun was often the last thing she would think of before returning to sleep when her rounds were complete.

Leaving the nuns' quarters, she turned down the long passage to the contemplation room. This night, for a reason she could not understand, the corridor seemed threatening. She paused by each of the widely spaced lamps that lit the corridor, insisting to herself that she was just checking the level of kerosene in the lamp, but knowing that she sought comfort from the light to sustain her as she walked through the area of near darkness that stood midway between the lamps. As she approached the intersection on her way to the contemplation room, she found herself walking more quickly. She always turned right, down the lit corridor. The darkness of the corridor that loomed straight ahead seemed like a fit place for an assailant to hide. Even more threatening was the empty corridor to her left, a place that could hold a frightening surprise. As she turned, she did not even glance down the left hallway, but stiffened her spine as if awaiting an unexpected blow from behind. She stopped at the first lamp, her heart racing, and forced herself to look behind, down the dark and vacant corridor.

"Nothing," she said, feeling that she had been made foolish by her fear and realizing that speaking out loud was a way to drive out the fear.

She continued on past the contemplation room, too nervous to take advantage of the altar and candles that could offer her a respite. She wanted to be outside in the night air. Walking quickly, almost running, she finally came to the door that led onto the street. When she emerged, she leaned back against the compound wall, letting her heart slow from her exertions and her fear. She checked that the door into the compound was locked behind her before continuing on to the hospital. She would reenter by the front door of the convent, as it was very near her quarters.

The hospital was only a few blocks away. She began the short walk with more confidence than she had felt inside the buildings.

The interior of the cathedral compound had become alien territory to her, and the graceful, cobbled streets were more to her liking. In the distance she could hear a wagon rolling over the stones. Above her, the bulk of the cathedral loomed comfortably. Even the fog that embraced her seemed friendly, though it made it difficult to see and made her footing on the dampened cobblestones hazardous. She crossed over the silent street.

As she approached the first of the street lamps, she noticed how the light reflected back off the fog, limiting the illumination from the lamp by diffusing its glow. She saw a nun passing under the street lamp ahead of her. She wondered which of her charges was leaving the hospital early. Perhaps she was ill. She was certainly moving strangely. While the habit they all wore made them seem to glide as they walked, there was nonetheless a movement in their gait that betrayed their humanity. This nun walked with a perfectly smooth step, floating over the sidewalk. Margaret could not tell which of her nuns it was. Her head was backlit by the street lamp, obscuring her face. Margaret stopped directly underneath the street lamp, her senses alert. Something was wrong about the nun coming toward her.

The approaching nun passed through the darkness between the lamps. About thirty feet from Margaret, the light began to reflect off of her face, though the mother superior could see nothing more than a vague white oval with no detail. Margaret prepared to greet the nun.

Then the light gave more detail, and a shiver passed over Margaret. A death's-head inhabited the wimple. Margaret could not move as the horrific apparition glided closer. Then, when it was almost upon her, the bony jaw moved. "Mother Superior," it said, just as if it were one of her nuns. It passed by her without touching. Margaret was shaking with terror. She spun around to watch the spectre depart and found that the street behind her was empty. The thing that had greeted her had vanished.

She ran back to the convent, angling across the cobblestones that were slick with the fog. In the middle of the street, she slipped and fell. She took most of the fall on her hands, but could not prevent her head from striking the stones hard enough to daze her. She sat up, then struggled to her feet. She finally made her way to the entrance to the convent. Once inside, she locked the entrance behind her. She walked as quickly as she could to her room. Dizzy from the fall, she was unsteady on her feet. Once inside her room, she threw the bolt on the door and lit every lamp and candle that she had. Shaking, she sat on her bed, waiting. She didn't know for what.

After a while, there was a slow knock on her door. Then silence. The knock came again. Steeling herself against what might be waiting outside her door, she did something that she had never done before. Instead of opening the door, she opened the grating to look out. When she saw that her visitor was Brigid, she threw the door open and embraced the other nun.

"Thank God," Margaret said.

Brigid did not know what to think. She had never been hugged by Margaret before. She certainly had never been hugged with the desperation that the shaking mother superior showed now.

"What is it, Mother Superior?"

"I was afraid. . . ."

"Afraid of what?"

Regaining her self-control, Margaret released her hold on the nun and stepped back from the door. "Please."

Brigid entered the room, noticing that the mother superior was very careful to lock the door behind her. She saw that the mother superior's face was cut above her left eyebrow and blood dripped slowly from her right hand.

"Your face!" Brigid exclaimed.

Margaret lifted her right hand to her face, surprised by the blood that was already there. She touched her wet fingertips to her wound above her eye. She had not even noticed that her face and hands were cut. "I fell in the street," she said, numbness in her voice.

Brigid stood to go and get help for the mother superior.

"No," Margaret said. "Don't leave."

"But you need your wounds bandaged."

"That can wait. Right now I need you." Margaret sat on the bed and motioned for Brigid to join her.

Brigid sat, and Margaret grasped her hand so tightly that Brigid winced.

"It looked like a nun," Margaret said.

"It?"

"The thing that glided down the street. When it got near, it was nothing more than a skull in a habit. It said, 'Mother Superior,' and vanished."

"I must tell Father Benito."

"Don't leave me. Not now. I feel safe with you here."

Brigid untangled her hand. "Then I will just step out in the hall and find someone. I will send her to get Father Benito." Feeling uncomfortably like a parent explaining something to a child, Brigid went to the door, unlocked it, and stepped out into the hall, leaving the door open so that the mother superior could see her. Sister Teresa was at the far end of the hall, looking toward the mother superior's room with a worried expression on her face. She immediately came to Brigid.

"What is it?" Teresa said, fearing the worst.

"Get Father Benito."

"Is the mother superior all right?"

"Terrified, with a few cuts, but otherwise all right," Brigid said. "Get Benito and something to clean and bandage some small wounds."

"What happened?"

"She saw something and fell in the street."

"What was it?"

"I don't know. Please, Teresa, get Father Benito and some bandages."

Not questioning Brigid's newly assumed authority, Teresa left to find the priest and fetch medical supplies.

Brigid returned to the room and sat by the mother superior. Margaret seemed to be beginning to reestablish control, but Brigid knew she was not ready to be alone.

While she waited for Luis's arrival, Brigid thought about her exchange with Teresa, as surprised by her new sense of command as she was by her becoming a talisman against evil. She was reminded of her aunt Emer, who had possessed a kind of authority that was never questioned. But Brigid was not becoming her aunt. She knew that she was becoming something else entirely.

Sister Teresa arrived shortly with the bandages and a message that Father Benito was on his way.

"Thank you, Sister Teresa," Brigid said.

The older nun went to sit beside the mother superior while Brigid bandaged Margaret's wounds.

"Are you all right, Mother Superior?" It was the only thing Teresa could think to ask.

The mother superior spoke slowly and with effort. "Shocked more than anything."

"What was it?"

"Something I saw, sent to frighten me."

"What did it look like?" Teresa asked.

"Not now. I'll tell you another time. But it's gone now." She took a breath. "You need to take charge of the convent. I need a little time to recover." Suddenly she said, "Brigid?" There was fear in her voice.

"I am here, Mother Superior." She finished tying off the bandage on Margaret's hand.

"Don't leave just yet."

"I won't." She looked at Teresa, who had stood up and was looking down at the mother superior. Teresa looked at Brigid. They both understood what shock was like. They had seen enough of it in the war.

"I'll see to the convent," Teresa said, then looked at Brigid again. "Do I need to stay with you?"

Surprisingly, Margaret replied, "No, Father Benito is on his way. They can take care of me."

Teresa realized that this realm was Brigid's. She and Benito could provide comfort to the mother superior. With a nod to Brigid, Teresa departed.

When Benito arrived, Brigid quickly outlined to him what had happened. Then they sat in silence and waited. Margaret finally fell asleep around two, but was startled into wakefulness by a dream. When she saw that Brigid and Luis were both with her, she fell back to sleep, and the pair resolved to stay with her until first light.

When they could both hear the soft breathing of a deep sleep, they realized that it was safe to talk, even about the events of the night, which they had done sparingly before out of respect for the mother superior's feelings.

Luis spoke softly. "I always regret it when the innocent become the victims."

"Wasn't I innocent?"

"Yes. But you also have discovered yourself in the process. So you have some gain. The mother superior will be haunted by the events of tonight, even after the shock and danger are gone."

They listened to the quiet ticking of a clock for a few minutes.

"Brigid, I have so much respect for you. You have a gift that I have studied all of my life to attain, yet, for you . . ."

"I didn't earn it. I was born with it. You are the one that awakened it in me."

"I don't think I can take full credit for that."

Remembering the other events that had happened to her, she said, "Maybe I would have gone further under my own inclinations, but that is only a possibility. Your lessons have given me keys that have begun to unlock the range of my abilities."

"Yes," Benito said, "and I would have not been here if the others had not been so arrogant as to kill Richardson. So their own acts end up working against them."

"Not if I don't survive this."

"You are more likely to survive than I am. Your shielding is stronger."

She absorbed what he had said, and then thought of the strange events of the evening. "I feel uncomfortable being in the role of protector of the mother superior. She relied on me as soon as she saw me tonight, like I was some sort of talisman. I don't know if I want people to do that."

"It isn't something that you can choose to do or not. It simply is."

"I feel comfortable around you, but I don't feel comfortable around those who were my closest friends."

"You're seen as different by them."

"But not by you."

"Not by me," he said.

"How will the others react?" She did not need to explain she was referring to the other Catholic magicians.

"I don't know. We will have to step carefully around them. I want you involved in the ritual, but the others don't have the same understanding of hereditaries that I do."

"Can't you tell them otherwise?"

"Yes, but they may not believe me."

She sighed. "What makes you different?"

"I think it's because I'm part Seminole. As a child, I spent time with the tribe. The medicine men there have real abilities. They are wise. They know medicines that Europeans don't know. They speak to the spirits, who are real enough. So I know that good magic is available outside the Church. Most others in the Church consider the legends of Europe, like the ones of the walkers, to be folktales. I gave up trying to convince them otherwise."

He seemed so sad that she reached out and took his hand. "Then it's good that you were the one to find me."

He looked at her and smiled. The candlelight flickered in her eyes. He nervously extricated his hand. "I am glad to have been the first of our order you met."

Neither mentioned their contact, though both were aware of it.

She asked, "So what should I do when the others arrive?"

"I will find out if you should become part of what we do or not. It will be up to Father Rimaldi."

"Who's that?"

"The leader of the Church's mages in North America. He is a Jesuit and a potent ceremonial magician."

"If he says no?"

"You will need to stay out of harm's way. But I will still meet with you when I can to continue your training."

"And what am I to do when you leave Savannah when all of this is over?"

"That is a problem. You need someone to work with you until you are ready to be on your own."

"On my own. I don't like that idea very much. They already see me as different here. I will always be set apart from the others. Even the mother superior will not be able to regard me as the same, though I am certain she will try."

They looked at the sleeping woman who was resting peacefully.

Luis said, "You can always write."

"Writing isn't the same as talking," she smiled, "or touching."

They both fell silent. The problem of her future was uppermost in their minds. While Luis, from long practice, could avoid thinking about the growing attraction between them, Brigid could not dismiss the forbidden topic as easily. They said little more as they awaited the first light of dawn.

CHAPTER FOURTEEN

Monday, October 19

AFTER leaving the mother superior, each was able to sleep for a few hours before the day began. They met in the training room in the late morning. When they arrived, a telegram was waiting for them. It had arrived early that morning. Benito opened and read it quickly.

"Father Rimaldi will be here by Wednesday."

"Good," Brigid said. "Is he a formidable magician?"

"There is no one superior outside of the Vatican. He's not merely a Jesuit, but the Father Provincial for the Jesuits in Maryland."

"And you think he will not want me involved?"

"I can't be certain, but I doubt he will want you to participate in the ritual we perform."

"Why?"

"You are untested in this type of situation. It may be very dangerous."

"I see," she said. "And going to Saint Julian Street today is not?"

"Not as dangerous. Even if the others perceive us, which is doubtful, they would not dare do anything in daylight."

"But I perceived you when you were attempting to conceal yourself. Couldn't they?"

"You are an hereditary. The perceptual ability you were born with is probably greater than their learned one. Those who serve evil are rarely hereditaries."

"Could there not be a first time?"

"There could be, at that. But most who have your level of talent are not able to serve the dark for long. They overreach themselves when young and end badly."

"Their power is taken?"

"After a fashion," he said. "They die young or become insane. Their souls are usually forfeit."

With that somber thought, he and Sister Brigid left the compound, emerging on the side of the cathedral. She automatically followed the priest. When he stopped, so did she. Benito turned to her. "You are the guide here. I need to follow you."

Embarrassed, she led the priest toward the square. She talked, partially to cover her nervousness. "We could go directly to Saint Julian Street, but I would like to approach it from another direction, the one I came from originally."

"Probably a good idea," he said.

They walked toward the river on Habersham Street. Colonial Park Cemetery lay to their left. Habersham, like most of the streets in Savannah, was hard-packed dirt and sand. A few of the streets in this area had been covered with cobbles, as Savannah had a surfeit of cobblestones. The empty ships arrived with the stones for ballast, and they were removed in Savannah, their weight more than replaced by a load of cotton, timber, and naval stores. Benito and Brigid walked down the long block of the cemetery and then covered the short block of Habersham that brought them to Columbia Square. The square's august precincts were overlooked by Mr. Davenport's house, one of the finest homes in the city. She stopped.

The priest looked up from his musings. "Are we near?"

She nodded. "From here it is a few blocks to Warren Square,

which is where I saw the darkness." She faced the square, but did not proceed.

"Is there something wrong?" he asked.

"I'm afraid."

"A reasonable reaction, especially after the events of last night. These people are not ones to be trifled with. But we should be safe. Your shielding is sufficient for this type of situation. I can protect both of us and probably keep us hidden as well. Make no effort to shield yourself unless it is necessary. I would prefer that they know little about your potential power at this point. Don't do more than observe with that Sight of yours. If you try to look into things, you will shine like a beacon. Let me do the examination."

Nodding, she led him down State Street. They said nothing, though it was unlikely they could communicate without shouting, as State Street was busy with traffic. Horses clopped their way down the street, and wagon wheels rumbled on the cobblestones. Though the sidewalks were crowded, the men were quite prepared to step to the side for the nun and priest. The two turned onto Houston and walked to Washington Square. Here the streets were less well traveled, as they were outside the commercial hub of the city. The streets in this residential area were almost deserted at this hour.

Brigid stopped near the middle of the square. "This is how I came upon the place. We're facing Saint Julian Street. The next square ahead of us is Warren Square. The block of Saint Julian after the square is the one that I saw darkened."

Benito gave Sister Brigid a few moments to gather her courage and quiet her mind. The street had been named for Saint Julian, the Hospitaller. He was the patron saint of innkeepers, travelers, and boatmen. As they began their walk down the street that bore the saint's name, Benito lifted a prayer to him for protection, thinking that mages are travelers, even though much of their travel occurs in unseen realms.

Benito avoided using his Sight until they had reached Warren

Square. Then he engaged it to look down the street. He pulled back immediately. There was no mistaking the darkness that hung across the street. The evil was palpable. A dark mist roiled the air.

"Brigid," he said, controlling his voice, "come with me." He led them away from the dark block of Saint Julian Street to the opposite side of the square. They stood so one of the large oaks was between themselves and the darkened block of Saint Julian. "I saw what you saw. The house is on the right side of the street, about halfway down the block."

"Yes."

"I have seen spirits driven from people's bodies, and I have been to places where evil has been practiced for a long time, but never have I seen a residue of evil to match this." He crossed himself. "We need to learn more. I want to know the exact address and see the house up close. I should wait for Father Rimaldi, but, once he arrives, they will be more on their guard."

"Then we should go now."

"I'm afraid so, but this I will do alone; you have no experience in these matters."

"Would you not be safer if I could join my power with yours?"

"Brigid, I honor your courage, but joining power is difficult, even for those with far more training than you have."

Brigid thought about what he had said for a moment. "I want to go with you."

He considered for a moment. "All right, we'll go together," he said. "But there's something else that surprised me. How did you know that we were safe once we were behind this oak tree?"

She frowned. "I didn't think about it. I just knew. Was I wrong?"

"No, not at all. No one can see through living oak. I just wondered how you knew. Did someone teach you?"

"I don't know if I was taught or not. It felt safe, and I know that the oak was the most sacred tree of the gods."

He let her sentence and its implications rest in the air though he wondered what other information lay buried in her mind.

She inclined her head toward the dark block of Saint Julian. "I guess we had best get it over with."

They walked out into the open area of the square and crossed it, bound for the darkness that lay across the street before them. To anyone seeing the street with normal sight, it was a pretty vista. Saint Julian was paved with cobblestones, and the brick sidewalks made it an easy walk. As was typical for late October, the day was sunny and warm, devoid of the brutal heat of August. Most of the houses were two story, and many had some sort of greenery bordering the street. Small fruit trees were planted along the curb. The houses were a mix of brick, wood, and tabby, a native and very durable building material made of concrete, gravel, and shells. The architectural effect, though eclectic, was pleasing. Saint Julian was one of the more beautiful streets in a city with a surfeit of beautiful streets.

Seen through the eyes of someone with the Sight, however, the view was very different. The eye was immediately drawn away from the houses to what extended across the street from one of the houses. The dark cloud was not merely a dimming or a grayness, but a swirling mass of black on gray, with a few dim streaks of red defining the darker areas. It looked alive, though it was not. It was like the residue of a windstorm, not a cleansing storm, but a whirlwind that trapped the dirt and filth of the thoughts and emotions that had been experienced in this house. Dark emotions had given their illness to the miasma. Terror and fear played the greater part, though lurid pleasure had meshed with the other feelings. Here was pleasure without joy, laughter without happiness. This pall hung like a funeral shroud. Its appearance was as frightening as the wind wall of a hurricane's eye.

The priest and the nun could both see what was before them. They locked their arms together for support and comfort. They did not think what someone seeing them might surmise about a priest and a nun walking arm in arm, clinging tightly to one another. The reality of what their Sight revealed to them was so overwhelming that it seemed impossible to them that others could not also see it. Other than the powerful impressions of the Sight, Brigid and Benito could see little. Their normal vision was largely obscured.

But another did see. Unnoticed by Brigid and Benito, dark eyes peered down on them through the lace curtains of a first-floor window. These eyes knew something of the turbulence in the street and the reasons for it. As the nun and priest approached, Esmerelda sensed from the way their bodies moved that they had an understanding of what they traversed. "So this," she thought to herself, "is what they sendin' to fight Streng and his demon. They gonna need help."

The two on the street stopped in front of the house, looked at it long enough to see the street number, then hurried away. Esmerelda watched them go, seeing the tension drain from them and their hands unclasp as they moved beyond the storm. She backed away from the curtain, glad that Streng was not at home. That the priest knew where Streng lived would have bothered him, perhaps even enough so that he might try to hurt these good people. The faint light they'd cast through the gloom of the street told her that they were good, but now she had to decide if she should try to help them or not. The *loa* had said she should avoid doing magic, but she could still talk to them, perhaps serve as their eyes and ears. If they failed, however, and Streng discovered her help, the result would be her death. Still, if she withheld her aid, how many more would die at Streng's hands? She shook her head. She did not like such decisions.

Shivering, Benito and Brigid emerged from the dark cloud before they reached the end of the block at Lincoln Street. They remained silent as they crossed Lincoln and continued on to Reynolds Square, where they both sat heavily on a bench as their breathing slowed.

Brigid was the first to speak. "Four fifty-four."

"Yes," he said. "I wonder if it is an accident that the numbers add up to thirteen?"

The quiet drew out between them.

"Luis, I do not think I shall willingly walk down that street again."

"Nor I."

Wanting to distance themselves from Saint Julian Street, they resumed their walk. When they came to another square, they took a longer rest. The square was peaceful, even beautiful. They sat on one of the benches. The gentle cooing of the pigeons, permanent residents of the squares, was a soothing sound, one that helped to quiet their thoughts. They had both seen the same things. Neither wished to discuss them until necessary. For a while they sat and simply drank in the loveliness of the square. Neither noticed how they were sitting, close enough to maintain contact and gain reassurance from it.

Benito stood and offered his hand to Brigid. She took it and rose. They turned toward the cathedral, both thinking of its cool dimness and sanctity. Perhaps it would serve to clean them of the taint of evil that had fallen on them like coal dust as they had walked past the house on Saint Julian. As they returned to the cathedral, they appeared to be a priest walking in his customary reserved manner and a nun with her arms crossed over her chest, guarded and serious. No one would take note of them or begin to guess their unusual mission. Jakob Streng certainly didn't, even though he passed within a few feet of them as he walked north on Abercorn Street. Automatically, he touched the brim of his hat in deference to the nun, his manners as carefully groomed as his beard.

⚜

WHEN Brigid and Benito returned to their training room in the cathedral compound, he was grim. She was both frightened and exhilarated. He looked across the table to her, surprised by her expression. "You found that exciting?"

"Yes. Exciting and frightening."

"I felt only fear."

"Luis, all of this is part of your life. For me it is new. I know it is childish to feel excited, but I feel as if I have just dodged death."

"Perhaps it is jaded of me not to feel the same."

She became thoughtful. "Luis, do you know what it is like to be a nun?"

"I think I have an idea, but tell me what you mean."

"Each day you arise at the same time. The routine never varies for six days a week. The only exception is Sunday, which has its own routine. So even every Sunday is the same. For those of us who work the wards in the hospital, there is some change week to week, but not much. I can tell you where I will be months in advance.

"Life was not meant to be so planned and predictable. During the war, things were disordered. I found pleasure in the fact that I never knew when I might be needed. I might have to work for twenty-four hours or longer. The diversion was such a novelty that, God forgive me, I almost wished the war would go on.

"It was a sign of desperation that I felt that way. Until the war came, every day was the same—the schedule of daily prayers that went on ceaselessly from year to year, the long hours of 'contemplation,' shut away from the world. In the war I felt useful. I was saving lives."

"But your vocation?"

"Vocation? I never had a 'calling' to the work of the Church. I was sent to the Church to keep from starving. I remained with the Church because it was all I knew, or maybe because I was too frightened to leave. Though other nuns may have chosen to take orders as a last resort, many do come to feel the calling, or they come to feel it over time. For them, this is the perfect life—work, prayer, meditation. No challenges to face in an outside world that is filled with chances and dangers."

"The convent life is not what you want." He made it a statement and not a question.

"No. It isn't." She sighed. "But I probably would have stayed here forever, being useful, taking care of the sick, were it not for the events of that night and my awakening memories."

He waited for her to continue.

"I knew that something evil had come, even before I heard Richardson's screaming. I felt its going. When the door to Richardson's room opened, I wanted to know what had happened. The other nuns held back. They did not know the creature was gone, but I did. The doctor entered because he has no belief. He did not think that there were powers that could threaten him. When I entered that room a part of me that had been asleep began to awaken." She paused. "Now, thanks to those events and your training, new thoughts drift into my brain. I know things. But it's not like the knowing I have when I see that someone is sick. That is my talent. What emerges within me is more subtle, like a gentle push or a thought to guide me down a path. Sometimes, I just know how to do something. The other night, when you were unconscious, I was left there with my shielding up. I relaxed, and I knew how to bring it down."

Father Benito was both troubled and inspired by what she had said. Troubled, because he realized that currents were rising in her that could lead her away from the Church. Inspired, to think that such desire for life dwelt inside her, to realize that she had such intuitive skills available.

"When we began our conversations," he said, "I should have admonished you for your change in beliefs away from the doctrine of the Church, but I knew, even then, that such an action would be a waste of time. Now I find that you test my faith."

"I don't intend to."

"I know." Benito took a deep breath. He found himself pulled ever more deeply into the world inside of Brigid's mind. It was all the more attractive since it was so alien to him. She had been raised as a true pagan, something that had become rare. Even stranger, neither he nor she knew the extent of these "remembered" powers. But he realized that they did not have time for that exploration now, no matter how seductive it might be.

He changed subjects. "What about the Voudon community? Have you decided whom you will talk with?"

"There is an old colored man, Isaiah, who works at the hospital. He's been here a long time and seems to know everything that goes on in the colored community. He's a freeman."

"I thought all of the slaves were freed."

"They are, but that's not how we think of it here. Isaiah was free before the war. His master, Isaac Meyer, died in the 1850s. Many of Meyer's slaves simply passed with his estate to his children, but Isaiah and his wife were freed by Meyer's will. So we call him a 'freeman.' It means he was freed by his master, not by Mr. Lincoln."

"Does that make a difference?"

"In Savannah, everything makes a difference. Isaiah gets special respect from the whites, since he was freed. Everyone knows that any colored man freed by his master must have done a special service."

"What was it?"

"No one knows. Mr. Meyer didn't say, and Isaiah doesn't talk about it. I can tell you, though, that he is wise, and the other members of the colored community look up to him."

Benito smiled. "Then it sounds like he's the man you should talk to."

THAT afternoon, Brigid found Isaiah in the basement. He was half inside the firebox of the boiler for the heating system. She stopped so she would not surprise him and called out, "Isaiah, it's Sister Brigid."

He stopped what he was doing inside the firebox and pulled his upper body out of the door.

"Sistah," he said, "you shouldn't be down here."

"And why's that?"

"Rats."

"Isaiah, I've been in this basement many times and there have always been rats. I wouldn't expect today to be much different."

He shook his head with the sense of both exasperation and wonder that he felt toward the nuns. "Yes, ma'am."

"So what are you doing down here?"

"Almost time to get the heat goin'. Tryin' to make sure this old furnace got some life in her."

"Is there doubt?"

"Always some, but it looks pretty good. I'll know better when I start a fire." He pronounced "fire" with two definite syllables. "Then there's gonna be lots of rats. When I light this off, I like to have me some cats around. Then the rats be too busy runnin' to have time to take any meat off my ol' bones."

She smiled. "Better you than me."

"So what brings you to Isaiah?"

"Let's talk for a minute." She walked over to the airy corner of the basement where an old table and two creaky ladder-back chairs stood waiting for the fireman and shoveler who would be here in the coldest weather. Isaiah and Brigid sat opposite each other. He busied himself with wiping the coal dust and soot from his face and hands. He was waiting for her to start, giving her time to collect her thoughts. He knew this talk would be serious; otherwise she would not have gone to the effort of finding him.

"Isaiah, do you know anything about the followers of Voudon in Savannah?"

"Voodoo? What you be messin' with that for?"

"Isaiah, I know that we aren't supposed to talk about Voudon, and I know it's not supposed to exist. The Church thinks that it is evil. I don't, and I need to talk to someone inside the Voudon community here in Savannah."

"Miss Brigid, I got no way—"

She interrupted. "Just please hear me out. Maybe you might know someone who might know someone?"

He appreciated that she was giving him every chance to give her information without saying who knew what. He said, "I'm thinking this is about that white man and Sistah Francis. Voodoo got nothin' to do with that."

"I know."

"You know? Then why you want to talk to them?"

"Because Voudon is the natural enemy of whoever killed them as much as the Church is. Maybe the local Voudon people might have information that would help us."

Isaiah sat and thought for a minute. Of course he knew about voodoo. He had talked to Esmerelda long ago. Though he was a Christian and did not practice voodoo, he wasn't about to betray those who did. At the same time, he also knew enough of what was happening in Streng's secret meetings to know that he had to be stopped.

"Sistah, I ain't saying I know anything, but I can talk to some might know."

"Thank you, Isaiah."

"Too early for thanking. But I need a promise."

She nodded.

"Whatever you find out, you got to promise you ain't going to use it to hurt any of my people. Don't want no priests botherin' the voodoo people."

"We're not trying to bother them. Right now, what we want is to find out if they know anything about who or what killed Mr. Richardson and Sister Francis. We also know there is something terribly evil on Saint Julian Street. The two things might be tied together. Maybe they can tell us. If they don't want to meet us, Benito and I can understand."

He thought for a moment. "How fast you need to know this?"

"Right now would be good."

"Ain't got nothing for you right now. But maybe I can find out somethin' by mornin'. Or it might take some time. No promises."

⌘

ISAIAH found Esmerelda while she was shopping for Streng's household at the city market. The midday crowd in the bustling market gave them a chance to slip away, unnoticed by others.

"So they want to meet with me?" Esmerelda asked.

"Didn't say you, just want to know what voodoo folks might know about the 'evil men' that called the demon that killed Richardson and the nun."

"Streng." It was a statement, not a question.

"Yeah, they saw the evil in the air round his house."

"I saw this nun, probably same one that visited you, when they come by the house," she replied.

"Then why you waitin'? We all want him gone."

"Not that easy. If they go after him and fail, things will just get worse."

"Yeah, but it ain't just Brigid and the priest from Florida."

"What do you know?"

"Thought you knew, too. They got a bunch of priests comin' from all over."

"Where you hear that?" she asked.

"From what one boy hears and passes on to another."

They looked at each other and smiled conspiratorially.

"Isaiah, the *loa* warned me about doin' magic, but I can talk. I ain't gonna talk to no priest. You bring this nun to me, tomorrow night, 'bout nine."

"You gonna let me take her to your place?"

"No, I'm gonna meet you on Jenkins Street, near Billie's. We'll go somewhere else to talk. You meet her in front of the big church and bring her to me. And don' leave before eight thirty. I'm gonna have some of the boys followin'."

"Why?"

"I don' want nobody to mess with you on the way. We got two ships in port, and lots of sailors are comin' to the colored part of town."

Isaiah nodded and rose to go.

"Isaiah," she called.

He turned, and she tossed him an apple.

"Thanks," he said.

"Don' thank me; Streng paid for it."

They both laughed as he walked away.

CHAPTER FIFTEEN

Tuesday, October 20

TUESDAY morning, Sister Brigid arrived in the basement before Isaiah came to work, glad for the time alone. She knew that she was being driven to a decision that she did not want to make. Her view of the world was shifting, becoming closer to the one she had held as a child, a perspective far different from that of the Church. Nonetheless, the Catholic faith that she had practiced much of her life held her powerfully. She was afraid to leave the spiritual cocoon of the Church.

Besides, there were practical matters to consider. Leaving the convent would not be simple. Where would she go? What would she do to make a living? Being in the outside world was unfamiliar. Simply living outside of a convent placed her at risk. In the convent the daily necessities—food, clothing, shelter—were taken care of, as they had been for all of her life. She had been a child, taken care of by her parents, until the time that she had left for school in Dublin. Since then she had effectively been a ward of the Church.

If she left, she didn't know how she would make a living. She could teach school or be a nurse. Maybe she would return to Ireland. Perhaps Siobhan could help her. As Brigid turned these thoughts over in her mind, she realized how sheltered she had been from the world beyond the walls of the convent.

She also knew that the practical issues of dealing with the real world were not the only things that held her in her orders. The issue before her had powerful spiritual implications. She was considering leaving the Church itself. The decision for her was not whether or not she should be a nun, but whether or not she should remain a Christian. From the time she was seven, she had attended a routine of Christian services. When she was a little older, the convent school had taken the girls to visit the great Catholic churches in Dublin. The magnificent buildings were, in themselves, like the creations of a god to a child raised in the poverty of Western Ireland. Over time, the teachings and daily practice had increased her belief in the Christian faith and the damnation that lay outside of it. Her years within the Church had imbued her with some faith in the Christian God. The thought of leaving that faith chilled her. How many times had she prayed to the Virgin for strength? How often had she risen from her knees reassured? To leave the faith was to leave security and assurance, spiritual and physical. A part of her cringed at the loneliness outside of the life she knew, yet another part of her sang sweetly.

When Isaiah entered the boiler room, he found the nun deep in thought. She was slightly startled by his arrival, but brightened when she recognized him.

Isaiah was surprised to see her. "Sistah, you up early."

"Well, I wanted to know if you'd found out anything. Besides, the early morning quiet gave me a chance to think."

"Seems like you nuns get lots of time to think."

"Not alone, not like this."

"I understan'. For me, I get my best thinkin' done when I can go down by the marsh at sunset. Twilight's the best time."

Brigid wondered what thoughts filled his mind then. Most white people never cared what filled the minds of colored people. These white people would probably be surprised by how similar their thoughts were. In Isaiah's case, they would probably be surprised at how subtle his thoughts were.

"So, Isaiah, do you have news for us?"

"Well, not exactly for 'us.' The *mambo,* the priestess, say she talk with you, but not to no priest."

"Why?"

He smiled. "She gonna trust a woman before she trust a man, specially if that man be a priest."

"She wouldn't trust a priest?"

"Priests done lots of bad things to her people. Voodoo people got no love for priests."

Brigid nodded. "So what do I do?"

"I be meetin' you tonight, just after eight thirty, in front of the cathedral."

"Is the time so important?"

He nodded. "The *mambo* gonna have some boys follow us."

"She doesn't trust me?"

"No, Sistah, she havin' us followed to protect you."

"What do I have to be afraid of?" After the events of the past few days, she did not know what to expect.

"White sailors. No colored man dare touch you, but white sailors, they tricky when they drunk."

She laughed. "Then I'll be glad for the escort."

Isaiah said, "Well, I got work to be doin'."

Sister Brigid stood. "Then I'll see you just after eight thirty."

⚘

FATHER Benito was not happy with the arrangement, even though he had expected that none of the practitioners of Voudon would meet with him. One thing particularly drew his attention.

"The *mambo* is meeting with you?"

"That's what he said."

"Then they must consider this important. The identity of the *mambo* is usually a closely guarded secret, especially from the Church."

"She's that important?"

"Here she would be. A city has only one *mambo,* which makes her the head of their local 'church.'"

Sister Brigid nodded and thought for a few moments, then smiled sweetly. "Do you think she'll want me to kiss her ring?"

Father Benito looked at her disapprovingly for a moment, then laughed. "I can see you're the right one for this task."

WHEN the clock over City Hall chimed the half hour after eight, Sister Brigid left the convent to go to the front of the cathedral. A minute or two later, she seated herself on the broad steps. She had hardly gotten herself settled when Isaiah emerged from the darkness across the street. She stood to greet him, brushing off the back of her habit.

"Evenin', Sistah."

"Evening, Isaiah."

He shook his head. "Ain't this somethin'."

"What?"

"I never seen a nun outside after dark. It's kind of spooky. When you was coming up the street, all I could see was your face and that white thing 'round it. Everythin' else just blended in with the night. Then when you turned to go up the steps, it was like you just blinked out."

"I never thought of that."

"I'm guessin' somebody did."

He didn't say any more about it, but she understood what he meant and appreciated the keenness of the observation. At night a nun would be hard to see from behind in her black habit. If she faced you, all that you would see was her face surmounted by a band of white. So her turning around gave the impression of appearing from nowhere. Brigid had never thought about that aspect of a nun's habit before. She wondered if it was an intentional effect. Isaiah seemed to think so.

"So, brother Isaiah, where to now?"

"Follow me." He turned into the darkness and headed toward the eastern end of town. They walked for several blocks before crossing East Broad Street. Here the streets sloped away from the bluff on which the town of Savannah was built. This part of the east side of the city was "colored town." It was the place where the maids and servants, the orderlies and janitors, lived. It was also the location of several taverns and brothels. Other colored neighborhoods lay to the south of town, but the people who lived there rarely came into the city.

Just as Isaiah and Brigid started down the slope, a drunken voice hailed them from between two of the ramshackle buildings. "So what we got here?"

An English sailor came lurching out of the darkness. "A nigger and a nun. Where you going to? Maybe the whorehouse? They'd pay plenty for somethin' like you."

Isaiah stepped between Brigid and the sailor. "Boss, we got no business with you." Brigid was immobilized by her fear. No one had ever talked to her like that. She did not, could not, know what to do.

"Out of my way, nigger." A knife suddenly appeared in the sailor's hand. "Always wanted to find out what a nun looked like under that rug they wear. Looks like this might be my best chance."

Isaiah slowly backed away. He stood no chance against a man thirty years younger than him who had a knife. The sailor mirrored his motions, moving closer to Brigid with each step.

Then an arm reached out of the darkness and wrapped around the sailor's neck. A dark face appeared over his shoulder. "I got my arm on your neck and a knife on your back. Drop that knife you got."

The sailor's face, which had been flushed with drunken confidence, turned to a mask of fear. The knife fell from his hand.

The large figure of a black man could be seen stepping away from the sailor. If he had a knife it could not be seen. "Now git out of here."

The sailor reached to recover his knife.

"No, suh, you leave that knife. Just git."

The sailor rushed at the big man. He was met by a fist that smashed into his face, knocking him unconscious. The black man reached down and picked up the sailor's knife and slipped it into his belt. "Might come in handy." He looked at Isaiah and Brigid. "Now you two get goin'; the *mambo* is waitin', and she don't like to wait."

Isaiah turned the terrified nun away from the scene of the fight. Brigid almost stumbled as he led her away. She stopped after a few steps and pulled away from him. She turned around to thank the man who had saved her.

"Sir," Sister Brigid said. For a moment the big man didn't know she was talking to him. Then he turned to face her. She continued, "Thank you for saving me. I don't think that sailor would have been satisfied with my honor; I think he would have taken my life as well. If I have any power to bless, I give my blessing to you."

A smile split his face. "Thank you, Sistah."

Isaiah tugged at her arm and pulled her away down the street. The figure behind them vanished in the gloom.

"Who was that, Isaiah?"

"Don' know him by name, but he's one of the boys that I see with the *mambo*. Likely she sent him to watch out for us."

"So she really did send someone to protect us?"

"Likely more than one."

"But why?"

"The *mambo* say you gonna be safe, you safe. The *mambo* always keeps her word."

They walked the next blocks in silence, Brigid pondering what she had just heard and looking about her at a part of town she had never before entered. A light fog had rolled onto the low-lying streets. Since there were no streetlights here, the only light was the occasional candle or lamp flame that glinted from a window or shone from an open door. The moon was hidden by clouds. But Isaiah knew his way, guiding Brigid around the cracked stones and broken bottles that lay on the sides of the dirt streets. He took a few more turns as they walked the final blocks, enough so that Brigid would have a hard time finding her way back to the place they were going.

Isaiah finally spoke. "She just ahead."

Esmerelda was sitting on an old packing crate in the middle of the narrow street. She stood as they approached. "Welcome, Sistah Brigid. Now, Isaiah, you wait here. We going a little bit from here to talk. I already hear about the trouble you run into on the way here. But don't you worry. One of my boys gonna escort that white sailor outta here, soon as he wakes up." She grinned. "The ones James puts down usually stay down awhile."

Brigid walked up to the woman. She extended both hands to the *mambo*. "An honor to meet you."

Esmerelda was surprised, but took both her hands in hers. "And I am just as happy to meet you." A glint of recognition passed across Esmerelda's eyes; then she added, "I think we gonna get along fine."

"I'm sure of it."

"Then let's get away from men with big ears."

Esmerelda led her to a small, deserted house nearby. A kerosene lamp burned on a small table. "Ain't my place, but it will do." She motioned to one of the two chairs that stood on either side of the table. "So what you need the *mambo* for?"

As they sat down, Brigid began, "There's an evil in this town."

Esmerelda laughed with grim amusement. "There's been bad evil in this place for a long time, but why you church folks suddenly get interested?"

"It's been here a long time?"

"Child, we known about the evil for years. There just ain't nothin' we can do about it."

"Couldn't you have asked for help?"

"If I go to the police with some story about devil worship, first thing they think about doin' is locking my black self up. Then if I tell them who the evil is, they gonna throw the key in the river."

"You know who it is?" She could not keep the excitement from her voice.

"Sure. Devil worshipers been here long as anyone can remember. Probably got their start in the early days, right after the white folk arrive. They like places where things ain't too regular. Lets 'em get away with more."

"But who is it?"

"Be patient with me. I need to know why you got so much interest."

"At the last new moon, a man was killed in the asylum ward at Saint Jo's. A spirit killed him."

"Mr. Richardson," Essie calmly replied.

"And early last Friday morning a nun died."

"Sistah Francis," the *mambo* said sadly. "She was a good woman."

"So you know about that, too?"

Essie nodded. "Seems like I know more than you. How come? Don't you have nobody with the eye?"

"The Church doesn't usually deal with such things. Publicly, we don't admit that they exist."

"How you be a religion and not deal with the spirits? Never has made sense to me. But, seein' what I have, I have to believe it."

They sat in silence for a moment. Then Essie went on. "How come you so sure that a spirit come for Richardson? Maybe he was just barking at the moon."

"No, something cold and evil came, killed him, and left."

Essie eyed her guest. "And you the one that felt it."

Brigid nodded.

"And with all these priests around, how come you be the one to feel it?"

Brigid realized that the *mambo* could probably understand her even better than Father Benito. "I am from Ireland. My great-aunt was the village wisewoman; I guess you could call her a witch. I was to take her place, but the famine came, and my family sent me to the convent. I became a nun because I didn't have a choice."

Essie nodded, digesting the story. "Well, you got the power. I look hard at you, and I see it. You got the gift."

"Thank you, I think."

"Good answer, child. The gift brings a lot with it. Some of it's not so good. You got a responsibility to help out others. Otherwise the gods, they get angry that you not using what they give you."

"I'm learning that."

"That's why you're not sure you should be grateful for the gift."

Brigid nodded.

The *mambo* composed her thoughts. "The evil ones are headed up by a man name of Jakob Streng. He's a powerful man in this town, rich. He's even more powerful when he does his magic. He's got followers, about two dozen. They meet once a month just before the new moon, most often at his house."

"You know where this house is?"

"On Saint Julian Street." Esmerelda smiled slowly. "You and that priest they send up from Florida already know."

"How'd you know that?"

"I'm Streng's housemaid. I see you and that monk stop in front of the house. I also saw that both of you saw a lot more on that street than sunshine."

Brigid stiffened.

"Don' worry, child. I got reasons for bein' in Streng's house. I got the job so I could keep an eye on him. Maybe I can help my own folks better if I know what he's about. But I ain't strong enough to stop him. He keeps right on killin' in the name of his devil. He's doin' more of it now than ever before."

"Doesn't he know who you are?"

"He figured out that I was in Voudon, but he's like most white people. He thinks Voudon's on the side of evil, so he thinks I'm on his side. He don't know that good got as many faces as evil do."

"Then you'll help us?"

"Much as I can. But I'm afraid of doin' magic against Streng. He's too powerful. If it goes wrong, my people will be in danger. And that spirit they call is way too strong for me to mess with."

"You're afraid?"

"Anybody not afraid don't have good sense. But I can keep my ears and eyes open. If anything happens you need to know, I'll tell you."

"Thank you."

"So now you tell me somethin'."

"All right," Brigid said cautiously.

"I hear you got others comin' to fight Streng. That's good. I known about the Church's magicians a long time. But they better be stronger than your priest. He got no chance against Streng."

"They are stronger, and they will work together."

"Good. You gonna be part of this?"

"I don't know yet, but I don't think they will let me be a part of it."

"Now that's plain stupid. You got more magic than that priest."

"I do?"

"You must have guessed it by now. You born to it. He learned most of what he knows. Oh, he got talent, but not like you."

"You can see all that?"

"And a lot more." She reached out to Brigid and took her hand. "Can I read you?"

Brigid was surprised by the question, but she needed to know more, especially about herself. "Yes. Tell me what you see."

Essie turned Brigid's hand palm up, and stared at it in the light of the lamp that lit the room, tracing the folds of skin with her fingertips, moving surely, gently.

Brigid relaxed and closed her eyes, feeling perfectly safe with this woman, though she wasn't sure why. Perhaps it was because she didn't need to keep any secrets from Essie. Even what Brigid said to Benito had to be monitored more carefully than what she might say to this Voudon priestess. As the fingertips slid over Brigid's skin, she felt a ripple of excitement, a quickening of her pulse, and a slight, delicious chill. When the *mambo* took her hands away, Brigid was sad they had gone. Brigid opened her eyes and saw the last of a luminous mist around the *mambo* fade into the darkness.

Essie missed nothing. "What you jus' see?"

"I saw a glowing mist around you. I've seen it before, around my great-aunt."

"So how long is your line of witches?"

"At least seven generations. The storytellers say longer. In almost every one of those generations someone had the Sight. Usually a woman, sometimes a man."

"Figured so. Power like you got don't come from nowhere."

"*Mambo,* can I ask your name? You haven't told me."

"I usually don' say, but time's past for secrets. I'm Esmerelda. Most people call me Essie or, in ceremony, just *mambo.*"

"Thank you. Brigid is both my birth name and my name as a nun, so it's the only one I have."

Essie had one more question. "Brigid, what's a 'walker'?"

"What do you know about walkers?"

Essie smiled. "The main thing I know is that Streng is scared of 'em."

"I've never seen one," Brigid answered. "I don't know if there are any left. But they are, or were, powerful magicians. My great-aunt saw one about fifty years ago. A demon was killing people and animals in the part of Ireland we are from. A walker came and killed the demon, but that was a long time ago, and I have not been with people of the old faith in a long time. Even the Catholic Church's magicians have almost no knowledge of them, outside of legend. So, if there are any walkers left, there must be very few."

"They had that big a power in them?"

"It was in them, or they could call it to them."

Essie nodded. "I believe they were real. Maybe some are still about. It only makes sense. The gods always make sure there be good to fight the bad. But the white man can be stupid, fighting against good men for the wrong reason. Then he's left to live with the evil he lets loose."

Brigid realized that the *mambo*'s perspective was broader than her own. "Esmerelda, I'd like to get to know you after all of this is over. I could learn much from you."

"Thank you. That would be good. But it may not be."

"Why?"

"What I saw in your hand. It was clear. I know it's true. You standin' at the crossroads. Two paths in front of you, and you not sure which you gonna take. But you be making the choice soon. One way and you become a priestess of your gods. That's the hard way, but it's your true way. Second path, you stay where you are. You be different from what you was, but a nun anyway."

"But won't I take what you called my 'true way'?"

"All of us are born with a place to go, a 'true way.' But we all got the chance to mess up as well as do right. Sometimes I read a hand and know the heart's gonna make the right choice. For you, I can't see. That don't mean you ain't gonna get it right. It don't even mean you ain't already made the right choice. It could mean they jus' ain't gonna let me see."

"But why?"

"Maybe 'cause you got to learn it without any help." Essie paused. "I also got to tell you to be careful. There's a short branch on your tree as well."

"A short branch?"

"Means you could die real soon. It's not likely; the line is faint. But it's there."

Brigid knew that she was involved in a dangerous battle, but she had no choice but to join in it. The *mambo*'s reading put a stamp of certainty on it. Brigid also knew that the other things that Essie said were right. Her heart could not be read because her heart had not decided. Some part of her longed for the old gods and the old ways, but she was afraid. How would she make her way in a world she knew nothing about? How would she eat? Where would she live?

She heard Essie's calm voice. "You best be gettin' back now. Isaiah ain't used to stayin' up this late."

"Thank you."

"Thanks ain't needed." She held Brigid with her eyes. "I be watchin' what happens around us. But I don't see everythin'. If I see somethin', I tell Isaiah. He'll see you for me. And if you hear anythin' I need to know, you can tell Isaiah you need to see me. You always welcome."

Brigid reemerged onto the porch of the small house. She saw that Isaiah was waiting for her just across the street. He came to meet her as she descended the uneven wooden stairs.

"So what you think about our *mambo*?"

"Impressive, a little scary."

"Scary?"

"She can look right through you and see what's inside."

He smiled. "That's why she's the *mambo*."

He led Brigid back to the main part of Savannah and then the cathedral without talking. The nun obviously had much to consider.

Brigid thought that the *mambo* had done little to bring her clarity. In fact, Essie's reading of Brigid's palm had given her one more thing to worry about. There was a short line in her hand. The reading had given her no answers. She already knew what was her true way, and she knew the reasons that she might not take it. She was left in the same confused state, except for the slight reinforcement about which way she should go. She just didn't know if she had the courage to do it.

CHAPTER SIXTEEN

Wednesday, October 21

RIMALDI looked out of the window of the train as it rumbled toward Savannah in the strengthening light of morning. The early train from Atlanta to Savannah held few occupants, and the majority of those few were dozing. The "passengers" who were the real reason for the train's schedule were bales of cotton, lying in the freight cars that nestled against the engine.

He regretted that it had taken so long for him to begin the trip to Savannah, but he had spent the time well. He had used his research library to prepare himself for the ritual ahead of him. He had also carefully reviewed the records of the members of his order. The ones he had summoned to join him in Savannah were the best he had at his disposal, but his best was not what it might once have been. A hundred years ago the secretive order of Catholic mages had possessed much more power and many more members.

Rimaldi knew the situation was partially a sign of the times. The magical order had never been public in its recruitment. Though most still believed in the hidden realm with which the members of his order dealt, many did not. As the percentage of believers was reduced, so were their recruits. Their very success had weighed against them. Fewer people had experienced the potency of malignant spirits, so fewer saw the need to participate in the long and often arduous training.

Rimaldi had summoned five other members of the magical order to join him in Savannah. Provided that health did not prevent any from traveling, he could depend upon seven mages for the rite that they must perform, counting himself and Benito. Rimaldi did not want to risk confronting the ones that they must face with less than that number. Benito had used the word "gorgon" in his telegram. If one of the less capable members of his order had included that word in his description, Rimaldi would have needed further confirmation. He trusted Benito.

To Rimaldi's knowledge, neither Benito nor any other member in North America had ever faced the kind of demon for which they used the name "gorgon." This demon had the capability of acting independently without possessing a human body. It could also exercise physical power in this realm in its own right. The coming battle would be a challenge. To Rimaldi, it would be a test of his abilities.

He had sent telegrams before he left to two members of his order; both would be needed to assure that he and Benito would be safe in Savannah until the arrival of the remaining mages. While Rimaldi traveled in his cassock, he had asked those two members to travel in mufti rather than clerical garb. The arrival of one priest would be unlikely to alert the suspicions of anyone, but the arrival of another might cause a reaction from their opponents, a reaction Rimaldi did not want to face until he had at least four of his order in Savannah.

Father Kirk would be coming from Duluth, Minnesota. He was the priest of a small congregation on the outskirts of the city. One of the larger parishes near him could easily provide someone to minister to his flock in his absence. Though Kirk was relatively new to the order and inexperienced, he had a tremendous natural talent for the magical arts. Rimaldi had chosen Kirk more for his innate abilities and the power he could summon than for his knowledge or discipline.

The second one Rimaldi had called, Sister Angela, had been a part of the order for some time, but had spent most of those years in Europe. Five years ago, the Church had sent her to join the Sisters of Mercy at their convent in Philadelphia. Though in her middle thirties, she was a formidable scholar, fluent in Italian, Greek, and French, as well as the expected Latin and English. Sister Angela came by her power by the most traditional of means. She was an hereditary, a descendant of Italian witches. Her great-grandmother had converted to Catholicism. Regardless of their conversion, Angela's family had not let her enter the convent until her eldest sister had given birth to a daughter, so that her family felt assured that there would be a female descendant. Daughters were very important in her family. They would carry on the legend of the Dellamorte clan.

In the tradition of some of the oldest Sicilian families, her family flouted Italian convention. Her father's name was Benelli, but her last name was interchangeably Benelli or Dellamorte. Outside of Sicily, she was a Benelli, but her wealthy father's name, that of an esteemed family that had grown fruit in southern Italy and on the island for centuries, took second place on the island of Sicily to the Dellamorte name. The Sicilians, always a little provincial about their island, claimed that the Dellamortes were descended from the Greeks who had built Syracuse. On one visit to Sicily an old man, after making the traditional sign against the evil eye, had "confided" to Rimaldi that the Dellamorte family was descended from Circe, the sorceress who played such a powerful role in the *Odyssey.*

Rimaldi had almost failed to discover the depth of Sister Angela's power. Her unassuming manner was not the only misleading factor about the nun. She was also disturbingly beautiful. The wimple could not hide her deep brown eyes and full lips. There was a hint of the Greek in her face. Though he had long ago steeled himself against the charms of a woman, he was glad that he could not glimpse the body beneath the shapeless habit.

With Father Kirk and Sister Angela joining himself and Benito in Savannah, he did not feel that they would be in any danger from their opponents before their next meeting, which he did not expect until the seventh or eighth of November, as the new moon would not occur until just after midnight on the ninth. He felt fairly certain that his opponents would choose the evening of the eighth to meet, as they could conduct their ritual at night and still finish before the moon would begin waxing.

He had summoned three more of his order by letter. Father Pascal was quite old and was the one whose health concerned Rimaldi the most, but Pascal had proven himself in serious situations. Father Anthony Siena, one of Rimaldi's oldest friends, would travel from New York City, Rimaldi's home. Siena was five years younger than Rimaldi and had grown from protégé to friend over the course of more than twenty years. His competence and good humor would be needed. Father Miguel Francisco was from the New Mexico Territory and was fluent in English, Spanish, and Latin. Rimaldi had never met Francisco, but Father Siena spoke highly of him. Though young, Francisco was accomplished in the arcane arts.

The coastal Georgia landscape outside the train window looked overbearing, even hostile, to Rimaldi. A wall of vegetation lined the tracks, with pine, sweet gum, sycamore, and oak trees competing for the sun. The space between them was filled with spiked palmetto bushes, scrub pine, and small flowering bushes he could not identify. Though he had known that summer in the far south simply faded into a warm fall that could extend into the new year, knowing about it was a different matter from experiencing it. A little more than an hour ago the train had started the gradual descent from the Piedmont plateau. Now, as they neared Savannah on the coastal plain, they were enmeshed in the lush vegetation that thrived in the sodden, hot climate. Spanish moss heavily draped the massive oaks. Resisting the strong sunlight, the oaken arms of the trees with their gray cloaks created a dark gloom beneath them.

The occasional field of a poor farm was a welcome respite from the wall of forest that lined either side of the tracks, but the farms were small and the shacks of the workers pitiable. Even the walls had chinks that would allow the wind to blow through on cold nights. Rimaldi thought that these workers could have easily taken wood from the surrounding forest and built better walls. Perhaps they were too lazy? Or perhaps, he chided himself, the effort was not justified by the few nights when the weather turned cold. It was almost November, and the temperature would probably reach eighty degrees by afternoon. The roofs of the shacks all looked sound. Protection from rain was clearly more important than protection from the cold. He had read that this area of the coastal plain received twice the annual rainfall as the great rain forests of the Amazon.

The sunlight dimmed, and, looking out the other side of the train, Rimaldi saw that dark thunderclouds had swept over them. The clouds' bellies seemed to scrape the trees, and the gray clouds were almost black where they were thickest, so black as to be fitting portents of God's judgment.

For a priest, he worried about God's judgment more than would be expected. Rimaldi knew that his sin of pride would weigh heavily against him. An arrogant man, assured of his brilliance, he had fought against the sin, but it was all too easy to embrace its heady pleasures. He had become a Jesuit partially in the hope of finding humility in that order. There were, after all, many brilliant Jesuits, but even that elite coterie of scholars had not produced many to match him. Unfortunately, he had found his compatriots in the order were frequently as tainted by arrogance as he was. Rimaldi was wise enough to know that this self-assuredness was dangerous. It led one into mistakes of overconfidence. Being wise enough to know that pride was dangerous, that it "goeth before the fall," did not necessarily grant him the ability to overcome the problem. In his lectures he often responded quickly and crushingly to questions, only to discover belatedly that there was more validity in the question than he had at first seen.

He felt the train slow as it approached the freight yards on the outskirts of the city. There the train would drop off some of the freight cars, and the engine would push the remaining freight and passenger cars into the station inside the city. He would be meeting with Benito, and then the bishop, within the hour. He was impatient with the need for Church formality. Meeting the bishop was a necessity, a Jesuit Father Provincial could not visit the diocese without making the obligatory call, but it wasted time. He wanted to be about his work.

He smiled in anticipation. A powerful demon backed by an old coven would be a challenge worthy of him and his best. This mission promised to be one that would be memorable.

RIMALDI'S impending arrival had finally resulted in enough conversation within the archdiocese that Streng's sources had news to pass on to him. Rimaldi's name drew Streng's attention. His reputation as a scholar was well known, and Streng realized that Rimaldi must be the one who had been summoned by Benito's telegram.

Streng had been serious when he had told Long that one exorcist did not concern him. Two were unlikely to be a problem. But the arrival of such a prominent scholar, a Jesuit Father Provincial no less, bore the stamp of something more serious. Streng sent word to the other two senior members of his coven to meet with him.

RIMALDI descended from the railcar to the platform in Savannah. The station itself was to his left, and he faced the street where coaches and carriages were ranked to accept passengers. The station was smaller than he had expected, but then the main business of Savannah was not the passengers who visited the city, but the cotton that passed through the city on the way to the harbor. Behind him, on the other side of the train, were more tracks and the immensely busy staging yard. Rimaldi recognized the short figure of

Father Benito as he approached him. He assumed the tall, distinguished-looking priest with Benito to be someone on the bishop's staff.

Benito immediately moved to greet Rimaldi. "Father Provincial, I am happy to see you again."

"Father Benito, while I may have wished for better circumstances, it is good to see you as well."

"Thank you, and may I introduce the bishop's secretary, Monsignor Robert Henry."

Rimaldi was pleased that the bishop was apparently taking this matter seriously. "A pleasure, Monsignor."

"We, and I speak for the bishop as well, are glad to see you arrive," the monsignor said.

"I look forward to our discussions."

While the greetings were passed, Benito noticed that there was a well-dressed young man who seemed to be paying a great deal of attention to the cluster of priests. Benito filed that fact away for another time and looked back to Rimaldi. "Let us retrieve your baggage and be off."

A young porter appeared at Benito's side. "I get it for you."

"Thank you, Daniel," the monsignor said.

Rimaldi turned to the porter. "Two black cases and a steamer trunk. Each marked with my name, Rimaldi."

The porter turned to fetch the baggage.

Rimaldi looked to the monsignor. "He knows where to take them? He'll get the right ones?"

The monsignor replied, "We told him your name before your arrival. He reads well, so he'll get your bags without a problem. We have a fair amount of travel to and from the archdiocese, and Daniel is also the bishop's coach driver. He is quite reliable. Shall we go?"

The three men turned toward Boundary Street, where the bishop's coach awaited them. After Daniel loaded the baggage, he assumed the coachman's seat, and they drove off.

Monsignor Henry was the first to speak. "I assume that you will first need some time to speak with Father Benito. We have set aside a room for your use. The bishop is anxious to see you after you have met with Father Benito. He would look forward to your taking lunch with him at twelve thirty."

The Jesuit nodded. "Please tell His Grace that it would be my privilege to join him."

"Good. Father Benito can take you to your meeting room as well as to your lodging. We are unsure how many of your order will be joining us, but we may need to make arrangements for some of them outside of the compound. We own a large house near the cathedral and thought of setting up something of a dormitory there. It is private and has the advantage of having little traffic near it at night. Initially, you will be near Father Benito inside the main compound."

"That seems excellent. I have asked for an additional five of my order to be here. So, with Father Benito and myself, the total should come to seven, but I am not certain that all will be able to join us." He looked to Benito.

"All have sent me telegrams and will be attending our conference. Two, Father Kirk and Sister Angela, are already in transit," the monk replied.

"Good."

The three men spent the remaining few minutes of their trip in silence. The other matters that needed discussion seemed far too weighty to broach after the trivialities of housekeeping.

Daniel took Rimaldi's bags to his quarters. The trunk would be delivered to the workroom set aside for them. Its weight made it clear that it contained books. After assuring Father Henry that Rimaldi would join the bishop for lunch, the other two priests went to the workroom, where Benito had been training Brigid. As they entered, Rimaldi looked around. The room was brightly lit by a bank of windows. The polished table and comfortable chairs had room enough for all of them.

"You have done well, Benito."

"Thank you, Father, but it was really the work of the bishop and the monsignor."

"Based on your requirements."

Benito nodded.

"So our first need is met; we have a place where we can gather and talk openly." He sat, automatically assuming a place at the head of the table. Benito sat in the chair to his right. Rimaldi asked, "So, Father Benito, what is your evidence for an independent demon?"

Rimaldi had quickly moved to the key point. The brief telegram had told him that someone had died at a demon's hands, and Rimaldi's first concern was the nature of their enemy. Benito was not surprised by the scholar's directness. He was prepared to present the evidence rapidly. Rimaldi listened intently to the details of Richardson's death and the condition of the room.

When Benito finished, Rimaldi said, "Taken together, the evidence makes it a virtual certainty that the demon had independent physical existence. Well stated, Benito. Is there anything else?"

Benito reached into his cassock and withdrew the damaged crucifix and laid it on the table. "As you can see, whatever was in that room had the power to melt silver. This crucifix was the property of Sister Mary Francis, one of the nuns in the convent. The last man to talk to Richardson directly was Dr. Gaston. He carried this crucifix into the room. It was also intact when Richardson forced him from the room. A few minutes later, it was in the condition you see."

The priest steeled himself to touch a thing that had been so defiled. He picked it up and turned it over. On the back, still partially readable, was the name of an esteemed silversmith in New York City. Rimaldi wondered what the nun might have done to have earned such a valuable gift. He turned the crucifix over slowly in his hands, sensing the corruption the demon had imprinted upon it. A sense of revulsion came over him. That the demon would take the time to defile the crucifix spoke to the creature's arrogance. Rimaldi could feel his anger rising. He quickly checked it, realizing that he was reacting just as the demon would wish. Anger weakened concentration, and lack of disciplined thought weakened magic. He laid the crucifix back upon the table.

"Our opponent is formidable," was all that he said.

"Yes, Father Provincial. That crucifix was Sister Francis's only valued possession. She had it constantly at her side for some twenty years. If any object can be considered to be sanctified by prayer, this one can. It is almost as if the demon wanted to make certain that we knew it had the power to destroy sanctified objects."

Rimaldi shook his head in sadness. "You did the right thing in using 'gorgon' in the telegram. I am glad I summoned our compatriots."

"Thank you, Father. When I first sent the telegram, I feared that I had overstated the danger of the situation, but, as the evidence mounted, I realized that it was as serious as I had feared it to be. And there is more."

"Go on."

Benito told him about the killing of Sister Francis, the ravaging of the rose garden, and the haunting of the mother superior. "I can't be certain about the event with the mother superior, but I sensed the remnants of the same demonic presence in Sister Francis's room as in Richardson's. The creature was clearly the one to destroy the roses."

Rimaldi said, "If they can summon so potent a demon, then it is likely that a formidable group of magicians opposes us here. I am glad I sent for as many of our members as I did."

"One of them paid me a visit in the night. It was strong, though its intent was only to frighten me. I have also been periodically watched since my arrival. They have a wide range of skills, but I have been able to gather some information about them, due to the help of one of the nuns. She was present the night of Richardson's death and has the gift of the Sight."

"An hereditary?" Rimaldi asked.

"Yes. She felt the creature come and go, and sensed some of its power. But, even more important, she has located where the satanists meet." Benito went on to explain what they had seen when she took him to Saint Julian.

"In the light of day this dark miasma was visible to her Sight?"

"And to mine. It has taken some time to build."

"Do you have any idea how long?"

"The monsignor that you met is in possession of a diary that has been kept for a century. A record of ritualistic killings of prostitutes and young girls goes back to 1786. There is a great similarity in the manner of the deaths and how the bodies have been disposed of. I suspect that this group has been in existence since at least that time. The killings have increased in frequency over the past few years. They have become more bold in their actions."

"Or perhaps the demon has grown more extreme in its demands."

That thought had not occurred to Benito, but it was more than plausible. As the group that summoned the demon was repeatedly exposed to its presence, the demon would begin to work its way inside of them. Though they might still believe themselves to be in control of the creature, in actuality the demon was increasingly in control of them.

"Have you found out who leads this group?"

"He is a very prominent citizen here. His name is Jakob Streng. He is a wealthy cotton factor with considerable influence in the city. So I think that we cannot hope for help from outside the Church. I had thought that the local Voudon community might be able to help, but they are too frightened to offer us anything more than information."

Rimaldi spoke sharply. "You contacted the local Voudon cult?"

"Yes. They are the ones who told us Streng's name."

"Father, you are too open in your discussions. Our magical order is a secret one, and now I find that you have brought the local voodoo cult into your confidence."

"My apologies, Father, but I thought that they might have some information for us."

"Information can come with too high a price. No doubt your motivations were right, but you must be more careful." Rimaldi softened his tone. "Nonetheless, your achievements have been remarkable. To know the name of the leader of the group and where they meet may prove to be of immense value to us." He paused. "What of this nun?"

"Sister Mary Brigid has been here for over ten years and is a nurse and teacher. I am certain that her gifts are hereditary. She was born in western Ireland. When the famine came, she was about seven years old and was sent to a convent to assure her survival, so she was never trained. Most of her family died in the famine. Her abilities are strong enough that I think she could be of use in our ritual."

"The ritual I have planned is one that requires immense discipline. I do not think it wise to incorporate the untrained, regardless of the strength of their gifts."

For a moment, Benito considered offering additional proofs of Brigid's abilities, but he refrained. He had promised not to share too much of what had passed between himself and Brigid. Benito bowed his head in assent. Rimaldi's reaction had told him that the Jesuit might not be receptive to further argument.

Benito said, "I have begun to train her in the rudiments of shielding. I think she may be in danger, since she was there the night that Sister Francis died."

"It's all right to continue her training, but don't let it diminish the time that might be spent more productively."

"Of course."

Rimaldi asked, "Do you think there is any value to be gained in my questioning this nun?"

"I believe I have all of the information that we will find of use, but I have made arrangements for her to be relieved of her duties and assigned to me."

"Then we shall let that stand for now. I may have Sister Angela speak with her. Sometimes a woman can find out more from a woman than a man." Rimaldi changed the topic. "When is Sister Angela expected?"

"Tomorrow morning."

"Excellent. You will meet her?"

"I have already arranged it," Benito replied.

"She will not be in her habit. I am concerned that our opponents may gain knowledge of what we are doing. Until I have both her and Father Kirk to bolster us, we are vulnerable. So I have asked both of them to wear conventional clothing for their journey. And don't take my criticism with regard to the voodoo community too severely. You have done well. I am glad that you were the first to arrive."

"Thank you, Father Provincial."

Rimaldi stood. "Unless there is something else, I think it is time to find my room and then see the bishop."

Benito said, "I will take you to your room." As he guided Rimaldi, he was glad that he had not told his superior that it was Brigid who had visited the *mambo*.

CHAPTER SEVENTEEN

RIMALDI sat alone in his room late into the night, enjoying the carafe of excellent wine that had awaited him on his return from dinner. He had much to keep him awake. Since his arrival, he had not been given enough time to think through the problem facing him and his small coterie of mages. The bishop had invited him to dinner during their lunch. Rimaldi had joined the bishop at seven, unaware until he arrived that the dinner was rather formal, with the monsignor and several of the parish priests joining them. The food and wine were superb, and, as often happens when such is the case, the diners lingered long. Rimaldi had hidden his restiveness, but was glad when the dinner finally adjourned at ten.

Rimaldi was not a man who was easily frightened, but the present situation caused him concern. Much of his anticipation of the coming battle had faded from him. A powerful demon, backed by a long-established coven of magicians, was the worst possible opponent. Their opponents might even have spies embedded in the cathedral staff, as they seemed to know a great deal about the daily routine, even the time that the mother superior made her nightly rounds.

Along with the wine, fresh-cut flowers brightened his room. The seriousness of his purpose made them seem out of place, but they were undoubtedly well meant. He slowly enjoyed a second glass of claret, careful not to overindulge when his arcane skills might be needed.

He finished his wine and went to bed. He had set everything in motion to confront the opponent. Tomorrow he would seek additional information. For now, there was nothing more he could do but pray.

When he awoke early the next day, he saw that the wineglass that he had been using had been shattered. It had not been knocked to the floor, merely shattered where it sat. He extended his senses and realized that the opposition had left a calling card. They were showing that they could send a projection into his room, a projection potent enough to shatter glass, without waking him. The broken wineglass was a chilling display of power and sophistication.

Rimaldi remembered that Benito had been visited in the night. Now Rimaldi had had his own visitor. Combined with all the other events, their opponents' actions meant that they were very confident of their own abilities. Rimaldi began to suspect that their confidence may not be unjustified. Their range of magical abilities was broader than that of any opponent he had faced. He dressed slowly, trying to push suspicion and fear from his mind before beginning his day.

BENITO stood on the platform awaiting the 9:10 train. He paced up and down, absorbed in his thoughts. However, he was not too absorbed to notice that the same young man who had been at the station the day of Rimaldi's arrival was again present at the station. Benito realized that this man's presence on two different days was an unlikely coincidence.

Daniel, as usual, was there to handle the luggage. Like many in his community, he served two masters. His other was the *mambo.* He was a Voudon *hounsis,* a student. He was trained well enough to be able to detect that Father Rimaldi had been what Daniel would call "stormy." Daniel didn't especially like him, but this Benito fellow was all right. Tonight the *mambo* would hear all he knew.

The rear car of the train was approaching the station. It was slowing as the flagman signaled the engineer where he should stop. Benito and Daniel awaited the train near the station, unsure of where the nun would descend. At last the train came to rest with a sigh of steam. The doors were opened, and the passengers began descending to the platform. As part of one of the main passenger runs from the north, this train was occupied by all manner of travelers.

Three cars forward, a woman descended to the platform. She was hardly to be missed. The green silk traveling dress and matching hat that she wore spoke of wealth and sophistication. Her lustrous dark brown hair surrounded a truly remarkable face, filled equally with humor, intelligence, and beauty. After directing the train porter where to stack her luggage, she set off down the platform toward the station. When her eyes fell on Benito, she smiled and approached him.

"Father Benito?"

"Ah," he stammered, "yes?"

"Wonderful. I was hoping they would have you meet me."

"And you are?"

"Sister Angela, of course." She beamed. "Oh, and you've been kind enough to bring a porter. How gracious." She beckoned to Daniel. "Come, young man. I have brought a few things with me and your help would be appreciated."

She turned and headed back to where her bags were stacked, with a smiling Daniel in tow. Benito could only shake his head and follow this unusual nun.

Sister Angela pointed out her bags to Daniel, who was more than ready to carry them anywhere. Daniel didn't think that he had ever seen a woman quite as beautiful as Sister Angela, yet it was more than her beauty and natural dignity that set her apart. Her sense of completeness, of containment, reminded him of Esmerelda.

Benito led the way to the bishop's carriage. As Daniel loaded the bags onto the carriage, Angela watched him closely. Daniel took every opportunity offered to look into her darkly luminous eyes. When he finished loading the carriage, she placed a silver dollar in his hand, an absurdly large tip, and something passed between their eyes, a glance of recognition. Daniel realized that he had let his guard down a little too much with Sister Angela. He had looked into her eyes too often, using skills of looking he had learned from the *mambo,* and Angela had discovered that he was studying magic. Strangely, he also knew that she was not troubled by it, because she herself was a magician. He would tell Esmerelda what he'd seen. This nun had power.

Benito saw the look that had flashed between them, but said nothing as he helped Angela into the carriage. They sat opposite each other as Daniel cracked the whip over the horses, and they moved off toward the archdiocese.

"Sister," Benito said, "that was quite an entrance."

She looked at him for a moment and then burst out laughing. When she saw the embarrassment on his face, she laughed harder. Recovering, she spoke. "First, when we are away from the formality of the Church, please call me Angela."

"As you should call me Luis."

"Wonderful. But you see, Luis," and she leaned over to whisper conspiratorially, "when our superior says to travel in conventional clothes, it gives me an opportunity to indulge a bit by wearing something a little better than a habit. I easily confess to the sin of having been raised by a wealthy Italian family. I take pleasure in dressing myself well. Besides, my father's family has given enough to the Church over the centuries to help me escape criticism."

"I would say that your dress is far beyond 'a little better than a habit.'" He had caught a whiff of her perfume as she had leaned close to him. The herbalist in him recorded the scents that he could identify, but there were smells there that were beyond his knowledge.

Angela smoothed the folds in her dress. "Well, this attire is normal for me. After all, I'm traveling under my father's name, as Angela Benelli. On my mother's side I am a Dellamorte." She sat back onto the cushions, pleased that the name had created a flash of recognition in Luis.

He, enjoying the banter, exhaled loudly, fell back on the cushions of the carriage, and theatrically exclaimed, "Madre de Dios, I am surrounded!"

She looked at him questioningly.

It was his turn to smile. "Here I am in a carriage with a daughter of the first family of Strega, while back at the archdiocese I have assigned to me another nun who is a seventh-generation Irish witch."

"Now that is fascinating. You must tell me more."

He looked pointedly toward the driver sitting in the front of the open carriage and said, "We have much to discuss once we get to the archdiocese."

She understood his warning and changed the topic. "This is certainly a beautiful city, with much kinder weather for this time of year than I have endured in Pennsylvania."

"Ah, yes, you are from Sicily. I am a native of Florida, so the weather here is similar to my own."

"So you were there before the Americans took over?"

"I was born after the departure of the Spanish, but I did experience some of the changes. My native tongue is Spanish, but it has become necessary for us all to learn English."

"The unification of Italy is causing changes in my homeland, but not as severe as the ones in Florida. At least we will not have to learn another language."

Keeping a carefully feigned expression on his face he said, "But won't you have to learn Italian?"

She laughed out loud. "Well said, Father." She appreciated his delicate skewering of the Sicilian dialect of Italian, which northern Italians often considered unintelligible.

With her laughter still floating in the air, she saw the cathedral towering over them and assumed a more demure air. "Ah well, back to black-and-white."

"Yes, I think we should get you changed before your meeting with Father Rimaldi. I doubt your dress would cause even an eyebrow to be raised by Mary Margaret, the mother superior, so we can pay our call in our present attire, but I fear our Jesuit might not take your rather liberal interpretation of 'secular attire' with the same equanimity."

Daniel slowed the horses to a stop at the front entrance to the convent. Helping her down from the carriage, Benito said, "Now let us see if we can astonish the mother superior."

AS convent protocol required, Sister Angela first met with the mother superior, who felt safer with each addition to the group of Catholic mages. Sister Angela's unconventional attire had little effect on Margaret, though it set quite a few tongues wagging in the confines of the convent. After a brief meeting, the mother superior and Benito escorted Sister Angela to the large four-bed guest room of the convent, which was adjacent to the main dormitory and close to the mother superior's quarters. The guest room was used for visiting nuns, and, on occasion, for the reverend mother of the order.

After changing into her habit, Sister Angela met with Benito for over an hour. When they were done, she realized the gravity of the situation and was glad that others would be with them soon. Before seeing Rimaldi, she returned to the mother superior's office, mindful as she was to the niceties of convent etiquette. She needed to ask the mother superior to move Brigid, as Benito was concerned for her safety. Brigid would be safer with Angela in the guest room than she would be in the convent dormitory.

Margaret looked up at the light tap on the door. "Enter."

Angela lifted the latch and entered the office.

"Ah, Sister Angela, welcome," Margaret said, eyeing her visitor. "You do look a bit more like a nun after changing."

Sister Angela smiled. "Well, it will be easier to move around the cloister without causing a disturbance. Besides, women's fashions are decorative, but they are less comfortable than a habit. They are designed to attract men, so they are rather constricting."

The mother superior's mouth turned up in a grin. "I see you have some humor about you."

"A necessary thing in the different worlds in which I move."

"Please have a seat. And, as for names, Margaret is more to my liking for those not under my jurisdiction."

Angela took the offered chair. "For me, 'Angela' will do fine."

"How can I help you?"

"I would like to know more about Sister Brigid."

"I'm not surprised."

"Why not?"

"During the war, we found that Brigid had special talents. She seemed to know who would survive and who would not. Maybe she would have been burned at Salem, but in a wartime hospital, with too few drugs and doctors and too many patients, she was a godsend. As her talent became known, she became part of the normal party that sorted the casualties as they arrived."

Sister Angela shivered. "That is a job I would never want—deciding who will live and who will die."

"That's not really what a sorting party does. They decide who can benefit from medical care and who is too injured to be helped. In war, wasting time on those who will not survive will result in the deaths of other men, those who might have been saved. It doesn't make the task any less brutal, but it does make it a task that is done to serve life."

"So she has a talent?"

"Actually more than one. But the others are harder to pin down. She seems to appear just when she is needed. Sometimes she will enter a room and it is as if no one saw her enter. It isn't that she tries to conceal herself; it's just that she moves with uncommon lightness of step and doesn't draw attention. In general, there's an air about her that causes gossip among the other nuns, especially the Irish ones."

"Why is that?"

"You have to understand that the Irish are notoriously superstitious."

"That I already know, but I am not certain they are any more superstitious than Sicilians."

"It's her eyes," the mother superior said. "When she is listening to you, watching you, she seems to be totally involved in what she's doing. The effect is amplified by the unusually deep blue of her eyes. Her focused attention is unnerving for those who feel that they have secrets to hide."

Angela commented, "I can see that little escapes your notice."

"Thank you, but I'm not so certain. There is so much to take note of and so little time to see it."

Angela paused before asking her next question. "Mother Superior, there is one thing that I would like to ask of you."

"What's that?"

"Father Benito believes that Sister Brigid may be in some danger. She might be safer if she were to stay with me in the convent's guest room."

"I understand. I will have her move. Besides, it will place her closer to me. Frankly, I'm glad that you and the others are here. The killings of Mr. Richardson and Sister Mary Francis have been shocking. Adding my own experience to that list makes certain things real that I am reluctant to accept or to believe."

Sister Angela waited for Margaret to continue, knowing that she had more to say.

The mother superior went to stand by the window in her office. The light slanted across her face. She had spent many hours thinking of what she might say to one of the Church's magicians, given the opportunity. Angela was the first person with whom she felt able to speak. "Most laypeople have their religious faith in a convenient place. They take it out on Sunday and burnish it, perhaps get a little emotional at Christmas and Easter, but, by and large, it is a matter of social custom. For us in the Church it is different. For some, like me, we do our duty to God. For some, like Sister Francis, belief is a tangible thing. They have a deep abiding faith that there is a God and there is a Satan, and that the Church is the only protection against the darkness that threatens to swallow us.

"But her faith did not protect her. She is dead, murdered within the walls of my convent, and I have been haunted by an apparition in the night."

"I know," Angela said quietly.

"I am frightened. What really is lurking out there in the darkness? What can come and kill us? How can we defend ourselves against what we cannot see?"

"I understand."

"Do you really?"

"Yes." Angela paused for a moment to gather her thoughts. "My group of magicians stays silent because some people would not believe we existed. But when we come to do the work that we do, there is no disbelief, because people have experienced something that has terrified them. They have been touched by a dark presence. For me, I have seen the creatures of the darkness. I know they are there. They have taken form before me and come for me. My skills have protected me." Angela looked at the mother superior with compassion. "It is terrible to face even a hint of the darker creatures without the knowledge that there is a power that can defeat them. You have been exposed to the darkness. You now believe in it. But you have not yet had time to adjust your knowledge to also include a different idea of the divine, not a cold statue in the chapel, but one who can wield a sword and cut down the darkness. I am more fortunate. I have seen evil destroyed. The reassurance that I can offer is to tell you that there is power to defeat the darkness and protect you."

"Thank God," Margaret said. The emotions that she had held largely in check since the night of her haunting threatened to overwhelm her. She trembled, remembering her desperate fear.

"Margaret, the Church is assembling the best that we have to fight this creature and the men who summoned it. Now that a few of us are here, the attention of our opponents will not be devoted to frightening you, but to trying to dissuade us from attacking them. They will not succeed. They will be defeated."

Margaret looked at the other nun. "You are certain?"

"That is always how it has been before."

Margaret regained control of herself, reassured by Angela's certainty.

Angela smiled. "And if there is more you wish to discuss, you and I will find the time to do it."

"I look forward to it."

Angela bowed and let herself out of the office, wishing that she was as confident as she had pretended to be.

Margaret sat in her office, thinking that her faith might well become stronger from all that she had seen and all that she would see. Sister Angela was right. The real terror was not the evil that lies in the darkness but believing in that evil without believing in the power to stop it.

THE interview with the mother superior had made clear to Angela how frightened the woman was. If the mother superior, with all of her experience, was this frightened, how much more frightened might the others on the cathedral staff be? Angela knew that fear was a difficult thing to control. It often led to hysteria, especially in the close quarters of a convent. Their opponents might attempt to make use of it.

Angela went to report to the Father Provincial. Rimaldi greeted her warmly when she entered the workroom.

"Are you settled in from your journey?"

"Quite well, Father. I'm in the convent's guest quarters. Father Benito has informed me of the recent events."

"Good. We will be taking a walk after Father Kirk arrives. I don't intend to walk past the house on Saint Julian at night, merely observe it in the day. Still, I think it prudent to wait for Father Kirk."

"Father Benito told me about the house and his visit to it. Should we go at all? I am wary of our opponents."

"Yes, but I hope to escape their notice by limiting our actions to observing and working no magic near them."

"Will that be enough?"

"I think so," he said confidently, and changed the subject. "Has Father Benito told you about Sister Brigid?"

"Yes, he has," she replied. "Father, I hope you don't object, I have asked the mother superior to move Sister Brigid to the guest room with me. Both Father Benito and myself feel that she may be in some danger."

"I think that is wise," he replied.

"Thank you. I will speak with her this evening."

"One other thing, Sister. You should review the Ritual of Solomon."

"The Ritual of Solomon?" She could not keep the edge of disbelief from her voice.

"Yes," Rimaldi replied firmly.

"That rite can be difficult to manage, even unstable," she said.

"I know, but it is quite potent."

"As you will," she acquiesced, though she felt that there was danger in choosing that ritual.

"Good. We can speak further tomorrow."

"Certainly, Father." She bowed and left the room.

JAKOB Streng arrived home before three in the afternoon. He barely had time to pour his customary bourbon before Jarred Cawthorne arrived. Essie showed him directly to the parlor.

As soon as she had shut the door, Cawthorne turned to Streng. "So what is the problem, Jakob?"

"The Church has summoned their principal exorcist."

Jarred grunted his disapproval. "Mind if I get a drink?"

"Not at all; I should have offered."

"I didn't give you time."

Cawthorne moved to the sideboard. Nearing fifty, he was ten years younger than Streng, but the difference was far greater than mere years implied. Streng was a heavily built man. In his youth, his broad shoulders had been much admired by young women, but, as he grew older, his girth had grown. He was not fat, at least not by the standards of the time, but he was what might be graciously called "prosperous." Jarred Cawthorne was a man who ran to height, not weight. Well over six feet, he towered over most men in the town. But he remained thin, partially because he would rather drink than eat. His favorite pastimes were riding and hunting. His public eccentricity was a penchant for slitting the throat of the game he shot rather than allowing one of his boys to do it, as would be more seemly. He never minded getting blood on his hands.

"So that fool Richardson has managed to create trouble, after all," Cawthorne commented.

They heard a knock at the door. They waited as Essie brought in the third member of the party, Micah Breeding. He was a little younger than Cawthorne, and his skin was so dark that he was rumored to be part Creek Indian. He moved with a threatening grace and spoke little. Though of normal height, he was a forbidding man. As more than one person had said, Breeding simply "looked dangerous."

Before Essie could leave, Streng stopped her. "Essie, lay out a cold supper for three in the kitchen. Then send the staff home. You can also leave as soon as you like."

"Thank you, Mr. Streng." Essie knew that Streng wanted the house empty of all of the servants, including her. She closed the door behind her, curious, but knowing it would be too risky to linger with all three of them in the house.

Streng looked at his new guest. "Something to drink, Micah?"

"Yes." He moved to the sideboard and poured himself a shot of whiskey as Cawthorne sat in one of the empty chairs. Streng was surprised. Micah rarely drank, preferring to take his pleasure from cocaine or laudanum.

"Something serious, Micah?" Cawthorne asked.

"Not certain. You probably have more information. I'll listen for a while."

Streng knew it was senseless to press him. Micah would add what he knew, quickly and efficiently, but only when he was ready.

"The Catholic Church has brought their principal exorcist here," began Streng. "He is Father Rimaldi, a Jesuit from Baltimore. One of our brother groups told me some time ago that he heads an order of magicians within the Church. Father Benito is also one of this order and another may have already arrived."

"Another is here," Micah interjected. "She arrived on the nine-ten train. I happened to be at the station and saw Benito meeting a woman, a very beautiful woman. If she is a nun, she neither dressed nor acted the part, but the fact that Benito met her with the bishop's carriage implies that she was a visitor of some note, so I would think that she may be part of their group."

"I agree," Streng said.

"Are they a threat to us?" Cawthorne asked.

"The actions we've taken, even killing Sister Francis, have drawn no magical response," Streng said. "They don't seem to be especially powerful, but they do not scare easily. I paid a visit to Rimaldi's room last night and left a reminder of their vulnerability. Still, they have not responded in any way."

"Do other groups like ours have any history with these Catholic magicians?" Cawthorne asked.

"Two of our groups have drawn their attention over recent years," Streng said. "Neither of those chapters had a spirit as potent as Belial at their disposal, and the problem was dispensed with quickly. In the trading of magic, none of our members was hurt, and two priests died. Apparently, the Church didn't have the stomach for more. Their magic presents no threat."

"So we can inflict damage on them," Micah said.

"Yes," Streng said. "If we were able to kill some of the members of their group, perhaps even before they assemble for their ritual, then it is likely that we would see little more interference from them. After they depart, we will remain quiet for a while."

"Is it worth the risk?" Micah asked.

"They are not impotent. They may have considerable ability when their full number is assembled. They might find out something that will lead them to us. Beyond that, Richardson might have talked."

Cawthorne said, "We will need to be more careful in the future."

"Agreed," Streng said. "As for our current course of action, I think that we need to gather information. Then we should strike before their full number is assembled. I intend to summon Belial on the first night of the waning moon."

"The twenty-sixth?" Cawthorne asked.

Streng nodded. "Monday night."

"What should we do?" Micah asked.

"I would attack one of the members of the group, but we should consult with Belial. He may have a different idea."

Cawthorne and Breeding nodded in reply. They would meet again in a few days and summon their creature. All of them felt a sense of fearful anticipation at seeing the demon again. They anticipated the feeling of sharing in its immense power. They feared the drained and hollow feeling that inevitably followed close contact with the creature.

Streng escorted his guests out into the night. Neither was interested in joining him for supper. Not hungry himself, he went upstairs to his study. He had not shared with the two men the full scope of his activities. He had directed Lilith to observe Benito, though she had learned almost nothing. Lilith had also aided him on his visit to Rimaldi's room. The Jesuit had not awakened, but Streng was not certain if it was the combined strength of himself and Lilith or Rimaldi's depth of sleep that had been the key difference.

Streng poured himself a glass of port and considered their plan. He felt an ache deep in his bowels when he thought of Belial. He knew the next days would be very taxing. The demon's connection to him was becoming stronger and more debilitating over time. As the years passed, the demon's presence was draining his vitality.

He did not like his train of thought, preferring to remember the pleasures that came courtesy of Belial and his own magic. The power he held over others was a heady pleasure. His sexual profligacy, lack of concern for others, and success in business were ample rewards for the drains on his energy and health.

Jakob needed a diversion. He stepped over to the door that led to Sally's room and opened it. The light spilling from the study illuminated Sally. She was not asleep. Her nude form was propped on one elbow. She had been expecting him.

He took a moment to enjoy the beauty of her sixteen-year-old body. Nothing sagged, not even her breasts, as she lay on her side. She was the perfect age, thought Streng, and she was becoming more avid for the varied pleasures the men offered her.

"I was hoping you'd like a little comfort tonight, Jakob."

He sat on her bed. "Undress me."

She slid out of bed, stood in front of him, and began unbuttoning his shirt. As she did, she leaned over next to his ear and whispered, "Is there anything particular you'd like me to do?"

Streng smiled through a haze of her jasmine perfume and allowed her to undress him. When she finished, he put his hands on her shoulders and brought her to her knees in front of him. She knew what was expected and smiled. As she bent her head to her work, Jakob ran his hands through her hair. They came to rest on the girl's shoulders. A delicate network of healed scars made a little spiderweb on the back of her left shoulder. A matching, though fainter, network was on her left shoulder. "Yes," he thought to himself, "Jarred is right handed."

Jarred was an artist at inflicting pain. He had told Streng that the first time that he had whipped her, he had expected her to cry and scream, which she did most engagingly. He had not expected her to enjoy the pain as well. Later she had told him that her father was fond of the belt and she had made herself learn to endure the pain. Over time, that endurance had become something else. She now enjoyed it when it had the overtone of sex. She had told Jarred, "Just don't mark me too much."

Jakob leaned his head back and groaned. The little girl was an artist.

❧

AFTER dinner Angela waited in the convent's guest quarters for Brigid's arrival. Angela had raised the intensity of her Sight to prepare herself for the other nun's arrival, hoping to learn as much as she could in advance of talking with her. She was aware of Brigid's approach long before she could hear her steps.

Brigid entered, carrying a small valise. She saw another nun sitting on one of the cots, her mouth open in astonishment. Brigid thought she had startled the woman, whom she assumed to be Sister Angela.

"I'm sorry, Sister; I didn't mean to surprise you," Brigid said.

Angela regarded her levelly, coolly, though her heart was racing. Then she reassured her guest, "Please, Sister Brigid, come in."

Brigid selected the nearest cot and set down her valise. Angela's eyes never left her.

"Forgive me for not introducing myself, Brigid. I am Angela." She stood and walked to Brigid. "My manners are getting terrible," she said more conversationally.

"And were you using some secret magical technique to peer into my soul?" Brigid said, half-joking.

"As a matter of fact, yes. For all the good it did."

Brigid looked at her questioningly.

Angela said, "I must apologize. I had intended to do that without your knowing. Normally, I would not have used my abilities without your permission, but these are unusual times."

"I have noticed," Brigid commented dryly.

"You have a great talent. Regardless of training, that talent can be seen by someone with the skill to do it. In looking as I did, I customarily learn something. In your case I was unable to see anything, since I was looking too hard."

"I don't understand."

"Do you know what happens when a photograph is overexposed?"

"Yes; you can't see much of anything except white."

"It's much the same. If you are prepared to look closely at someone with the Sight, as I was, and she turns out to be a potent hereditary, you are unable to see any detail, only light. Benito told me you were an hereditary, but I did not expect the level of power that I saw."

"Please, Sister Angela, I am nervous enough already."

Angela indicated they should sit on their cots. "This must seem rather strange to you."

"Yes and no. It is strange because everything around me is moving very quickly. A month ago I was a nun with some odd gifts. Now I'm told that I am a person with powers. On the other hand, no, it's not strange. I saw things in my childhood, and they have prepared me in some way for what is occurring now."

"Your family is like mine," Angela said.

"What do you mean?" Brigid was intrigued.

Angela composed herself. "I am also an hereditary. I come from an old family of Sicilian witches. They have been practicing magic, *magia,* for as long as anyone can remember, which in Sicily is a very long time. My great-grandmother's conversion to Catholicism was an important event in Sicily."

"Your family remained pagan until then?"

"Yes, though the priests were not very pleased. My family was able to remain non-Christian because they were feared and respected, but the triumph of the Church was only a matter of time. My grandmother realized that fact and took the practical course of publicly becoming Catholic, though she continued to train her children in the old ways."

"My great-aunt never converted," Brigid said. "She remained a worshiper of the old gods."

"I have heard that was true in the remote parts of Ireland. Why did you become a nun?"

"The famine was killing thousands. My family sent me to the Church so I wouldn't starve."

"Do you stay in touch with your family?"

A hint of anger came into Brigid's voice. It was an old anger, one that she had endeavored to forget. "My family was destroyed by the famine. Both the English and the Church sent very little help. They blamed the famine on the 'lazy Irish.'" She relaxed her voice. "Perhaps the Church didn't understand how dire the situation was. So many died and so many left that staying in touch with anyone during the famine years was difficult. Mail was always unlikely to get through.

"One of my brothers, Benedict, survived the famine, but we lost touch with him. I don't even know if he is still alive. In that kind of chaos, it is easy to lose people. My older sister, Siobhan, still lives near where we were born. My other two brothers died, as did my great-aunt, mother, and father. In my area of Ireland, one in two died from hunger or disease. My sister and I stay in touch by the occasional letter, but the distance is great. We are not that close. I was so little when I left."

"I didn't know how bad it was."

"Few outside of Ireland did."

They sat in silence for a moment. The reaction was common when others heard how devastating the famine had been in Ireland. The percentage of the Irish population that had died from the famine was similar to the devastation wreaked by the Black Plague centuries before.

"So why did you take holy orders?" Brigid asked.

"Though our family is publicly Catholic, that is not our true faith. We believe in the old gods. My mother chose me to enter the Church and find if it still presented a danger to us. In general, it does not. There are, however, other things that threaten all of us, all of humanity; there are dark spirits and people foolish enough to unleash them.

From within the Church's magicians, I can lend my skills to the destruction of these things. So I remain."

"Is the power of this order enough to deal with this thing that has come here?"

"I don't know. The demon we are facing here is powerful. Rimaldi seems confident that it can be dealt with, but I am less certain. Still, this group of magicians is the most potent that I am aware of. If there is any chance of defeating this creature, it lies with Rimaldi."

"Does Rimaldi know that you are not really a nun, I mean in the sense of what you believe?"

"No. Do not forget that Rimaldi is thoroughly a Christian. If he suspects the truth about me, he is ignoring it because he needs my strength for what we do. Rimaldi, or any honest magician for that matter, understands that magic is not limited to one faith or another. It is a skill, a craft in the truest sense."

"I don't understand."

Angela sighed. "Luis was right. You know so little." She paused. "I'll try to explain. There are three types of magical power. The first is personal ability. Almost everyone can do some things. Some can sense when a loved one dies or is in danger. Others can sense the health of an individual or the presence of spirits. Some are born with a high level of talent, like you were. We call them 'hereditaries,' since they almost always come from a family of recognized abilities.

"The second type of magic is ritual or ceremonial magic. To do it all you need is the ritual itself."

"Like exorcism?"

"Yes. All that is needed is a priest with the force of will and the courage to keep to the words of the ritual. He will be successful, unless the opponent is too strong. You can become much stronger if you have an aptitude for magic that is magnified by years of education, training, and discipline. In ceremonial magic, some rituals allow magicians to join their abilities together. The more magicians present, the stronger the magic. Ritual magic is based on formulae and incantations." Angela paused. "Then there is the magic that no one really understands, or, at least, we don't anymore."

Brigid felt a chill up her spine.

"The third magic is high magic. Much of it is something the magician simply 'knows' how to do. We don't know where high magic comes from, and we don't know how to awaken or strengthen it. The legends say that there once were trained high magicians. They supposedly worked alone. What they were capable of is like the old legends of the magicians who could destroy demons or lift tons of stone. Unfortunately, we no longer know how to train someone to allow high magical abilities to manifest.

"We would think that all of this talk about high magic was just nonsense, except that there have been too many instances of someone being able to perform the kind of magic that only a group of ceremonial magicians could normally accomplish."

"Such as?" Brigid asked.

Angela thought for a moment, seeming to evaluate Brigid, before answering. "When I was fourteen, I was wandering in the hills near my home in Sicily. My parents were not concerned that I was alone. No one would hurt a Dellamorte, at least not intentionally, but there are some in Sicily who do call upon dark forces, using *magia nera,* black magic, and I stumbled upon one such ritual.

"A shepherd and two women were sacrificing a lamb. I came across a hill as night was descending and saw them below me. A full moon had just risen, and I could see them as clearly as if it were daytime. They had scribed a circle on the ground and were casting herbs into a fire. The lamb was tethered near the fire and was bleating in fear. I knew I should not watch, but I did anyway. I could not make out their chant, but it did not sound like Italian or Latin. When the chant reached its zenith, the man seized the lamb and one of the women slit its throat and let the blood pour onto the fire. Out of the bloody smoke a dark form began to rise.

"I became frightened and screamed. All three turned to me, and the dark shape swept up the hill and wrapped itself around me. I felt like I was being crushed by oily smoke. I couldn't breathe. I was terrified.

"Then, from some knowledge I didn't know that I had, I reached down inside of me. I felt a sudden rush of power from within. As the power rushed out of my body, it passed through the dark form and shattered it. Some fragments of the dark being still remained. They coalesced, and it fled from me, rushing down the hill like a wind, back to the doorway the three had opened for it. One of the women stood between it and the fire, and she backed away from its approach, stumbling backward and falling into the fire. She screamed as the hot coals ignited her clothes. The creature vanished into the fire and returned to its own realm.

"I was dizzy and fell to my knees. I may have even blacked out for a few moments. When I looked up again, the woman was still screaming. Her two companions had dragged her out of the fire and were putting out the fire in her clothes. When they got the fire out, they lifted her up between them and stumbled away as rapidly as they could.

"My sister Lucia later heard that the woman who fell into the fire died that night. We never found out who the others were. Though the incident added to the legend of the Dellamortes, I didn't even know how I'd done what I'd done. The entire event had been an accident. A few days later an old man from a village near our home visited us. He was a shepherd and brought us a lamb as a gift.

"My mother met him at the door. He insisted on giving her the lamb and thanking us for saving his granddaughter. Apparently, the young man who had taken part in the ritual had enlisted the aid of two of the darker sisters of Strega to place a curse on the man's granddaughter, who had refused the young man's proposal of marriage. By accident, I had saved her from the curse. So the old man came with a gift and swore allegiance to the Dellamortes.

"It was all by accident, but I felt good about what I had done, though I had had no intent to kill the witch. Very little dark magic was done for some time in the surrounding area, since the Dellamortes had again proven that the villagers were under their protection."

Angela sat down again opposite Brigid. "So that is what high magic is like. It is a natural extension of personal power, but with unimaginably greater force. Learning how to harness that magic is the 'holy grail' of our order. In order to be a true high magician, one who can control the power at will, we surmise that you must be a hereditary, and you must know certain keys, certain mental disciplines. But we are guessing. It may be that all there is to high magic is some special ability that appears unpredictably. It may be that the legendary high magicians never really existed.

"If anyone once possessed the knowledge of the ways of high magic, no one knows them now. Even those like me, who have had a flash of high magical power, do not really understand what to do to make it reoccur. I and many others have searched for the keys to high magic, but we have all failed. Though my personal magical power is far greater than Rimaldi's, his overall power is greater than mine, because of his vast ritual knowledge. For now, ceremonial magic is the greatest power we know of."

Angela looked sadly at the floor, then once again looked up at Brigid. "So we do the best with what we have."

"Then you should come to Ireland."

"What do you mean?"

Brigid told Angela the story of the old man who had come to the village to stop a marauding demon.

Angela sat in astonishment when Brigid finished her story. "This was less than fifty years ago?"

"Yes."

"Do such men still exist?"

"I don't know. The man who came was very old. Perhaps he was the last of his kind."

"With such a magician," Angela said, "we could face any demon these people might summon."

"Even Satan himself?"

"There is no Satan," Angela said distractedly.

Brigid looked at her strangely. "You don't believe in Satan either?"

"Any magician should know that. There are evil and powerful things that can do all manner of harm, but there is no Lord of Evil whose power is nearly as great as that of the gods. If you could bring down only a fraction of the power of the divine, nothing that seeks to do ill could stand against you. The gods are not frivolous enough to allow such creatures to exist."

"Then why does Father Benito call them satanists?"

"It is convenient and matches doctrine. When Benito uses the term he means people who worship evil, who do magic to satisfy their own greed and desires. They seek to destroy, control, and even kill. Since they think the evil is named 'Satan,' they call on Satan, and evil responds. They, as any other magician, get what they ask for."

"Where does evil come from?"

"The great question," Angela said. "Some of the dark demons were created by magicians who fashioned them to do their bidding. Demons also come from hate, fear, and ignorance. When a large number of people hold any thought for a length of time, be it good or bad, they have the ability to create something. But most of these dark creatures simply 'are.' They exist, and we have no idea of their origins. Perhaps they hid in some fold of creation; perhaps they were mistakes. Perhaps they are combinations of ghosts or spirits that were misbegotten.

"Look at the thing that we are facing here. Potent magicians are calling up evil forces to do their bidding. Why? To gratify their own desires for power or dominance or promiscuity. Are they foolish enough to think that they will not eventually pay a price? No, but they might not believe that they will pay." Angela shrugged. "I cannot comprehend wishing to do evil. Ultimately, it is senseless."

The two sat in silence, absorbed in their own thoughts. Then

Angela remembered the thread of the conversation. "Brigid, if such a magician as the one you speak of were to still exist, how would we find him?"

"Father Benito said that the Church is unlikely to be able to call a man such as this. He would have too much to fear from the Church and would remain hidden."

"I understand," Angela said.

"But that doesn't really matter," Brigid said quietly. "I've done all that can be done to call him."

"What?" Angela replied. "How?"

"As shattered as Ireland may have been after the famine, there are still those who follow in the ways of the old gods. My sister knows of them, and I have written her. She will pass the message on, and perhaps it will reach the right person. I don't know if such a powerful magician still exists. And if there is one, I don't know if he would come. He may not wish to risk exposure by being in-volved." She sighed. "I wish there weren't so many 'ifs.'"

"Brigid, you know what it means if we fail?"

"Not really."

"Most of us would be killed."

"Even you?"

"Against the thing that we face, I might die as well. This creature is no minor demon called by a local shepherd. It is far more powerful. The ritual that Rimaldi has chosen also may leave us more vulnerable. It is the most powerful that we know, but it has a weakness. If it fails, the defenses that are part of the ritual fail as well. Each of us would be left with only our own protection."

"So we would succeed and survive or fail and likely die?"

Angela slowly nodded.

"And I," Brigid said, "am supposed to have all of this ability, but it is undeveloped and likely useless."

"What do you mean?"

Anger laced her voice. "I should have been trained. I should have learned how to use my abilities. Luis has awakened some of my capabilities, but everything else is still dormant, and you don't have enough time to teach me everything I need to know."

"We still have some time. . . ."

"But not what we should have had. When I listened to your story about the ritual you stopped, I couldn't help but think that you went home after that, surrounded by your family and people who could explain what had happened. I envy you for that. When I was fourteen, I was a novice, on my way to becoming a nun. By that age, I had learned to suppress my Sight and keep my abilities to myself."

"It wasn't your fault, Brigid."

"No, it wasn't," she admitted more calmly, "and there is another side to the coin. Staying with my family might have meant the death of my sister and brother. They had barely enough food to sustain two. One more person might have meant that all three starved. Or maybe we would all have survived, and I would have come into my birthright. Then I wouldn't be so powerless in the face of evil."

"And you still wouldn't be here to help us. You'd be in the far reaches of Western Ireland, not here."

Brigid smiled wanly. "There is that."

"Often the gods choose strange pathways for us."

Brigid noticed how easily she said "gods" and wondered what it might be like to say such a thing and not have the term bring confusion to her. This woman was so different from her, yet they shared so much in their heritage.

Angela sat, waiting for the next question, sensing the confusion in Brigid.

"Angela," Brigid said, "have you ever been with a man?"

"Of course."

Brigid had been timid in asking her question, afraid that the subject that had often come to her mind would be one that would offend another nun. The near casual answer that Angela gave shocked her. "You have?"

Angela smiled comfortably. "That is another advantage of only pretending to be a nun. In my religion, which I suspect should also be our religion, the pleasures of the flesh are not condemned."

"What about getting pregnant?" she blurted.

"There are herbs that let you avoid that."

"I . . . I am dumbfounded." Brigid fell silent, too astonished to continue.

"You shouldn't be," Angela said. "Even within the strictures of the Church, a few hundred years ago, some nuns and priests broke their vows of chastity with one another. It still happens, but rarely, and the nun is usually the one to suffer. In the older religions, there were goddesses and gods that took lovers, from both humans and their fellow gods. Passion was celebrated."

"But I was taught that the great goddesses were virgins."

"A convenient mistranslation. Yes, they were virgins in the Greek sense, which meant that they were not married. It didn't mean that they were sexually innocent."

"You and Luis are making me dizzy. I don't know where I stand anymore."

"You're confused."

"Very."

"That's a good thing. Socrates said that confusion is the beginning of wisdom," Angela said. "But sometimes, too many new pieces of information do tend to overwhelm us. Then we need time to think and someone to ask," Angela said. "Take all the time you want to think, and you can ask me anything. After all, we're sisters in a sense far different than the Church usually means it."

"How?"

"We are both hereditaries. There are few of us around. I, more than anyone, even Luis, can understand what you are because I am one as well."

Brigid sighed. Angela was right. She was overwhelmed, but she was also challenged. Her future was beginning to take shape, just as the *mambo* had promised. Brigid only hoped she would live long enough to be able to choose her destiny.

CHAPTER EIGHTEEN

Friday, October 23

FATHER Benito had just sat down to breakfast when the monsignor entered the dining hall with a tall blond man, heavily muscled and powerfully built. He gave every appearance of being a farmer. With an amused smile on his face, the monsignor led the man to Father Benito.

"It seems that another of your people has arrived, though a bit earlier than expected," the monsignor said.

The big man extended his hand. "I'm Father Steven Kirk."

Benito, recovering from his surprise, stood to take the offered hand. "Father Luis Benito. Pleased to meet you. We didn't expect you would arrive this early today."

"I was fortunate enough to catch an earlier train."

"Then please join me for breakfast."

"A fine idea," Kirk said, smiling.

The monsignor, who seemed to be taking a great deal of amusement from the situation, interceded. "I haven't eaten yet today, so I can help Father Kirk get his breakfast. Then we'll both join you."

Benito nodded. He watched as the monsignor led the other priest back to the serving tables at the back of the dining hall. Benito watched Kirk carefully as they fetched their food, and understood why Rimaldi had chosen him. The young man was a magical engine, capable of drawing up large amounts of raw power. Even though he did not appear to have the skill to focus it yet, he would be very valuable in a group working. Father Kirk's deep laughter sounded through the dining room as he and the monsignor stopped in front of the large pot of grits that was one of the central features of a southern breakfast. The two priests rapidly filled their platters and returned to the table.

They joined Benito, and each said grace over his food. The cheerful Kirk then looked to Benito and said, "The monsignor was kind enough to explain that the white substance was not Cream of Wheat, but grits."

"I hope you enjoy them," the monsignor said.

Kirk, moving with surprising delicacy for a big man, sampled the substance in question. He frowned slightly. "For something that is spoken of so often, these grits seem to taste mainly of butter and salt."

"That's what makes them the perfect breakfast food. They go just as easily with bacon and ham as they do with shrimp or crab," the monsignor said. "Here, sprinkle some crabmeat on them."

Kirk tried the crab on the grits and was pleasantly surprised by the combination. "Now that is excellent. We don't get too much seafood in the Midwest."

"I'd imagine not." Benito smiled, affected by Kirk's cheerful good humor. "I'm also beginning to appreciate the sense of humor of our order. Sister Angela arrived dressed as a grand lady, and you arrive dressed as a farmer."

"The apple never falls far from the tree," he remarked with a smile. "At least you have substantial breakfasts here. Some of the places I've visited with the Church have a smaller interpretation of breakfast than we do in farm country."

"We don't have that problem in Savannah," the monsignor said.

Benito commented, "You are younger than most of the members of our order. You are in your thirties?"

"Thirty-two, to be precise. At most gatherings, I feel like the child of the group."

"And you are a bit larger than the average scholar."

Steven laughed. It was a simple, uncomplicated sound. He was someone who took joy from life at every possible occasion. "I can see that Father Rimaldi did not warn you about me. Regardless of the Scottish name, one side of my family is pure Swedish, and the other is mostly good Bavarian Catholics. I grew up on a farm outside of Minneapolis. Tossing around hay bales when you're a youngster does a bit to build you up. I also help the occasional parishioner with a barn raising. Helping with building serves to forge a stronger bond with my parish. It is quite rural, outside of Duluth, Minnesota."

After their breakfast, Kirk and Benito went to the workroom. Benito had just finished giving Kirk a quick summary of the situation when Angela joined them. As she entered, Steven stood up from his chair and went to take her hand.

"I'm Father Steven Kirk." He smiled his infectious grin.

Angela gave a muted smile. "And I am Sister Angela."

"A pleasure to meet you. I am glad to be able to add my modest strength to that which is already gathered here."

"Help is always appreciated. I pray that our strength will be enough," Angela said.

"You doubt that?" Kirk asked.

"I am always careful to overestimate my opponent. It avoids unpleasant surprises," she answered.

Before anyone could frame a response, the door swung open to reveal Father Rimaldi and Monsignor Henry.

Father Kirk moved to shake his superior's hand. "Father Provincial, it is good to see you again."

"And I am glad to see you, as well. We are now armed well enough to begin some further explorations." He turned to the monsignor. "Monsignor Henry, thank you for taking care of Father Kirk this morning."

The monsignor smiled. "When we met, I was glad to discover

that he was a priest. When I first found him, he was asking for Father Rimaldi, and I feared you might have imported a large Swedish farmer as a bodyguard."

Steven, who had not yet changed his clothes, laughed loudly. "Good. A sense of humor. We shall all need one to strengthen us through this business."

The five sat around the table in their workroom.

Rimaldi began. "Have you and Father Benito discussed the problem we face?"

"Yes," Steven replied. "This demon could prove to be a fearsome opponent."

"It concerns me, as well, Steven," Rimaldi replied. "I have selected the Ritual of Solomon to use against the demon, but we are all aware of the challenges of that ritual."

"There cannot be any weak points in the triangles," Angela said, looking around the table. She, like the others, knew that the Ritual of Solomon used two groups of three to feed power to the central and seventh mage. Each group formed an equilateral triangle, with the two overlapping to form a Star of David. The groups maintained their own shielding and protected the center mage while feeding power to him. If either of the two groups failed, the other would continue the ritual, though with less power available to the primary magician. However, if one person failed in the remaining triangle, that would bring down the entire triangle, leaving everyone vulnerable.

"It is my intent," Rimaldi went on, "to be at the center. Benito and Angela will be in different triangles, and the other mages will work with them."

"Who else will join us?" Benito asked.

"Fathers Pascal, Siena, and Francisco. I know that you do not know Francisco, but he is quite potent."

Angela raised a question. "Isn't Pascal old for such a task? I know his health has been failing."

Rimaldi nodded. "Yes, but I saw him recently, and I think he is fit enough. Besides, there is no other who can do the job as well, considering the limited people that I have to choose from. Unless," he added, "you have a suggestion?"

She paused for a moment. "No, I don't. There is not another on this side of the Atlantic whom I would select."

Benito asked, "Could we wait for the Vatican to send us another?"

"I do not want this to continue for another month, and it would take that long for the Vatican to send a magician to replace Pascal."

They realized that there was risk in moving quickly, but knew that waiting would jeopardize more lives, perhaps even their own.

"Father Provincial?"

"Yes, Steven?"

"Are you certain that I am the best choice? After all, I am one of the newest members of the order. Perhaps someone with more experience would be better?"

"I have considered that, as well as your talents. You are very potent and can draw up a large amount of power to feed into the center. Besides, I will place our next most powerful people with you to help focus that energy."

Steven nodded in response.

Benito bit back his own thoughts. Steven was capable of drawing up power, but Brigid was much stronger. Again Benito regretted that she was not with them.

"Father Benito," Rimaldi continued, "has been able to discover where the opponents' rituals are held. We will have an advantage in that way. Also, we know the name of the leader of the group."

He looked around the table. "Then we are agreed on the Ritual of Solomon?"

There were no objections, merely uneasiness.

"There is one other topic that we must look into, and that is the matter of our own ritual's location. That is why I have asked the monsignor to join us. He will take us to a house that the diocese has available. There is a ballroom on the second floor for our ritual. The house is also large enough to serve as our lodging. I am of the opinion that we should move there as the time for our working approaches."

"Why not work from a more sanctified space within the cathedral?" Benito asked.

"I am concerned about the damage that might be done to the cathedral, and we are aware that the cathedral itself has provided little protection against our opponents. Also, I think that this house will offer us greater privacy."

"Then let's see this house," Angela said. "We should have a chance to feel its suitability in advance."

Rimaldi rose, bringing the others to their feet. Monsignor Henry led them from the room, down several corridors, and into the bright morning sunshine.

The house lay on the southern side of York Street, a few blocks from the cathedral. It was not quite a mansion, but it was large and imposing. Monsignor Henry opened the door and led them in. "It was a significant legacy left to us by Mrs. Grayson."

"Quite good fortune on your part," said Steven.

"Yes, it was. But our good fortune came about by her lack of it. Her husband and both of her sons died in the war. She rarely left the house after her second son's death. Her daughter-in-law tried to maintain a semblance of a normal life, even though she had lost her husband, but this house became too somber for her child.

"Seeing the problem, Mrs. Grayson was the first to recommend that her daughter-in-law return to her family. Mrs. Grayson died shortly afterwards, leaving the house to the Church. Her land and money she left in trust for her granddaughter. The daughter-in-law had no objection. She wanted no more to do with this house. She had lived here with her husband before the war, and the ghosts of happier times were always around her."

"Sad," Angela remarked. "It is a beautiful home."

"Yes," the monsignor said. "We have spent some time maintaining the house and adding furniture more suited to our purposes. The ballroom is empty, but there are five bedrooms, all fitted with beds for two, so it gives us a place to lodge visitors. It has been very useful over the past years." He looked from the foyer into the drawing room with its leather chairs, book-lined shelves, and large fireplace. "It can also be a good retreat from the business of the cathedral."

He turned back to the group. "Come, let me show you around."

The quarters for the staff, the pantry, and the cellar on the ground floor were simply empty rooms. The first floor held the drawing room, a formal dining room, a sitting room, a breakfast room, and the kitchen. The second floor of the house was divided by a hallway that ran perpendicular to the street. One side had two smaller hallways leading off of it. The front hallway gave access to the master bedroom, which looked out over York Street. It was twice as large as the other bedrooms. Off the rear hallway were four small bedrooms.

The other side of the house was occupied by the ballroom, which had a high ceiling and was approximately forty feet deep and thirty feet wide, east to west. The shorter side that faced north looked out over York Street, and the opposite wall overlooked the rear yard and coach house. The room was unobstructed by pillars. It seemed to be an excellent room for the planned ritual, the open space allowing them to position themselves to best advantage.

"So what do you think?" Monsignor Henry asked.

"It appears to be exactly what we need," Rimaldi responded. "Give us a few moments, please."

The four magicians all closed their eyes, searching with their skills for signs of disharmony in the building or the location. After a few minutes, they each emerged from their examination.

Sister Angela was the first to speak. "I sensed no real discord, though there is a pall of sadness and resignation over the house."

Benito added, "I sense much the same. The widow apparently had made peace with her situation before she died."

Rimaldi summed up the impressions. "You see, Monsignor Henry, sometimes a place can look right, but there might have been reasons that we might not want to use it. Fortunately, the atmosphere of this house is good. It will be quite suitable for conducting our rituals, so, assuming there are no objections, that is what we would like to do."

"The entire house is at your disposal," the monsignor replied. "I will have the staff make up the bedrooms. Will you require any staff while your people are in residence here?"

The Jesuit responded, "It would be better if only the members of our order are present for any length of time from now until we complete our business." He looked to the monsignor. "You, of course, are excepted from that, but I don't think you'll want to be here when we are actually working."

"That is a privilege I will happily forgo."

"Sister Angela, could you curtain off an alcove for yourself in the northeastern corner?"

"Of course," she replied.

"Then, Monsignor, if you'll excuse us, I think the four of us would like to meet in the drawing room for a few minutes. Then we'll return to the dining hall for lunch."

"Certainly. I will leave the key on the table in the foyer."

They followed the monsignor downstairs, and the four turned into the drawing room as he continued to the front door. In the drawing room they arrayed themselves in the comfortable chairs, all facing the center of the room.

"There is one other task we need to discuss," Rimaldi said. "We need to view the house where our enemies meet."

"Should all of us go?" Sister Angela asked.

"I think so. That would give us the best impression of their abilities. Do you think we shouldn't?"

"Father Benito has already been there. If we all go, we are likely to draw attention to ourselves."

"Father Benito has much to gain from a second look. And you, Sister, have not seen it at all. I think the risk of being noticed is well justified. Any other objections?"

No one spoke.

"Good. Then we will meet in our workroom at the archdiocese

tomorrow morning at ten." He rose. "I will return to my studies for now."

Father Kirk rose as well. "I have some unpacking to do. I also need to change into more appropriate attire."

The two men left together. Angela and Luis were left alone in the drawing room. They listened to the conversation of Kirk and Rimaldi as they disappeared down the street.

"I am not happy," Angela said.

"Our superior is a little," he paused, "impervious."

"Luis, I do not know you well, so perhaps I am speaking out of turn, but he seems resistant to suggestions."

"I have known him a long time, and it's his Achilles' heel."

"In this case, it may prove deadly for all of us. The Ritual of Solomon is powerful, but it is dependent upon everyone doing his task without fail. What concerns me even more is his refusal to bring Brigid into the ritual."

"So you have discussed that with him as well?"

"You mean to say that you made the same suggestion?" Angela asked.

"Yes," Benito replied.

"Given two weeks to train her, which we apparently have, she would be able to add more power to our ritual than all but a few members of the order, especially that doddering Pascal."

"Angela," he said with a slight tone of rebuke, "Father Pascal is one of our most knowledgeable members."

"When was the last time you saw him?"

"Three or four years ago."

"I saw him three months ago. He has slipped badly in the last few years. It took him some time to remember my name. I am worried that he might not be able to maintain concentration during the ritual."

"Do you wish me to bring it up with Rimaldi?"

"Do you think it would do any good?" she said.

He shook his head slowly.

She changed the subject. "You know we're being watched."

"Both physically and magically," he replied.

"Magically?" she said, alarmed.

"I don't think it is constant, but I have detected an observer, faintly, on more than one occasion. I sense someone's attention focused on me, and, if I attempt to examine it, it vanishes."

"That worries me. Our opponents have strong abilities. I was talking about physical observers," she said.

"I saw a young man at the train station when I was picking up both you and Father Rimaldi. I assume he is with the satanists."

"I didn't notice him," Angela said.

"So to whom were you referring?"

"The porter that you brought with you to the train station."

"Daniel?" he asked.

"Yes. And he has enough magical training to attempt to assess me."

He shook his head with an expression akin to resignation. "I don't believe it."

"You don't believe me?"

"No, no, Sister. That's not what I meant. I don't know if Brigid told you, but I sent her on an errand to discover if there was an active Voudon cult in Savannah."

"And there is one," she stated with no surprise in her voice.

"Yes. Brigid met with their *mambo,* who turned out to be an unexpected ally. She is Streng's housemaid, and she took the job with him to be able to have as much knowledge as possible about what he was doing. From what you're telling me, she is also having her members keep watch on us. I can only assume that he is one of them."

"Can they aid us in the working?"

"They are too afraid of Streng to be involved. Besides, Father Rimaldi does not want them involved."

"Why?" she said sharply.

"He was angry that I had contacted the Voudon followers here.

He felt that I had not observed proper discretion. But it was from them that I learned Streng's name."

"Observing his niceties could prove dangerous."

"Well, he doesn't know that I was not the one to talk with the *mambo*. It was Brigid who met with her."

"Brigid's beginning to interest me more and more."

"She has unexpected depth."

"That is certain. I wonder if she could gain me an audience with the *mambo*? I have always wanted to meet one."

"I think she could arrange it. The Voudon followers here don't like priests very much, but seem to be quite comfortable around nuns." He paused. "But you're not worried about meeting followers of voodoo?"

"Why? They serve the same gods, regardless of what they may call them."

"Gods? Sister, are you a nun or a witch?"

"Am I a Benelli or a Dellamorte?"

He paused before hesitantly saying, "Both?"

"The right answer."

Benito knew that the situation in Savannah was more complex than he had suspected. Disturbingly, he was also finding that his secret order of magicians had secrets, even from each other. Angela had taken a risk to reveal so much to him. Then again, Benito himself had withheld information from Rimaldi that he had shared with Angela. His sharing of information so easily with her and not Rimaldi bothered him, though he understood why. He was a person who trusted his gut feelings. Angela's openness encouraged him to speak freely. Rimaldi's self-assurance mated with his dedication to doctrine often made him difficult to talk with. The lack of communication could impact their work. He did not mention any of this to Angela; instead he said, "I think I will avoid further complexities and go back to reviewing rituals."

"For myself," she said, "I will see if I can meet this *mambo*. Come to think of it, our mysterious Daniel might be a more direct route than Brigid. Where does Daniel normally spend his afternoons?"

"In the stables."

"Well, I seem to have a sudden desire to visit them." She rose and let herself out of the house, leaving Benito alone to think about the ritual Rimaldi had chosen.

Benito remembered the ritual well. The interlocked triangles of the Ritual of Solomon were the distinguishing feature of the ancient ritual. They formed a Star of David. Legend had it that the ritual had been created by Solomon himself. The legends also said that Solomon did not need anyone else to establish the points of the star. He had brought up both triangles from the center and then done his magic securely within the shielding. Each apex of the star was guarded by a spirit whom he had summoned. Each was named for a point on the Kabbalist Tree of Life. Some speculated that his spirits were those that actually composed the Tree. If the old texts were to be believed, Solomon was an extraordinarily powerful magician. He had safeguarded Israel with his magic as much as with his wisdom and his armies.

Benito had read many of the hidden Vatican manuscripts. The old texts indicated that the legend of Solomon's power was more than a tale that had grown over the millennia. The ancient king had been a consummate ceremonial magician. However, much of what he had known was lost. All that remained were fragmentary documents that did not describe complete rituals.

The powerful Ritual of Solomon was rarely used. It was difficult to control unless all of the participants could maintain absolute concentration. Benito knew of at least one case when the ritual had disintegrated with unpleasant consequences. The uncontrolled power had folded back on itself and killed one of the participants. Benito knew that Rimaldi had chosen it because of its potency, but that potency came at a price. Benito hoped the aging Pascal and the novice Kirk could maintain their concentration well enough to make the ritual succeed.

The question that they would all soon be facing was whether or not they had the means to defeat their opponents. At every turn Streng, his minions, and the disturbingly strong demon had proven themselves to be more potent than Benito would have expected. Angela had already voiced her concern, and Benito was beginning to share her perspective—they might be underestimating their opponents. Rimaldi seemed to be operating under the assumption that their enemies were bound to be defeated. His viewpoint was guided by the dogma in the Church, that no spirit could stand against the soldiers of God. If Rimaldi had any doubts, he was keeping them to himself and operating as if their opponents' defeat was assured. Benito did not have such blind faith. The Church was not always wise, not always right. The memories and impressions of pain that were imbued in the walls of the cathedral at Toledo were enough to convince Benito that mistakes had been made in the past.

⟡

THE smells of the stable called to Angela's mind childhood memories of long rides through the Sicilian countryside. Though she had not been on horseback for years, she had grown up riding and still knew how to handle a horse. She enjoyed being in the company of animals, beings who were neither good nor evil. Animals were simply what they were. From the rear of the stable she heard the sound of a brush as one of the stable hands groomed a horse. She hoped it would be Daniel.

She was not disappointed. Daniel's face rose over the back of the horse and brightened in recognition.

"Sistah Angela, nice a you to visit."

She walked over to the horse and laid a hand on her, feeling the rough horsehair. "Daniel, I think that you should call me Angela."

"Not proper, ma'am. You might be fine with it, but some white folk might take it wrong."

"Proper or not, I definitely am not a ma'am." She smiled, and he returned her smile sheepishly.

"Daniel, I might as well get to the point. I'd like to meet the *mambo*."

His face blanked. "What's a *mambo*?"

"Well, Daniel, let's put it this way. If you don't know what a *mambo* is, then you don't. If you do know what a *mambo* is, then I would greatly appreciate the chance of meeting with her. We have much more in common than it would appear."

"Don't know no *mambo*," he repeated, not quite convincingly.

"I saw it in your eyes at the train station as clearly as you saw it in mine. We both have training in magic." She smiled as she rubbed the horse's neck and avoided looking Daniel in the eyes. "But you do what you think is right."

"Yessum," he said tentatively.

"This is a fine mare you have here."

He was relieved to be able to change the subject. "She's my pride. Course she's not really mine, but the bishop never rides her. I'm the only one who takes her out. She's a highbred quarter, gentle as a lamb, but she needs to run from time to time."

"All of us girls need to run from time to time." Angela patted the horse fondly. "Don't we, sweetheart?"

The horse neighed in response.

As Angela left the stable, she could feel Daniel looking at her. She knew the *mambo* would hear of her request. Whether or not she agreed to that request was another matter.

CHAPTER NINETEEN

Saturday, October 24

ANGELA and Benito arrived in the workroom just before ten the next day. Rimaldi and Kirk had not yet arrived, but were expected any moment, so they sat in uncomfortable silence. Each had things to say to the other, but neither wished to speak, since they might be overheard. They did not want to face Rimaldi with their questions, at least not yet.

The Jesuit soon entered with Father Kirk in tow. The younger priest obviously had total confidence in his superior. "Well," Rimaldi said, taking his chair at the head of the table, "I think we should review the situation before we go. Father Benito?"

"When Brigid and I went to the house, we came from Warren Square. It's a good direction to approach from, as it will give us the opportunity to look directly down the street that the house is on. Then we can walk down Saint Julian on either side. The last time, I was on the same side of the street as the house."

"And?"

"The residue of evil was easily visible to the Sight, even in the light of day. It grows more dense as you approach the house. Within it, the air is cold and penetrating. The residual power might test your shielding."

"Do you think we need to work together, or do you think that the shielding each of us has would be enough?" Angela asked.

"For yourself and Father Rimaldi," Benito said, "you can resist it on your own. I have experienced the place and feel confident that I can protect myself. As for Father Kirk, I am unfamiliar with your capabilities."

"And I," said Steven, "am unfamiliar with the abilities of these magicians."

"I think it would be prudent to assume that Father Benito and I need to be wary of your shielding, Steven, as well as each other's. We may need to support you should there be a problem."

"Isn't Sister Angela going with us?" Steven asked.

Benito smiled. "Yes, she is, Steven, but she is a Dellamorte. She is more than able to protect herself."

"Hereditary?" Steven asked.

Angela nodded.

His curiosity was aroused. "How long?"

"We don't know exactly. Generations," she replied.

"Impressive," Steven said.

"She does not like to say it," Rimaldi interjected, "but we suspect that her family has passed the gift down for more than a thousand years."

Steven had heard that such people existed, but had never expected to meet one. "I am honored."

Angela smiled graciously. She was accustomed to the reaction.

"Then," Rimaldi said, "let us be on our way."

Father Benito led the way. He doubted he would ever forget the way to this particular house. They walked in silence, each keeping his own counsel. Several people on the street greeted them, though some stared at the mismatched group. Father Kirk was almost a foot taller than Benito, and at least a head taller than Rimaldi. Angela looked like a porcelain doll next to him. Benito led them to Warren Square.

"Saint Julian Street would bisect the square if it ran straight. The block we are concerned with is on the far side of the square." He indicated the direction with a slight movement of his head.

"Then let us prepare ourselves," Rimaldi said. They calmed themselves and touched upon their magical centers. "Are we ready?"

Steven and Benito nodded.

Benito said, "Remember, Steven, we must all remain within a few feet of one another and move together, or we could lose touch."

"See with the Sight," the Jesuit added.

As Benito changed his perspective to see with the Sight, he noticed that Kirk's protection was relatively weak. Both Angela and Rimaldi appeared to be encased in a glowing mist, while there was just a hint of brightness around Kirk.

Steven reacted as his normal view of the street was overlaid by the Sight. "The evil is palpable. I have never seen its like."

Rimaldi said, "Let us pass down the street as quickly as we can without drawing notice. We will walk down the side opposite the house."

The three men began to move in unison. Benito remembered that he had told Brigid that he would not return to this street willingly, and he had not. Rimaldi led them forward with grim determination. Kirk was cautious. Benito followed him, keeping a close eye on the young priest. Angela followed in their wake, perhaps three paces behind. She saw with more detail than the priests, and what she saw disturbed her. This evil had needed many years to take root.

When they entered the block, Benito felt the hair on the back of his neck stand up. In the full light of a warm day, he could feel the chill. It was a chill that only those with the Sight could fully experience, though this place would give anyone a sense of disquiet.

Overlaying the peaceful and sunny street were swirling black tendrils, whipping about like the tentacles of an octopus. Benito wondered what Rimaldi and Kirk saw, as he thought that their Sight was less strong than his. He could only imagine what Angela, with her stronger senses, was seeing. Before Benito's eyes, the smoke and darkness folded in on itself, swirling back to the center of the storm. Tendrils extended out from the center of the dark mass. Some were tainted red. Each time one swept over him, he felt a chill. When the darkest tendrils swept over him, he felt an echo of fear and terror, mated with a joyless pursuit of carnality. Beneath the tentacles was a roiling gray mass that grew darker and more dense as they came closer to Streng's house. Finally the darkness almost blotted out the view of their normal vision.

Rimaldi stopped the group directly across the street from 454 Saint Julian. They turned to face the house.

"Useless bravado," Angela thought to herself. She did not need to concentrate on her shielding, even though she felt impacts as the tendrils swept by. Once inside the gray mass, she felt a constant pressure against her defenses. Her shielding was far too solid to be penetrated and required little of her attention. As a result, she was the first to see the face of a man looking down on the priests from a second-story window. She realized that the man must be Streng. He was enjoying the display of the darkness he had helped to create. More important, he was assessing his opponents.

Benito, Rimaldi, and Steven looked up to the same window. Rimaldi was examining the magician he would be facing. Then Benito noticed that Rimaldi had moved a little too far ahead of Steven. Before Benito could say anything, the tendrils began a different dance and reached out to draw the three men across the street. It was a minor show of power. Streng was playing with them, letting them know how easily he could strike at them when they, unshielded by ritual, dared traverse his home ground.

Benito and Rimaldi were aware of the change in the tendrils, but not affected. Then Benito was horrified to see Steven falling prey to the tendrils. The young priest began to slowly move toward the house, walking almost mechanically. Rimaldi did not notice; his vision was locked onto Streng, attempting to assess his power. Kirk had almost reached the middle of the street. Angela was preparing to attack the hold that Streng had established on the young man. In that moment, Benito quickly stepped into the street, grabbed the young priest's cassock, and pulled him back to the sidewalk. Benito's sudden action drew Rimaldi's attention away from Streng, and he belatedly saw his pupil being almost dragged away from Streng's house. Rimaldi was angry with himself that he had allowed his awareness of Steven to waver. Benito pushed Steven toward Rimaldi, squeezing the younger man between the two more experienced magicians.

Rimaldi quickly led them down the street and away from the house. Streng moved his gaze from the priests to Angela and leered at her. Then he let the curtain fall and vanished from view. Streng's arrogance almost caused Angela to strike out at him, but she realized it would not be wise. He had seen weakness. It was better if he saw no show of strength.

The three men moved toward the corner and turned left at the next street. Angela was just behind them. Rimaldi stopped to evaluate Steven, but Angela pushed into them.

"Not here," she said.

For a moment, Rimaldi was offended; then he turned and led the way back to the cathedral.

❧

STRENG remained standing at the second-floor window. He heard a knock on the door.

"Come in."

Essie cautiously entered. "I felt somethin', Mr. Streng."

"Please come in, Essie. I'm afraid you missed the excitement."

She closed the door behind her. "What did I miss?"

"Four of the Catholic magicians came down Saint Julian. They were here to investigate my house. Unfortunately, they were not up to the task."

Carefully keeping her face blank, Essie responded. "They weak?"

"More so than I thought. I did not even use a spell, I just called out to them, and one began to leave the others and come across the street to me." Streng was very pleased with himself.

"I knew you didn't need no help. We got nobody can do that."

"I still wish you would join us, but you are right. We will not need anyone's help." He turned to face the window and said quietly to himself, "Soon, we will begin to pick them off, one by one."

"Excuse me, Mr. Streng, I didn't hear."

"Not for you anyway, Essie." He turned away from the window to face her. "Monday night, we will have dinner for four. Seven o'clock."

"Yes, Mr. Streng." Esmerelda turned to go, glad that she'd been able to conceal that she'd heard what he had said.

❧

CONCERNED about Steven, Rimaldi quickly led them back to their workroom in the cathedral. Rimaldi knew that Angela had been right. He had been wrong to stop so near the house. He had also been wrong to focus so much of his attention on Streng that he had allowed himself to become too distant from Steven. Steven's abilities had not been up to the task. Rimaldi realized that he should not make that kind of error when dealing with opponents this powerful.

They sat the young priest in a chair. Rimaldi asked, "Steven, are you all right?"

"I am all right," he said haltingly. His voice was weak, and he seemed dazed. "I think I am more frightened than anything else."

"You have a right to be," Rimaldi said.

"I don't know what happened. I stopped thinking and began walking toward the house. It seemed so," he searched for a word, "natural."

"He used a simple gathering gesture, which was enhanced by the place we were in, a place where his power has built up," Benito said. "We should have guarded you better."

"We should not have gone at all," Angela said.

"It was necessary," Rimaldi said. "It is unfortunate that we made the error we did, but no lasting harm was done. We will not repeat that mistake."

Angela said, "I hope not," and left the room angrily.

Stunned by her abrupt departure, Benito said, "I will go after her."

"No, she is who she is, and bringing her back will only force an argument. Our time is better spent in assuring that Steven has sustained no damage." The Jesuit looked down at the young priest, whose color was returning. Kirk looked less dazed, and he ventured a weak smile.

"I'm not certain that I am ready to face this strong an opponent," Steven said. "He certainly frightened me enough today, and he had not called his demon."

"We will see, Steven," he said kindly. "We have two weeks to prepare you better. They will not dare attempt anything of any consequence until the new moon. We can help you with the disciplines to strengthen your resistance to their magic."

Benito had been examining Kirk with his Sight. He saw that the normal, faint aura around Steven was disrupted but not damaged.

"You're fine," Benito said. "And by the time you have a little more training, you'll be ready to shield yourself. Attacking is harder than defending."

"I will work with him," Rimaldi said.

"I'd like to start after lunch," Steven said. "For now, I think I need a little time alone."

"Certainly," Rimaldi responded.

Steven left to go to his room. He was shaken, but more like himself than he had been a few minutes before.

Rimaldi looked questioningly at Benito. "Well?"

"He is undamaged. Thank goodness for the resilience of youth."

Rimaldi shook his head. "We should have watched more care-fully."

Had he been expecting an objection from Benito, he did not re-ceive it.

"The events today have made it clear that these people are not to be trifled with," Rimaldi said; then he took a long breath and ex-haled slowly, calming himself. "Fathers Siena and Francisco should arrive on Tuesday on the nine-ten train. We can discuss these events with them. Their arrival will give us a greater level of security."

"I will meet them at the station," Benito responded automati-cally.

"Thank you," Rimaldi said perfunctorily. "I would like some time alone now."

"Of course." Benito bowed slightly and let himself out of the room. The Benedictine also needed some time alone. The events of the morning had further shaken his confidence. Steven would re-cover, but would they succeed when they formed their ritual to combat the darkness?

ᏇᎯᎧ

ANGELA found the guest quarters unoccupied when she re-turned. Brigid had begun to assist during the day shift in the hospi-tal since Rimaldi had made it clear that she would play no part in the ritual. She would not return to her temporary quarters with An-gela until after four.

Angela sat on her cot, wanting to scream in frustration. She was not afraid for herself, but for the others. If they could not hold shielding against such a minor intrusion, what chance would they have against a demon? If the dynamics of the ritual that Rimaldi had planned were disrupted, she might be the only one who could protect herself, and she wasn't even certain about that.

She thought back to what she had said to Brigid about high magic and about the gods. How sad that the world had come to a point where people might be left defenseless against the terrors that men like Streng could unleash. A few, such as herself, might be able to defend themselves, but she could not destroy the creature alone. For the coming ritual, all that she could do would be strengthen her defenses and prepare to raise as much power as she could, perhaps enough to make the ritual a success. Other than that, prayer was the only solace, but, for the first time in her adult life, she felt her faith in Artemis slipping from her. What good was prayer if no one was able to bring the power of the gods to bear?

The rest of the day passed slowly for her. She ate and performed the necessary functions of life. Her mood was grim. The memory that haunted her was not the leering face of Streng, peering down from his second-floor window, but the face of Rimaldi, locked in concentration on Streng and forgetful of Steven. The Father Provincial was wrapping himself in a cloak of arrogance and authority. He would not listen, so he was putting all of them in danger.

Benito came to talk to her, but she refused to do more than answer the door and send him away. He could offer her nothing in her present mood. She avoided Rimaldi, and he made no approach to her. At lunch she saw him sitting with his acolyte, Steven. The young priest, she thought of him as young, though he was almost the same age as she, had felt his world shaken that morning. Now he sought solace from Rimaldi. Angela wondered if Steven would ever realize that their superior was the one most responsible for having put him in danger. Had it not been for Benito, Steven might have walked in Streng's front door.

She felt very alone. Brigid was the person she wanted to see because of the kinship she felt with her, built on their common birthright. Perhaps she would walk with Brigid tonight beneath the full moon. The very act of seeing the moon, so sacred to Angela's goddess, would give her some hope.

When Brigid returned from her shift in the hospital, she found Angela lying on her cot, thinking and waiting. "Sister Angela, what's wrong?"

Angela looked up at her. "I think I would feel better if you simply called me Angela."

"Certainly, but what happened?"

Angela related the events of the morning. She told her everything that had happened and everything that she had thought. Anger clouded her voice. She finished by saying, "So that is why I don't want you to call me Sister Angela. These people, even Rimaldi himself, have too little power to threaten my family in Sicily. When all of this is over, I will renounce my vows, leave the Church, and return home."

Brigid sat silently for a while. She remembered what the *mambo* had said to her. She had not yet made the decision to leave the Church. She felt torn by indecision. "I, too, have considered renouncing my orders and leaving the faith."

Angela was surprised. "You are not certain?"

"I am afraid. The Church is all that I've known. To give up the Church and return to Ireland sends me back to a place that I remember as covered in death," she said. "And the problems are difficult. I have no family that I can rely on, except in Ireland, and no money to pay for passage. I have to find some way to survive in the world."

"That," Angela said, "is at least something I can do to bring some good out of this sad trip. You don't need to worry about what you will do or where you will go. My family is wealthy, and they would be honored to have someone with gifts as strong as yours. Or, if you'd prefer, I would pay for your passage back to Ireland."

"Are you certain? That is a great gift." She felt a bubble of emotion rising in her throat.

"Please, allow me to lift that problem from you. It is a small enough thing to do, and it would please me to do it. I may not think of myself as 'Sister Angela' anymore, but I am still your sister."

"Thank you." Brigid burst into tears. "No, no, it's all right. I had never expected such kindness, and I didn't realize the weight that all of this had placed on me. With your offer, I can make my decision with my heart and head, not with fear." She wiped the tears from her face and smiled at Angela.

"It is no more than you deserve," Angela said. "For myself, I hope you decide to join me. But, should you return to Ireland, I may come with you. I have wanted to visit your island for a long time."

They were interrupted by a knock on the door. It was Isaiah.

"Isaiah, I didn't expect to see you," Brigid said.

"We need to talk. In private."

"Then come in."

He came into the room hesitantly, not certain if it was right for him to be in a white woman's bedroom, even if she was a nun. Then he saw Angela.

"You the one they call Angela?"

She rose. "Yes, I am."

"Then you can stay. What I got to say is for both a you."

"Please, Isaiah, have a seat." Brigid pointed to one of the empty cots.

"Won't be stayin' that long. I jus' come to tell you the *mambo* wants to see you tonight. We meet just like we did last time. In front of the church, jus' past eight thirty."

"Of course," Brigid said.

He looked at Angela. "Sistah, the *mambo* is sorry, but she don't want no one else new comin' to see her. Maybe after all this mess is over, but not now."

"I understand," she responded.

"Good. I see you tonight, Sistah Brigid." He left, and his light footsteps receded down the quiet corridor.

Angela said, "That's discouraging. I had hoped to meet her."

"I think that will happen before your visit is over. But this summons is disturbing."

"Why?"

"The *mambo* is very private; at least that is what she told me. If she wants me to see her, then something has happened. I suspect she has information, and I don't think it will be anything good."

✺

AT 8:35 Brigid was in front of the cathedral. As on the other night, Isaiah appeared out of the darkness.

"Just stay with me." He led the way down the street.

Brigid talked quietly to him. "Do you know why she's called me?"

"She just say she wants to meet with you."

They continued in silence until Isaiah motioned for them to stop when they reached East Broad Street. He looked up and down the street, outlined in the light of the nearly full moon. He saw no one and led her across the street. When he reached the other side, he looked back to see if the street was still deserted. It seemed to be. Then he saw a dark shadow detach itself from one of the oaks and cross the street a block to their north. It was one of the *mambo*'s men. Isaiah led Brigid away from East Broad and took them a few feet down a side street and stopped. They waited until Daniel came up the same side street.

Daniel quietly approached them. He nodded in greeting. "Sistah Brigid."

"Hello, Daniel," Brigid said.

Daniel smiled in response.

Isaiah spoke to Daniel. "Let James follow us down, but you stay here a bit. See if any white men cross East Broad that look like they followin' us."

Daniel nodded.

Isaiah led her farther into the colored section of the city.

"Isaiah," Brigid asked quietly, "why are we being so much more careful this time?"

"The *mambo* tell you. For now, we need to be goin'."

Brigid glanced back and saw the comfortingly immense figure of James.

Isaiah led her down different streets than he had the last time. The streets here were lined by closely packed, ramshackle houses. More people were out on the street than in Savannah proper. The street life here was lively and complex. People chatted, clumped irregularly on the dirt streets. Groups of children played among them. The white nun garnered curious glances from the people on the street, but Isaiah's presence let them know that this white person had reason to be in their part of town.

Isaiah was more relaxed here than he had been in the white section of the city. "You gettin' to see what few white folks ever see. We got our own city here, and it's a good one. The other part of our town you saw was the part that white folks visit when they need somethin' from us. Either a colored gal for some fun or some bad business done."

He turned down an even smaller side street, more an alley than a street. No carriage could enter this area. He stopped and knocked on a door. Even in the faint light, they could see that it was painted a bright blue.

Esmerelda opened the door. Her smile of greeting could not hide the seriousness of her expression. "Come in."

They entered, and Isaiah quietly took a chair to the side of the room, leaving the center of the room to the women. Esmerelda seated Brigid and herself at a table.

The room was lit by two kerosene lamps, the walls festooned with many things that could be used in Voudon and in magic. Masks, carved carefully of wood and painted to represent spirits, stared down on the women. Charms of feathers and bone cluttered the walls. A cloak of raven feathers was surmounted by a carved beak. Brigid was most surprised by a bookshelf that sat on one side of the room. She wondered what books a *mambo* might read. She focused on the *mambo,* who was surrounded by a strong aura.

"I feel safer here than anywhere I've been in a while," Brigid said.

"My strength's greater here than anywhere. This is my home. I've built up magic here. Around here I'm safe from the demon or from the pryin' eyes that Streng might send after me. But outside this little piece of town . . ." She didn't need to finish the statement.

Regardless of the serious reminder of the demon's power, Brigid felt very secure with this woman, even more than she did around Benito. Esmerelda, like Angela, was her sister in a craft and a belief system that crossed all boundaries, except the one that the Church had drawn about itself.

Esmerelda said, "If they got such as you and that other nun here, why they send such a weak one to visit Streng? That boy you brought almost got himself in real trouble."

"Rimaldi is our leader, and he insisted that we all go to Saint Julian Street," Brigid said.

"This Rimaldi your abbé?"

"He's not really an abbot, but he is our leader."

"He knows what he's messing with?"

Brigid hesitated. "He's read about creatures such as this, but he, in fact, none of us have dealt with such a thing before."

"He's proud, and that pride gonna get people killed. That's one reason why you can't ask us to help. Always some priest thinks he knows, when he don't." She smiled ruefully. "Not that we could do much good against Belial."

"Is that its name?"

"Thought I'd told you before."

"No. That name could be important information."

"Maybe. But not from what I seen. I'm not sure you got the power to face him."

They were silent for a moment. Then Brigid said, "We have three more magicians arriving."

Esmerelda looked at her steadily. "Then maybe you can do it. I know your priests got some powerful spells. If your abbé has time to get set up, maybe he can." She paused. "But that's not why I asked you here."

Brigid waited.

"Streng's going to do somethin' real soon. Gonna be before the moon goes dark. Maybe in a day or two. He's gonna go after one of your people."

"Are you certain?"

"He don' tell his plans to me. But I hear things around his house."

"Thank you. That's an important warning."

"Not if your abbé don't listen."

"I'll try to make him."

"I be havin' some of my folk keep an eye on Streng's house for you. Daniel will let you know about the comings and goings."

"Won't that put you at risk?"

"White folk don't see us. We're everywhere, and they don't look." The *mambo* smiled. "Besides, we hard to see in the dark."

Brigid, seeing the amusement in Esmerelda's eyes, laughed in response.

After her joke, the *mambo* became somber again. "Brigid, I got a responsibility. Streng's been killin' people, white and black, for a long time. His kind of evil got to die. The *loa* warned me not to do magic, but that don't mean I won't help where I can."

"So there is a risk?"

"Always is when people like Streng are around. But I need to help out; this ain't just Church business no more."

"Because of what he's doing?"

"No, that's been the same for a long time. It's different because you're tied up in this business."

"Me?"

"I felt it when I first met you. We both part of somethin' that goes back a long, long way. Who do you think kept these things off of people before there was a Church, before there was a Jesus?"

Brigid had no answer. She was surprised she had never made

the simple logical connection. All she could do was stare dumbly into the *mambo*'s eyes.

Esmerelda realized that Brigid had simply never thought about what must have been before. "It just makes sense. Somebody had to. And those that did passed their blood on to their children and the children of those children, right on down to today. When I look at you the other night I saw a line of women stretching back and back. All the ones that gave down the power."

"Seven generations."

"No, wasn't no seven generations. This line stretched back 'til I couldn't see it no more. Dozens of women back."

Brigid fell silent. She had never thought about what being an hereditary really meant. She had never considered that the power she was born with might reach back far in time, back to a place more ancient than she had ever imagined. With her new knowledge, she felt honored, but she also felt a sense of responsibility to her ancestors, a duty that frightened her. She was so unprepared to take on the responsibility. Had her birthright not been stolen, she would not have to rely so much on "knowing" the right thing to do, as she had when she had suddenly known how to bring her shielding down during the lesson with Luis. Her feeling the right things to do was not enough. She needed to be taught things as well, things that she might have learned had her own training gone on. The lack of knowledge pained her. The Church may have saved her life, but she had sacrificed so much to avoid hunger. She looked at the *mambo,* thinking that the wisewoman understood much about her that even she did not know. Esmerelda looked back at her regally, encased in the subtle glow of her power. Brigid had so many questions that she ended up not having any at all.

Esmerelda said, "You better go on and get back. Don't do for too many to see you down here."

Brigid was called back to the present and looked into the *mambo*'s eyes. "Whatever happens, thank you for what you just told me and thank you for your warning. And the information from Daniel will be of great help."

The *mambo* replied, "If you live through this, come visit and bring that other nun with you."

"If?"

"All hell's gettin' ready to come after you."

CHAPTER TWENTY

Sunday, October 25

FATHER Benito sat in the visiting nuns' quarters, his sadness apparent. Angela angrily paced back and forth. "So he wouldn't listen?"

"Listen? He was upset by my first contact with the Voudon community. To hear a warning from them was intolerable. He told me that Christians need pay no attention to primitive religions, even if they were the ones to supply us with the names of the creature and the man who summoned it."

"Idiot," Angela said.

Benito wanted to say something in Rimaldi's defense, but he realized there was nothing he could say that he could also believe.

"Then we shall all do our best in his ritual," Angela said, calming herself. "But there is one thing that we must do. I am almost certain my shielding can withstand that thing that Streng calls. Perhaps we can train Brigid so that she may also withstand it, but you must do all you can to strengthen your own personal defenses. If the *mambo*'s warning is correct, it may come for you soon, and if the ritual fails, it will certainly come for you then."

"Is it necessary to work without his knowledge?" Benito asked.

"He is the one that has cut himself off from open communication. What we must do is prepare for our own protection. If the ritual fails, then the only way someone can survive to tell the Church what happened is for us to be ready to protect each other."

"We must do all we can to make the ritual succeed."

"Of course, but we also have to be ready to abandon the ritual the moment it becomes apparent that it is failing."

Heeding her warning, they spent much of Sunday in the workroom, teaching Brigid everything they could that might serve to protect her. Angela taught Brigid how to control the power that she drew up. Benito taught her how to achieve the stillness that must lie at the center of every magician when working, as well as the different ways that shielding could be used. Brigid remembered the ancient names that Emer had taught her in the late nights of her childhood.

Benito was envious. "You are so fortunate. You are the fastest study I have ever taught."

Brigid half-smiled, half-blushed.

"Luis," Angela said, "in a few hundred years, you will be, too. You just haven't lived enough lives yet to have the same adeptness."

"Angela, you know I do not believe in reincarnation."

"That doesn't matter." She smiled with a glint in her eyes.

"Belief doesn't matter?" he asked.

"Does a plant need to believe in its need for light to turn toward the sun? No, it simply turns. Reincarnation is the same. Natural law does not require belief in order to function."

"Keep this up, and you two will turn me into a heretic."

"Then you can be even better company for us." The women laughed.

Benito grew somber. "And what of our superior? He has not entered the workroom today."

Angela responded, "He is with Steven, helping him with his own protection."

Brigid asked, "Why don't we work together?"

"The training for someone like Steven is very different than it is for someone like you. His shielding is based more on ritual, on chants and spells, than his own strength. Yours is based almost solely on the strength inside of you."

"And for Luis?"

He answered, "For me, it is both."

Brigid nodded, surprised that she understood. This realm of magic was strange, but it did have rules and principles. She hoped that she would quickly learn to protect herself if the demon came for her. For now, she was glad that she slept in a room with Angela.

Benito stifled a yawn. "For myself, it is off to bed."

"A good idea, Luis. Brigid and I will do the same."

They went their ways to their quarters, aware that this night was the last night of the waxing moon. As the moon waned, the power of their opponents would increase.

UNLIKE her small room, the visiting nuns' quarters had windows that faced out onto the street. The moon was just past full and Angela had opened the curtains to the night, enjoying the pale illumination that flowed into the room. In their beds, the combination of the moonlight and the sturdy walls imparted a sense of security that they both needed, and they fell into a deep sleep.

They were startled awake by screams coming from the nuns' quarters. They both sat up, immediately awake and remembering the *mambo*'s warning. Angela's senses reached out, perceiving nothing amiss.

"I sense nothing," she said to Brigid, who was already half out of her bed and moving to the door.

Angela grabbed her robe and followed Brigid out of the door. Brigid, clad only in her nightdress, was ten feet ahead of her, disappearing through the door into the nuns' corridor. When Angela followed her through the door, she was surprised by the scene. Almost every member of the convent was halfway down the long corridor, formed into a rough semi-circle around the door to Sister Maria's room. Maria had been the one to find the body of Sister

Francis. The faces of the nuns were etched with fear and apprehension. No one would approach the door.

Angela sensed the approach of the mother superior. She could feel the fear radiating from the woman, yet Angela knew, without turning, that none of that fear would ever be seen by anyone without the Sight. As the mother superior came next to her, Angela held out her arm, stopping Margaret gently.

"Wait, Mother Superior. There is no danger here, and this is Brigid's time."

Though puzzled, the mother superior waited, her heart slowing with Angela's reassurance.

Angela watched Brigid as she strode toward the circle of nuns, her long black hair unleashed and flowing like an unruly cloud. The thin nightdress was like a simple robe over her dancer's body. Angela wondered how long it had been since she had seen someone who looked so much like Artemis. The nuns parted before Brigid, tacitly assenting that this was her realm. She stopped in front of the door.

"What happened?"

The voices overlaid one another. "Maria started screaming . . . we came." "She hasn't come out. . . ." "What's wrong?"

"Have any of you opened the door?"

A silence. "We were afraid," Sister Fiona reluctantly said.

Brigid opened the door with no hesitation and saw Sister Maria kneeling by her bed, praying. She looked up with fear in her eyes. "What is it?"

"Did you scream?"

"Yes," she said hesitantly. "I had a nightmare. I kept seeing Sister Francis's face, with her eyes gouged. Then I thought I wasn't alone, and I screamed and woke up. So I prayed." She looked past Brigid. "I didn't know I had screamed out loud."

Margaret had heard everything. She moved down the hall with Angela behind her. "So what is this nonsense?" Margaret called. The nuns turned to her. Those farther away bolted for their rooms; those nearer her had no choice but to stand their ground.

"Mother Superior," Sister Ursula said, "we heard screams in the night and came to see what the matter was."

"Obviously nothing was, just a bad dream. Back to bed, all of you." They scattered back to their rooms. Margaret and Angela came to stand beside Brigid.

Sister Maria was now standing. "I'm sorry, Mother Superior, very sorry. I didn't know I had screamed out loud. I didn't hear them come to the door. I was praying to the Blessed Virgin for protection. . . ." She stopped, her face shifting from apologetic to fearful. "I was so afraid, I remembered Sister Francis, how she was . . ." She sat on her bed and began crying.

The mother superior pushed past Brigid and went to sit beside her nun. "It's all right, Maria. We have all been afraid these past few days." She hugged the younger woman to her.

Margaret turned to face Brigid and Angela. "Thank you. I'll come to see you in your quarters as soon as she's calm."

The two nuns returned to the guest quarters. When they entered, Brigid moved to light a candle.

"No," Angela said.

Brigid watched the other nun go to stand in front of the largest window. The angle of the moon let the blue-white beams fall directly into the room. Amazed, Brigid looked on as Angela slipped off her robe, then her nightdress, to stand naked in the moonlight. She leaned back her head to look up at the moon and spread her arms, turning her hands so that the beams fell on her open palms. Her exquisite body was perfectly formed, and she looked like a statue lit by moonlight. Slowly, gracefully, she sank to one knee, her eyes never leaving the face of the moon. Then she lowered her head in reverence. She held that position for a minute, then rose and bent to pick up her nightdress and robe. She slipped the dress on and turned to Brigid.

"Prayer?" Brigid asked.

Angela nodded, then went to light one of the candles in the room. She did not discuss her prayer, but focused on Brigid. "Tonight was important for you. I stayed behind and held back the mother superior for a few moments."

"Was that a test?"

"In a way. You took command of the situation. The other nuns obeyed you. I was as curious what their reactions would be as what yours might be."

"I didn't feel like I was giving them orders. I just did what needed to be done."

"I know," said Angela. "You did what was natural to you."

"Why is that important?"

"You were born to be not only one of us, but a leader among us."

"A leader?"

There was a gentle knock on the door, interrupting their conversation. Brigid opened the door for the mother superior. She entered the dimly lit room and asked, "Are you comfortable in the dark?"

Brigid responded to the implied need for light by lighting two of the kerosene lamps, which drove the shadows from the corners of the chamber.

Margaret went to sit on one of the other beds. "It's what I have been fearing."

"Hysteria," Angela said.

The mother superior nodded.

"I have seen it before. Other places we have been. It will spread, but it always begins with the nuns."

"Why?" Brigid asked.

"A conclave of women, locked away from the world," Angela replied. "Some came to the convent because they did not want to face the world. They wanted safety, security, and have lived a quiet existence, away from the dangers and problems of life. They have no experience of fear, and now they are afraid."

"Especially after one of their own has been killed," Brigid added.

"Is there anything you can do?" Margaret asked.

"What should we do? Tell them that the danger isn't real? No, the only thing we can do is try to control the fear until the time comes when we can face the darkness."

"When will that be?" the mother superior asked.

"A week, maybe longer."

"So, until then, we wait." The mother superior rose from the bed. She stopped by the door. "Thank you for tonight. Without your presence, tonight would have been much harder." She shook her head. "And it was only a nightmare." She let herself out.

Brigid listened to her light footfalls recede down the corridor. "Was that all it was, a nightmare?"

"I'm not sure," Angela responded. "I thought for just a moment that I detected an impression of something leaving the convent. It might have been a nightmare planted by our opponents."

"Then they could do it again."

Angela nodded. "Planted nightmare or one out of her own experience, the real danger is still hysteria."

"Angela, what we were talking about earlier . . ."

Angela gently held up her hand. "Enough for now." She blew out the candle and the lamps. In the room still lit by the moon, Angela slipped between the sheets, leaving Brigid alone with her questions.

CHAPTER TWENTY-ONE

Monday, October 26

ON Monday the three met early to continue Brigid's training. Brigid felt a sense of urgency. The *mambo* had been clear in her warning. Angela and Benito concentrated on working with Brigid more than before. Benito was more confident in his shielding, and both he and Angela were worried that Brigid might lose her concentration. If she did lose focus, then her own power, which should give her greater shielding than Benito possessed, would be weakened. They worked, undisturbed, through the day.

That night the three sat together in the dining hall for dinner. Father Kirk, at loose ends since Rimaldi was dining with the bishop, joined them. Monsignor Henry rounded out the five at the table. The two new people at the table brought a welcome respite to Brigid, who was exhausted from the lessons of the afternoon.

"So, Father Benito," asked the monsignor cheerfully, "any news other than the nun's nightmare?"

Father Kirk looked uncomfortable, knowing that the monsignor should not know of the events of the previous day.

Benito glanced around himself and realized how isolated their table was before commenting truthfully, "Only that we must wait. The other members of our order begin arriving tomorrow. Until we are at greater strength, we are at risk."

"That is a disturbing thought," the monsignor said, keeping his voice low.

Angela said, "None of us has ever faced anything of this power."

The monsignor responded, "Even Father Rimaldi?"

"Such creatures are rare," Benito replied. "He has never faced a threat of this strength before. However, of all of us, he certainly knows the most about it. He spent time before leaving Maryland in reviewing all of the information on the subject that he had. What he knows is extensive. He has the greatest library of its kind on this side of the Atlantic."

"That eases my mind somewhat," the monsignor said.

"But reading, Monsignor Henry," said Angela, "is not experience."

The monsignor felt that he was entering deeper water than he wished to traverse.

"You need not be concerned," Father Kirk added. "With the addition of the other members, we are certain to prevail."

"Good," the monsignor said, taking heart from Steven's reassurance.

Angela bit back her comment. She kept it to herself that confidence was necessary, but less so than power.

"Sister Brigid," Father Kirk asked, "is your training going well?"

"I believe so."

"Are they planning to take you away from us?" the monsignor asked, partially in jest.

"If they are, Monsignor, they have not told me."

The monsignor was surprised by the considered tone of her response. He had unintentionally asked a question that, apparently, had greater implications. As the monsignor was determined to be a gracious host, he slipped away from unsteady ground to a safer topic, hoping to keep the conversation from becoming too serious. He turned to Angela, who reflected neither the piety of Steven nor the sobriety of Benito, as a possible savior in the conversation. "And what do you think of our city?"

Angela sensed the monsignor's need to lighten the conversation. She also felt that dinner should be a respite from business. "It is a beautiful place. I have been to all of the great capitals of Europe, except Berlin, and only Rome can eclipse the beauty of this place. It is not only the beauty of the land but the plan of the city that makes it so special. I love the open squares. Whoever planned the city must have been determined to keep part of the natural world in it."

"You are a true romantic, Sister. That has been the outcome, but the squares were originally places where men from the neighborhoods could muster to defend the city."

"From whom?"

The monsignor glanced at Benito.

"From Spain," Benito answered.

"Was there an attempt to invade from Florida?" Angela asked.

"Right after the city was founded," Benito answered, "the Spanish sent an expedition north, but they found that the English of Georgia were well prepared. It was a small battle, but it was important, nonetheless. It stopped the Spanish from reaching to the north, so Georgia fulfilled its purpose, which was to protect the more valuable colonies in the Carolinas."

"And what was the name of this small but important battle?" Angela asked.

Benito smiled. "The Battle of Bloody Marsh."

"That," Angela said, "is certainly a fearsome name."

"Supposedly, the marsh ran red with blood," Benito said. "But, given the small list of casualties, I fear the name was an exaggeration."

Talk of history gave the five a subject for discussion that avoided the menacing events that had brought them together. They lingered over dinner, glad for the company and the brightly lit dining room.

Father Kirk retired for the night to his bedroom in a wing of the compound where male clerical visitors and the monsignor were housed. When Father Kirk entered his room, he again noted the advantage of a powerful and numerous congregation. This room was nicer than his own at his church in Minnesota. He lit the oil lamp above his desk and picked up the notes he had taken in his meetings with Father Rimaldi. He reviewed the details of the planned ritual and the lessons on personal shielding. He would not fall prey to Streng again. It was merely a matter of concentration and focus, he had learned.

One of the ways that he could improve that concentration was memory exercises. He read over the words of the ritual, careful not to speak any of them aloud. Though there was little chance that they would have any effect outside of a ritual circle, he knew that speaking them could possibly create unwanted results. He spent over an hour learning the words of the main section of the ritual. When he had committed them to memory, he laid the ritual aside and picked up a novel to relax his mind before bed. It was one of the novels of Dumas, *The Three Musketeers,* a good yarn and thoroughly engaging.

A FEW blocks away, Streng and his inner circle were beginning their ritual in his basement. The group was made up of Streng, Cawthorne, Breeding, and Lilith Claire. Lilith was in her late forties and had an air of sensuality about her, but few knew how much of a libertine she really was. She retained her beauty, long after it should have faded. Her hair kept its dark luster and framed the olive skin of her face, which was dominated by a sharp, hawk-like nose.

The four stood at the cardinal points of the compass just within the bounds of their ritual circle. Streng began their rite by invoking air from his place in the east. Lilith picked up the chant in the north, invoking earth. In turn, Cawthorne added his own invocation in the west for water. Breeding completed the circle at the south, the point of fire. When each had achieved the desired response, they all began moving counterclockwise around their circle, bowing to each of the cardinal points.

When they had completed their circuit, Streng moved to the front of the altar. He lit the three black candles there and scattered sulfur on a smoldering brazier in the middle. Then all four went to stand around the portal stone in the center of their circle. Made of dark granite, the flat slab was set into the floor. Roughly circular and almost five feet in diameter, the single slab had been polished so smoothly that the light of the candles was reflected in it. Streng muttered a spell and threw more of the sulfurous powder on the portal stone. The four then sat on the floor, forming a tight arc around the stone. They faced the altar over the stone.

Streng began to mutter the chant that would summon their demon, and the others joined in. They were quickly rewarded. The polished stone began to change. The shining granite hazed over, and the slab became a dark, flat gray. As they continued the chant, the gray began to fade as it became a translucent window into another realm. Then the portal became nearly clear, and they could distinguish a few features on the other side, mainly rock outcroppings and a red-orange sky. The chant changed again as they began calling Belial.

Inside the basement room, the temperature rose. The four magicians began to sweat profusely underneath their robes, and a bitter, fetid odor flowed from the portal to suffuse the room. They continued their monotonous chant. Finally, the landscape on the other side of the portal was bathed in a ruddy glow, which grew in intensity to a fiery red. Belial was coming.

Its nightmarish shape began to emerge from the portal. It did not climb out of the portal; rather, it floated upward through it. The immense shape was vaguely humanoid and dominated the room. They never quite knew how Belial would appear to them, but it was not its appearance that made it terrible; rather, it was the sense of contained cruelty and ruthless power that flowed out from the demon that truly terrified. Heat and the smell of brimstone and offal rose from its body. Streng and the others abased themselves on the floor in worship of this terrible power. Tonight they had a task for their demonic ally, one that it would enjoy.

THE cathedral dormitory was silent. A few oil lamps had been placed along the corridor, but the light was quickly swallowed by the rough walls. In their separate rooms, Benito and Rimaldi slept deeply. The thick tabby walls around them imparted a sense of security.

In his own room off the corridor, Father Kirk was so involved in his reading that he did not see a space in a darkened corner of the room behind him become even darker. The space then began to glow with a faint red light. The light increased and began to solidify into a ruddy shape. Belial took form.

Belial came across the room and stood a few feet behind the priest. The creature made no sound. Kirk did not even look up from his book. Then Belial, knowing the ways of fear and surprise, gently chuckled. Kirk spun around at the noise, finding himself facing the belly of the beast. Kirk attempted to stand, but he was partially entangled with the chair. He lost his balance and threw his arms out to the side to avoid falling. Just as he regained his balance, Belial grabbed him by the throat with an iron grip. Being a physically strong man, Kirk made the critical mistake of reaching for the arm that held him and attempting to pull it away. Physical strength was useless against the demon. It was many times stronger than Kirk. Only magic could weaken the creature's physical power. Kirk's hands burned where they touched the beast, and the priest jerked his arms away.

The demon lifted him from the floor, where Kirk's legs flailed uselessly against its body. The priest continued to struggle, though he did not make a sound. He could not speak or cry out with Belial's hand around his throat. Kirk realized that he could not fight the demon physically and attempted to concentrate upon a spell in his mind, closing his eyes against the face of the demon that now leered at him from a few inches away. Kirk could feel the heat radiating from the creature's face.

Belial sensed the change in tactics and pulled the face of the priest toward its own. Where they touched, Belial's skin was so hot that the heat seared Kirk's skin, breaking the priest's concentration. Then Belial loosened its grip around the priest's throat enough to let the screams of pain escape him. Belial was burning him with its fiery hands. A second, louder scream ripped from Kirk to reverberate down the empty stone hallway. The scream and the fear were like manna to Belial. This was its food, the screams and struggles of the ones it would kill. Belial would have enjoyed letting its pleasure go on, but it was wary. It knew that the screams would bring the others, and it was not sure of what power they might bring. Knowing that Streng, like all humans, was stupid, Belial did not trust Streng's reassurance that these people had little power, even though it felt no stir of answering magic. Kirk writhed and screamed in Belial's hands, kicking his feet in the empty air. Blood was running down Kirk's face where the fire had burned through the skin. Kirk's nose was now more a charred gash in his face than a physical feature. Blood began to run into the priest's mouth as his screams of pain contorted his face.

Belial heard doors being thrown open in the hallway. In response, it tightened its grip on the priest, cutting off his screams. It shook the priest like a doll and squeezed Kirk's neck, strangling him and snapping his spine in one motion. Belial lifted the dead priest with one hand and ripped open the guts of the corpse with the other. It threw Kirk's body at the door, where it slumped, blocking entrance into the room.

Belial folded in upon itself and slid back to the corner. Its shape became smaller and more indefinite. Then there was only a red mist, which faded to a darkened place in the air and vanished. Belial was gone, returning to the circle of magicians on Saint Julian.

Benito and Rimaldi emerged from their rooms, seeking the

source of the screams. Benito immediately sensed the presence of another in Kirk's room. As they ran to the door, the screaming stopped. Benito was the first to arrive, knowing whatever had been in there with Kirk was now gone.

Rimaldi shouted, "Steven, what's wrong?"

He threw his shoulder into the door and it opened a few inches. Benito joined him. They pushed again, and the door yielded a few more inches. Monsignor Henry arrived. The three men pushed together and drove the door open enough for them to enter. Rimaldi was the first inside the room, closely followed by the other priests. He slipped on the blood on the stone floor and almost fell. He looked for Kirk and was horrified by what he found.

The room was lit by a reading lamp. Father Kirk lay behind the partially open door. His head was at an odd angle. His face was blank, holding nothing more than the vacant stare of death. His nose was a charred ruin, and his forehead was creased with burn marks. Blood leaked from the burns on his face and neck. The entire room stank of sulfur, burned flesh, and blood.

The Jesuit lurched away from the disfigured corpse. The war had conditioned Benito and Henry to such sights, so they did not react as violently, even though they were as horrified as Rimaldi. Steven had been their friend, and they had heard his screams as he died. What frightened them the most was the thought of what had done this to their friend.

Monsignor Henry was the first to speak. "I'll send for Dr. Gaston."

"Why him?" Benito asked.

"I want someone who can examine the body without being too disturbed by its condition. Also, he knows something about what we are fighting here. I don't think we want too many others to know." The monsignor left quickly.

Benito began examining the body.

"We need to cover him," Rimaldi said as he rejoined Benito.

"We should wait," Benito said calmly. "This is our chance to examine what this demon does firsthand. The doctor will be here soon."

Rimaldi nodded. "I'll get Sister Angela."

"And Brigid."

"Why Brigid?"

"Because she saw the first killing," Benito said, "and because her Sight is strong."

The Jesuit's confidence was shaken, but he was still unsure. "Are you certain?"

"As certain as I can be, Father Provincial."

Rimaldi, stepping carefully through the blood that now blocked the entire doorway, left to fetch the nuns.

The monsignor returned. "I've sent for Dr. Gaston. He should be here soon." He squatted next to Benito. "Are we safe here?"

"I don't know if this creature has to wait before it kills again, so I don't know if we are safe. Rest assured that you are as safe here as anywhere. The creature is not interested in you. It wants those of our order dead. Besides, Angela will be here soon. Together we can give you more protection than you're likely to find anywhere this side of Heaven."

"Magic didn't seem to help Kirk."

"No, but he was not as strong as I am, and he was definitely weaker than Angela. You're better off here."

The monsignor nodded. "What can you tell from the body?"

"See here." Benito touched the exposed portion of the neck, turning the head slightly. "If his killer faced him, which I think it did, then it has a very human-like hand, except that Steven's skin is burned where the hand touched him. It is as if a mechanical hand, red-hot, grabbed him about the neck. Based on the size of the grip, this creature must be immense."

"Comforting to know," the monsignor commented.

"I fear that there is not much to be found in the way of comfort. It appears that the actual cause of death was the hand's grip about the neck. The neck is thinner and elongated. The grip was powerful enough to actually elongate the neck while snapping it."

"So death was by a broken neck and strangulation, both at once."

"It appears so," Benito continued. "Then the demon gutted him. It is trying to frighten us, just as it did when it killed Sister Francis."

Their conversation was interrupted by the sound of light footsteps running down the hall. They slowed outside the door, and the two nuns entered the room, carefully avoiding slipping in the blood.

"Mother of God," Angela said.

Benito nodded. "Will you check the room?"

The energy of her magic rose about her, so potent that even the monsignor, who was not gifted with the Sight, could feel the change in the air.

Brigid stepped around her fellow nun and pointed to the dark corner of the room. "It came in there. It left there."

Angela swept her eyes about the room. "She is right. The demon took form within the room."

Brigid looked penetratingly at Steven's body. "His spirit is gone. May the gods stand ready to receive it." Then, incongruously, she crossed herself. The three others did the same.

The monsignor decided that commenting on Brigid's unusual blessing could wait for another time.

Benito asked, "Where is Father Rimaldi?"

Angela replied, "He went to meet the doctor."

"Then we shall wait." Benito stood from where he had squatted next to Steven and walked to the washbasin. He carefully washed his hands of the blood that had come from Steven's body.

Angela looked sadly at Steven. "He was so young."

"He was about your age, Angela," Luis said.

"Not really," she responded.

The four of them sat in the room with the corpse, awaiting the arrival of Dr. Gaston. They had little to say. Brigid felt rage and a desire for vengeance clotting in her throat. She looked at her companions. Angela was clearly as angry about what had happened as she was saddened by Kirk's death. Benito was folded into himself. Whatever thoughts he may have had, they did not show on his face. The monsignor was shaken, glancing nervously from time to time at Steven's body, then slowly shaking his head. He did not need to explain his thoughts, at least not to Brigid. She was as inured to the sight of corpses killed by brutal means as he was, but she felt what was plainly on his face. Even Richardson's body had not been so brutally handled.

Rimaldi rejoined them, bringing Dr. Gaston with him. The smell of whiskey clung to the doctor.

The monsignor rose to greet him. "David, thank you for coming."

"Couldn't sleep anyway," Gaston replied.

The monsignor indicated the corpse to him. Even Gaston felt a moment of shock. He had thought his days of mangled corpses were behind him. "I need more light."

Brigid went to the bed table and brought a second lamp to the desk, where she lit it. Then she carried the lamp to stand over the body. She had too much experience as a nurse to need any further direction. Gaston began his examination around the neck area, where the worst wounds were. He turned the head to look at the wounds on either side. Then he felt the forehead where the lesser burn marks had been imposed. The nose received only a cursory glance, as it had been charred beyond recognition. The ripped stomach needed no explanation.

"Knees are gettin' old, Sister. Mind giving me a hand?"

Brigid reached down her free arm and helped the doctor to his feet.

The doctor turned to the monsignor. "Robert, it's pretty plain that he was strangled by a very powerful hand. Only one was used, but it is much larger than a man's hand should be. The hand also left burn marks on his neck. Death was by strangulation or a broken neck, both near simultaneous. There are ragged pierce marks at the ends of the fingers. The hand was clawed."

"Are you certain?" Rimaldi asked.

Gaston nodded. "I've seen men killed by bears and other animals, and the signs of claws are unmistakable. But it's the marks on the forehead and the damage to his nose that trouble me. Don't see any reason for it. Unless the killer spent time playing with him before it killed him."

"So what killed him?" Benito asked.

"From what I see, a big, maybe eight-foot-tall, animal with a clawed red-hot iron glove and a taste for inflicting pain."

"Such a thing doesn't exist," Rimaldi blurted.

"Didn't think so," Gaston said.

CHAPTER TWENTY-TWO

Western Ireland
Tuesday, October 27

SIOBHAN was surprised to receive Brigid's letter in the post. It was unusual for Brigid to write so soon after her previous letter, so it was with some sense of concern that Siobhan sat down at the kitchen table to read it. She always treasured hearing from Brigid. She dreamed that she might one day see her sister again. Brigid's letter was uncharacteristically abrupt.

> *My dear sister:*
> *I hope this letter finds you well. From your last letter, it seems that the Ireland you are enjoying is very different from the one that we grew up in, but I pray that some of the old Ireland remains. Last night, at the new moon, a thing of horror, a demonic spirit, came to our hospital. It had been sent to kill a man who had tried to leave a cult that worships the left hand. He betrayed them by leaving, and they sent a spirit to kill him.*
> *Please believe me when I say that it was a creature of immense power. His passing forced awake abilities I thought I'd lost in my childhood. The Church may not be able to cope with it. The creature can act in the physical realm without need of possessing a human body. If you have any ties*

*remaining with those who follow the old ways, please let
them know that we need help here. I do not believe that this
beast will be satisfied with one death.*

Brigid

Siobhan was not a person to flinch in the face of such thoughts. In the famine she had seen horrors that few could imagine—a house where a woman and three children had starved to death together, a village of nothing but corpses and a half-eaten horse. Having lived through the famine had changed Siobhan's perspective on life. To her, each new day was a beautiful one. She had food to eat, a good husband, four beautiful children, and a warm house.

Now her sister was in danger. Siobhan knew how she might help, though she could not be certain. She called upstairs, "Nessa, I have a task for ya."

In a few moments the girl appeared in the kitchen, silent and composed. Her red hair framed her translucent complexion.

"Brigid has sent us a letter." Siobhan handed it to the girl, who quickly read it. A frown creased her perfect forehead.

"I've never asked about your lessons," her mother said, "in all the years you've studied the old ways. But yer aunt needs help that only the old ways can give. Do ya know of someone who can get a message to them that might help?"

"Yes, Mama." Nessa slid the letter inside the pocket of her dress.

"Then you be about findin' 'em. Take Windmark and ride where you need to go. I'll expect ya when I see ya again. Do ya need money?"

"I've enough. And I should be back on the morrow, at latest."

"Then ride, darlin', and remember this letter took a fortnight to get here. Only the gods know what's happened since."

Nessa went to change as Siobhan saddled Windmark. The horse seemed to sense the urgency of the mission. He impatiently stood still for the bridle and feather of a saddle that Nessa preferred. Nessa used no bit with Windmark. By the time Siobhan finished,

Nessa was there to take the bridle and lead him from the barn. She had a bit of bread and wrapped cheese in a small bag. She swung lightly into the saddle, and the big stallion pawed the ground, anxious to be going. There was nothing Windmark loved more than a run with Nessa on his back, her light hand on his neck, and her voice whispering in his ear.

Siobhan smiled to her daughter. "On yer way, darlin'."

Nessa leaned over Windmark's neck. "Fast, my love, fast." Her hand came down on his flank in a light slap, but it was all that Windmark needed. He reared, just for the pure pleasure of it. Before his front hooves came down, he launched himself toward the main road. The closed gate of the farmyard was no obstacle. He and Nessa cleared it without a nick.

Siobhan could have sworn she felt the earth vibrate when the big stallion's front hooves struck the ground after he cleared the gate. His rear hooves threw up clods of dirt with every stride. How that horse loved to run.

⚮

NESSA slowed Windmark to a trot as she approached the village in the early twilight. Best not to make too much of a stir, though anyone who saw what house she went to would know that it was the business of the old ways that had brought her. The house was on the edge of the village, near a meadow. She dismounted on the verge of the meadow and dropped the bridle to the ground.

"Here ya go, love. Plenty of grass and even a stream nearby fer a drink. I won't be long."

Windmark whinnied his acknowledgment.

Nessa turned from the horse without a thought that her beautiful stallion might be stolen. Irishmen never stole horses, unless they belonged to the English. Besides, Nessa knew that Windmark would never allow strangers to get too close.

Her knock on the door was quickly answered. The old man regarded her calmly. "Nessa, isn't it?"

"Yes."

"You've never come before without your teacher."

"No time for that."

He gestured for her to come into the cottage.

A HALF hour later she emerged from the cottage and gently whistled to Windmark. The horse came quickly. She reached up and scratched his massive head. Windmark nuzzled her in return. She swung up into the saddle, and the stallion pointed himself back the way that they had come. She gently prodded him into motion, not wishing to rush home. She had passed the message from Brigid on, and it had taken much of its sense of urgency with it.

Nonetheless, Nessa was still concerned about her aunt. Brigid was facing something innately terrifying. Though Nessa had never met her aunt, she felt a kinship with her. They shared the same unusual talents and the same deep blue eyes. All her life Nessa had heard about Brigid, how precocious she had been, how the powers had begun to show in her so early. Nessa also knew the story of why Brigid had been given to the Church; everyone in Ireland knew about the horror of the famine. The Church had done very little to help the starving, but had been more than happy to take Brigid for a nun.

Nessa resented the Church for its lack of help for the starving Irish, but she resented it even more for her having to grow up without the help and counsel that Brigid might have offered her. The Church had taken Brigid away by having the power to offer her parents the surety that their child would be fed.

Nessa felt the anger rise up in her. The village priest, now in his dotage, had seen an opportunity to remove the one that Emer had chosen to carry on the old ways. His desire to break the line of village wisewomen had removed Brigid and left Nessa to grow up feeling separated and alone. Others could not comprehend what she had experienced. Emer was long dead. Siobhan did all she could to help her daughter understand the odd things she saw, the curious abilities she possessed, but her mother was not like Nessa. She did not know from experience. All Siobhan had to offer her child were memories of what she had seen Brigid undergo at the same age. Not until Nessa began her studies in the old ways was she able to speak with someone who understood. Even then, it was not the same as having an aunt close at hand, an aunt who shared so much with her.

Nessa let the anger drain from her. Dwelling on the past offered nothing. It could not be changed. She leaned down and hugged Windmark's neck. The great beast was mystified by his rider's action, but felt it as affection, an affection he wholeheartedly returned. She luxuriated in the strength of the horse, the rough hair and powerful muscles quieting her mind and giving a sense of rightness back to the world.

Nessa sat back in the saddle. Looking up, she saw an abandoned village ahead of her, a common enough sight in the west of Ireland. Between the famine and the waves of emigration that had followed it, much of the area had been depopulated. As much as sixty percent of the people, maybe more, had died or left, mainly for America or the mills in the cities of England. Ireland as a whole had suffered little better. The population in 1845 had been well over eight million. By 1870 it had dropped below five million, and the emigration went on.

The village was a strange kind of ghost town. The cottage walls, many built of stone, still stood, though the thatched roofs had fallen in and rotted away years ago. Even the wooden furniture in the cottages was mostly gone, as were the wooden buildings. Most people avoided the abandoned villages, especially at night, afraid that the shades of the dead might come to haunt them. Nessa had no such fears. She knew there would be no haunting here. Her special senses told her that the village was dead and empty; no shades lingered to trouble the living.

In the years after the worst of the famine, burial parties had come to move the bodies, sometimes the skeletons, of the villagers to better resting places. Words said over the graves had ensured a peaceful rest for those who had died from starvation or disease. All that remained behind in the village was an aching sadness in the stones. As Nessa stopped in the middle of the village, the sadness triggered rebellious thoughts in her. Since the 1600s, the English had kept their boot on the necks of the Irish, draining them of food and dignity, often refusing to even acknowledge their humanity. The sadness etched in the stones reached further back than the famine, back through all of the campaigns to subdue England's troublesome colony. One day they would be free of that English boot.

She called Windmark to a gallop to escape this dismal place. On the other side of the village they slowed again, and Nessa's heart was lifted by the rare beauty of the land. The late afternoon sun cast long shadows over the gently rolling hills and fields. A copse of trees here and there gave accent to the fertile landscape. This late in the year the fields were harvested and the cattle fat from a summer of feasting. The herd had already been culled. The last full moon had been the Blood Moon, as it had been the time for the slaughter and butchering of cattle as herds were thinned for the winter.

The descending sun had let a chill grow in the air. Nessa shifted in her saddle, pushing Windmark into a faster walk. She intended to ride until she reached home. The night bore no fear for her. The chill was not enough to bother Windmark, and, with her legs wrapped securely about the horse, she was immune to it as well.

CHAPTER TWENTY-THREE

Savannah
Tuesday, October 27

RIMALDI'S chastened group met after breakfast. The monsignor joined the meeting, as he was their liaison with the bishop. The monsignor had already reported the events of the previous evening to his superior. Bishop Shea had asked that the monsignor convey his deepest condolences. Brigid had been invited as she had been present for the aftermath of the demon's visit.

Rimaldi cleared his throat and began with the mundane. "We need to stay aware of the time. Fathers Siena and Francisco will be on the nine-ten this morning."

"I can meet them for you," the monsignor said.

"Thank you, Monsignor," Benito said, unable to dislodge the sadness on his face.

Father Rimaldi looked as if he carried the full weight of his years and more. "Steven was my responsibility. I brought him here because he had a powerful gift, a natural talent for magic. I also wanted to continue his training. It may have been an ill-considered decision, even though I am not certain that I could have made a better choice." Almost speaking to himself, he said, "Our numbers have become so diluted over time. It has been so long since we were so direly needed." Rimaldi regained his focus. "I must confess that

I erred in not taking the warning of our friends in the Voudon community more seriously."

In the silent room, Benito nodded. His respect for this often arrogant man had increased. Rimaldi could admit mistakes.

"But now, we must decide what to do. We are in danger. I had originally thought that this creature was limited to being called at the dark of the moon. I was wrong, as the deaths of Sister Francis and Father Kirk have shown us. Each day, more of our members will join us, but that increase in numbers will do us no good if we are individually killed before we strike at them."

"Can we act earlier?" Sister Angela asked.

"Any of the most potent rituals will need at least four of us. Six would be better. We have only three, with two more arriving today. Father Pascal should be here anytime."

"I am willing to help," Brigid said.

"I know, and I have considered adding you. But, especially after what happened to Steven, I am unwilling to risk someone new against such an opponent."

Angela spoke. "Father, she is a true hereditary. I think that she would be able to help us a great deal."

"And I believe that it is still too early for her," Rimaldi responded, though without sounding as if the matter was closed.

Benito objected. "Father Rimaldi, I have felt the strength of her shielding. It is more powerful than mine. Alone, Kirk could not stand against the demon; none of us probably could. But Brigid and Angela together just might be able to. Their shielding is based on their hereditary strength, which none of us truly understand."

"A valid point," Rimaldi conceded.

Benito continued, "I probably have the second greatest ritual knowledge of all of us here. I confess that I have my doubts about the Ritual of Solomon, but we may need a ritual that potent to succeed. With Brigid in our company, we can attempt that ritual once the others arrive. Without her, we are too few."

"Angela, you have some sense of the creature's power. What do you think?" Rimaldi asked.

"The Ritual of Solomon, for all of its vulnerabilities, is the most potent one we can do with seven. I can have Brigid ready to work in one of the triads in a few days."

"But it places her in danger," Rimaldi objected, still unwilling to risk someone so new to their realm.

Brigid spoke up. "I am already at risk. The creature may have sensed me the night that Richardson died. Even if it did not, I have become linked with you. If we do not defeat it together, then it will come for me. Part of your order or not, I am part of what you do here. I do not mean to sound disrespectful, but I have the right to decide how to face this creature, and I would rather face it with all of you."

"But," he said, anger creeping into his voice, "what if protecting you weakens our ability to fight?"

Her shielding momentarily flared about her, a natural response to his anger. "Pride, Father Provincial, goeth before the fall."

Even the monsignor could feel the power in the air. He gasped, both at the affront to the Father Provincial and at the strange electricity in the air about the nun.

Rimaldi remembered his own thoughts aboard the train and was chastened. "Then you shall join us."

Angela reached over to clasp Brigid's hand.

Rimaldi took a minute to regain his calm before speaking. "We have to wait for the others to arrive to attack. However, that course leaves us with the problem of our own defense until then. I think that we should all move to the ballroom in the house on York Street. We will stay together for mutual protection. The monsignor can take our new arrivals directly to the house."

The monsignor nodded his assent.

"Then let us move to York Street."

As the meeting broke up, the monsignor approached Rimaldi.

"Father Provincial, I think we need to visit the bishop; he is very concerned."

"Of course," Rimaldi replied.

⟡

THE bishop paced back and forth in his office as they explained what had happened to Kirk. Since the monsignor had told the bishop of the previous evening's events, he had had little room in his mind for anything else.

"Three dead," the bishop said, "a patient, a nun, and now one of your own. I thought you were here to remove the problem, but you seem to be making it worse."

"Our opponent, Your Grace," Rimaldi replied, "is more powerful than we had expected, more powerful than we have ever faced in America."

"But can you defeat it?"

"Once my magicians are assembled, I believe we can."

"Believe?" The bishop ran his hand through his uncharacteristically tousled hair. "And what if you fail?"

"Rome will send someone else."

"And what will we do in the meantime?" The fear of his own experience and the concern for his diocese were obvious in his voice.

"Your Grace, I will send a telegram to Rome today to tell them that you need help here immediately if I do not contact them once a week and assure them that the threat has been dealt with."

"Do it daily. Making it weekly would only add another week of danger to the situation."

"But I do not think that we will fail."

"So far, Father Provincial, your 'thoughts' have not impressed me. I was appointed by the Holy Father to see to the spiritual needs of this diocese, and I will decide what is needed. You will send a telegram every day, and the monsignor will have the address in the event that you are unable to send it."

"Yes, Your Grace," Rimaldi replied.

"See to it, Monsignor," the bishop said, dismissing them.

"Yes, Your Grace," the monsignor also replied.

✺

AS Streng returned from the morning session at his factoring house, he did not imagine that things could be proceeding any better, regardless of the piercing pain deep within his shoulders and the unusual ache in his bowels that had plagued him all morning. The pains were a common enough occurrence after a ritual. Each summoning of Belial drained his strength, sometimes for as long as a week. His physical condition was deteriorating more rapidly with each passing year.

Nonetheless, Streng was elated with the events of the previous night. Belial had come when they had called and had immediately set about their bidding. Their instructions to the demon had been to seek out and kill the most vulnerable member of the group. The idea had occurred to Streng just as Belial had emerged. In the quiet time after Belial had returned through the portal to its realm, they had congratulated themselves on picking a good strategy, in testing the strength of the priests in a real situation. None of them considered how often a new strategy occurred to them just as Belial appeared.

Streng and the others had seen the priest through Belial's eyes and shared in the demon's emotions. The priest had been easy prey. Even someone with many times his strength would not have been a challenge to Belial. The image that remained with Streng and the others was that of the priest's ruined body slipping down the door.

"This," a smiling Streng thought to himself, "was a pleasure worth the price." The priests he had seen as a child had always been so sure of themselves, so self-righteous, even the one who had always let his hand linger a little long on a boy's shoulder. Yes, he knew the interior of the cathedral all too well, even those nooks where a young boy might disappear for a while and see what he was not supposed to see. Humiliating a priest, crushing him as Belial had done, terrifying him, and draining the blood from his body were pleasures that Streng had never hoped to experience. But now he had. He chuckled softly to himself. What pleasures he would have, all thanks to Belial.

Streng was so closely attuned to Belial that they could wordlessly communicate. Immediately before returning through the portal, the demon had placed a message in Streng's mind. Belial wanted to return in two days, and Streng realized the wisdom of the plan. It would give the priests a night to recover from the terror, and then the terror would return. Belial would whittle down their numbers. When Belial and Streng and his group finally struck in full force at the priests, the priests' numbers would be less, and they would be demoralized. Streng, backed by Belial and the full power of his group on that final night, looked forward to destroying them.

As he completed his walk home, he began to wonder who might be their next victim. Perhaps that lovely Italian nun. Streng hugged his power to him like a bloody sword. No matter what price he had to pay, he was sure that it would not be enough to balance the elation that he felt. This power that he wielded over the Catholic priests was true command. It was the ability to decide life and death. No man could feel more godlike, at least not in Streng's definition of what being godlike entailed.

MONSIGNOR Henry went to his office after the meeting. He had a few minutes before he would have to leave for the train station, and he needed to calm himself after the meeting with the bishop. The normally soft-spoken bishop had shown an edge of steel that the monsignor had rarely seen as he had sliced through Rimaldi's self-assurance.

Though Monsignor Henry was calm to all outward appearances,

his emotions were in turmoil. Rimaldi's group had been chosen by the Church to defend against the darkness. They were the ones who were supposed to wield the sword of God in retribution. Now one of them was dead. About them was the feel of desperate men, ones who knew they were in a battle that they might well lose.

As Henry walked to the side entrance of the cathedral where Daniel would meet him with the carriage, he realized that he was seeing a new view of the Church itself, a view at odds with the one he was accustomed to—that of the potent, all-encompassing Catholic Church, whose outposts ringed the world. The Church he saw represented by the magicians was a handful of people, waiting for reinforcements, huddled in their sanctuary on York Street. They were so unsure of their own safety that he, a noncombatant, was needed to bring reinforcements to the battle. Even worse, they needed a new recruit, one of his nuns, to fill their ranks.

After the monsignor boarded the carriage, Daniel snapped the reins and drove it over the cobblestone street. The clean morning air was bracing, but the monsignor could not dispel the dark cloud in his thoughts. He kept a fixed smile on his face, waving to the many on the street who greeted him, sometimes giving an automatic reply. None suspected anything was wrong. In truth, the monsignor himself was only now beginning to comprehend the deadly nature of this arcane battle.

The monsignor could not even rely on his allies in the police department, men who were normally more than happy to oblige him. He could imagine the result of approaching them about these murders. If they even took him seriously, which he doubted, they would focus their investigation on the wrong things. They would look for a perverse man who had tortured, then killed, the victims, but the monsignor already knew who the culprit was, and this culprit could not be brought to trial or caged. Nor would the police move against Streng. There was no evidence linking him to the crime, at least none that could be seen by anyone without the strange perceptual skills held by people like Benito, Brigid, and Angela. No court would recognize the testimony of anyone, priest or not, who claimed to see spirits. In a legal contest, Streng's lawyers would embarrass the police and the Church publicly. The world had become so confident in its secularity that the truth of what was occurring would never be accepted. Paradoxically, secularity made people more vulnerable to an attack from the spirit realm. The Church was left to fight on alone with scant resources left over from a different time, when men had believed in evil.

Henry emerged from his reverie when Daniel began to rein in at the front of the station. Three, not two, priests were waiting for them.

The monsignor stepped down from the carriage and extended his hand to the new arrivals. "Hello, I'm Monsignor Robert Henry. Father Provincial Rimaldi sent me to meet you."

"Ah, good," the jovial priest to the right said. "I am Father Anthony Siena." He indicated the priest on the left. "This is Father Miguel Francisco, and between us we have Father Armand Pascal. We met by chance in Atlanta yesterday and joined for the remainder of the journey."

Father Pascal looked into the monsignor's eyes. Regardless of the frail state of his body, Pascal's eyes were bright and penetrating. "A pleasure, Monsignor." He shook the younger man's hand. There was a slight palsy in his grip.

Father Siena said, "I had thought that Father Benito would be meeting us."

The monsignor answered, "There was an incident last night."

"Incident?" Siena asked. The cheerfulness fell from his face.

"It's best we not discuss it here."

Siena nodded, frowning. He did not expect that the incident would be good news.

As Siena and Francisco loaded the bags for all three priests into the carriage, the monsignor looked at the new arrivals. Father Siena was a rotund, cheerful man of about fifty. His olive skin was pale compared to that of the younger Father Francisco, who looked as if he was a mix of Spanish and Indian parents. He was thin and moved quickly and economically. The monsignor became aware that Father Pascal was muttering something.

"Excuse me, Father?" the monsignor asked.

The old man looked up into his eyes. The brightness had vanished, to be replaced by a vacant stare. In a singsong chant, the old man repeated, "Holy Mary, Mother of God, pray for us sinners, now and at the hour of our death."

The monsignor found that these few familiar words, spoken on a sidewalk in full daylight, frightened him more than anything else he had seen or heard in the past days.

⚬⋏⚬

THE mages, including the new arrivals, met in the ballroom at the York Street house at a little past ten. The servants had brought a large table for the group as well as cots to sleep on. There was an abundance of chairs in the ballroom. They could hear the staff busily working downstairs, cleaning and moving in food. Both the monsignor and the mother superior had come with the staff to ensure that the group would have everything that they needed.

Rimaldi quickly explained the situation to the new arrivals. They were stunned to hear of Steven's death.

Siena was the first to speak. "One of our own. Brutally killed."

Father Francisco shook his head. "I have not heard of such a thing in living memory, a demon who can attack a magician in the physical world."

"Few of us have been misfortunate enough to feel the wrath of a demon that can take physical form," Angela said. "Yes, Father, it is hard to believe, but the demon has killed three people recently. It will kill again."

A momentary silence fell.

"I am sorry I did not have the opportunity of meeting Father Kirk," Father Siena said. "I had heard many good things about him."

"He is already missed," Rimaldi said. "We will bury him this afternoon. Needless to say, we will all go as a group."

"How are we to proceed now?" Siena asked.

Rimaldi looked around the room. "If any have suggestions about what I propose, please feel free to make them." He cleared his throat. "I think we must remain together at all times. We shall stay in this room to the greatest extent possible and avoid being alone. At night, one of us will always be awake and alert, ready to awaken the others in the event that anything out of the ordinary happens.

"In the meantime, we must hone our skills. I think that we should wait for them to come to us, so as to give us the advantage of place. It would be more difficult for us to attack them in a place where they have built up so much power. Sister Angela will work with Sister Brigid to ready her for the ritual. We must remain as rested as possible, even at the close of the day. Undoubtedly, our greatest danger will be in the night."

"Will Father Pascal be standing watch?" Angela asked. The question sounded more like a challenge.

"I do not think that would be wise," Rimaldi replied. "Anything else?"

He drew no response. Everyone knew that the most important task was to stay alive until they would have the opportunity to fight as a group. For some, the first step of that task was to overcome the dread of what they faced.

Father Pascal was tired from his journey and lay down to rest in one of the bedrooms. Siena accompanied him as his guardian. Francisco did not know any of the others, except for Siena, whom he had met once before this trip. His interaction with Rimaldi had been through letters. Father Francisco made it his first objective to get to know these people upon whom his life might depend. He gravitated to Benito, who also spoke Spanish as his first language.

❧

THE funeral was held in mid-afternoon at Laurel Grove Cemetery. The Church owned most of the few vacant plots that remained
in the old cemetery. When they returned to York Street after the funeral, Angela said that she was not ready to return to the ballroom
yet. She turned into the drawing room. Luis and Brigid accompanied
her. The three had become inseparable. They sat arrayed around the
room.

"At least Rimaldi seems less confident about the reality that we
face," Angela said.

Benito nervously glanced at the door, as Brigid did. "Angela,"
he said admonishingly, "confidence is needed in our work."

She kept her voice low and level. "Luis, I know that you have
been longer under the Church hierarchy than I have been. But confidence is a danger when you are too certain of your strength."

"Yes, it is."

Brigid had been drawn out of her reverie and said in a strangely
distant voice, "Now perhaps we have a chance."

"You don't think we did before?" Luis asked.

"No, I didn't think our prospects were particularly good, but
Siena and Francisco both add to our abilities."

"And Pascal?" Angela said.

"I don't count assets that I can't be certain of," Brigid replied.

"Wise," Angela said.

Nothing more was said, or needed to be. Each selected a book
that could help divert the sense of dread that followed them. Having
improved chances, as they now did, was not the same thing as feeling confident of the outcome. They read for perhaps an hour, when
they returned to the main room. The others were just beginning a
discussion of dinner and what they would prepare. Planning dinner
and helping in its preparation gave them all a respite from the study,
contemplation, and prayer that had filled most of the hours of the

day. By the time dinner was served, the mood had lightened. When dinner was over and the cleaning done, their leader drew them all together, made the watch assignments, and bid them a good night. Father Pascal would not be called upon to watch, though he would be sleeping in the ballroom with them. Rimaldi was afraid that the demon might come during a time in which Pascal was less than lucid.

Father Francisco was the first to stand watch, followed by Benito, Angela, Siena, and Rimaldi. The night passed without incident. Rimaldi spent his time on his predawn watch wondering about the best course of action. He carefully reviewed the reasons for and against each ritual. The greatest question remained. Could they take the battle to their opponents?

Rimaldi looked up from his musings at the first steel gray light of dawn. He saw that one other was awake. Brigid regarded him levelly, as if wondering what manner of odd creature he was. He looked into her eyes as they caught the strengthening light of dawn. In this light, their deep shade of blue seemed eerie, almost supernatural. He comprehended, as he had not before, that she was a sister to Angela, not as a nun, but as an hereditary witch from an ancient line. Within themselves, these women held a power that he could not match. It fit none of his rituals, none of his magic. They could lend much of their power to a ritual, but not all of it. Inside of them was a sacred place, an untouchable sanctuary. He wondered if the demon, in all of its power, could really harm them.

Another movement from a stirring sleeper caught his attention and the moment was broken. When he looked back to Sister Brigid, she was leaning close to the waking Angela, whispering to her.

As he watched the two women, he thought about the talent they shared. Rimaldi had met hereditaries only a few times in his life. All of them, male and female alike, though males were rare, possessed an inner stillness that Rimaldi found unsettling. Though they had been born with a talent that allowed them to be trained in very little time, they were not proud. They did not think of themselves as being better than others, only different. Other mages, himself included, often took pride in the skills they had mastered. Hereditaries seemed to feel that they had an unearned gift. They took even more responsibility upon themselves than others, as if they owed the world service for the gift they had.

Perhaps their attitude, their lack of boastfulness, came from the fact that they were often alone. Rarely did they meet another hereditary who shared their odd world. When they did, as Brigid and Angela had done, they quickly formed deep friendships. Yet, even when alone, Rimaldi had noticed, they did not act as if they were alone. They always acted at ease with the world around them, remaining unthreatened. Maybe they really did possess a direct line to the divine forces and knew that there was something there to support them. Perhaps, he thought, they were not proud because they were in touch with something so much more powerful than they were that they knew they were not that special. The other thing, whatever that was, was where the real significance and power lay.

This territory was dangerous for him. Catholic doctrine did not allow for reincarnation, but that was one of only two ways that Rimaldi could explain their unusual powers. The other was pure inheritance. It really came in the blood, like blond hair or green eyes. That was unsatisfactory to him as well, since it implied that God had not dealt the hand evenly to all humans. Yet Rimaldi and every other serious student of the craft knew that hereditary power flowed along family lines. The Dellamortes had one or two hereditaries in every generation.

What bothered him the most about the capability of the hereditaries was that this power seemed to have nothing to do with which god they worshiped. If their power was based on a connection with the divine, it did not seem that the name of the divine or its sex had anything to do with whether they had power or not. This ground was dangerous theologically, since it implied that there were many gods, not one. The hereditaries were living proof that the Christian doctrine of one god was flawed.

The light of dawn flooded the room as the sun rose. Rimaldi looked up to see the subjects of his thoughts and found that they were gone. In the kitchen, he suspected, making coffee.

CHAPTER TWENTY-FOUR

Beddgelert, Wales
Wednesday, October 28

WHILE Rimaldi was experiencing dawn, it was five hours later in the day in Wales. The information that Brigid had sent had finally reached someone who could act on it. He lived in a small village in Wales, Beddgelert. The village lies in the heart of Snowdonia, the most mountainous section of the county of Gwynedd in Wales. Beddgelert is set in what might be the most lovely valley in a country filled with lovely valleys. Surrounded by mountains that wall it off from the world, Snowdonia has always remained out of the reach of any enemy. Even the Norman English, who conquered Wales, never penetrated the mountain strongholds of the Welsh. In the thirteenth century they surrounded these mountains with their great castles at Caernarvon, Beaumaris, Conwy, and Harlech, then burned the grain fields in the lowlands and on the Isle of Môn until the Welsh were starved from their aerie. In 1282, with the death of the last native Prince of Wales, Wales became a part of Britain, with the eldest son of the British monarch being the one to carry the title of "Prince of Wales." The isolation of the village had allowed it to retain much of its ancient Celtic character and the traditions that went with it.

Even after English tourists discovered the beauty of Beddgelert and its mountains in the nineteenth century, the village retained an "otherworldly" aspect. The terrain was not the only barrier that separated the tourists from the locals. Though most of the natives could speak English, the daily language of Beddgelert, in fact of much of Gwynedd, was Welsh. The simple salutation "sut mae'r" separated the Welsh from the visitors.

The retention of the language also signified their link to the history of Wales. The Welsh were Celts, and they had occupied Britain long before the coming of the Angles and the Saxons. Beddgelert itself was linked to the old myths of Wales, lying close to Dinas Emrys, the place where Merlin was said to have given his first prophecy. Beddgelert was also the only village in Scotland, Ireland, or Wales to have two walkers. In centuries past, many towns had had more than one walker, but those days were long past, except in Beddgelert.

By late October the tourists left, and the village returned to a more sedate pace. The farmers and herders were at work. Owain Llywelyn had few customers in his apothecary shop. Beddgelert was not large enough to support a shop that sold only medicines, so he also had a small bookstore and an herb shop within the apothecary. The shop suited him. His was a quiet life. He lived over his shop and had enough to see to his needs. But on this day that quiet life had been disrupted by a telegram that had come from across the Irish Sea. He had been called to his true work, to the job to which he had been born. That very morning, he and the other Beddgelert walker, Gwynfor Jones, had sent a letter to a third walker, Dafydd Bevan, who lived in Betws y Coed.

Owain and Gwynfor had taken the information in the telegram seriously enough. The Irish walker who had sent it knew of Brigid's family, but the Irish had no walkers in America. The Irish walkers not only had faced the depredations that had occurred over the centuries as their religion faded about them but had also lost many to the famine. When the call for help had come from America, they had turned to their Welsh brothers. The two walkers in Beddgelert hoped that there were some of their calling in America. Dafydd

Bevan might know if there were. Owain had to wait for his compatriot's arrival before he could take any action.

The walkers had always been independent of the pagan religious rites of the British Isles, even though they shared the same beliefs. They stayed to themselves, as had been their habit for many
hundreds of years before the coming of Christianity. Their task was
not a public one. It was to safeguard people against those things
from the dark realms that could threaten the lives and sanity of others.
Walkers worked silently and anonymously, drawing as little attention as possible. Yet even that caution had not protected them from
the fires of the Inquisition. Some had been caught and killed. Some
had renounced their ancient duties, feeling that renunciation was
the appropriate response to a society that no longer wanted their
services.

Wales had more walkers than Ireland, even though it was much
smaller and had no areas that were truly pagan, as Ireland did. In
the western reaches of Ireland, pagan customs and even the practice of the old religion remained alive, though sorely weakened.
Wales, on the other hand, was a thoroughly Christian country, but it
had not seen the same cultural brutality as Ireland. A high percentage of the Welsh still spoke their own language, and the oral literature of Wales extended further back than that of England. Much of
that literature dealt with the tales of the old gods, of Bran and
Branwen, Manawyddan and Llyr.

A special pride existed among the Welsh of Gwynedd, stemming
from the province's claim to be the birthplace of Merlin, though they
had to argue that claim with every place between Cumbria and Land's
End. As a result of their honoring their pagan past, men like Owain
were left to themselves, and if they were less than dutiful in their ob-
ligations to the Church, nothing was said. Everything was done with a
nod and a wink, for the Welsh were always looking for ways to be
"different" from the English. Travelers in Wales soon learned that the
Welsh could be referred to as "Welsh" or as "British," but referring
to a Welshman as "English" was to be avoided.

The walkers of Wales were left to themselves for other, more subtle reasons. Wales is a mountainous land that distorts the sense of distance. Things seem farther apart in Wales. Being alone in a valley at night between two Welsh villages is very lonely indeed. Everyone knew the old tales that had been written down over a millennium ago, the stories of lords of the underworld who would ride from the sides of mountains to carry mortals off to lands from which they might never return. All knew of Manawyddan's bargaining with one such lord to return the people of Dyfed to human form. A good way for a traveler to ward off the fear in the night was with a memory of Merlin, who was said to still wander the land in human form, protecting his people. So, if a traveler glimpsed a solitary stranger walking a road in the night, the traveler greeted him with courtesy and very little curiosity.

For the walkers, the courtesy with which they were met was not a matter of superstition. Merlin might be gone, but he had been one of them all the same. The dragons with whom he had spoken still lay sleeping beneath the spines of the Welsh mountains.

CHAPTER TWENTY-FIVE

Savannah
Wednesday, October 28

THAT evening, the watch assignments were the same as for the previous night. Each two-hour shift of watch passed in its turn. At 2:00 A.M. Siena relieved Angela, who immediately fell deeply asleep. Siena watched her breathing slow to a sleeping rhythm in a few minutes. Some of the others seemed to sleep shallowly, like soldiers in their trenches, aware that an attack could come at any time.

As the clock progressed to three, he realized that he was having trouble staying awake, so he stood and began moving around the ballroom, walking barefoot so as not to awaken the others. He did not like the feel of the room. Was it just apprehension or was there really something to fear hovering outside in the darkness? He walked to one of the rear windows of the ballroom, away from the front windows where the sleepers were clustered. The window looked down onto a small backyard with a gazebo that needed repainting. "No," he thought to himself, "nothing there."

He heard a loud intake of breath and Angela crying hoarsely from the alcove, "It's coming!"

At the same moment, one of the front windows of the ballroom shattered inward. Belial emerged through the shattered frame, fire running down its arms. The immense figure immediately went for the nearest priest, Father Pascal.

Muttering a spell, Father Siena raced across the floor toward Pascal. Sister Angela emerged from the alcove, shouting to wake the others. Pascal was struggling, trying to get to his feet. Belial struck the still-waking Pascal, knocking him down. As Siena neared the demon, a faint glow of his own magic grew about him. Belial turned from Pascal and swatted Siena to the side. The priest slid across the floor and came to rest against a wall, dazed but conscious. Belial turned its attention back to Pascal, but the old priest had been given time to awaken. As he struggled to his knees, a marginal glow of his own power began to build. A protective barrier formed in the air between himself and Belial. The demon concentrated its strength, knowing it had little time to work. The others were awakening. Belial pressed against the shielding that had been thrown up by the old priest. The protective shell began to buckle.

The others were awake enough to call their own magic to them. Rimaldi was the first to launch his personal power against the demon, but it was more of an annoyance to Belial than a threat. Pascal was trying to stay within the protective orb of his collapsing shield. Then Angela was at Pascal's side, with Brigid a few steps behind. Though the other magicians were throwing their power against Belial, it was not a joined effort, and their individual thrusts could not divert the demon from its kill. Angela cast no spells, but her own shielding glowed as she insinuated herself between Belial and Pascal. Her shielding was not like Pascal's. Its greenish shell was powerful and could hold against the full brunt of the demon's power. Belial tried to go around her, but collided with Brigid, who had slipped between the demon and Pascal from the other side and stood next to Angela. Brigid's dull red shielding looked like steaming blood against the fiery orange-red of Belial. The demon could not quickly break through the protective power of the two nuns but continued to hammer at it. While the demon battered at the nuns, Rimaldi, Benito, and Francisco were given a minute's respite. They began a coordinated spell. Finally, Belial uttered a bellow of rage and retreated through the broken window.

Brigid sat heavily on the floor, drenched with sweat. Angela turned to help Father Pascal as the other priests moved to them. Benito went to examine the injured Siena.

Father Rimaldi pushed in close to Pascal. "Are you all right?"

The old priest looked dazed but alert. He took several breaths before replying. "That was a close thing. Thank you, Sister," he said to Angela. "I appear to owe you my life."

"I could not have done it without Brigid. Our combined power was too strong for it to penetrate quickly."

Brigid said, "I doubt I could have held out much longer against it without Angela."

"You are all right?" Rimaldi asked again.

"I seem to be," Pascal replied. "What about Father Siena?"

Benito answered for the other priest. "Outside of a nasty bump on the head and a few cuts on his feet from running barefoot through broken glass, he seems to have survived."

Rimaldi sighed in relief. It was their first victory, small though it may have been. A victory in defense is far easier than destroying a demon, but it was nonetheless a victory. Father Francisco reached down to help Pascal to his feet.

"Ah, thank you. I didn't know this old man had that much left in him." He smiled. "But it is the sisters—" He broke off and grabbed at his chest. He cried out once in pain, then collapsed to the floor. Broken glass crunched beneath him.

"Benito!" Rimaldi cried.

Father Benito was beside them immediately and pressed his hand against Pascal's carotid artery. He held it there for several seconds, then slowly pulled his hand away. He leaned over, close to Pascal's face, hoping for some faint sign of breath. He looked up and said sadly, "I saw what happened. It was a heart attack. Undoubtedly brought on by the strain. There's nothing I can do."

"If we called a doctor?" Rimaldi said hopefully.

"There's nothing he can do either," Brigid replied for Father Benito.

In the aftermath of the attack, the sadness of Father Pascal's death left them all numb. They went back to their cots, though none could sleep. The power of the magic still hung in the air, like the smell of powder after an artillery barrage. The electricity in the air would take time to dissipate. Brigid and Angela sought solace in each other's company. Luis sat with Francisco. Siena came to sit by Rimaldi.

"I'm sorry, Father Provincial," Siena said. "I had sensed something was wrong, but I did not expect such a sudden explosion of power."

"There is nothing to apologize for. I have certainly made much more serious mistakes myself."

Siena looked at him in puzzlement.

"Brigid," he said. "Had I brought her into our preparations earlier, perhaps tonight's death would not have happened."

"She," said Siena, "is an hereditary?"

"Yes."

"I would have assumed so from the odd color of her shielding. Deep red is a disturbing color for the shield of one on our side."

"We normally think of it as being the province of darkness, but her shield held better than Pascal's against the strength of the demon." Rimaldi looked old and dismayed. "I should have done something earlier with her."

"Father Provincial, we all know it is hard to assess hereditaries. Their talents are often hidden."

"Yes, but I now realize that both Luis and Angela were trying to tell me that she had access to power."

"I didn't realize that . . ." Siena trailed off.

"Maybe she could have saved him."

"I think not. I was the only one fully awake when Belial attacked, and I felt the force of what was only a backhanded blow. It is very powerful. Angela and Brigid arrived very soon to protect him. I might have been dazed, but I did see what happened. The only way they could have saved him is if they had both been awake and fully ready to protect him. Belial seized him because he was nearest the window. And what killed him was not Belial, but a heart not strong enough to bear the strain." He looked intently at the Jesuit, one of his oldest friends. "And, Joseph, second-guessing yourself helps no one."

Rimaldi straightened his shoulders. "Thank you, Anthony. I could also criticize myself for calling him here, when I should have called another. But you are right. What has happened, already has. Now, for the future, I must make certain that we gain everything we can from Brigid's abilities."

"What can I do to help?"

"Be aware of everything that happens. If I miss something, or misinterpret it, tell me."

Anthony nodded, knowing his friend's weaknesses as well as his strengths.

CHAPTER TWENTY-SIX

Thursday, October 29

THURSDAY'S dawn in Savannah was gray, filled with clouds and rain. The priests hurriedly boarded up the shattered window. The few people who passed by in the early dawn did not seem to want to inquire. The police, knowing enough of the strange happenings at the cathedral to be certain that they did not want to know more, were sent away with little trouble. The priests and nuns ate breakfast in silence. There would be another funeral that afternoon.

Angela stood at one of the unbroken windows in the front of the house and looked down at the street. She saw Daniel looking up at her, sadness creasing his normally cheerful face; then he turned away in the rain. She let her hands slide gently over the glass in the window. The pane had the gentle waviness of glass that has been in place for a very long time. The replacement windows would never match. She traced a drop as it slid down the pane.

Brigid came up behind her. "Father Pascal seemed like such a good man."

"He was, and we did manage to keep the creature from killing him. His heart just gave out on him."

"Whatever the reason, he is dead, and we have one less magician."

Neither the grayness of the mood nor the grayness of the day lifted. Father Siena was bruised and limping, but had no serious physical injury. However, Belial's blow had disturbed more than his body, and Rimaldi knew that Siena would not be as effective a magician as he could be until his psychic wounds had healed. Brigid would take his watch that night.

In the early afternoon, Benito, Angela, and Brigid buried Father Pascal. Rimaldi had wanted them all to stay together, but Benito dissuaded him, assuring him that Angela, Brigid, and he would be in no danger. Rimaldi, Francisco, and Siena stayed behind at the house on York Street.

When they finished the service for Father Pascal, they each tossed a handful of muddy dirt onto the coffin and turned away from the wooden box lying in the dark and damp earth. The grave diggers came behind them to cover the coffin. Some moved with fear, looking over their shoulders as they rapidly shoveled dirt into the freshly dug hole.

The day had become a beautiful one. The clouds and rain had moved on, and the afternoon sun was warm on their faces. None of them had any desire to return to the grim house on York, though they knew that they must. They simply sought to delay that return. When they reached the street, they approached the waiting coach.

"Daniel," Benito called up to the driver.

The young man looked down at him. He did not speak. He was almost as affected by the deaths as they were.

"Go back to the stable without us," Benito said. "We will walk."

"It's a good ways," Daniel replied.

"We know. Thank you for your concern."

Daniel nodded and snapped the reins. They watched the coach drive off and followed in the same direction, heading toward the cathedral. For a while they walked without talking.

Brigid broke the silence. "Is there any other source of help?"

Angela was the first to respond. "I have sent a telegram to my family. There may be some help possible from there, but I do not know. Even we have little experience with such creatures."

Benito continued the train of thought. "Father Rimaldi and I discussed the same thing after breakfast. We have sent a telegram to the Vatican, requesting help, but such help would take weeks to arrive, even assuming that it is available."

"What do you mean by 'assuming that it is available'?"

"What he means, Brigid," Angela answered, "is that there are few magicians in the Church more powerful than Rimaldi. We have others here to feed power to him. Given that circumstance, our group is probably as potent as any that the Church could assemble anywhere. If we cannot defeat this thing under Rimaldi's leadership, then it is quite possible that the Church cannot defeat it at all."

Brigid said, "Then I guess that it was wise to try to send for a walker."

Benito stopped in astonishment. "You did what?"

"I sent for a walker," Brigid said quietly.

"But I thought there weren't any walkers left."

"I don't know if there are or if there aren't, but I sent a letter in hopes of finding one."

"To whom?" Benito asked.

"My sister. She may still have some contacts with those that follow the old ways."

"Why didn't you say something to me earlier?" Benito asked.

"I think I was afraid to say anything. I was confused. On the one hand, I wanted to see this thing killed. On the other, I didn't want my family or those involved in the old ways to be in any danger." She paused. "I'm not even sure there are any walkers left. If there are, would they come? Their relations with the Church have probably been less than pleasant."

Angela said, "I should have said something to you, Luis. I just assumed you knew."

"So I was the only one left out of this particular piece of news?" he said.

"I am sorry," Brigid said. "But you weren't the only one left out. Angela was the only one other than myself to know."

"It's all right, Brigid," Benito said. "I am just disappointed that you didn't trust me enough to tell me."

"I wrote to her the day after Richardson's death, before I met you."

"So you thought this might be beyond the Church from the beginning?"

"I don't know what I thought. I just felt that I should."

"Then it was the right thing to do," Angela said. "I would assume that you would not want Father Rimaldi to know of this?"

Brigid nodded thankfully. "I would appreciate it."

Benito added, "Then think no more of it. Besides, he doesn't need something else on his mind, especially something that might not occur. The subject will remain between the three of us, unless the walker actually arrives."

They resumed their walk.

"How long will it take the letter to get to Ireland?" Benito asked.

"About two weeks. It may already have arrived."

"We cannot count on a walker's arrival," Benito said. "Even if one exists and will help us, we are a long way from Ireland. It is doubtful that one could reach us in time."

They fell silent again. Each was left to his or her own thoughts, but they were all glad to be away from the oppressive atmosphere in the house on York Street, at least for a while. As they walked in the sunshine, the city itself worked its magic of beauty upon them, and they began to heal from the sadness of the events of the previous days. Angela and Benito each recalled the story that Brigid had told of the walker that had come when her great-aunt had been young. It gave them hope that a savior might appear, as unlikely as his arrival, even his very existence, might be.

That afternoon the Catholic mages met and discussed if they might be able to strike at their enemies. Sooner would be better, since Belial's power would grow as the new moon approached. But the disheartened magicians could make no plan. They were intimidated by the power of the demon and by the strength of the residual magic on Saint Julian. Belial itself was frighteningly strong. What would happen when Streng's magicians added their power to the battle? Besides, the Catholic mages were no longer able to perform the Ritual of Solomon. Pascal's death had left them one short. Reaching no decision, they postponed their discussion to the next day.

Rimaldi and Benito thought that conducting a summoning ritual two nights in a row would be too trying a task for their opponents, so it was not likely that Belial would strike them again that night. The priests and nuns went to sleep that evening comforted by the expectation that the events of the previous night would not be repeated. They did not stand watch, trusting that Angela would sense an attack, as she had the night before, if one came.

Brigid remained awake for a while and reflected on their situation. She had no way of knowing if Siobhan had been successful in her attempt to find a walker, nor was she likely to know soon. The situation in Savannah was growing more grim. If their opponents' intent had been to undermine their courage and confidence, they had succeeded. The shock of two additional deaths was almost more than the Catholics could bear.

The Catholics were supposed to be the ones wielding the sword, carrying out the will of God, but now they felt more like prey. Would Streng wait for the new moon, or would he call his coven together before the last night of the waning moon to destroy the remaining magicians of the Church? Brigid tried to resign herself to whatever might happen, hoping that she and Angela might survive.

Brigid knew little about ceremonial magic and was frustrated by her own ignorance. Reluctantly she realized that, even if she knew more, that knowledge would not help her. Streng would strike at the time of his choosing. Until then they must wait, because what they had to destroy was Belial, the creature that their opponents summoned.

At first, she had been angry that Rimaldi had not included her in their meetings. Now she had gained the questionable honor of being attacked by the demon itself. Its blows upon her defenses had not stopped at the bloodred barrier. Each one that had impacted her shielding had resonated inside of her, leaving her weak from the effort to resist them. Her intestines had clenched in response to the unfamiliar energy pounding against her. Still feeling battered and in need of rest, she lay down to sleep until breakfast.

CHAPTER TWENTY-SEVEN

Beddgelert
Friday, October 30

DR. Dafydd Bevan stopped his carriage in front of Owain's apothecary as the sun first penetrated to the floor of the valley. He had brought a fourth walker, Cerridwyn Evans, with him.

Thomas Humphries, Owain's apprentice, was just arriving at work, having first done his morning chores on his family's farm.

"Bore da," Thom greeted Dr. Bevan and Miss Evans.

"Good morning to you as well, Thom," Dr. Bevan replied.

Cerridwyn smiled her greeting.

Thom approached the doctor, whom he knew from his previous visits. "Looks like your horse could use a little water and a rubdown. Should I take care of him for you?"

"I would appreciate it, Thom."

As the young man led the horse around to the small stable in the back of the shop, Dafydd and Cerridwyn entered the apothecary shop. At the sound of the door, Owain looked up.

"I thought that might be you." He smiled. "And you've brought another. Always good to see you, Cerridwyn."

"I thought that we might have need for her special skills," Dafydd said. "So I stopped by to pick her up on the way."

"A good thought. We have a serious situation. As soon as Thom arrives we must go to meet with Gwynfor at his farm. We are less likely to be disturbed there than here."

"Well, I'd best get Thom for you. He's arrived and is taking care of my horse. From what you've said, it appears we'll have immediate need of my carriage."

"We can let your horse rest a bit while the two of you have a cup of tea upstairs. There's a fresh pot on the hob. Go on up. I'll talk to Thom."

Dafydd led Cerridwyn up the stairs to Owain's living quarters. The room was sparsely furnished. Owain had little attachment to things, other than books, and his walls were lined with them. Some were in English, others in Latin or Greek. The few precious Welsh texts were the most prized parts of his collection. Dafydd also knew that behind one of the bookcases was a small but even more valuable cache of books. Those texts were handwritten in ancient Welsh and contained the methods for training a walker. Every walker had a copy of them, and every walker just as surely had four people, each of whom knew where the books were so that they could be removed after his death.

Dafydd and Cerridwyn poured tea and looked out into the small village. Owain was below, talking to Thom.

"That's his apprentice walker?" Cerridwyn asked.

"Yes," Dafydd responded. "What do you think of him?"

She blew softly over her tea to cool it. "He'll do. In fact, I think he'll do quite well."

Dafydd smiled over his teacup. Cerridwyn was notoriously sparing with her praise. Thom had just received a high compliment.

Within a half hour, the three walkers were on their way to Gwynfor's farm. They would not be meeting at his house, but in a cave about a half mile distant from it. Owain told the others what he knew about the problem in America as they made the short trip. They did not stop the carriage near their final destination. Instead, they pulled into a copse of trees a good distance away from the cave. Gwynfor met them there.

"Expected you'd stop here. Didn't know you were coming, Cerridwyn. Good to have you."

The other three climbed down. They had already begun to assume the laconic manner of the walkers, quite different from their daily manner as typically talkative Welshmen. The four knew the way to the cave by heart. They could easily walk it in the dark, as they had on more than one occasion. A few hundred feet from where they had stopped the carriage, they crossed a brook and continued on through a small meadow and a grove of trees, which ended in what appeared to be a blank rock face. The face actually had a diagonal crevice in it, though it was well hidden by the trees. The crevice was wide enough for a man to slip through, provided that he leaned against the rock and slid along his back. After a transit of about ten feet, the cleft turned. A few feet farther on, it emerged into a small glade that sat like a grassy bowl in a stone cup.

The occasional person passing through the meadow on the outer side of the rock face presented no danger to the security of the walkers' meeting place. Already difficult to see, the crevice was magically protected in subtle ways. The first discouragement was a spell that tended to make others overlook it. A second spell had been cast that would discourage anyone from entering. If someone were daring enough to enter the cleft, a third spell assured that he would experience a feeling of claustrophobia that would drive him back out of the rocks. The third spell became stronger the deeper into the cleft one went.

The four emerged from the cleft, then crossed the glade, which rose as it met the root of the mountain that loomed over them. They entered a dense growth of shrubbery that clung to the face of the mountain. Behind that shrubbery was the entrance to the cave.

Not even they knew how long the cave had been used by the walkers, but it was certainly more than two thousand years. The deeper chambers of the cave held various artifacts that had been brought back as souvenirs by the walkers before them. In the chamber were Roman coins that dated from the reign of Claudius, who had died

FRANCIS CLARK

in A.D. 37. Other items were even older, but the walkers did not have the inclination to date them. The walkers already knew that their order was immeasurably old.

Owain led the way into the cave. They stopped in the second chamber, which was an oval about fifteen by twelve feet. It was lit by two small natural shafts in the rock that let in enough light to provide some illumination in the day. At night, they could build a small fire. They sat and felt the security of the rock about them before speaking.

Gwynfor began, "So someone has been foolish enough to open a portal."

Dafydd nodded. "We can't be certain, but this incident seems similar to the one that occurred in Scotland forty years ago."

Owain said, "Quite possibly these people are from the same type of group."

"Dafydd, Owain tells me that you know of one of us in America," Gwynfor said.

"I know of him; I don't know him," Dafydd replied.

"I do," Cerridwyn said. "I trained him. He is capable, but I don't know what he might be facing. As well, he is far away from them in New York. It would take him days to get there."

"Should we alert him?" Dafydd asked. "The Catholics will undoubtedly send their own magicians, just as they did in Scotland."

"That complicates things," Owain said.

"And we don't know what has happened since the letter was sent," Cerridwyn added. "It may be three weeks since it was mailed."

"What are you suggesting?" Dafydd asked.

"That I take a look," she answered.

"It's a long way, Cerridwyn, almost four thousand miles, and we have no object to tie you to your objective. Our information came by telegram."

"I know. I had decided what needed to be done as we came over this morning. But I need to go now. It is still dark there, and I would prefer to look while it is still night. Less chance of my being observed."

"Well," Owain said, "you are the one who is the far-seer."

She lay down on the floor of the cave. The others could do nothing while she was gone except watch her body. They heard her breathing slow as she pulled up the power for the task. The next moment, they could see that she was insensate. Her body lay still on the floor and would not move again until she returned.

Only a truly talented far-seer could bridge the immense distance that she was trying to reach across. The talent was not one that any of the other three possessed. Far seeing was a very different skill from sending a projection of a magician's essence. The far-seer sent only perceptual abilities.

Time was not important in the task. Her perceptions would reach across the miles as fast as her power could take them. Far seeing takes the magician into a silvered realm, an ether that diminishes distance. She could see nothing of the everyday world as she flew through that realm. She was a ghost flashing across the ocean at unimaginable speeds. The trouble in trying to reach so far was that she had to be precise. She was traveling so fast that it was difficult to judge when she was near her objective, which needed to be near when she came out of the ether. If not, she would have to reenter and fly farther. Each transition taxed her strength.

Cerridwyn was very experienced at the task. She emerged over the Savannah River, just east of the city where it entered the ocean. Dawn was perhaps an hour away. She ghosted up the river to the city. As she crossed over the low-lying eastern part of the city, she sensed that someone observed her. But the observer seemed more curious than defensive. Cerridwyn continued into the city and saw the cathedral.

No magicians were in the cathedral. She floated higher so that she could see more of the city. The house on York immediately caught her attention. She could sense the presence of six magicians there. All were asleep. As she came closer, she could distinguish the two hereditaries. Both were potent; both were women. One of them must be Brigid. Cerridwyn drifted into the ballroom where they slept. The four men were all ceremonial magicians, though one seemed to possess more talent than the others. The two women were sleeping behind a curtained corner of the room. One was Italian. Cerridwyn drifted closer to the pale skin of Brigid and touched her thoughts, moving deftly so as not to disturb the others. In a few moments, she learned what she needed to know and quickly slipped back outside the house. Again she rose in the air, and saw the house where Streng slept. The dark miasma in front of the house told her of the power and intent of the rituals conducted there. Having learned all she needed, she fled back to Wales before the first stabs of light from dawn illuminated the city streets.

In the cave near Beddgelert, the men awaited her return. They were considering the dangers that their compatriot might have to face. As always, the first problem was the power of the creature that the American walker would have to confront. Would their American member have the power to defeat it? The second problem was potentially revealing themselves to the Church.

"I do not know what you would recommend," Owain said, "but we have always had to confront these creatures ourselves. The Christians have never proven themselves against one of them. They will likely fail, and, if they do, the creature might become more rapacious. Others might die."

They mulled over what Owain had said.

"And," Gwynfor said, "the situation is made more difficult by the presence of this nun, Brigid, who comes from a family that has long been devoted to the gods. We are obligated to help her."

"But she is a nun," Dafydd objected.

"The famine forced poor choices on many Irish," Owain reminded him.

Gwynfor said, "There are innocent people in danger. I think that outweighs other considerations."

"I agree," Owain said.

They waited for a few more minutes. Then they felt her return. Her eyes fluttered. Cerridwyn lay still, needing some time to readjust herself to perceiving through her eyes and ears and not through her other senses.

Dafydd leaned over her with a pocket flask. "Something stronger than tea?"

She sat up on her elbows and reached for the offered flask. She took a short drink and let the whiskey slide down her throat, bringing with it a welcome warmth and a slight overtone of peat. "I see that the poor country doctor retains his taste in single malts."

Dafydd grinned. "I do have a few indulgences."

She sat up. The men awaited her discoveries.

"Six Catholic magicians. Part of their group are two hereditaries of significant strength, one is an Italian nun and the other is Brigid. She is a nun, but leaning to return to the old ways. Their opponent has already killed three. It is a first-order demon, summoned by a large and long-established group of dark magicians with ceremonial power. Without their demon, the Catholics could probably defeat them. With the demon, none but the hereditaries are likely to survive, and even that is questionable.

"Of greater importance, I could sense a latent ability for high magic in both of the nuns. In Brigid's case it is very strong. With training she could join us."

"You know the strength of the opponent and the strength of our member in New York. Can he defeat the demon?" Owain asked.

"Probably. But it will take him days to get there. I cannot be certain, but I feel that the demon will strike again, perhaps even tonight. He would likely arrive too late to help. If they can survive the next attack and we can find a way to strengthen Brigid, then they have a chance."

"What can we do?" Gwynfor asked.

"Cerridwyn, is her talent great enough that we might be able to send her the keys?" Owain asked.

"It is worth a try, but without one of us to explain their usage, she might not understand. Even then, we may be too late. We must wait until she sleeps again, and I fear an attack may come before then."

"Then let us prepare a dream for her and send it tonight," Owain said. "That is the best we can do. If she fails, then we will need to send our walker in America to dispose of this demon."

CHAPTER TWENTY-EIGHT

Savannah
Friday, October 30

TO brighten the mood at York Street, the monsignor made dinner on Friday, the traditional day for fish, into a special meal. He arranged for an afternoon delivery of fresh shrimp, red snapper, and grouper. He had insisted that the bishop's chef, Benjamin, prepare dinner. Benjamin and his staff arrived at four, bringing several bottles of wine from the bishop's cellar.

Father Rimaldi had asked that the mother superior join them. As a show of support, she had accepted the invitation. They gathered just after five around the large table in the ballroom. The atmosphere was quiet, but was nonetheless in marked contrast to the funereal affair that dinner the previous evening had been. Benjamin was an excellent chef, and a feast began appearing from the kitchen around six. The centerpiece was his specialty, red snapper smothered with roasted sweet peppers. Other dishes—red rice, shrimp creole, baked grouper, and a bounty of local fresh vegetables—were delivered to the table, still steaming from the kitchen. As the wine disappeared, it was replaced by Chatham Artillery Punch. The punch was a Savannah tradition, a rum drink that hid its potency in the tastes of fruit juice and sugar. Knowing the seriousness of recent events and the danger that they shared, the monsignor was careful to warn all present that it was not a drink to be trifled with.

The conversation was light, as all of them gratefully grasped the opportunity to evade the dark that surrounded them. Still, those who had witnessed the deadly actions of Belial could not completely escape their memories. Rimaldi was the most affected. He felt a sense of personal failure, feeling that his excessive confidence had played a role in the loss of two of their members. As well, he was concerned that they might be overmatched. Though Angela and Brigid had been able to withstand Belial and protect Father Pascal, their defense had only needed to last a minute or two. What might be the result if they had to resist Belial much longer? What would be the results if the creature were aided by the others? Rimaldi sensed that Streng was a potent magician in his own right, and this worried him.

Rimaldi could not hide the dark current of his thoughts. After they finished eating and were served their coffee, he slipped away from the table and went to stand at one of the back windows that looked down on the dark yard behind the house. The light that spilled from the kitchen windows cast a feeble illumination against the darkness and was swallowed by the dense foliage that surrounded the patch of grass directly behind the kitchen.

As the Jesuit looked down at the yard, a red glow began to suffuse the air outside the window, and tendrils of glowing red fire swept by. In the heart of the red glow, just outside the window, a horrible, leering face began to take shape. Rimaldi quickly threw a defensive shell around himself and prepared to strike against the apparition.

Behind him, the room fell quiet as the magicians sensed his working and turned toward him. Benito and Angela rushed to his side. By the time they arrived, the illusion had vanished. Rimaldi himself almost doubted what he had seen.

"What is it, Father?" Benito asked.

"I saw Belial, or an illusion of it."

"Where?"

"Outside, hovering in the air. Just the red glow, but it began to move and grow stronger. There was the suggestion of a face."

"It was probably an illusion," Angela said.

Rimaldi nodded. "Nonetheless, I think we should end our dinner. It may be too dangerous for the others to remain."

"I agree," she said. "This could be a prelude to an attack. We need to be prepared."

Benito went back to the table. "Monsignor, we all appreciate the extraordinary hospitality you've shown, but we need for you, the mother superior, and the staff to leave for a safer place."

The monsignor wiped his mouth with a napkin as he stood. The mother superior was already on her feet.

Rimaldi faced back into the room. "Sister Angela, Sister Brigid, could you help them prepare? The rest of us will remain in the room, together. Monsignor, I apologize for the sudden interruption."

"Of course, Father Provincial. We understand," the monsignor said. He, the mother superior, and the two nuns made their way downstairs to speed the kitchen staff on their way.

In the ballroom, Rimaldi looked at the others. All were shaken. None of them had experienced an opponent with anything like Belial's power. They were like soldiers who had never faced a cannon in war. The first time a cannon is fired against them, many are afraid.

It took a half hour for the house to be cleared of the staff and the visitors. Once the food, wine, tablecloths, and china had been taken away, the ballroom appeared to be what it was—a wartime barracks. Cots were lined up on the floor, and chairs stood randomly around the room. Clothes and blankets were stacked in the corner.

Rimaldi called them all together. Benito saw the strain on his face. The Jesuit needed his support, even though Benito could also see that Rimaldi had become more determined because of the intrusion on their small celebration. The fighter in him was awakening.

Rimaldi spoke slowly, but with decision. "Two of our members have been killed. And we know from the information provided by the Voudon group that the full coven has not yet been called. The demon, Belial, is the greatest threat, but some members of this group are magicians of power.

"Until now I've thought that we must wait for their attack so that we could destroy the demon and the ones who called it. But we cannot wait any longer as they pick us off one by one. We must strike at the magicians who call this creature. It may not be necessary to destroy the demon if we can assure that the portal will remain closed. We know the identity of one of the opposing magicians, Streng. If we strike at Streng, the others might still be able to summon the demon. But, even with that risk, we can't just wait. I advocate that we attack him tomorrow night."

Benito supported him. "I, too, am tired of waiting."

Angela and the others nodded in agreement.

Rimaldi continued, "We have six magicians at our disposal if we include Sister Brigid. She and Sister Angela were able to stop the attack on Father Pascal. Had his heart not failed him, he would still be with us.

"We have several rituals we could use. I recommend that we use the pentagram. It is the most powerful for our current number."

They all felt more reassured. Going on the offense was dangerous, but simply waiting for the enemy's next attack now seemed even more so.

They heard a furious pounding on the front door of the house. Rimaldi and Benito went down to answer it.

A breathless Daniel stood outside. He had run from Streng's. "Streng and five of his people there," he said, speaking between gasps.

"When did they arrive?" Rimaldi asked.

"Three carriages come in the last few minutes. I wait a few more minutes, but no more came. So I run here. He got five people in there, plus his self."

"Thank you, Daniel," Rimaldi said quickly.

"I go back to see if any more come." Daniel turned to go.

"You shouldn't. It's too dangerous."

"You sure?"

"I am."

Daniel vanished back into the darkness.

Rimaldi shut the door and ran up the stairs. "Streng has assembled a total of six magicians. They may be calling Belial. We must form the pentagram immediately."

"So the visitation . . . " Angela said.

"Was a prelude to an attack," Benito finished for her.

Rimaldi formed their group into a pentagram in the open area of the room. He stood in the center and faced east. Benito stood in front of Rimaldi at the east point. Brigid and Angela were at the northeast and southeast points. Siena and Francisco were at the northwest and southwest points. The dispositions were made hastily. They had not practiced the new ritual. Each performed his or her own ritual to draw up power; then they made the connections between them. First Benito to Angela, then Angela to Francisco, and so on, until they had formed the five sides. Rimaldi was in the center of the wall of power they had raised. The power flowed around the pentagram, intensifying as soon as the final connection was made. Rimaldi reached out and tapped into it. His power, already called up, joined to the strength of the others. Now they had to maintain concentration and wait.

❦

AT Streng's house, the triad of Streng, Jarred Cawthorne, and Micah Breeding was augmented by the three next most powerful of their group, Lilith Claire, Frank Ames, and Hans Rimmer. As the hour crept past midnight, they began the summoning of Belial. This ritual was different from the one that they had used to summon Belial to kill Father Kirk. Tonight the three senior magicians would go with Belial, adding their power to its. Claire, Ames, and Rimmer had a different task. They placed themselves in a rough triangle at the edges of the room and linked their power together. They were there to protect the portal while the other three went with Belial.

Streng, Cawthorne, and Breeding sat around the portal stone in the floor of the room. It was through this portal that Belial would emerge. The only thing that would hold it in their control was their ability to close the portal, marooning the demon in the normal realm, which would eventually destroy it, or, at least, that was what they believed. They did not realize how firmly they were under Belial's control, that their souls would one day be forfeit to it. They began their chant, and were soon rewarded, as the stone shifted to a dull gray, then to a clear opening into another realm. Belial was waiting for them and quickly flowed through the portal.

With difficulty, Lilith pulled her eyes away from Belial and accepted control of the portal from the inner group, leaving Streng, Cawthorne, and Breeding free. They lay down on the floor of their ritual room. Muttering spells, they separated their spirits from their bodies. These spirits carried their essences and left their bodies on the floor as living, but insensate, husks. At first their projected spirits looked like their physical bodies, but they changed their appearances to mimic Belial's. The three projections left the room with Belial. Together, they flew to the house on York.

Inside the ballroom on York Street four "Belials" appeared. The priests and nuns were confused. Neither Rimaldi nor any of the others knew which was the real Belial.

Taking advantage of the momentary confusion, Streng launched himself at Siena from the north. Cawthorne and Breeding threw themselves against Francisco from the south and west. The two nuns both turned to the west to see if they could help Siena and Francisco. Then the real Belial, far more potent than the shades of the magicians that had accompanied it, attacked Benito. Benito reeled backward from the force of the blow and dropped to his knees. The band of power that had linked the magicians in the pentagram shattered.

Rimaldi shouted to the nuns, "Behind you."

The two women had already sensed the presence of their most powerful opponent at their backs. Turning east, they moved between Benito and Belial, just as the demon launched a tongue of fire at the monk. The fire was caught on the shielding of the two witches and went no farther. Even though Rimaldi was no longer being fed power by the others, he launched his own spell at Belial. If it had an effect, Belial showed no sign of it.

Father Francisco screamed. He was caught between Cawthorne and Breeding, and his protection was failing. Their spells were licking about him like flames, searing his flesh. Rimaldi moved to help him, abandoning the ritual he had proposed.

Siena was falling to his knees from the potent spells being launched against him by Streng. The priest was no match for his powerful adversary alone, and the attention of the others was focused on the more immediate dangers that Belial, Cawthorne, and Breeding presented. The magical force of Streng hammered against Siena. The priest was losing ground in his battle, but stubbornly refused to call for help. His shielding gave way. Instantly he felt smothered, as if buried in hot wool. Collapsing onto the floor, he felt his life seeping out of him. He did not even have the ability to cry out for help.

Belial kept up its relentless pressure against the nuns, who were totally occupied in protecting Benito. He was sheltered behind them, dazed but still struggling to return to the fight. Brigid and Angela were having difficulty protecting themselves and preventing Belial from reaching the weakened Benito. Brigid felt that her strength was being tested beyond measure. Even though she was just able to withstand the onslaught from the demon, she felt the air around her grow hot. Without Angela beside her, she would never have been able to hold off the power that Belial was directing at them. Brigid saw that Angela was sweating as well, though she did not seem to be as near the end of her strength as Brigid.

Sensing movement behind her, she saw Streng approaching. Unthinking, Brigid threw out her arm, not using a spell, simply directing her own power at the shade of Streng. A lance of deep crimson flame spouted from her arm. It smashed against an overconfident Streng. His projection was thrown back ten feet. His spirit form wavered, then blinked out as he was thrown back to the refuge of his body.

With Streng gone and Rimaldi joining the faltering Francisco, Cawthorne and Breeding departed. Belial, even without their support, was in no danger. The powerful demon slashed again at Benito. Its blow fell on Angela's shielding and dissipated, though enough power flowed around her to knock Benito to the ground. A sudden burst of fire erupted around Belial, but it was one of the demon's own making. As the others instinctively drew back, the demon vanished from their sight. Brigid felt Belial fly from the room and disappear into the night.

The room was enveloped in darkness. The oil lamps that had lit the room had been snuffed out in the brief magical battle. Father Rimaldi went to a lamp and lit it. Then he lit two more. The scene revealed brought no comfort to anyone. The room was quiet, except for the pained gasps of Francisco, who was severely burned.

Benito struggled upright, aided by Sister Angela. Brigid went to Siena, who had not stirred. She sensed that he was dead even before she came to stand over his body. Rimaldi hovered over Father Francisco, who was in severe pain. Brigid went to him as soon as she had assured herself that Siena was beyond help. Rimaldi was stunned. He realized that the wreckage was more than physical. This attack had struck at the thing that every magician must have, confidence. They were the ones confused, while their enemy played a game, a game that would lead to a denouement on a night of the enemy's choosing.

Sister Brigid's voice brought him back to the room, away from his thoughts. "I need some help; we must undress him."

"Undress him?"

"He is burned," Sister Brigid explained. "The great risk is infection. The only way to prevent it is to get his clothing away from the burned areas."

"But shouldn't we wait for the doctor?" Rimaldi asked.

"No, his blood is clotting now. The longer we wait, the worse it will be."

"But you're a nun."

Exasperated by his provincial tone, she struggled to control the anger in her voice. "Right now I am a nurse. And unless you have more medical knowledge than I do, you can help best by getting a doctor. The monsignor will know who to call." She turned toward Angela. "Please get my bag." Then she looked to Benito. "Father Benito, if you can, I need you. We cannot wait to get the clothing off him. Time is precious."

"Yes," he said, "of course." Benito moved to her assistance.

Rimaldi left to go to the monsignor. Then he noticed Siena. He knelt on the floor next to his old friend. "Sister?" he cried out.

Brigid looked up at him briefly. She saw the anguish on his face, and, as gently as possible, said, "I'm sorry, Father Provincial. Father Siena is dead. There is nothing more that we can do for him. But we must help the living. I need a doctor for Father Francisco—"

"I'll go," Angela interrupted, setting Brigid's medical bag by the nurse's side.

Brigid nodded and turned her attention back to Francisco. Rimaldi remained crouched by the body of his friend. Angela left for the cathedral.

Brigid instructed Benito, "He may go into shock. We need to get some morphine in him for the pain, then elevate his feet. Someone should build a fire; it's too cold in this room. He needs to be warm to prevent shock. We should leave him uncovered until a doctor arrives."

"Can a doctor save him?" Benito asked.

"I don't know, but I hope they fetch Gaston," she said. "He may be an irritable old drunk, but he knows more about saving a man's life than anyone else I know."

Brigid soon had a carefully measured dose of morphine in the injured priest, who had been silently crying in pain. As the drug stole through his veins, he began to relax. Benito lit the fire in the room. The fireplace had been prepared by him earlier in the day. The kindling began to catch quickly. Brigid elevated her patient's feet and began to remove Francisco's burned cassock.

Benito knelt at the fireplace, stoking the fire. Brigid called to him as she worked over Francisco, "Father Benito, as soon as you get that fire going, please go to the kitchen and find some whiskey or strong spirits. We'll need it to clean the wounds."

Benito nodded from his place next to the fire.

Rimaldi quietly said, "I'll go." He disappeared down the stairs.

When Benito was satisfied that the fire would catch, he returned to where Francisco lay. Brigid worked carefully over their patient. The task was laborious and slow, even though she moved as quickly as she could. At times Francisco would gasp as the pain of removing some shard of clothing proved too severe for the morphine to mask.

"What do you need?" Benito asked.

"More light."

Benito went back to the fireplace. He tended the blaze and was rewarded with a burst of illumination that seemed to dispel some of the chill from the room. Then he brought two of the oil lamps over to Brigid so that she could see better as she endeavored to pick fabric from the burns that covered a large part of Francisco's upper body.

"Thank you, Father," she said.

Rimaldi reemerged from downstairs. "All I found was rum," he said.

"Good enough," Brigid replied. She sat back on her heels. Much of Francisco's burned skin was now exposed to the air. She washed her hands in the rum, then handed the bottle to Benito. "You should do the same if you want to help me clean the wounds."

Benito washed his hands in the alcohol and began removing fabric from the areas that Brigid had not yet reached. They heard someone coming up the stairs. It was Angela, followed by the monsignor and Dr. Gaston.

Gaston quickly glanced around the room and decided that he did not want to know what had happened. He moved to Francisco.

"Are all of his burns exposed to the air?" Gaston asked Brigid.

"Most are, but we haven't cleaned them yet. I gave him morphine for the pain and had the others start a fire to keep him warm. I elevated his feet against shock."

"Good work, girl," Gaston said as he lowered himself to the ground beside the patient. "I need more light," he called to no one in particular. "And a disinfectant."

Father Benito handed Gaston the rum. "Your idea, Brigid?" the doctor asked.

She nodded.

"Knew you'd make a fine nurse one day." He took a drink of the rum before washing his own hands. "Let's get to work." Benito fetched another lamp to add to the light.

"What about the other one?" Gaston asked, tilting his head toward Siena.

"Dead," Brigid replied.

The doctor and Brigid set about finishing the task of picking pieces of charred cloth and threads from the burns on Francisco's body. As they finished each wound, Gaston cleaned it with the alcohol he had in his bag. When they ran out of the alcohol, they used the rum. Sister Brigid covered the wounds with a salve from the doctor's bag, sealing them from the air. Finally they bandaged Francisco with light gauze. The cleaning had taken most of an hour, but it had been thorough.

Finally, Gaston got to his feet, helped by Rimaldi, who asked, "Will he live?"

"Not my department any longer, Padre," said the doctor. "It's yours. Up to God. But there's nothing else that man can do, 'cept make sure he's got plenty of water to drink."

"Did we do the right thing?" Rimaldi asked.

"About what?"

"Caring for the priest?"

"Couldn't have done better myself." Gaston paused. "As for what else happened in this room, I don't care to know. Probably wouldn't believe it if I did." He looked at the monsignor. "You need to get him over to the hospital. I'll look in on him in the morning." The doctor picked up his bag. Then he knelt by Siena and checked on him. Gaston shook his head. Siena's body was already cooling. Gaston left; his heavy tread could be heard retreating down the stairs.

"Nothing seems to affect him," said Father Rimaldi.

"He's seen a lot of death," the monsignor said, "more than most men could stand."

❧

NO one wanted to sleep after what they had experienced, but they had to try. Sleep was now a weapon. Without it, they would be tired and weak and easy prey. They were all exhausted. Soon the room was dark, and sleep came quickly for all of them.

As Brigid lay on the cot, she drifted into the dark waters of her mind. She floated even deeper into sleep and heard music playing, Celtic music that reminded her of her childhood. She found herself walking along a forest path, though she was a younger version of herself, perhaps fourteen. She realized that she was in a dream, since she had no such memories. She felt safe and secure in the dreamscape. The path was covered in soft grass, and the healthy smell of the forest filled her nostrils. After some minutes, she came to a clearing and found a woman sitting there, someone she did not know, but someone she felt honored to be with. The woman beckoned to her to join her on the soft grass. Brigid sat.

"You have asked about the walkers," the woman began.

Brigid thought or said, "Yes."

"It is not as you think it is. Walkers are more born than made."

"How?"

The clearing faded away as pictures played in her mind. The woman was doing magic. Brigid could see her reaching down inside herself, opening places of strength. Symbols and words ran through Brigid's mind. She could make no sense of them. Then she was drawn into the other woman and became so small that she could float along the bright pathways within the woman. Brigid tumbled joyously inside of the bright places. Finally she came to the end of the journey. There, waiting for her, was a man. He shone so brilliantly that her eyes hurt to look at him. He was immensely strong and beautiful, a father of many thousands. She curled up in his arms, no bigger than a kitten to him. As she floated, warm and secure, back to sleep, she thought, "So this is what a god is like."

CHAPTER TWENTY-NINE

Saturday, October 31

THE sun rising over Savannah illuminated the ballroom on York, revealing the full extent of the destruction that Belial, Streng, and the others had left behind them. The magical battle had left burn marks on the walls and floor. Father Francisco was not with them. He had been taken to the hospital the night before. The most terrible reminder was the corpse of Father Siena, lying where they had covered it the previous night.

Brigid awoke to this dismal scene, though her mind was still filled with the beauty of her dream. Those thoughts were chased from her mind by seeing Rimaldi in a solitary vigil over the body of his friend. Rimaldi was exhausted by his efforts and by the loss of life. He was frustrated by his seeming inability to find the correct strategy to oppose Streng's group.

The others awoke and silently clustered around him.

He raised his head to look at them. "I did not choose the right way to defend ourselves. I have failed you all."

None of them expected Rimaldi's humility or his acceptance of the truth of their situation.

"No, Father, you have not." Angela's voice rose in the dull quiet of the room. "The problem was not your strategy. The problem is that Belial is simply too strong."

Rimaldi looked hopeless. "Then what do we do?"

The silence drew out. The women had nothing to contribute. Brigid knew little of ceremonial magic. Angela had no suggestions. Benito was the first to find a different way to look at things.

"It is possible that we are being misled by our own training. We were taught that number is the secret to power in magic. The more magicians, the more power. While that is undoubtedly true, there is more to it than just numbers. The vulnerability of the magician must also be taken into account. The four that we have left are the strongest of those that were gathered here. That is no accident. Angela and Brigid have held off Belial on two occasions without assistance. If that power, added to mine, could be channeled through you, then perhaps we could succeed in striking at Belial."

"Streng killed Father Siena by himself," Rimaldi reminded him.

"But Siena was not your equal," Angela said.

"Are you certain?" Rimaldi asked.

"Father," Angela said, "my Sight is stronger than yours. I can see the power that you carry inside yourself. You have more than twice the power of Siena. Father Benito is almost as strong as you."

Rimaldi gained some confidence from her words. "And Brigid?"

"She is stronger than either of you," Angela said. "She may be stronger than me."

Benito added, "From the beginning we have been out of our depth against Belial, but the problem may be that we have concentrated on ceremonial techniques. This situation is different. We have two hereditaries with us. We may, in fact, be stronger with a smaller number, if we join our power."

Rimaldi looked at the priest. "Are you suggesting that now we will be able to defeat it?"

"If we form a triad protecting you and channel our power to you, we stand a chance." He looked to Brigid in explanation. "Small number rituals are the easiest ways to join power." He looked back to Rimaldi. "But we cannot be prepared in full every night," Benito said. "We can manage that for two or three days at the most. The question we must answer is how do we protect ourselves until the crisis?"

"Simple," Angela stated. "We do not try to stay ready. We sleep."

"And what," asked Father Benito, "prevents us from being attacked?"

"I can sense Belial's approach in my sleep. And I can wake Brigid swiftly. Together, we can hold the demon off for a few minutes. If it comes, we will wake you."

They looked to Rimaldi for a final decision. "It might work, but the odds are very much against us. The plan is a desperate one. It might turn out to be futile. But I would rather fail in the attempt than run from the battle. I would not think less of any of you if you were to decide not to participate."

Benito knew his heart. He looked to the two nuns and saw the same grim decision on their faces. "Father Provincial, we might fail. But we will fail together."

The Jesuit looked gratefully at the other three. "Then we are decided."

When the small meeting ended, Rimaldi and Benito went to sit at the large table where they had gathered for meals. Brigid followed Angela back to the curtained alcove.

Once inside, Brigid came up behind Angela and whispered, "I have something to ask you."

The two women sat on their cots, facing each other. Angela whispered as well, since she assumed that Brigid wanted to discuss something privately with her.

"Last night I had a dream. It was clearer in my mind when I first awoke. I've lost some of it since then."

"That often happens."

"All that I can remember is sitting beside a beautiful woman in a meadow. She told me, 'Walkers are more born than made.' Then strange signs that I have never seen before were in my head. I fell asleep, feeling safe and protected in the arms of a god."

"Anything more? Can you draw any of the symbols you saw?"

"No, that's all I have now. Do you know what it means?"

"There's not enough there for me to do much. But I think that it means you will be protected by either the god or the goddess. The elder gods are a natural part of human life, not distant from us. Perhaps someday you may become a walker. It fits with what I know. Maybe one day you just wake up and are a walker."

"And the symbols?"

"Unless I see them, I can't tell what they mean."

"I mean what would a train of symbols be?"

Angela frowned, then said hesitantly, "Information?"

"About what?"

"Brigid, sometimes dreams are meant for a deeper part of the mind. The gods put things there to have effect at a later time. If we survive all this, you must try and understand what they mean."

Brigid lowered her head and sighed. She looked back up to Angela. "I am frustrated and confused. Angela, I feel like I am being a fool. I feel like there is so much to be learned, but it is just barely out of my grasp."

"Time will make things more clear."

"But what if we have no time?"

CHAPTER THIRTY

Sunday, November 1

THE monsignor came to speak with Rimaldi around nine in the morning. The day before, when the monsignor had come to arrange the removal of Siena's body, he knew that it was not a time for questions. Rimaldi was still too overcome with the death of his friend. Today the monsignor found a somber but determined Rimaldi.

"So, Father Provincial, you seem more ready for the battle."

Rimaldi said, "Yes, things are better today." Then he motioned for the monsignor to follow him. He led Henry out of the ballroom to the drawing room downstairs.

Benito watched them go, knowing what was in the mind of the Jesuit. Rimaldi was putting up a brave front, but was not certain that they could succeed. Benito worried about those doubts, because they undermined the confidence that was necessary for a magician to work at his best. Doubt would blunt his capabilities, but Rimaldi would have to deal with his doubt. Benito went back to training Brigid how to blend her power in the triad ritual.

Once Rimaldi ushered the monsignor into the drawing room, he slid the door shut. The monsignor waited expectantly.

"Monsignor Henry?" Rimaldi began.

"Yes." Robert was put on guard by the formality.

"As you know, the situation here is a very unusual and dangerous one. We have devised a new strategy, one that stands some chance of succeeding, but it is only a chance. We may be defeated and killed by the next attack of Streng's group. If that occurs, the city will have no protection against this demon." He handed the monsignor an envelope. "Inside that envelope is a draft of a telegram. If we fail, you must send the telegram immediately to Rome. Send it instead of the daily telegram that we have been sending. Use the same address we have been using."

The monsignor looked at him with a stunned expression on his face.

"Do you understand?" Rimaldi asked.

"Yes. But do you think you will fail?"

"I think it is probable. I hope we do not, but I must prepare for the worst."

"Is there anything that I can do?"

"Pray."

Rimaldi left to rejoin the others in the ballroom. The monsignor left the house on York, slipping the telegram into his cassock. He must tell the bishop what had happened. The battle was almost over, and the Church was the likely loser. The magicians who remained to carry on the battle did so more from pure obstinacy and a sense of duty than from the hope that they would succeed. Henry could not help but think of the South's struggles in the last months of the Civil War. So many had died even after it was clear that the cause was lost.

The monsignor walked slowly back toward the bishop's office. The gentle fall sunshine cascaded down on Robert. He felt tears welling and went to sit in the square in front of the cathedral. He sat on one of the benches that faced the mighty building and looked up at the towering steeples above the nave. The bells were ringing, as they did every morning at 9:30, signaling the ten o'clock Mass.

He knew that the parishioners who would come to Mass would

soon be approaching. It would not do for them to see their monsignor sitting on a park bench crying. He lowered his head, still listening to the bells. Perhaps the parishioners would think he was in prayer. He knew that the Church's magicians were determined, but they could not extinguish the horrors he had seen in the last weeks. Siena, Pascal, and Kirk were dead. Francisco was in the hospital, severely burned. Monsignor Henry needed to calm his emotions before he went to report to the bishop.

❧

SHORTLY after lunchtime, Benito felt that he had Brigid as prepared as she could be. He and Brigid stood with Angela to form the triad. The results were encouraging. The power between them might be strong enough to withstand Belial, but they would not know until the actual test came. Rimaldi then joined in their practice.

He stood in the center as they re-formed the triad around him. They channeled a small amount of strength to him. He raised his hands, as if preparing to launch a spell, and smiled. "Very good. This is far more power than I had to direct before. Maybe we can generate enough to protect ourselves and possibly do some damage to our opponents."

"Do you want us to channel all we can to you?" Benito asked.

"Only in the actual battle. For now, we should conserve our strength."

They spent the remainder of the day resting, since they did not know when they would be attacked again.

As night fell, they cleared away dinner and remained in the ballroom, talking. Around eight, they heard a rapid knocking on the kitchen door. Brigid went down and opened the door. Daniel was on the front porch.

He did not enter, just said, "They all comin' tonight. Must be twenty, maybe thirty of 'em." Then he turned and escaped back into the gloom.

The nun carried the message back to Rimaldi, who said, "So the battle will be tonight. Let us prepare."

The four went to the ritual space in the room. Brigid stood in the east, Angela in the southwest, and Benito in the northwest. Each was separated from the others by about ten feet. Rimaldi stood in the center of the triangle. No altar was used for this rite.

They heard footsteps coming up the stairs. No one had any idea who it might be. They looked expectantly at the door.

Esmerelda appeared at the doorway. "Figured you could use a hand."

Brigid smiled. "*Mambo,* it is good to see you. But aren't you afraid of what Streng might do to you?"

"That I am, girl. The *loa* even warned me. 'Work no magic, 'less you have to.' Well, I'm thinkin' I have to. Time for fence-sittin's gone. We got to stand together if we gonna stand at all." She looked at the other nun. "Sistah Angela, sorry we didn't meet the other night."

Angela nodded in smiling acquiescence. "I understood."

Rimaldi looked at Esmerelda. "I take it you are the voodoo *mambo.*"

Guardedly she replied, "You must be the abbé."

"Whatever I am, you're welcome. We need all the help we can get."

She smiled at his welcome. "So how I fit in here?"

"Could you take the north?" Rimaldi asked.

They shifted positions, with the *mambo* at the north, Brigid in the east, Angela in the south, and Benito in the west. Rimaldi remained in the center. They began to bring up their power, which quickly spanned the distance between them, casting a faint glow in the air.

The ritual was like none that Rimaldi had ever seen. The *mambo* had brought a new influx of power. Rimaldi had never been part of such a potent grouping. The interplay of colors showed how different the magic of each of them was. Yet the power all blended together. Ultimately, power is simply power, no matter its source.

They settled in to wait. They did not expect to have to wait for long.

❧

STRENG was certain of victory. Though he had surprised the priests with the last attack and managed to kill one and disable another, his opponents had not yet seen the extent of his power. Tonight he had the might of his full coven at his command, with all twenty-five members present. After their ritual two nights before, he had decided that they should attack with full force while the priests were still in shock rather than wait for the new moon.

At seven Cawthorne, Breeding, and Lilith arrived. They helped Streng with the preparation for the ritual. The others had been told not to arrive until eight. Almost exactly at eight, the other twenty-one members converged on Saint Julian Street within a few minutes of each other. Shortly thereafter they assembled in the ritual room.

Four of the coven's most senior members formed a circle around the portal. Streng stood alone in front of the altar, which they had formally prepared for this rite. On the altar was a goat-legged statue of Satan. Thirteen candles, each formed of solid black wax, were lit on the altar. Held between the crossed legs of the statue was a large incense burner, which Streng fed with sulfur until the acrid fumes drifted to every corner of the basement ritual room. The windows on the sides of the basement were masked and sealed to prevent any light, odor, or sound from escaping. In addition to the candles on the altar, light was provided by sconces set about the walls of the room. The light in the room was dimmed by the heavy, sulfurous smoke.

The nineteen junior members formed a second circle outside the inner one. The final senior member, Lilith Claire, stood between the two circles. She would call the rhythm of the dance. Streng began the ritual, tossing more sulfur onto the brazier and speaking a solitary incantation. The four around the portal began muttering a spell. Lilith directed the nineteen to begin a counterclockwise dance.

They started a slow motion, keeping time to her clapping and chanting Belial's name.

As she clapped her hands slowly, she called, "Give power to the center. Give worship to Satan. Honor his servant, Belial." The nineteen on the outside began to repeat the phrases in a chant that was timed with their steps.

The inner group's incantation changed. They chanted, "We summon you, Belial, servant of Satan. We summon you to do as we bid, to rid the earth of those who oppose us. Come forth." They repeated the chant, growing louder with each repetition. The effect of the two different chants in the room was cacophony. The sounds rang confusingly in the air. Each person concentrated on his or her own chant, though the inner ring watched as well as chanted.

The portal stone in the circle's center began to glow with a dull red fire. As the chant continued, the light grew in intensity. The inner ring stopped its chant when the stone became a portal into Belial's realm. The outer ring kept up its chant, funneling its power to the inner ring. Lilith sped up the chant to the outer ring, moving them to a faster walk. She could feel the strength coming from the outer ring to fuel the power of the inner group.

As Belial emerged from the portal, Lilith gave the signal to stop the dance, and those in the outer ring knelt in honor of the massive creature. Belial had changed its appearance again in order to look more like what they might expect a demon to be. It looked about, thriving on the devotion of so many worshipers. It growled deep in its throat. It directed its gaze to Streng and said in its low voice, "You and two others shall come with me. Tonight we kill our enemies."

Streng said, "Jarred. Micah."

The three lay down on the earth before the altar. Rimmer and Ames remained beside the portal and were joined there by Lilith. They would guard the portal for Belial's return.

The outer ring remained kneeling on the ground. Each gazed at the magnificently evil mass of Belial. They felt invincible. Silver-hued, ghostly shapes arose from the bodies of Streng, Cawthorne, and Breeding. Each shape looked like the man it had risen from; each was a projection of the man's presence. Belial led them upward and out of the room. The spirits flew toward the house on York.

⚭

ANGELA was the first to feel their approach. "They are coming."

The Catholics focused their concentration. Then, audaciously, the demon materialized in front of them on the eastern side of the ritual circle. Streng and his two companions manifested themselves, arrayed in an arc in the west. Streng was shocked to find Esmerelda allied with the priests, but said nothing. For a moment everyone seemed to wait, to assess the other side. Then Belial threw itself against the shielding, aiming directly for Brigid at the eastern point of the square. The impact threw her back almost a yard, but she was protected by her own power as well as that being channeled to her by the others.

For a few moments, Brigid was able to push back toward her original position. Then, regardless of all of the power given to her defense, she began to yield by inches. The sweat was pouring down her face. At this moment, Rimaldi launched their first spell at Belial. White fire poured from him and crashed against the demon, who cried out in rage. For a moment, Belial drew back, allowing Brigid to regain her position. Quickly Belial renewed its assault on Brigid with even greater force, this time throwing her back almost into Rimaldi.

The three satanists, who had been ignored by the five magicians as they struggled against Belial, joined in. Streng launched his power toward Benito. Cawthorne attacked Angela, attempting to drive her back toward Rimaldi. Her power was weakened by the need to support Brigid. Breeding came at Essie from the north and was initially repulsed by the *mambo*.

The spells launched by the satanists were potent. They were drawing on the power of the nineteen who were sending them strength from the ritual room on Saint Julian. The square began to crumble. Only Angela and the *mambo* were holding their own against Cawthorne and Breeding. Brigid was faltering before Belial, regardless of the stream of spells launched at the demon by Rimaldi. The others were unable to furnish her enough power to drive off the demon. Benito was being relentlessly driven back by Streng.

Benito collapsed and fell to the floor, unconscious. The power joining the square together collapsed. Streng did not continue his attack and kill Benito; rather, he directed his power against Esmerelda, who had betrayed him. Streng and Breeding began to squeeze Esmerelda between them, and her shielding, though formidable, was wavering under the attention of the two magicians who were drawing on the power of the nineteen at Saint Julian. Brigid was finally pushed aside by Belial, who now dove on Rimaldi. Brigid fell, barely conscious, aware of the battle going on around her. Benito was lying dazed on the floor. Angela was holding off Cawthorne. Belial was ripping through the shielding around Rimaldi. Essie was drawing up the last of her strength to protect herself against the two magicians who were relentlessly pressing her.

As Brigid lay dazed on the floor, images from her dream returned to her. She saw the woman's face, heard her saying, "Walkers are more born than made." She saw the woman reach inside of herself for the center of her power, a power that led to the laughing face of a god. Desperately, Brigid tried the same thing, reaching inside of herself, mimicking what the woman had done in her dream.

She found it, the seat of her power, and strength flowed back into her, a strength that she had never known before. Still lying on the floor, she lashed out at Streng, shattering his projected form and leaving Essie to battle only Breeding, who became the entire focus of the *mambo*'s strength. Brigid looked at Belial, who was driving Rimaldi down with heavy blows. Brigid reached inside again and pulled up raw power. She directed it at the demon's back. It smashed into Belial with immense force, stopping it, forcing it upright, ending the attack on Rimaldi.

In the house on Saint Julian Street, Streng's body cried out in pain as his spirit reentered; then he lay still. The ritual around him lost focus as the astonished worshipers saw their high priest lying still on the ground. Lilith could sense that something was very wrong. The power supporting Breeding and Cawthorne fell to nothing for a brief moment. That was all the respite that Esmerelda needed. With a final exertion of her energy, she drove Breeding back. His projection wavered and vanished. Angela, who had been barely holding her ground against Cawthorne, sensed his weakness. She focused her strength and tore his projection apart. It would not return to Saint Julian. Jarred Cawthorne was dead.

Rimaldi looked up from beneath the shreds of his protection and saw the face of the astonished demon. Belial had never felt such power from a human magician. Slowly the immense beast turned toward Brigid. The exhausted Rimaldi looked toward Brigid, still lying on the floor. Angela stared at her, as did Essie. Why was she lying down? Was she defeated or preparing a new spell? Time was suspended.

A white mist floated up from Brigid, who seemed to fall asleep as the mist rose from her. The mist turned in on itself and re-formed. First it looked like her; then it expanded and turned a pure and opaque white. Wings sprouted from its sides. Clawed arms appeared; a tail jutted out behind. Even taller than the humanoid form of Belial, a white dragon formed from the mist. The dragon faced the immobile Belial and roared. Rimaldi covered his ears against the roar, which rattled the windows in their frames.

Belial was afraid. In its thousands of years of existence, it had never seen a thing like this rise from a human magician. The demon fled, dashing toward the window, but it was too late.

The dragon leapt on Belial's back, her teeth sinking into the back of the demon's neck. Claws ripped at Belial's back, tearing bloody gashes in its form. The demon was being forced down, helpless as a buck under the onslaught of a lioness. The claws tore at Belial relentlessly. Hunks of its flesh were ripped out only to fall on the floor and vanish. The red blood of the prey stained the scales of the dragon. Finally the demon was crushed to the floor. The dragon raised her head and gave an immense bellow of victory. Then she leaned down and exhaled fire on the defeated demon. Belial writhed as it burned. In a matter of seconds, it was incinerated, leaving only a dusting of ash behind.

Before anyone could speak, the dragon bounded over Esmerelda's head and smashed through the wood covering the front windows, vanishing into the night.

Angela moved toward Brigid's body where it lay on the floor. Esmerelda joined her. Rimaldi went to the awakening Father Benito. They were awestruck. The two women sat on either side of Brigid's body.

Angela said, "She's still breathing."

Outside, the white dragon banked high in the sky, then dove like a peregrine on the house on Saint Julian. Inside the ritual room, all was chaos. Streng and Breeding were unconscious. Cawthorne was dead. The ritual that Lilith had been leading had stopped. When the dragon materialized in the room, ducking her head beneath the low rafters, the assembled worshipers panicked. They raced for the door and streamed out into the night. They had thought that Belial was awesome, but this creature reached deep inside of them, frightening them on a more primal level. They were children in the face of a god. Terrified, two were knocked unconscious at the door. Three more suffered broken limbs and dragged themselves away. The cold and ruthless eyes of the dragon followed their flight with disinterest.

The creature faced back into the room. Lilith was gibbering in fear, backed against the altar. The other two who had guarded the portal with her had fled. The dragon reached out and tore Lilith in half. Then the dragon went to the form of Breeding and gutted him. She sniffed the corpse of Cawthorne and stepped beyond him.

Only the dragon and Streng were left in the room. The dragon delicately prodded the body, seeking signs of life. When she found them, she reared back her head and breathed fire on him. With the crackle of a roaring blaze for accompaniment, the dragon waited until Streng's body had been reduced to ash. As an afterthought, she smashed the portal stone.

Once done, she took flight and returned to York Street. When she reentered the window, she began to change again, shifting from the shape of a dragon to that of Brigid. The projection slipped back into her unconscious body.

Brigid's eyes fluttered open. "Streng is dead." She passed out.

Reverently, the others carried her to a bed in one of the bedrooms. It seemed safe now.

CHAPTER THIRTY-ONE

Monday, November 2

THE first light of dawn was erasing the darkness as Esmerelda walked the last blocks to Streng's house. Few were about at this hour. Most of the people on the street were servants, arriving to prepare breakfast. She turned the corner onto Saint Julian and stopped. The dark cloud, the one that had been so dense that she could almost see it without her Sight, was gone. She looked harder and saw that only a few wisps of it remained. She slowly moved toward Streng's house. The basement gate that let out from under the front porch onto the sidewalk was standing wide open. She stopped to look at it. That gate was never opened except to let Streng's followers into or out of the basement ritual room. Now it, and the door into the house behind it, were open.

Esmerelda extended her senses into the house. She smiled. The entire house had a different feel to it. Though some of the taint of evil remained, much of the house felt new and clean. She cautiously entered the gate and stepped under the porch, then entered the basement through the open door. The stairs up to the first floor were in front of her. To the right was Streng's wine cellar and cool storage for vegetables and perishables. She had been in there many times. To the left was the door to the ritual room itself. She had never seen that door open, but it was open now.

Inside the ritual room was dim. It was illuminated only by the light filtering in from the street through the door behind her. No other light lit the room. The windows were still covered. On a small table at the foot of the stairs were two hurricane lamps that she used when she went into the wine cellar. She picked up the matches and lit one. She carried it before her into the ritual room. Though her senses told her it was safe, habit made her cautious. Long ago Streng had told her never to enter that room.

As she entered she smelled the death and blood. On the floor were three corpses and a charred ruin that must be a fourth corpse. The three corpses next to the charred one were Lilith, Breeding, and Cawthorne. Esmerelda bent over the fourth corpse and held her hands over it. Her senses could not pick up anything, not even a remnant of the person it had once been. Then she saw a piece of partially molten jewelry on one of the hands. The last corpse was Streng. She smiled and stood.

She saw the smashed portal stone. Then her eye was caught by the statue on the altar. It was a five-foot-high porcelain image of what Streng must have thought of as Satan. The goat legs and the horns on the head were as black as the rest of the statue. The smooth finish reflected the light from the kerosene lamp. A residue of the old evil still clung to it. In the right setting, the statue might have been frightening to some. It only annoyed the *mambo.*

A smile split her broad face. She set the lamp down and went to a cupboard under the stairs where Streng kept tools for workmen. Still grinning, she selected a five-pound sledge and went back to the ritual room.

"Statue," she said, "you got no reason to be." She brought the hammer down onto the statue, shattering one shoulder and knocking off an arm. Then she knocked the head off of the statue and went to work on the rest of it. When she had reduced it to shards, she rested. She went back and replaced the hammer in the cupboard. Then she went out onto the street to find a policeman.

～※～

BRIGID awoke late. A strong morning sun slanted through the window that looked out over the yard. Angela was in the other bed, waiting for Brigid to awaken.

"Do you remember what happened?" Angela asked.

"You mean I didn't dream it?"

"If you remember becoming a white dragon and tearing a demon to shreds, no, you didn't dream it."

～※～

A FEW minutes later, the two women made their way to the ballroom. Brigid was still unsteady on her feet. Benito and Rimaldi rose when she entered. Benito made no attempt to hide his admiration. Rimaldi looked respectful but uncomfortable. He had never been in the presence of a magician whose abilities dwarfed his own. What he had seen last night had humbled him. He was in awe and a little afraid of Brigid. She was something he had never expected to meet.

Angela and Brigid sat, and the men regained their seats. An uncomfortable silence fell over them. No one knew how to begin.

Finally, Benito asked, "How?"

"I don't know." Brigid was still dazed. "Friday night I had a dream, which must have given me the key to unlock something, though I don't see how. I barely remember the dream." She faltered, searching for words. "Last night, when I first fell to the floor, I thought I would soon be dead. The demon had struck me down and was attacking Father Rimaldi. I reached into myself and found a power. I used it to destroy Streng's projection. Then I attacked the demon. I had to, or Father Rimaldi would have died.

"When I saw the demon stop its attack and stand upright, I knew I needed to remain on the floor. I had to leave my body to fight Belial. My human form would not be enough. I needed claws to match Belial's; I needed fire to burn it; I needed jaws to bite it. I drifted up, out of my body. Everything became hazy, and suddenly I was a dragon.

In my eyes, Belial was no longer frightening." She fell silent, looking at the burned spot on the floor where she had breathed fire on the demon. "It was like I was two beings in one body. One was me, and the other was the dragon. We destroyed Belial."

"Then what happened?" Angela asked.

"Streng had to die. I went to Saint Julian Street and killed him and two other members of his coven. I let the rest flee into the night. One of his members was already on the floor, dead. I think it was the one who'd fought Angela."

"So high magic is not a myth," Benito said.

"I don't know what to call it. I can't even explain it."

They heard someone entering the front of the house. Esmerelda soon appeared at the doorway to the ballroom. "Any of you folk thought of making breakfast?"

They looked back at her, bewildered at the mundane request.

"Thought so." She turned and called down the stairs, "Daniel, you go fetch Streng's cook, Callie. Tell her I said come over here and make these people some breakfast. And tell her I said come quick, don' want no dawdling."

⋙⋘

THEY gathered for breakfast one final time. Their mood reflected their confused emotions. None of them had really expected to survive the previous evening. They had each made peace with death, but now they found themselves alive and astonished by what they had seen.

Brigid's transformation had caused Benito and Rimaldi to rethink who and what they were. Before this battle, they had thought of themselves as the magicians who fought the enemies of man. Now they knew themselves as the ones who managed the lesser enemies, the ones within their scope, but their feeling of diminution was more than overwhelmed by their gratitude. Brigid had not only saved their lives but also removed the threat of the demon.

Benito spoke the thought that had haunted him in the hours

since Belial's defeat. "I find it impossible to believe that such power was in you and I had no hint of it."

Angela responded, "She was given the keys to high magic in her dream."

"But is that all it takes, a set of keys, a message that can come in a single dream?" Benito asked, looking toward Brigid.

"No," Brigid said, and they fell silent. "First you must have the power inside of you. The one thing in my dream that I clearly remember is the thought that walkers are more born than made. I must have brought the power into the world with me."

"Then you learned the skills in a previous life," Angela said with finality.

Benito thought of objecting, but realized that he had no better explanation. The power that had risen from Brigid had awed him as well. Nothing he knew could refute what he had seen.

"Now is as good a time as any to say it," Angela announced. "I have decided to leave the Church and return to my family in Sicily. I will not be returning to the convent."

"You're renouncing your Holy Orders?" Rimaldi asked.

"Yes," Angela said.

"And I am as well," Brigid said. "I am going back to Ireland."

Rimaldi nodded, not surprised by her decision.

They were quiet for a moment. "Why?" Benito asked.

"I cannot speak for Angela," Brigid said. "But, for me, the decision to leave was actually made the night that Richardson died. I don't know how I knew, but from the beginning I suspected that this demon we were fighting was out of the reach of the Church. That is why I sent for a walker. The walkers are the ones who must have sent me the dream.

"The truth that I have come to know is that I am not Catholic. I am not even Christian. I still believe in the old gods, and it is time that I devoted my life to them. I'm not certain what I am, or what I am becoming, but my path lies along the old way."

Benito began to speak, but Rimaldi held up his hand to stop him and said, "After what we have seen, I am not surprised. I can begin to understand what Angela is, but you, Brigid, are something that I cannot comprehend. The only way I can describe it is that what you became last night is godlike." He paused. "You have tested not merely my faith, but my understanding of how the world is made.

"I would wish you good fortune on whatever path you choose, as I do Angela, but to bless you would seem . . . arrogant."

Angela reached across the table to take the Jesuit's hand. "Thank you, Father."

Rimaldi was embarrassed by such an open display of affection. To cover his emotion, he turned to Brigid. "I owe you my life, and a profound debt of gratitude for what you did. The least that the Church can do is help with your return. We can provide you with clothes for the trip, passage on a ship, and the money you will need to reach your final destination. Do you know where you will go?"

"Home. To Ireland. I have not seen my sister in almost thirty years. I will visit her. From there, the gods will tell me."

"Will you tell others what happened here?" Rimaldi asked.

"Who would believe me?' she responded.

The answer was not what Rimaldi had hoped for, but he was reluctant to press further.

"I will accompany you," Angela said. "I had hoped you would come to Sicily with me, but your roots run deep in Ireland. I do want to meet this sister of yours. I want to meet the members of any family that can give birth to dragons." Angela smiled and turned to the *mambo*. "I assume you've already visited Streng's."

"Looks like I'm gonna need a new job."

"Tell us."

"I got there 'bout two hours ago. Basement door was wide open. So I go in and find the door to the ritual room open. In there was four corpses. The bodies of the meanest people I ever knew." She grinned. "Lord, it was a pretty sight, Streng's body especially. Brigid took special care of him. He was near turned into charcoal.

"You know, that's the first time I been in that room. They even had a porcelain statue of Satan. I took a hammer to it 'fore I called the police. It broke up right smart."

Angela and Brigid laughed with Esmerelda. They could imagine the *mambo* setting about thoroughly destroying the statue in a no-nonsense way.

Esmerelda looked at the two women. "And before you go worryin', I'm gonna have some of my people collect every piece of that statue we can find. We'll spread it out over fifty miles of salt marsh. Drownin' it in salt water ought to leach the evil out of it."

"It will," Angela agreed.

"Brigid, you done us a powerful favor," the *mambo* said. "Evil men and the demons they call be as bad for my people as for you. If I'd thought I could have taken on Streng, I would have done it a long time back."

"But you were part of his destruction," Brigid protested.

"If it hadn't been for you, my joining you folks woulda killed me. Streng and Breeding were winning until you got rid of Streng."

"You said you called the police?" Benito asked. "What do they think of all of this?"

"Well, they called for Doc Gaston. Guess they figured he was the only one who could make sense out of that mess."

"Are they going to have an investigation?"

"Sure. But it's not gonna be a real one. Probably end up sayin' it was a bad house fire."

"They aren't going to question it any more deeply?" Rimaldi asked, relieved.

"Lots of strange things go on in this town. The police here know when to look and when to look away."

❦

AT Saint Julian Street, Dr. Gaston knelt over the last of the bodies. The first three he had examined had already been covered with sheets, as much out of respect for the dead as to hide the massive claw marks two bore on their chests. Cawthorne did not have a mark on him. He was simply dead from unknown causes. As for the fourth, who Gaston supposed had been Streng, the corpse was completely charred.

In his long career, Gaston had seen about every way there was for a human to die, but what he saw this morning was new to him. These deaths were as mysterious as Kirk's and Siena's deaths. The only corpse that made any kind of sense was Streng's. He had died by fire, but he had been cremated, not merely burned to death. Gaston knew there was no way that Streng could have been burned like that without the entire house having gone up in smoke.

Gaston had once believed in God. He had been a devout Catholic, but he had seen too many ruined bodies at Shiloh, Antietam, and so many other battlefields. He had stopped believing, stopped thinking there could be a God if he allowed this carnage.

"But," Gaston thought, "war is the work of man. Perhaps God does not choose to interfere. Maybe he becomes involved only when man's evil calls something into being that shouldn't be here. Then he sends his soldiers, and the evil dies." There was comfort in that thought.

Gaston stood, wiping his hands on a cloth, and spoke to the senior policeman in the room. "You can cover the last one, Cap'n."

The police captain signaled to the officer who had a sheet ready to cover the last body.

"What killed them?" the captain asked. His eyes betrayed that he wanted a reason, not the truth.

"Must have been a hell of a fire," Gaston said.

"That's what we thought." The policeman nodded with finality.

❦

GASTON walked out onto Saint Julian Street. It was early November, but the day was warm. Graceful oaks shaded the squares. The azalea bushes were replete with their dark green leaves. In the spring, they would explode in white, pink, and red blooms, producing so many flowers that the bushes themselves could barely be seen.

For the first time since before the war, Gaston noticed the beauty of the city. It was a fine morning.

FATHER Benito said his good-byes to the others and left to return to his monastery that same day, carrying a letter to the abbot from Rimaldi. Aboard the overnight train to Saint Augustine, Benito gave every appearance of calm, though his mind was in turmoil. The events of the past weeks, especially those of the final night, had disrupted his certainty, his view of the world. He needed the quiet peacefulness of his garden. By the early afternoon of the next day he found it.

For the first few hours he found comfort in working with his hands. He carefully watered the herbs and flowers that appeared dry. Then he applied himself to removing the tiny sprouts of weeds that had intruded into his beds. The comfrey plants attracted a host of interlopers, more than any other plant except his tobacco. The foxglove, whose powerful medicine could stop a heart attack, was often preyed on by a small beetle that seemed to like the taste of the plant. As he picked off the few bugs, he realized that he was making work for himself. His assistant had done a fine job of tending to the garden in Benito's weeks of absence. The tiny sprouts that he pulled could easily have waited a few days to be removed, but the act of clearing the garden of any intrusions served to clear his mind as well.

As the sun dipped low in the western sky, Benito sought out his favorite spot in the garden, an old branch that had bent low to the ground, a natural chair that looked down on the water of the marsh creek that bordered his garden. It sat on a bluff perhaps ten feet above the water. On the opposite side of the creek, marsh grass extended east as far as he could see. The tall trees behind him threw their shadows from the west, leaving Benito in a cool shade.

As he sat, he turned over the thoughts that had been troubling him. The Church, as he knew, had played an important role in eliminating the old religions of Europe, the same religions that had lent their power to the destruction of the demon that had threatened

Savannah. The demon had killed Pascal, Kirk, Richardson, and Sister Francis. How many more deaths could be attributed to that brutal presence Benito did not know. What if the Church had succeeded in killing off all of those who knew the old magic? What if there had been no Brigid, Angela, and Esmerelda to fight against it? Neither he nor the Church possessed a spell to call a dragon.

What of the dragons themselves? Saint George had supposedly slain them, killing the ones that feasted on the village virgins and destroyed crops in the fields. In all of Christian Europe the dragon had been the most feared beast, a representative of the forces of darkness. One of the old words for dragon, "Drakul," had become the name of a bloody tyrant who had tortured his own people even as he had waged war against the armies of the Ottoman Turks. Now Benito had seen a dragon, or the shape of one at least. He had watched the claws rend apart a demon and burn its body until nothing but a wisp of ash remained. The awesome dragon had been terrifying but had also been an ally in their battle.

The Church had much to answer for. Benito heard a crunch of gravel behind him. The slowness of the step and the small crunch of a cane told him that it was the abbot. The older man came around the end of the branch and sat next to Benito.

"Father Abbot," Benito said in quiet welcome.

The abbot nodded and looked out over the peaceful marsh, enjoying the sight as much as Benito. They sat, side by side, enjoying the slow approach of sunset in the humid air. The green marsh grass began to lose its color as the light of the sun turned red.

"I have read the letter from Rimaldi," the abbot said.

The comment hung in the silent air.

"Brother Benito, you have seen what few have ever seen. The spirits that possess men are hard enough to believe in. But a demon, then a dragon. You have been honored."

"But have we, has the Church, done what it should?" Benito said.

The abbot waited before replying, "How many possessing spirits have you driven out in the name of the Christ? How many people have you healed in the name of the Church? How many pregnancies have you eased? And that work has been done by thousands of monks and priests over centuries." The abbot paused. "No, we do not always get it right. The Church makes mistakes, but the Church is made of men. It is a thing of man. And we always seek ways to make the Church not only stronger, but wiser.

"Great evils have been done in the name of the Church. But we have also done great good. Our monasteries in Ireland preserved the knowledge of Rome in the centuries after the fall of that empire. The knowledge was waiting for us when the dark times were over. The Church has ended wars, brought peace to millions. On balance, the Church has been a force for good in the world, though the men that comprise it have made many errors, perhaps even unforgivable ones."

Benito nodded.

"Put your faith in God, as you always have." The old man rose, his cane leaving a strong imprint in the soft soil. "Dinner will be in a half hour. We will expect you."

Benito looked up into the kind and wise eyes of the abbot. "I'll join you."

The abbot nodded and smiled, then turned toward the monastery.

Benito listened as the abbot's slow step receded. Over the marsh a bird swept low, still alert in the failing light. Soon he would head home to a nest, probably high in a tree overlooking the marsh. As the light dimmed, Benito felt a familiar sense of peace wash over him.

⚮

THREE days later a steamer left Savannah, bound for Belfast. Two women had booked the first-class cabin for the crossing at the last minute. Though grateful for paying passengers, the captain thought they were an odd pair. One was an Italian woman, obviously wealthy and stunningly beautiful. The other was Irish. Though lovely, she was dressed as plainly as a schoolteacher.

The first day out, they caught a strong wind that would speed them on the way to Ireland. The women came out on deck to watch the crew set sail. The captain saw no sense in burning fuel if the wind was this favorable.

Once he was certain that the setting of the sails was going well, he walked across the deck to greet his passengers. "Miss Benelli, Miss Rourke, good to see you taking the air."

"Thank you, Captain," the Italian replied.

"Switching to sail might add a day to the trip, but it will save us all from breathing smoke."

"It's fine with us, Captain," Miss Rourke replied.

"We don't often get weather this nice, so I figure to use it as long as it lasts."

Miss Rourke smiled. "I wouldn't worry. It should stay like this for the entire crossing."

The two women looked at each other and grinned conspiratorially.

"I look forward to seeing you at dinner," the captain said, turning back to the helm.

Being superstitious, as all sailors are, he crossed himself.